Flora Curiosa

Flora Curiosa

Cryptobotany, Mysterious Fungi,
Sentient Trees, and Deadly Plants
in Classic Science Fiction and Fantasy

CHAD ARMENT, EDITOR

COACHWHIP PUBLICATIONS
Landisville, Pennsylvania

Flora Curiosa
Published 2008 Coachwhip Publications
Coachwhipbooks.com

ISBN 1-930585-56-X
ISBN-13 978-1-930585-56-0

Front cover image: Robert Brown

Contents

Rappaccini's Daughter
Nathaniel Hawthorne

A young man, named Giovanni Guasconti, came, very long ago, from the more southern region of Italy, to pursue his studies at the University of Padua. Giovanni, who had but a scanty supply of gold ducats in his pocket, took lodgings in a high and gloomy chamber of an old edifice, which looked not unworthy to have been the palace of a Paduan noble, and which, in fact, exhibited over its entrance the armorial bearings of a family long since extinct. The young stranger, who was not unstudied in the great poem of his country, recollected that one of the ancestors of this family, and perhaps an occupant of this very mansion, had been pictured by Dante as a partaker of the immortal agonies of his Inferno. These reminiscences and associations, together with the tendency to heart-break natural to a young man for the first time out of his native sphere, caused Giovanni to sigh heavily, as he looked around the desolate and ill-furnished apartment.

"Holy Virgin, signor," cried old dame Lisabetta, who, won by the youth's remarkable beauty of person, was kindly endeavoring to give the chamber a habitable air, "what a sigh was that to come out of a young man's heart! Do you find this old mansion gloomy? For the love of heaven, then, put your head out of the window, and you will see as bright sunshine as you have left in Naples."

Guasconti mechanically did as the old woman advised, but could not quite agree with her that the Lombard sunshine was as cheerful as that of southern Italy. Such as it was, however, it fell upon a garden beneath the window, and expended its fostering influences on a variety of plants, which seemed to have been cultivated with exceeding care.

"Does this garden belong to the house?" asked Giovanni.

"Heaven forbid, signor!—unless it were fruitful of better pot-herbs than any that grow there now," answered old Lisabetta. "No; that garden is cultivated by the own hands of Signor Giacomo Rappaccini, the famous Doctor, who, I warrant him, has been heard of as far as Naples. It is said he distils these plants into medicines that are as potent as a charm. Oftentimes you may see the Signor Doctor at work, and perchance the Signora his daughter, too, gathering the strange flowers that grow in the garden."

The old woman had now done what she could for the aspect of the chamber, and, commending the young man to the protection of the saints, took her departure.

Giovanni still found no better occupation than to look down into the garden beneath his window. From its appearance, he judged it to be one of those botanic gardens, which were of earlier date in Padua than elsewhere in Italy, or in the world. Or, not improbably, it might once have been the pleasure-place of an opulent family; for there was the ruin of a marble fountain in the centre, sculptured with rare art, but so wofully shattered that it was impossible to trace the original design from the chaos of remaining fragments. The water, however, continued to gush and sparkle into the sunbeams as cheerfully as ever. A little gurgling sound ascended to the young man's window, and made him feel as if a fountain were an immortal spirit, that sung its song unceasingly, and without heeding the vicissitudes around it; while one century embodied it in marble, and another scattered the perishable garniture on the soil. All about the pool into which the water subsided, grew various plants, that seemed to require a plentiful supply of moisture for the nourishment of gigantic leaves, and, in some instances, flowers gorgeously magnificent. There was one shrub in particular, set in a marble vase in the midst of the pool, that bore a profusion of purple blossoms, each of which had the lustre and richness of a gem; and the whole together made a show so resplendent that it seemed enough to illuminate the garden, even had there been no sunshine. Every portion of the soil was peopled with plants and herbs, which, if less beautiful, still bore tokens of assiduous care; as if all had their individual virtues, known to the scientific mind that fostered them. Some were placed in urns, rich with old carving, and others in common garden-pots; some crept serpent-like along the ground, or climbed on high, using whatever means of

ascent was offered them. One plant had wreathed itself round a
statue of Vertumnus, which was thus quite veiled and shrouded in
a drapery of hanging foliage, so happily arranged that it might have
served a sculptor for a study.

While Giovanni stood at the window, he heard a rustling behind a screen of leaves, and became aware that a person was at
work in the garden. His figure soon emerged into view, and showed
itself to be that of no common laborer, but a tall, emaciated, sallow,
and sickly looking man, dressed in a scholar's garb of black. He
was beyond the middle term of life, with gray hair, a thin gray beard,
and a face singularly marked with intellect and cultivation, but which
could never, even in his more youthful days, have expressed much
warmth of heart.

Nothing could exceed the intentness with which this scientific
gardener examined every shrub which grew in his path; it seemed
as if he was looking into their inmost nature, making observations
in regard to their creative essence, and discovering why one leaf
grew in this shape, and another in that, and wherefore such and such
flowers differed among themselves in hue and perfume. Nevertheless,
in spite of the deep intelligence on his part, there was no approach
to intimacy between himself and these vegetable existences. On
the contrary, he avoided their actual touch, or the direct inhaling
of their odors, with a caution that impressed Giovanni most disagreeably; for the man's demeanor was that of one walking among
malignant influences, such as savage beasts, or deadly snakes, or
evil spirits, which, should he allow them one moment of license,
would wreak upon him some terrible fatality. It was strangely
frightful to the young man's imagination, to see this air of insecu-
rity in a person cultivating a garden, that most simple and innocent of human toils, and which had been alike the joy and labor of
the unfallen parents of the race. Was this garden, then, the Eden
of the present world?—and this man, with such a perception of
harm in what his own hands caused to grow, was he the Adam?

The distrustful gardener, while plucking away the dead leaves
or pruning the too luxuriant growth of the shrubs, defended his
hands with a pair of thick gloves. Nor were these his only armor.
When, in his walk through the garden, he came to the magnificent
plant that hung its purple gems beside the marble fountain, he
placed a kind of mask over his mouth and nostrils, as if all this
beauty did but conceal a deadlier malice. But finding his task still

too dangerous, he drew back, removed the mask, and called loudly, but in the infirm voice of a person affected with inward disease:

"Beatrice!—Beatrice!"

"Here am I, my father! What would you?" cried a rich and youthful voice from the window of the opposite house; a voice as rich as a tropical sunset, and which made Giovanni, though he knew not why, think of deep hues of purple or crimson, and of perfumes heavily delectable.— "Are you in the garden?"

"Yes, Beatrice," answered the gardener, "and I need your help."

Soon there emerged from under a sculptured portal the figure of a young girl, arrayed with as much richness of taste as the most splendid of the flowers, beautiful as the day, and with a bloom so deep and vivid that one shade more would have been too much. She looked redundant with life, health, and energy; all of which attributes were bound down and compressed, as it were, and girdled tensely, in their luxuriance, by her virgin zone. Yet Giovanni's fancy must have grown morbid, while he looked down into the garden; for the impression which the fair stranger made upon him was as if here were another flower, the human sister of those vegetable ones, as beautiful as they—more beautiful than the richest of them—but still to be touched only with a glove, nor to be approached without a mask. As Beatrice came down the garden-path, it was observable that she handled and inhaled the odor of several of the plants, which her father had most sedulously avoided.

"Here, Beatrice," said the latter,— "see how many needful offices require to be done to our chief treasure. Yet, shattered as I am, my life might pay the penalty of approaching it so closely as circumstances demand. Henceforth, I fear, this plant must be consigned to your sole charge."

"And gladly will I undertake it," cried again the rich tones of the young lady, as she bent towards the magnificent plant, and opened her arms as if to embrace it. "Yes, my sister, my splendor, it shall be Beatrice's task to nurse and serve thee; and thou shalt reward her with thy kisses and perfume breath, which to her is as the breath of life!"

Then, with all the tenderness in her manner that was so strikingly expressed in her words, she busied herself with such attentions as the plant seemed to require; and Giovanni, at his lofty window, rubbed his eyes, and almost doubted whether it were a girl tending her favorite flower, or one sister performing the duties of affection to another. The scene soon terminated. Whether Doctor Rappaccini had finished his labors in the garden, or that his watchful eye had caught the stranger's face, he now took his daughter's arm and retired. Night was already closing in; oppressive exhalations seemed to proceed from the plants, and steal upward past the open window; and Giovanni, closing the lattice, went to his couch, and dreamed of a rich flower and beautiful girl. Flower and maiden were different and yet the same, and fraught with some strange peril in either shape.

But there is an influence in the light of morning that tends to rectify whatever errors of fancy, or even of judgment, we may have incurred during the sun's decline, or among the shadows of the night, or in the less wholesome glow of moonshine. Giovanni's first movement on starting from sleep, was to throw open the window, and gaze down into the garden which his dreams had made so fertile of mysteries. He was surprised, and a little ashamed, to find how real and matter-of-fact an affair it proved to be, in the first rays of the sun, which gilded the dew-drops that hung upon leaf and blossom, and, while giving a brighter beauty to each rare flower, brought everything within the limits of ordinary experience. The young man rejoiced, that, in the heart of the barren city, he had the privilege of overlooking this spot of lovely and luxuriant vegetation. It would serve, he said to himself, as a symbolic language, to keep him in communion with Nature. Neither the sickly and thought-worn Doctor Giacomo Rappaccini, it is true, nor his brilliant daughter, were now visible; so that Giovanni could not determine how much of the singularity which he attributed to both, was due to their own qualities, and how much to his wonder-working fancy. But he was inclined to take a most rational view of the whole matter.

In the course of the day, he paid his respects to Signor Pietro Baglioni, Professor of Medicine in the University, a physician of eminent repute, to whom Giovanni had brought a letter of introduction. The Professor was an elderly personage, apparently of genial nature, and habits that might almost be called jovial; he kept the young man to dinner, and made himself very agreeable by the freedom and liveliness of his conversation, especially when warmed by a flask or two of Tuscan wine. Giovanni, conceiving that men of science, inhabitants of the same city, must needs be on familiar terms with one another, took an opportunity to mention the name of Doctor Rappaccini. But the Professor did not respond with so much cordiality as he had anticipated.

"Ill would it become a teacher of the divine art of medicine," said Professor Pietro Baglioni, in answer to a question of Giovanni, "to withhold due and well-considered praise of a physician so eminently skilled as Rappaccini. But, on the other hand, I should answer it but scantily to my conscience, were I to permit a worthy youth like yourself, Signor Giovanni, the son of an ancient friend, to imbibe erroneous ideas respecting a man who might hereafter chance to hold your life and death in his hands. The truth is, our worshipful Doctor Rappaccini has as much science as any member of the faculty—with perhaps one single exception—in Padua, or all Italy. But there are certain grave objections to his professional character."

"And what are they?" asked the young man.

"Has my friend Giovanni any disease of body or heart, that he is so inquisitive about physicians?" said the Professor, with a smile. "But as for Rappaccini, it is said of him—and I, who know the man well, can answer for its truth—that he cares infinitely more for science than for mankind. His patients are interesting to him only as subjects for some new experiment. He would sacrifice human life, his own among the rest, or whatever else was dearest to him, for the sake of adding so much as a grain of mustard-seed to the great heap of his accumulated knowledge."

"Methinks he is an awful man, indeed," remarked Guasconti, mentally recalling the cold and purely intellectual aspect of Rappaccini. "And yet, worshipful Professor, is it not a noble spirit? Are there many men capable of so spiritual a love of science?"

"God forbid," answered the Professor, somewhat testily— "at least, unless they take sounder views of the healing art than those adopted by Rappaccini. It is his theory, that all medicinal virtues are comprised within those substances which we term vegetable poisons. These he cultivates with his own hands, and is said even to have produced new varieties of poison, more horribly deleterious than Nature, without the assistance of this learned person, would ever have plagued the world withal. That the Signor Doctor does less mischief than might be expected, with such dangerous substances, is undeniable. Now and then, it must be owned, he has effected—or seemed to effect—a marvellous cure. But, to tell you my private mind, Signor Giovanni, he should receive little credit for such instances of success—they being probably the work of chance—but should be held strictly accountable for his failures, which may justly be considered his own work."

The youth might have taken Baglioni's opinions with many grains of allowance, had he known that there was a professional warfare of long continuance between him and Doctor Rappaccini, in which the latter was generally thought to have gained the advantage. If the reader be inclined to judge for himself, we refer him to certain black-letter tracts on both sides, preserved in the medical department of the University of Padua.

"I know not, most learned Professor," returned Giovanni, after musing on what had been said of Rappaccini's exclusive zeal for science— "I know not how dearly this physician may love his art; but surely there is one object more dear to him. He has a daughter."

"Aha!" cried the Professor with a laugh. "So now our friend Giovanni's secret is out. You have heard of this daughter, whom all the young men in Padua are wild about, though not half a dozen have ever had the good hap to see her face. I know little of the Signora Beatrice, save that Rappaccini is said to have instructed her deeply in his science, and that, young and beautiful as fame reports her, she is already qualified to fill a professor's chair. Perchance her father destines her for mine! Other absurd rumors there be, not worth talking about, or listening to. So now, Signor Giovanni, drink off your glass of Lacryma."

Guasconti returned to his lodgings somewhat heated with the wine he had quaffed, and which caused his brain to swim with strange fantasies in reference to Doctor Rappaccini and the beautiful Beatrice. On his way, happening to pass by a florist's, he bought a fresh bouquet of flowers.

Ascending to his chamber, he seated himself near the window, but within the shadow thrown by the depth of the wall, so that he could look down into the garden with little risk of being discovered. All beneath his eye was a solitude. The strange plants were basking in the sunshine, and now and then nodding gently to one another, as if in acknowledgment of sympathy and kindred. In the midst, by the shattered fountain, grew the magnificent shrub, with its purple gems clustering all over it; they glowed in the air, and gleamed back again out of the depths of the pool, which thus seemed to overflow with colored radiance from the rich reflection that was steeped in it. At first, as we have said, the garden was a solitude. Soon, however,—as Giovanni had half hoped, half feared,

would be the case,—a figure appeared beneath the antique sculptured portal, and came down between the rows of plants, inhaling
their various perfumes, as if she were one of those beings of old
classic fable, that lived upon sweet odors. On again beholding
Beatrice, the young man was even startled to perceive how much
her beauty exceeded his recollection of it; so brilliant, so vivid in
its character, that she glowed amid the sunlight, and, as Giovanni
whispered to himself, positively illuminated the more shadowy
intervals of the garden path. Her face being now more revealed
than on the former occasion, he was struck by its expression of
simplicity and sweetness; qualities that had not entered into his
idea of her character, and which made him ask anew, what manner of mortal she might be. Nor did he fail again to observe, or
imagine, an analogy between the beautiful girl and the gorgeous
shrub that hung its gem-like flowers over the fountain; a resemblance which Beatrice seemed to have indulged a fantastic humor in
heightening, both by the arrangement of her dress and the selection of its hues.

Approaching the shrub, she threw open her arms, as with a
passionate ardor, and drew its branches into an intimate embrace;
so intimate, that her features were hidden in its leafy bosom, and
her glistening ringlets all intermingled with the flowers.

"Give me thy breath, my sister," exclaimed Beatrice; "for I am
faint with common air! And give me this flower of thine, which I
separate with gentlest fingers from the stem, and place it close
beside my heart."

With these words, the beautiful daughter of Rappaccini plucked
one of the richest blossoms of the shrub, and was about to fasten
it in her bosom. But now, unless Giovanni's draughts of wine had
bewildered his senses, a singular incident occurred. A small orange
colored reptile, of the lizard or chameleon species, chanced to be
creeping along the path, just at the feet of Beatrice. It appeared to
Giovanni—but, at the distance from which he gazed, he could
scarcely have seen anything so minute—it appeared to him, however, that a drop or two of moisture from the broken stem of the
flower descended upon the lizard's head. For an instant, the reptile
contorted itself violently, and then lay motionless in the sunshine.
Beatrice observed this remarkable phenomenon, and crossed herself, sadly, but without surprise; nor did she therefore hesitate to
arrange the fatal flower in her bosom. There it blushed, and almost

glimmered with the dazzling effect of a precious stone, adding to her dress and aspect the one appropriate charm, which nothing else in the world could have supplied. But Giovanni, out of the shadow of his window, bent forward and shrank back, and murmured and trembled.

"Am I awake? Have I my senses?" said he to himself. "What is this being?—beautiful, shall I call her?—or inexpressibly terrible?"

Beatrice now strayed carelessly through the garden, approaching closer beneath Giovanni's window, so that he was compelled to thrust his head quite out of its concealment, in order to gratify the intense and painful curiosity which she excited. At this moment, there came a beautiful insect over the garden wall; it had perhaps wandered through the city and found no flowers nor verdure among those antique haunts of men, until the heavy perfumes of Doctor Rappaccini's shrubs had lured it from afar. Without alighting on the flowers, this winged brightness seemed to be attracted by Beatrice, and lingered in the air and fluttered about her head. Now here it could not be but that Giovanni Guasconti's eyes deceived him. Be that as it might, he fancied that while Beatrice was gazing at the insect with childish delight, it grew faint and fell at her feet;—its bright wings shivered; it was dead—from no cause that he could discern, unless it were the atmosphere of her breath. Again Beatrice crossed herself and sighed heavily, as she bent over the dead insect.

An impulsive movement of Giovanni drew her eyes to the window. There she beheld the beautiful head of the young man—rather a Grecian than an Italian head, with fair, regular features, and a glistening of gold among his ringlets—gazing down upon her like a being that hovered in mid-air. Scarcely knowing what he did, Giovanni threw down the bouquet which he had hitherto held in his hand.

"Signora," said he, "there are pure and healthful flowers. Wear them for the sake of Giovanni Guasconti!"

"Thanks, Signor," replied Beatrice, with her rich voice that came forth as it were like a gush of music; and with a mirthful expression half childish and half woman-like. "I accept your gift, and would fain recompense it with this precious purple flower; but if I toss it into the air, it will not reach you. So Signor Guasconti must even content himself with my thanks."

She lifted the bouquet from the ground, and then as if inwardly ashamed at having stepped aside from her maidenly reserve to respond to a stranger's greeting, passed swiftly homeward through the garden. But, few as the moments were, it seemed to Giovanni when she was on the point of vanishing beneath the sculptured portal, that his beautiful bouquet was already beginning to wither in her grasp. It was an idle thought; there could be no possibility of distinguishing a faded flower from a fresh one, at so great a distance.

For many days after this incident, the young man avoided the window that looked into Doctor Rappaccini's garden, as if something ugly and monstrous would have blasted his eye-sight, had he been betrayed into a glance. He felt conscious of having put himself, to a certain extent, within the influence of an unintelligible power, by the communication which he had opened with Beatrice. The wisest course would have been, if his heart were in any real danger, to quit his lodgings and Padua itself, at once; the next wiser, to have accustomed himself, as far as possible, to the familiar and day-light view of Beatrice; thus bringing her rigidly and systematically within the limits of ordinary experience. Least of all, while avoiding her sight, should Giovanni have remained so near this extraordinary being, that the proximity and possibility even of intercourse, should give a kind of substance and reality to the wild vagaries which his imagination ran riot continually in producing. Guasconti had not a deep heart—or at all events, its depths were not sounded now—but he had a quick fancy, and an ardent southern temperament, which rose every instant to a higher fever-pitch. Whether or no Beatrice possessed those terrible attributes—that fatal breath—the affinity with those so beautiful and deadly flowers—which were indicated by what Giovanni had witnessed, she had at least instilled a fierce and subtle poison into his system. It was not love, although her rich beauty was a madness to him; nor horror, even while he fancied her spirit to be imbued with the same baneful essence that seemed to pervade her physical frame; but a wild offspring of both love and horror that had each parent in it, and burned like one and shivered like the other. Giovanni knew not what to dread; still less did he know what to hope; yet hope and dread kept a continual warfare in his breast, alternately vanquishing one another and starting up afresh to renew the contest. Blessed are all simple emotions, be they dark or bright! It is the lurid intermixture of the two that produces the illuminating blaze of the infernal regions.

Sometimes he endeavored to assuage the fever of his spirit by a rapid walk through the streets of Padua, or beyond its gates; his footsteps kept time with the throbbings of his brain, so that the walk was apt to accelerate itself to a race. One day, he found himself arrested; his arm was seized by a portly personage who had turned back on recognizing the young man, and expended much breath in overtaking him.

"Signor Giovanni!—stay, my young friend!" —cried he. "Have you forgotten me? That might well be the case, if I were as much altered as yourself."

It was Baglioni, whom Giovanni had avoided, ever since their first meeting, from a doubt that the Professor's sagacity would look too deeply into his secrets. Endeavoring to recover himself, he stared forth wildly from his inner world into the outer one, and spoke like a man in a dream.

"Yes; I am Giovanni Guasconti. You are Professor Pietro Baglioni. Now let me pass!"

"Not yet—not yet, Signor Giovanni Guasconti," said the Professor, smiling, but at the same time scrutinizing the youth with an earnest glance. "What, did I grow up side by side with your father, and shall his son pass me like a stranger, in these old streets of Padua? Stand still, Signor Giovanni; for we must have a word or two before we part."

"Speedily, then, most worshipful Professor, speedily!" said Giovanni, with feverish impatience. "Does not your worship see that I am in haste?"

Now, while he was speaking, there came a man in black along the street, stooping and moving feebly, like a person in inferior health. His face was all overspread with a most sickly and sallow hue, but yet so pervaded with an expression of piercing and active intellect, that an observer might easily have overlooked the merely physical attributes, and have seen only this wonderful energy. As he passed, this person exchanged a cold and distant salutation with Baglioni, but fixed his eyes upon Giovanni with an intentness that seemed to bring out whatever was within him worthy of notice. Nevertheless, there was a peculiar quietness in the look, as if taking merely a speculative, not a human interest, in the young man.

"It is Doctor Rappaccini!" whispered the Professor, when the stranger had passed.— "Has he ever seen your face before?"

"Not that I know," answered Giovanni, starting at the name.

"He *has* seen you!—he must have seen you!" said Baglioni, hastily. "For some purpose or other, this man of science is making a study of you. I know that look of his! It is the same that coldly illuminates his face, as he bends over a bird, a mouse, or a butterfly, which, in pursuance of some experiment, he has killed by the perfume of a flower;—a look as deep as Nature itself, but without Nature's warmth of love. Signor Giovanni, I will stake my life upon it, you are the subject of one of Rappaccini's experiments!"

"Will you make a fool of me?" cried Giovanni, passionately. "*That,* Signor Professor, were an untoward experiment."

"Patience, patience!" replied the imperturbable Professor. "I tell thee, my poor Giovanni, that Rappaccini has a scientific interest in thee. Thou hast fallen into fearful hands! And the Signora Beatrice? What part does she act in this mystery?"

But Guasconti, finding Baglioni's pertinacity intolerable, here broke away, and was gone before the Professor could again seize his arm. He looked after the young man intently, and shook his head.

"This must not be," said Baglioni to himself. "The youth is the son of my old friend, and shall not come to any harm from which the arcana of medical science can preserve him. Besides, it is too insufferable an impertinence in Rappaccini thus to snatch the lad out of my own hands, as I may say, and make use of him for his infernal experiments. This daughter of his! It shall be looked to. Perchance, most learned Rappaccini, I may foil you where you little dream of it!"

Meanwhile, Giovanni had pursued a circuitous route, and at length found himself at the door of his lodgings. As he crossed the threshold, he was met by old Lisabetta, who smirked and smiled, and was evidently desirous to attract his attention; vainly, however, as the ebullition of his feelings had momentarily subsided into a cold and dull vacuity. He turned his eyes full upon the withered face that was puckering itself into a smile, but seemed to behold it not. The old dame, therefore, laid her grasp upon his cloak.

"Signor!—Signor!" whispered she, still with a smile over the whole breadth of her visage, so that it looked not unlike a grotesque carving in wood, darkened by centuries— "Listen, Signor! There is a private entrance into the garden!"

"What do you say?" exclaimed Giovanni, turning quickly about, as if an inanimate thing should start into feverish life.— "A private entrance into Doctor Rappaccini's garden!"

"Hush! hush!—not so loud!" whispered Lisabetta, putting her hand over his mouth. "Yes; into the worshipful Doctor's garden, where you may see all his fine shrubbery. Many a young man in Padua would give gold to be admitted among those flowers."

Giovanni put a piece of gold into her hand.

"Show me the way," said he.

A surmise, probably excited by his conversation with Baglioni, crossed his mind, that this interposition of old Lisabetta might perchance be connected with the intrigue, whatever were its nature, in which the Professor seemed to suppose that Doctor Rappaccini was involving him. But such a suspicion, though it disturbed Giovanni, was inadequate to restrain him. The instant he was aware of the possibility of approaching Beatrice, it seemed an absolute necessity of his existence to do so. It mattered not whether she were angel or demon; he was irrevocably within her sphere, and must obey the law that whirled him onward, in ever lessening circles, towards a result which he did not attempt to foreshadow. And yet, strange to say, there came across him a sudden doubt, whether this intense interest on his part were not delusory— whether it were really of so deep and positive a nature as to justify him in now thrusting himself into an incalculable position— whether it were not merely the fantasy of a young man's brain, only slightly, or not at all, connected with his heart!

He paused—hesitated—turned half about—but again went on. His withered guide led him along several obscure passages, and finally undid a door, through which, as it was opened, there came the sight and sound of rustling leaves, with the broken sunshine glimmering among them. Giovanni stepped forth, and forcing himself through the entanglement of a shrub that wreathed its tendrils over the hidden entrance, he stood beneath his own window, in the open area of Doctor Rappaccini's garden.

How often is it the case, that, when impossibilities have come to pass, and dreams have condensed their misty substance into tangible realities, we find ourselves calm, and even coldly self-possessed, amid circumstances which it would have been a delirium of joy or agony to anticipate! Fate delights to thwart us thus. Passion will choose his own time to rush upon the scene, and lingers sluggishly behind, when an appropriate adjustment of events would seem to summon his appearance. So was it now with Giovanni. Day after day, his pulses had throbbed with feverish blood, at the improbable idea of an interview with Beatrice, and of standing with her, face to face, in this very garden, basking in the oriental sunshine of her beauty, and snatching from her full gaze the mystery which he deemed the riddle of his own existence. But now there was a singular and untimely equanimity within his breast. He threw a glance around the garden to discover if Beatrice or her father were present, and perceiving that he was alone, began a critical observation of the plants.

The aspect of one and all of them dissatisfied him; their gorgeousness seemed fierce, passionate, and even unnatural. There was hardly an individual shrub which a wanderer, straying by himself through a forest, would not have been startled to find growing wild, as if an unearthly face had glared at him out of the thicket. Several, also, would have shocked a delicate instinct by an appearance of artificialness, indicating that there had been such commixture, and, as it were, adultery of various vegetable species, that the production was no longer of God's making, but the monstrous offspring of man's depraved fancy, glowing with only an evil mockery of beauty. They were probably the result of experiment, which, in one or two cases, had succeeded in mingling plants individually lovely into a compound possessing the questionable and ominous character that distinguished the whole growth of the garden. In fine, Giovanni recognized but two or three plants in the collection, and those of a kind that he well knew to be poisonous. While busy with these contemplations, he heard the rustling of a silken garment, and turning, beheld Beatrice emerging from beneath the sculptured portal.

Giovanni had not considered with himself what should be his deportment; whether he should apologize for his intrusion into the garden, or assume that he was there with the privity, at least, if not by the desire, of Doctor Rappaccini or his daughter. But Beatrice's manner placed him at his ease, though leaving him still in doubt by what agency he had gained admittance. She came lightly along the path, and met him near the broken fountain. There was surprise in her face, but brightened by a simple and kind expression of pleasure.

"You are a connoisseur in flowers, Signor," said Beatrice with a smile, alluding to the bouquet which he had flung her from the window. "It is no marvel, therefore, if the sight of my father's rare collection has tempted you to take a nearer view. If he were here, he could tell you many strange and interesting facts as to the nature and habits of these shrubs, for he has spent a life-time in such studies, and this garden is his world."

"And yourself, lady"—observed Giovanni— "if fame says true— you, likewise, are deeply skilled in the virtues indicated by these rich blossoms, and these spicy perfumes. Would you deign to be my instructress, I should prove an apter scholar than under Signor Rappaccini himself."

"Are there such idle rumors?" asked Beatrice, with the music of a pleasant laugh. "Do people say that I am skilled in my father's science of plants? What a jest is there! No; though I have grown up among these flowers, I know no more of them than their hues and perfume; and sometimes, methinks I would fain rid myself of even that small knowledge. There are many flowers here, and those not the least brilliant, that shock and offend me, when they meet my eye. But, pray, Signor, do not believe these stories about my science. Believe nothing of me save what you see with your own eyes."

"And must I believe all that I have seen with my own eyes?" asked Giovanni pointedly, while the recollection of former scenes made him shrink. "No, Signora, you demand too little of me. Bid me believe nothing, save what comes from your own lips."

It would appear that Beatrice understood him. There came a deep flush to her cheek; but she looked full into Giovanni's eyes, and responded to his gaze of uneasy suspicion with a queen-like haughtiness.

"I do so bid you, Signor!" she replied. "Forget whatever you may have fancied in regard to me. If true to the outward senses, still it may be false in its essence. But the words of Beatrice Rappaccini's lips are true from the heart outward. Those you may believe!"

A fervor glowed in her whole aspect, and beamed upon Giovanni's consciousness like the light of truth itself. But while she spoke, there was a fragrance in the atmosphere around her rich and delightful, though evanescent, yet which the young man, from an indefinable reluctance, scarcely dared to draw into his lungs. It might be the odor of the flowers. Could it be Beatrice's breath, which thus embalmed her words with a strange richness, as if by steeping them in her heart? A faintness passed like a shadow over Giovanni, and flitted away; he seemed to gaze through the beautiful girl's eyes into her transparent soul, and felt no more doubt or fear.

The tinge of passion that had colored Beatrice's manner vanished; she became gay, and appeared to derive a pure delight from her communion with the youth, not unlike what the maiden of a lonely island might have felt, conversing with a voyager from the civilized world. Evidently her experience of life had been confined within the limits of that garden. She talked now about matters as simple as the day-light or summer-clouds, and now asked questions in reference to the city, or Giovanni's distant home, his friends, his mother, and his sisters; questions indicating such seclusion, and such lack of familiarity with modes and forms, that Giovanni responded as if to an infant. Her spirit gushed out before him like a fresh rill, that was just catching its first glimpse of the sunlight, and wondering, at the reflections of earth and sky which were flung into its bosom. There came thoughts, too, from a deep source, and fantasies of a gem-like brilliancy, as if diamonds and rubies sparkled upward among the bubbles of the fountain. Ever and anon, there gleamed across the young man's mind a sense of wonder, that he should be walking side by side with the being who had so wrought upon his imagination—whom he had idealized in such hues of terror—in whom he had positively witnessed such manifestations of dreadful attributes—that he should be conversing with Beatrice like a brother, and should find her so human and so maiden-like. But such reflections were only momentary; the effect of her character was too real, not to make itself familiar at once.

In this free intercourse, they had strayed through the garden, and now, after many turns among its avenues, were come to the shattered fountain, beside which grew the magnificent shrub with its treasury of glowing blossoms. A fragrance was diffused from it, which Giovanni recognized as identical with that which he had attributed to Beatrice's breath, but incomparably more powerful. As her eyes fell upon it, Giovanni beheld her press her hand to her bosom, as if her heart were throbbing suddenly and painfully.

"For the first time in my life," murmured she, addressing the shrub, "I had forgotten thee!"

"I remember, Signora," said Giovanni, "that you once promised to reward me with one of these living gems for the bouquet, which I had the happy boldness to fling to your feet. Permit me now to pluck it as a memorial of this interview."

He made a step towards the shrub, with extended hand. But Beatrice darted forward, uttering a shriek that went through his heart like a dagger. She caught his hand, and drew it back with the whole force of her slender figure. Giovanni felt her touch thrilling through his fibres.

"Touch it not!" exclaimed she, in a voice of agony. "Not for thy life! It is fatal!"

Then, hiding her face, she fled from him, and vanished beneath the sculptured portal. As Giovanni followed her with his eyes, he beheld the emaciated figure and pale intelligence of Doctor Rappaccini, who had been watching the scene, he knew not how long, within the shadow of the entrance.

No sooner was Guasconti alone in his chamber, than the image of Beatrice came back to his passionate musings, invested with all the witchery that had been gathering around it ever since his first glimpse of her, and now likewise imbued with a tender warmth of girlish womanhood. She was human: her nature was endowed with all gentle and feminine qualities; she was worthiest to be worshipped; she was capable, surely, on her part, of the height and heroism of love. Those tokens, which he had hitherto considered as proofs of a frightful peculiarity in her physical and moral system, were now either forgotten, or, by the subtle sophistry of passion, transmuted into a golden crown of enchantment, rendering Beatrice the more admirable, by so much as she was the more unique. Whatever had looked ugly, was now beautiful; or, if incapable of such a change, it stole away and hid itself among those shapeless half-ideas, which throng the dim region beyond the daylight of our perfect consciousness. Thus did Giovanni spend the night, nor fell asleep, until the dawn had begun to awake the slumbering flowers in Doctor Rappaccini's garden, whither his dreams doubtless led him. Up rose the sun in his due season, and flinging his beams upon the young man's eyelids, awoke him to a sense of pain. When thoroughly aroused, he became sensible of a burning and tingling agony in his hand—in his right hand—the very hand which Beatrice had grasped in her own, when he was on the point of plucking one of the gem-like flowers. On the back of that hand there was now a purple print, like that of four small fingers, and the likeness of a slender thumb upon his wrist.

Oh, how stubbornly does love—or even that cunning semblance of love which flourishes in the imagination, but strikes no depth of root into the heart—how stubbornly does it hold its faith, until the moment come, when it is doomed to vanish into thin mist! Giovanni wrapt a handkerchief about his hand, and wondered what evil thing had stung him, and soon forgot his pain in a reverie of Beatrice.

After the first interview, a second was in the inevitable course of what we call fate. A third; a fourth; and a meeting with Beatrice in the garden was no longer an incident in Giovanni's daily life, but the whole space in which he might be said to live; for the anticipation and memory of that ecstatic hour made up the remainder. Nor was it otherwise with the daughter of Rappaccini. She watched for the youth's appearance, and flew to his side with confidence as unreserved as if they had been playmates from early infancy—as if they were such playmates still. If, by any unwonted chance, he failed to come at the appointed moment, she stood beneath the window, and sent up the rich sweetness of her tones to float around him in his chamber, and echo and reverberate throughout his heart— "Giovanni! Giovanni! Why tarriest thou? Come down!" And down he hastened into that Eden of poisonous flowers.

But, with all this intimate familiarity, there was still a reserve in Beatrice's demeanor, so rigidly and invariably sustained, that the idea of infringing it scarcely occurred to his imagination. By all appreciable signs, they loved; they had looked love, with eyes that conveyed the holy secret from the depths of one soul into the depths of the other, as if it were too sacred to be whispered by the way; they had even spoken love, in those gushes of passion when their spirits darted forth in articulated breath, like tongues of long-hidden flame; and yet there had been no seal of lips, no clasp of hands, nor any slightest caress, such as love claims and hallows. He had never touched one of the gleaming ringlets of her hair; her garment—so marked was the physical barrier between them—had never been waved against him by a breeze. On the few occasions when Giovanni had seemed tempted to overstep the limit, Beatrice grew so sad, so stern, and withal wore such a look of desolate separation, shuddering at itself, that not a spoken word was requisite to repel him. At such times, he was startled at the horrible suspicions that rose, monster-like, out of the caverns of his heart, and stared him in the face; his love grew thin and faint as the morning-mist; his doubts alone had substance. But when Beatrice's face brightened again, after the momentary shadow, she was transformed at once from the mysterious, questionable being, whom he had watched with so much awe and horror; she was now the beautiful and unsophisticated girl, whom he felt that his spirit knew with a certainty beyond all other knowledge.

A considerable time had now passed since Giovanni's last meeting with Baglioni. One morning, however, he was disagreeably surprised by a visit from the Professor, whom he had scarcely thought of for whole weeks, and would willingly have forgotten still longer. Given up, as he had long been, to a pervading excitement, he could tolerate no companions, except upon condition of their perfect sympathy with his present state of feeling. Such sympathy was not to be expected from Professor Baglioni.

The visitor chatted carelessly, for a few moments, about the gossip of the city and the University, and then took up another topic.

"I have been reading an old classic author lately," said he, "and met with a story that strangely interested me. Possibly you may remember it. It is of an Indian prince, who sent a beautiful woman as a present to Alexander the Great. She was as lovely as the dawn, and gorgeous as the sunset; but what especially distinguished her was a certain rich perfume in her breath—richer than a garden of Persian roses. Alexander, as was natural to a youthful conqueror, fell in love at first sight with this magnificent stranger. But a certain sage physician, happening to be present, discovered a terrible secret in regard to her."

"And what was that?" asked Giovanni, turning his eyes downward to avoid those of the Professor.

"That this lovely woman," continued Baglioni, with emphasis, "had been nourished with poisons from her birth upward, until her whole nature was so imbued with them, that she herself had become the deadliest poison in existence. Poison was her element of life. With that rich perfume of her breath, she blasted the very air. Her love would have been poison!—her embrace death! Is not this a marvellous tale?"

"A childish fable," answered Giovanni, nervously starting from his chair. "I marvel how your worship finds time to read such nonsense, among your graver studies."

"By the bye," said the Professor, looking uneasily about him, "what singular fragrance is this in your apartment? Is it the perfume of your gloves? It is faint, but delicious, and yet, after all, by no means agreeable. Were I to breathe it long, methinks it would make me ill. It is like the breath of a flower—but I see no flowers in the chamber."

"Nor are there any," replied Giovanni, who had turned pale as the Professor spoke; "nor, I think, is there any fragrance, except in your worship's imagination. Odors, being a sort of element combined of the sensual and the spiritual, are apt to deceive us in this manner. The recollection of a perfume—the bare idea of it—may easily be mistaken for a present reality."

"Aye; but my sober imagination does not often play such tricks," said Baglioni; "and were I to fancy any kind of odor, it would be that of some vile apothecary drug, wherewith my fingers are likely enough to be imbued. Our worshipful friend Rappaccini, as I have heard, tinctures his medicaments with odors richer than those of Araby. Doubtless, likewise, the fair and learned Signora Beatrice would minister to her patients with draughts as sweet as a maiden's breath. But wo to him that sips them!"

Giovanni's face evinced many contending emotions. The tone in which the Professor alluded to the pure and lovely daughter of Rappaccini was a torture to his soul; and yet, the intimation of a view of her character, opposite to his own, gave instantaneous distinctness to a thousand dim suspicions, which now grinned at him like so many demons. But he strove hard to quell them, and to respond to Baglioni with a true lover's perfect faith.

"Signor Professor," said he, "you were my father's friend—perchance, too, it is your purpose to act a friendly part towards his son. I would fain feel nothing towards you save respect and deference. But I pray you to observe, Signor, that there is one subject on which we must not speak. You know not the Signora Beatrice. You cannot, therefore, estimate the wrong—the blasphemy, I may even say—that is offered to her character by a light or injurious word."

"Giovanni!—my poor Giovanni!" answered the Professor, with a calm expression of pity, "I know this wretched girl far better than yourself. You shall hear the truth in respect to the poisoner Rappaccini, and his poisonous daughter. Yes; poisonous as she is beautiful! Listen; for even should you do violence to my gray hairs, it shall not silence me. That old fable of the Indian woman has become a truth, by the deep and deadly science of Rappaccini, and in the person of the lovely Beatrice!"

Giovanni groaned and hid his face.

"Her father," continued Baglioni, "was not restrained by natural affection from offering up his child, in this horrible manner, as the victim of his insane zeal for science. For—let us do him justice—he is as true a man of science as ever distilled his own heart in an alembic. What, then, will be your fate? Beyond a doubt, you are selected as the material of some new experiment. Perhaps the result is to be death—perhaps a fate more awful still! Rappaccini, with what he calls the interest of science before his eyes, will hesitate at nothing."

"It is a dream!" muttered Giovanni to himself, "surely it is a dream!"

"But," resumed the Professor, "be of good cheer, son of my friend! It is not yet too late for the rescue. Possibly, we may even succeed in bringing back this miserable child within the limits of ordinary nature, from which her father's madness has estranged her. Behold this little silver vase! It was wrought by the hands of the renowned Benvenuto Cellini, and is well worthy to be a love-gift to the fairest dame in Italy. But its contents are invaluable. One little sip of this antidote would have rendered the most virulent poisons of the Borgias innocuous. Doubt not that it will be as efficacious against those of Rappaccini. Bestow the vase, and the precious liquid within it, on your Beatrice, and hopefully await the result."

Baglioni laid a small, exquisitely wrought silver phial on the table, and withdrew, leaving what he had said to produce its effect upon the young man's mind.

"We will thwart Rappaccini yet!" thought he, chuckling to himself, as he descended the stairs. "But, let us confess the truth of him, he is a wonderful man!—a wonderful man indeed! A vile empiric, however, in his practice, and therefore not to be tolerated by those who respect the good old rules of the medical profession!"

Throughout Giovanni's whole acquaintance with Beatrice, he had occasionally, as we have said, been haunted by dark surmises as to her character. Yet, so thoroughly had she made herself felt by him as a simple, natural, most affectionate and guileless creature, that the image now held up by Professor Baglioni, looked as strange and incredible, as if it were not in accordance with his own original conception. True, there were ugly recollections connected with his first glimpses of the beautiful girl; he could not quite forget the bouquet that withered in her grasp, and the insect that perished amid the sunny air, by no ostensible agency save the fragrance of her breath. These incidents, however, dissolving in the pure light of her character, had no longer the efficacy of facts, but were acknowledged as mistaken fantasies, by whatever testimony of the senses they might appear to be substantiated. There is something truer and more real, than what we can see with the eyes, and touch with

the finger. On such better evidence, had Giovanni founded his confidence in Beatrice, though rather by the necessary force of her
high attributes, than by any deep and generous faith on his part.
But, now, his spirit was incapable of sustaining itself at the height
to which the early enthusiasm of passion had exalted it; he fell
down, grovelling among earthly doubts, and defiled therewith the
pure whiteness of Beatrice's image. Not that he gave her up; he
did but distrust. He resolved to institute some decisive test that
should satisfy him, once for all, whether there were those dreadful
peculiarities in her physical nature, which could not be supposed
to exist without some corresponding monstrosity of soul. His eyes,
gazing down afar, might have deceived him as to the lizard, the
insect, and the flowers. But if he could witness, at the distance of a
few paces, the sudden blight of one fresh and healthful flower in
Beatrice's hand, there would be room for no further question. With
this idea, he hastened to the florist's, and purchased a bouquet
that was still gemmed with the morning dew-drops.

It was now the customary hour of his daily interview with
Beatrice. Before descending into the garden, Giovanni failed not
to look at his figure in the mirror; a vanity to be expected in a beautiful young man, yet, as displaying itself at that troubled and feverish
moment, the token of a certain shallowness of feeling and insin-
cerity of character. He did gaze, however, and said to himself, that
his features had never before possessed so rich a grace, nor his eyes
such vivacity, nor his cheeks so warm a hue of superabundant life.

"At least," thought he, "her poison has not yet insinuated itself
into my system. I am no flower to perish in her grasp!"

With that thought, he turned his eyes on the bouquet, which
he had never once laid aside from his hand. A thrill of indefinable
horror shot through his frame, on perceiving that those dewy flowers were already beginning to droop; they wore the aspect of things
that had been fresh and lovely, yesterday. Giovanni grew white as
marble, and stood motionless before the mirror, staring at his own
reflection there, as at the likeness of something frightful. He remembered Baglioni's remark about the fragrance that seemed to
pervade the chamber. It must have been the poison in his breath!
Then he shuddered—shuddered at himself! Recovering from his
stupor, he began to watch, with curious eye, a spider that was busily
at work, hanging its web from the antique cornice of the apartment, crossing and re-crossing the artful system of interwoven

lines, as vigorous and active a spider as ever dangled from an old ceiling. Giovanni bent towards the insect, and emitted a deep, long breath. The spider suddenly ceased its toil; the web vibrated with a tremor originating in the body of the small artizan. Again Giovanni sent forth a breath, deeper, longer, and imbued with a venomous feeling out of his heart; he knew not whether he were wicked or only desperate. The spider made a convulsive gripe with his limbs, and hung dead across the window.

"Accursed! Accursed!" muttered Giovanni, addressing himself. "Hast thou grown so poisonous, that this deadly insect perishes by thy breath?"

At that moment, a rich, sweet voice came floating up from the garden: "Giovanni! Giovanni! It is past the hour! Why tarriest thou! Come down!"

"Yes," muttered Giovanni again. "She is the only being whom my breath may not slay! Would that it might!"

He rushed down, and in an instant, was standing before the bright and loving eyes of Beatrice. A moment ago, his wrath and despair had been so fierce that he could have desired nothing so much as to wither her by a glance. But, with her actual presence, there came influences which had too real an existence to be at once shaken off; recollections of the delicate and benign power of her feminine nature, which had so often enveloped him in a religious calm; recollections of many a holy and passionate outgush of her heart, when the pure fountain had been unsealed from its depths, and made visible in its transparency to his mental eye; recollections which, had Giovanni known how to estimate them, would have assured him that all this ugly mystery was but an earthly illusion, and that, whatever mist of evil might seem to have gathered over her, the real Beatrice was a heavenly angel. Incapable as he was of such high faith, still her presence had not utterly lost its magic. Giovanni's rage was quelled into an aspect of sullen insensibility. Beatrice, with a quick spiritual sense, immediately felt that there was a gulf of blackness between them, which neither he nor she could pass. They walked on together, sad and silent, and came thus to the marble fountain, and to its pool of water on the ground, in the midst of which grew the shrub that bore gem-like blossoms. Giovanni was affrighted at the eager enjoyment—the appetite, as it were—with which he found himself inhaling the fragrance of the flowers.

"Beatrice," asked he abruptly, "whence came this shrub!"

"My father created it," answered she, with simplicity.

"Created it! created it!" repeated Giovanni. "What mean you, Beatrice?"

"He is a man fearfully acquainted with the secrets of nature," replied Beatrice; "and, at the hour when I first drew breath, this plant sprang from the soil, the offspring of his science, of his intellect, while I was but his earthly child. Approach it not!" continued she, observing with terror that Giovanni was drawing nearer to the shrub. "It has qualities that you little dream of. But I, dearest Giovanni—I grew up and blossomed with the plant, and was nourished with its breath. It was my sister, and I loved it with a human affection: for—alas! hast thou not suspected it? there was an awful doom."

Here Giovanni frowned so darkly upon her that Beatrice paused and trembled. But her faith in his tenderness reassured her, and made her blush that she had doubted for an instant.

"There was an awful doom," she continued,— "the effect of my father's fatal love of science—which estranged me from all society of my kind. Until Heaven sent thee, dearest Giovanni, Oh! how lonely was thy poor Beatrice!"

"Was it a hard doom?" asked Giovanni, fixing his eyes upon her.

"Only of late have I known how hard it was," answered she tenderly. "Oh, yes; but my heart was torpid, and therefore quiet."

Giovanni's rage broke forth from his sullen gloom like a lightning-flash out of a dark cloud.

"Accursed one!" cried he, with venomous scorn and anger. "And finding thy solitude wearisome, thou hast severed me, likewise, from all the warmth of life, and enticed me into thy region of unspeakable horror!"

"Giovanni!" exclaimed Beatrice, turning her large bright eyes upon his face. The force of his words had not found its way into her mind; she was merely thunder-struck.

"Yes, poisonous thing!" repeated Giovanni, beside himself with passion. "Thou hast done it! Thou hast blasted me! Thou hast filled my veins with poison! Thou hast made me as hateful, as ugly, as loathsome and deadly a creature as thyself—a world's wonder of hideous monstrosity! Now—if our breath be happily as fatal to ourselves as to all others—let us join our lips in one kiss of unutterable hatred, and so die!"

"What has befallen me?" murmured Beatrice, with a low moan out of her heart. "Holy Virgin pity me, a poor heartbroken child!"

"Thou! Dost thou pray?" cried Giovanni, still with the same fiendish scorn. "Thy very prayers, as they come from thy lips, taint the atmosphere with death. Yes, yes; let us pray! Let us to church, and dip our fingers in the holy water at the portal! They that come after us will perish as by a pestilence. Let us sign crosses in the air! It will be scattering curses abroad in the likeness of holy symbols!"

"Giovanni," said Beatrice calmly, for her grief was beyond passion, "Why dost thou join thyself with me thus in those terrible words? I, it is true, am the horrible thing thou namest me. But thou!—what hast thou to do, save with one other shudder at my hideous misery, to go forth out of the garden and mingle with thy race, and forget that there ever crawled on earth such a monster as poor Beatrice?"

"Dost thou pretend ignorance?" asked Giovanni, scowling upon her. "Behold! This power have I gained from the pure daughter of Rappaccini!"

There was a swarm of summer-insects flitting through the air, in search of the food promised by the flower-odors of the fatal garden. They circled round Giovanni's head, and were evidently attracted towards him by the same influence which had drawn them, for an instant, within the sphere of several of the shrubs. He sent forth a breath among them, and smiled bitterly at Beatrice, as at least a score of the insects fell dead upon the ground.

"I see it! I see it!" shrieked Beatrice. "It is my father's fatal science? No, no, Giovanni; it was not I! Never, never! I dreamed only to love thee, and be with thee a little time, and so to let thee pass away, leaving but thine image in mine heart. For, Giovanni—believe it— though my body be nourished with poison, my spirit is God's creature, and craves love as its daily food. But my father!—he has united us in this fearful sympathy. Yes; spurn me!—tread upon me!—kill me! Oh, what is death, after such words as thine? But it was not I! Not for a world of bliss would I have done it!"

Giovanni's passion had exhausted itself in its outburst from his lips. There now came across him a sense, mournful, and not without tenderness, of the intimate and peculiar relationship between Beatrice and himself. They stood, as it were, in an utter solitude, which would be made none the less solitary by the densest throng of human life. Ought not, then, the desert of humanity around them to press this insulated pair closer together? If they should be cruel to one another, who was there to be kind to them? Besides, thought Giovanni, might there not still be a hope of his returning within the limits of ordinary nature, and leading Beatrice—the redeemed Beatrice—by the hand? Oh, weak, and selfish, and unworthy spirit, that could dream of an earthly union and earthly happiness as possible, after such deep love had been so bitterly wronged as was Beatrice's love by Giovanni's blighting words! No, no; there could be no such hope. She must pass heavily, with that broken heart, across the borders of Time—she must bathe her hurts in some fount of Paradise, and forget her grief in the light of immortality—and there be well!

But Giovanni did not know it.

"Dear Beatrice," said he, approaching her, while she shrank away, as always at his approach, but now with a different impulse— "dearest Beatrice, our fate is not yet so desperate. Behold! There is a medicine, potent, as a wise physician has assured me, and almost divine in its efficacy. It is composed of ingredients the most opposite to those by which thy awful father has brought this calamity upon thee and me. It is distilled of blessed herbs. Shall we not quaff it together, and thus be purified from evil?"

"Give it me!" said Beatrice, extending her hand to receive the little silver phial which Giovanni took from his bosom. She added, with a peculiar emphasis: "I will drink—but do thou await the result."

She put Baglioni's antidote to her lips; and, at the same moment, the figure of Rappaccini emerged from the portal, and came slowly towards the marble fountain. As he drew near, the pale man of science seemed to gaze with a triumphant expression at the beautiful youth and maiden, as might an artist who should spend his life in achieving a picture or a group of statuary, and finally be satisfied with his success. He paused—his bent form grew erect with conscious power, he spread out his hand over them, in the attitude of a father imploring a blessing upon his children. But those were the same hands that had thrown poison into the stream of their lives! Giovanni trembled. Beatrice shuddered very nervously, and pressed her hand upon her heart.

"My daughter," said Rappaccini, "thou art no longer lonely in the world! Pluck one of those precious gems from thy sister shrub, and bid thy bridegroom wear it in his bosom. It will not harm him now! My science, and the sympathy between thee and him, have so wrought within his system, that he now stands apart from common men, as thou dost, daughter of my pride and triumph, from ordinary women. Pass on, then, through the world, most dear to one another, and dreadful to all besides!"

"My father," said Beatrice, feebly—and still, as she spoke, she kept her hand upon her heart— "wherefore didst thou inflict this miserable doom upon thy child?"

"Miserable!" exclaimed Rappaccini. "What mean you, foolish girl? Dost thou deem it misery to be endowed with marvellous gifts, against which no power nor strength could avail an enemy? Misery, to be able to quell the mightiest with a breath? Misery, to be as terrible as thou art beautiful? Wouldst thou, then, have preferred the condition of a weak woman, exposed to all evil, and capable of none?"

"I would fain have been loved, not feared," murmured Beatrice, sinking down upon the ground.— "But now it matters not; I am going, father, where the evil, which thou hast striven to mingle with my being, will pass away like a dream—like the fragrance of these poisonous flowers, which will no longer taint my breath among the flowers of Eden. Farewell, Giovanni! Thy words of hatred are like lead within my heart—but they, too, will fall away as I ascend. Oh, was there not, from the first, more poison in thy nature than in mine?"

To Beatrice—so radically had her earthly part been wrought upon by Rappaccini's skill—as poison had been life, so the powerful antidote was death. And thus the poor victim of man's ingenuity and of thwarted nature, and of the fatality that attends all such efforts of perverted wisdom, perished there, at the feet of her father and Giovanni. Just at that moment, Professor Pietro Baglioni looked forth from the window, and called loudly, in a tone of triumph mixed with horror, to the thunder-stricken man of science: "Rappaccini! Rappaccini! And is *this* the upshot of your experiment?"

The American's Tale
Arthur Conan Doyle

"It air strange, it air," he was saying as I opened the door of the room where our social little semiliterary society met; "but I could tell you queerer things than that 'ere—almighty queer things. You can't learn everything out of books, sirs, nohow. You see it ain't the men as can string English together and as has had good eddications as finds themselves in the queer places I've been in. They're mostly rough men, sirs, as can scarce speak aright, far less tell with pen and ink the things they've seen; but if they could they'd make some of your European's har riz with astonishment. They would, sirs, you bet!"

His name was Jefferson Adams, I believe; I know his initials were J. A., for you may see them yet deeply whittled on the right-hand upper panel of our smoking-room door. He left us this legacy, and also some artistic patterns done in tobacco juice upon our Turkey carpet; but beyond these reminiscences our American story-teller has vanished from our ken. He gleamed across our ordinary quiet conviviality like some brilliant meteor, and then was lost in the outer darkness. That night, however, our Nevada friend was in full swing; and I quietly lit my pipe and dropped into the nearest chair, anxious not to interrupt his story.

"Mind you," he continued, "I hain't got no grudge against your men of science. I likes and respects a chap as can match every beast and plant, from a huckleberry to a grizzly with a jaw-breakin' name; but if you wants real interestin' facts, something a bit juicy, you go to your whalers and your frontiersmen, and your scouts and Hudson Bay men, chaps who mostly can scarce sign their names."

There was a pause here, as Mr. Jefferson Adams produced a long cheroot and lit it. We preserved a strict silence in the room, for we had already learned that on the slightest interruption our Yankee drew himself into his shell again. He glanced round with a self-satisfied smile as he remarked our expectant looks, and continued through a halo of smoke.

"Now which of you gentlemen has ever been in Arizona? None, I'll warrant. And of all English or Americans as can put pen to paper, how many has been in Arizona? Precious few, I calc'late. I've been there, sirs, lived there for years; and when I think of what I've seen there, why, I can scarce get myself to believe it now.

"Ah, there's a country! I was one of Walker's filibusters, as they chose to call us; and after we'd busted up, and the chief was shot, some of us made tracks and located down there. A reg'lar English and American colony, we was, with our wives and children, and all complete. I reckon there's some of the old folk there yet, and that they hain't forgotten what I'm agoing to tell you. No, I warrant they hain't, never on this side of the grave, sirs.

"I was talking about the country, though; and I guess I could astonish you considerable if I spoke of nothing else. To think of such a land being built for a few 'Greasers' and half-breeds! It's a misusing of the gifts of Providence, that's what I calls it. Grass as hung over a chap's head as he rode through it, and trees so thick that you couldn't catch a glimpse of blue sky for leagues and leagues, and orchids like umbrellas! Maybe one of you has seen a plant as they calls the 'fly-catcher,' in some parts of the States?"

"Dionaea muscipula," murmured Dawson, our scientific man par excellence.

"Ah, 'Die near a municipal,' that's him! You'll see a fly stand on that 'ere plant, and then you'll see the two sides of a leaf snap up together and catch it between them, and grind it up and mash it to bits, for all the world like some great sea squid with its beak; and hours after, if you open the leaf, you'll see the body lying half-digested, and in bits. Well, I've seen those flytraps in Arizona with leaves eight and ten feet long, and thorns or teeth a foot or more; why, they could—But darn it, I'm going too fast!

"It's about the death of Joe Hawkins I was going to tell you; 'bout as queer a thing, I reckon, as ever you heard tell on. There wasn't nobody in Montana as didn't know of Joe Hawkins— 'Alabama' Joe, as he was called there. A reg'lar out and outer, he was, 'bout the darndest skunk as ever man clapt eyes on. He was a good chap enough, mind ye, as long as you stroked him the right way;

but rile him anyhow, and he were worse nor a wildcat. I've seen
him empty his six-shooter into a crowd as chanced to jostle him
agoing into Simpson's bar when there was a dance on; and he
bowied Tom Hooper 'cause he spilt his liquor over his weskit by
mistake. No, he didn't stick at murder, Joe didn't; and he weren't
a man to be trusted further nor you could see him.

"Now at the time I tell on, when Joe Hawkins was swaggerin'
about the town and layin' down the law with his shootin'-irons,
there was an Englishman there of the name of Scott—Tom Scott, if
I rec'lects aright. This chap Scott was a thorough Britisher (beggin'
the present company's pardon), and yet he didn't freeze much to
the British set there, or they didn't freeze much to him. He was a
quiet simple man, Scott was—rather too quiet for a rough set like
that; sneakin' they called him, but he weren't that. He kept hisself
mostly apart, an' didn't interfere with nobody so long as he were
left alone. Some said as how he'd been kinder ill-treated at home—
been a Chartist, or something of that sort, and had to up stick and
run; but he never spoke of it hisself, an' never complained. Bad
luck or good, that chap kept a stiff lip on him.

"This chap Scott was a sort o' butt among the men about Montana for he was so quiet an' simple-like. There was no party either
to take up his grievances; for, as I've been saying, the Britishers
hardly counted him one of them, and many a rough joke they played
on him. He never cut up rough, but was polite to all hisself. I think
the boys got to think he hadn't much grit in him till he showed 'em
their mistake.

"It was in Simpson's bar as the row got up, an' that led to the
queer thing I was going to tell you of. Alabama Joe and one or two
other rowdies were dead on the Britishers in those days, and they
spoke their opinions pretty free, though I warned them as there'd
be an almighty muss. That partic'lar night Joe was nigh half drunk,
an' he swaggered about the town with his six-shooter, lookin' out
for a quarrel. Then he turned into the bar where he know'd he'd
find some o' the English as ready for one as he was hisself. Sure
enough, there was half a dozen lounging about, an' Tom Scott
standin' alone before the stove. Joe sat down by the table, and put
his revolver and bowie down in front of him. 'Them's my arguments, Jeff,' he says to me, 'if any white-livered Britisher dares
give me the lie.' I tried to stop him, sirs; but he weren't a man as
you could easily turn, an' he began to speak in a way as no chap

could stand. Why, even a 'Greaser' would flare up if you said as much of Greaserland! There was a commotion at the bar, an' every man laid his hands on his wepin's; but afore they could draw we heard a quiet voice from the stove: 'Say your prayers, Joe Hawkins; for, by Heaven, you're a dead man!' Joe turned round and looked like grabbin' at his iron; but it weren't no manner of use. Tom Scott was standing up, covering him with his Derringer; a smile on his white face, but the very devil shining in his eye. 'It ain't that the old country has used me overwell,' he says, 'but no man shall speak agin it afore me, and live.' For a second or two I could see his finger tighten round the trigger, an' then he gave a laugh, an' threw the pistol on the floor. 'No,' he says, 'I can't shoot a half-drunk man. Take your dirty life, Joe, an' use it better nor you have done. You've been nearer the grave this night than you will be agin until your time comes. You'd best make tracks now, I guess. Nay, never look black at me, man; I'm not afeard at your shootin'-iron. A bully's nigh always a coward.' And he swung contemptuously round, and relit his half-smoked pipe from the stove; while Alabama slunk out o' the bar, with the laughs of the Britishers ringing in his ears. I saw his face as he passed me, and on it I saw murder, sirs—murder, as plain as ever I seed anything in my life.

"I stayed in the bar after the row, and watched Tom Scott as he shook hands with the men about. It seemed kinder queer to me to see him smilin' and cheerful-like; for I knew Joe's bloodthirsty mind, and that the Englishman had small chance of ever seeing the morning. He lived in an out-of-the-way sort of place, you see, clean off the trail, and had to pass through the Flytrap Gulch to get to it. This here gulch was a marshy gloomy place, lonely enough during the day even; for it were always a creepy sort o' thing to see the great eight- and ten-foot leaves snapping up if aught touched them; but at night there were never a soul near. Some parts of the marsh, too, were soft and deep, and a body thrown in would be gone by the morning. I could see Alabama Joe crouchin' under the leaves of the great Flytrap in the darkest part of the gulch, with a scowl on his face and a revolver in his hand; I could see it sirs, as plain as with my two eyes.

"'Bout midnight Simpson shuts up his bar, so out we had to go. Tom Scott started off for his three-mile walk at a slashing pace. I just dropped him a hint as he passed me, for I kinder liked the chap. 'Keep your Derringer loose in your belt, sir,' I says, 'for you might chance to need it.' He looked round at me with his quiet smile, and then I lost sight of him in the gloom. I never thought to see him again. He'd hardly gone afore Simpson comes up to me and says, 'There'll be a nice job in the Flytrap Gulch tonight, Jeff; the boys say that Hawkins started half an hour ago to wait for Scott and shoot him on sight. I calc'late the coroner'll be wanted tomorrow.'

"What passed in the gulch that night? It were a question as were asked pretty free next morning. A half-breed was in Ferguson's store after daybreak, and he said as he'd chanced to be near the gulch 'bout one in the morning. It warn't easy to get at his story, he seemed so uncommon scared; but he told us, at last, as he'd heard the fearfulest screams in the stillness of the night. There weren't no shots, he said, but scream after scream, kinder muffled, like a man with a serape over his head, an' in mortal pain. Abner Brandon and me, and a few more, was in the store at the time; so we mounted and rode out to Scott's house, passing through the gulch on the way. There weren't nothing partic'lar to be seen there—no blood nor marks of a fight, nor nothing; and when we gets up to Scott's house, out he comes to meet us as fresh as a lark. 'Hullo, Jeff!' says he, 'no need for the pistols after all. Come in an' have a cocktail, boys.' 'Did ye see or hear nothing as ye came home last night?' says I. 'No,' says he; 'all was quiet enough. An owl kinder moaning in the Flytrap Gulch—that was all. Come, jump off and have a glass.' 'Thank ye,' said Abner. So off we gets, and Tom Scott rode into the settlement with us when we went back.

"An all-fired commotion was on in Main Street as we rode into it. The 'Merican party seemed to have gone clean crazed. Alabama Joe was gone, not a darned particle of him left. Since he went out to the gulch nary eye had seen him. As we got off our horses there was a considerable crowd in front of Simpson's, and some ugly looks at Tom Scott, I can tell you. There was a clickin' of pistols, and I saw as Scott had his hand in his bosom too. There weren't a single English face about. 'Stand aside, Jeff Adams,' says Zebb Humphrey, as great a scoundrel as ever lived, 'you hain't got no hand in this game. Say, boys, are we, free Americans, to be murdered by any darned Britisher?' It was the quickest thing as ever I seed. There was a rush an' a crack; Zebb was down, with Scott's ball in his thigh, and Scott hisself was on the ground with a dozen men holding him. It weren't no use struggling, so he lay quiet. They seemed a bit uncertain what to do with him at first, but then one of Alabama's special chums put them up to it. 'Joe's gone,' he said; 'nothing ain't surer nor that, an' there lies the man as killed him. Some on you knows as Joe went on business to the gulch last night; he never came back. That 'ere Britisher passed through after he'd gone; they'd had a row, screams is heard 'mong the great flytraps. I say agin he has played poor Joe some o' his sneakin' tricks, an' thrown him into the swamp. It ain't no wonder as the body is gone. But air we to stan' by and see English murderin' our own chums? I guess not. Let Judge Lynch try him, that's what I say.' 'Lynch him!" shouted a hundred angry voices—for all the rag-tag an' bobtail o' the settlement was round us by this time. 'Here, boys, fetch a rope, and swing him up. Up with him over Simpson's door!' 'See here though,' says another, coming forrards; 'let's hang him by the great flytrap in the gulch. Let Joe see as he's revenged, if so be as he's buried 'bout theer.' There was a shout for this, an' away they went, with Scott tied on his mustang in the middle, and a mounted guard, with cocked revolvers, round him; for we knew as there was a score or so Britishers about, as didn't seem to recognise Judge Lynch, and was dead on a free fight.

"I went out with them, my heart bleedin' for Scott, though he didn't seem a cent put out, he didn't. He were game to the back-bone. Seems kinder queer, sirs, hangin' a man to a flytrap; but our'n were a reg'lar tree, and the leaves like a brace of boats with a hinge between 'em and thorns at the bottom.

"We passed down the gulch to the place where the great one grows, and there we seed it with the leaves, some open, some shut. But we seed something worse nor that. Standin' round the tree was some thirty men, Britishers all, an' armed to the teeth. They was waitin' for us evidently, an' had a businesslike look about 'em, as if they'd come for something and meant to have it. There was the raw material there for about as warm a scrimmidge as ever I seed. As we rode up, a great red-bearded Scotch-man—Cameron were his name—stood out afore the rest, his revolver cocked in his hand. 'See here, boys,' he says, 'you've got no call to hurt a hair of that man's head. You hain't proved as Joe is dead yet; and if you had, you hain't proved as Scott killed him. Anyhow, it were in self-defence; for you all know as he was lying in wait for Scott, to shoot him on sight; so I say agin, you hain't got no call to hurt that man; and what's more, I've got thirty six-barrelled arguments against your doin' it.' 'It's an interestin' pint, and worth arguin' out,' said the man as was Alabama Joe's special chum. There was a clickin' of pistols, and a loosenin' of knives, and the two parties began to draw up to one another, an' it looked like a rise in the mortality of Montana. Scott was standing behind with a pistol at his ear if he stirred, lookin' quiet and composed as having no money on the table, when sudden he gives a start an' a shout as rang in our ears like a trumpet. 'Joe!' he cried, 'Joe! Look at him! In the flytrap!' We all turned an' looked where he was pointin'. Jerusalem! I think we won't get that picter out of our minds agin. One of the great leaves of the flytrap, that had been shut and touchin' the ground as it lay, was slowly rolling back upon its hinges. There, lying like a child in its cradle, was Alabama Joe in the hollow of the leaf. The great thorns had been slowly driven through his **heart** as it shut upon him. We could see as he'd tried to cut his way **out**, for there was a slit in the thick fleshy leaf, an' his bowie was **in his** hand; but it had smothered him first. He'd lain down on it **likely** to keep the damp off while he were awaitin' for Scott, and **it had** closed on him as you've seen your little hothouse ones do on **a fly**; an' there he were as we found him, torn and crushed into pulp by the great jagged teeth of the man-eatin' plant. There, sirs, I think you'll own as that's a curious story."

"And what became of Scott?" asked Jack Sinclair.

"Why, we carried him back on our shoulders, we did, to Simpson's bar, and he stood us liquors round. Made a speech too—a darned fine speech—from the counter. Somethin' about the British lion an' the 'Merican eagle walkin' arm in arm for ever an' a day. And now, sirs, that yarn was long, and my cheroot's out, so I reckon I'll make tracks afore it's later"; and with a "Good-night!" he left the room.

"A most extraordinary narrative!" said Dawson. "Who would have thought a Dionaea had such power!"

"Deuced rum yarn!" said young Sinclair.

"Evidently a matter-of-fact truthful man," said the doctor.

"Or the most original liar that ever lived," said I.

I wonder which he was.

The Man-Eating Tree
Phil Robinson

(Before committing this paper to the ridicule of the Great Mediocre—for many, I fear, will be inclined to regard this story as
incredible—I would venture on the expression of an opinion regarding credulity, which I do not remember to have met before. It is
this. Placing supreme Wisdom and supreme Unwisdom at the two
extremes, and myself in the exact mean between them, I am surprised to find that, whether I travel towards the one extreme or
the other, the credulity of those I meet increases. To put it as a
paradox—*whether a man be foolisher or wiser than I am, he is
more credulous.* I make this remark to point out to those of the
Great Mediocre, whose notice it may have escaped, that credulity
is not of itself shameful or contemptible, and that it depends upon
the manner rather than the matter of their belief, whether they
gravitate towards the sage or the reverse way. According, therefore, to the incredibility found in the following, the reader may
measure, as pleases him, his wisdom or his unwisdom.)

Peregrine Oriel, my maternal uncle, was a great traveller, as
his prophetical sponsors at the font seemed to have guessed he would
he. Indeed he had rummaged in the garrets and cellars of the earth
with something more than ordinary diligence. But in the narrative
of his travels he did not, unfortunately, preserve the judicious caution of Xenophon between the thing seen and the thing heard, and
thus it came about that the town-councillors of Brunsbüttel (to whom
he had shown a duck-billed platypus, caught alive by him in Australia, and who had him posted for an importer of artificial vermin)
were not alone in their scepticism of some of the old man's tales.

41

Thus, for instance, who could hear and believe the tale of the man-sucking tree from which he had barely escaped with life? He called it himself more terrible than the Upas. "This awful plant, that rears its splendid death-shade in the central solitude of a Nubian fern forest, sickens by its unwholesome humors all vegetation from its immediate vicinity, and feeds upon the wild beasts that, in the terror of the chase, or the heat of noon, seek the thick shelter of its boughs; upon the birds that, flitting across the open space, come within the charmed circle of its power, or innocently refresh themselves from the cups of its great waxen flowers; upon even man himself when, an infrequent prey, the savage seeks its asylum in the storm, or turns from the harsh foot-wounding sword-grass of the glade, to pluck the wondrous fruit that hang plumb down among the wondrous foliage." And such fruit!— "glorious golden ovals, great honey drops, swelling by their own weight into pear-shaped translucencies. The foliage glistens with a strange dew, that all day long drips on to the ground below; nurturing a rank growth of grasses, which shoot up in places so high that their spikes of fierce blood-fed green show far up among the deep-tinted foliage of the terrible tree, and, like a jealous body-guard, keep concealed the fearful secret of the charnel-house within, and draw round the black roots of the murderous plant a decent screen of living green."

Such was his description of the plant; and the other day, looking it up in a botanical dictionary, I find that there is really known to naturalists a family of carnivorous-plants; but I see that they are most of them very small, and prey upon little insects only. My maternal uncle, however, knew nothing of this, for he died before the days of the discovery of the sun, dew, and pitcher plants; and grounding his knowledge of the man-sucking tree simply on his own terrible experience of it, explained its existence by theories of his own. Denying the fixity of all the laws of nature except one, that the stronger shall endeavor to consume the weaker, and holding even this fixity to be itself only a means to a greater general changefulness, he argued that—since any partial distribution of the faculty of self-defence would presume an unworthy partiality in the Creator, and since the sensual instincts of beast and vegetable are manifestly analogous—the world must be as percipient as sentient throughout. Carrying on his theory (for it was something more than hypothesis with him) a stage or two further, he arrived at the belief that, given the necessity of any imminent danger or urgent self-interest, every animal or vegetable could eventually revolutionize its nature, the wolf feeding on grass or nesting in trees, and the violet arming herself with thorns or entrapping insects.

"How," he would ask, "can we claim for man the consequence of perceptions to sensations, and yet deny to beasts that hear, see, feel, smell, and taste, a percipient principle co-existent with their senses? And if in the whole range of the animate world there is this gift of self-defence against extirpation, and offence against weakness, why is the inanimate world, holding as fierce a struggle for existence as the other, to be left defenceless and unarmed? And I deny that it is. The Brazilian epiphyte strangles the tree and sucks out its juices. The tree, again, to starve off its vampire parasite, withdraws its juices into its roots, and piercing the ground in some new place, turns the current of its sap into other growths. The epiphyte then drops off the dead boughs on to the fresh green sprouts springing from the ground beneath it,—and so the fight goes on. Again, look at the Indian peepul tree; in what does the fierce yearning of its roots towards the distant well differ from the sad struggling of the camel to the oasis, or of Sennacherib's army to the saving Nile?

"Is the sensitive plant unconscious! I have walked for miles through plains of it, and watched, till the watching almost made me afraid lest the plant should pluck up courage and turn upon me, the green carpet paling into silver gray before my feet, and fainting away all round me as I walked. So strangely did I feel the influence of this universal aversion, that I would have argued with the plant; but what was the use? If only I stretched out my hands, the mere shadow of the limb terrified the vegetable to sickness; shrubs crumbled up at every commencement of my speech; and at my periods great sturdy-looking bushes, to whose robustness I had foolishly appealed, sank in pallid supplication. Not a leaf would keep me company. A breath went forth from me that sickened life. My mere presence paralyzed life, and I was glad at last to come out among a less timid vegetation, and to feel the resentful spear-grass retaliating on the heedlessness that would have crushed it. The vegetable world, however, has its revenges. You may keep the guinea-pig in a hutch, but how will you pet the basilisk? The little sensitive plant in your garden amuses your children (who will find pleasure also in seeing cockchafers spin round on a pin), but how

could you transplant a vegetable that seizes the running deer,
strikes down the passing bird, and once taking hold of him, sucks
the carcass of man himself, till his matter becomes as vague as his
mind, and all his animate capabilities cannot snatch him from the
terrible embrace of—God help him!—an inanimate tree?

"Many years ago," said my uncle, "I turned my restless steps
towards Central Africa, and made the journey from where the
Senegal empties itself into the Atlantic to the Nile, skirting the
Great Desert, and reaching Nubia on my way to the eastern coast.
I had with me then three native attendants,—two of them brothers, the third, Otona, a young savage from the gaboon uplands, a
mere lad in his teens; and one day, leaving my mule with the two
men, who were pitching my tent for the night, I went on with my gun,
the boy accompanying me, towards a fern forest, which I saw in the
near distance. As I approached it I found the forest was cut into two
by a wide glade; and seeing a small herd of the common antelope, an
excellent beast in the pot, browsing their way along the shaded side, I
crept after them. Though ignorant of their real danger the herd was
suspicions, and, slowly trotting along before me, enticed me for a
mile or more along the verge of the fern growths. Turning a corner
I suddenly became aware of a solitary tree growing in the middle
of the glade—one tree alone. It struck me at once that I had never
seen a tree exactly like it before; but, being intent upon venison for
my supper, I looked at it only long enough to satisfy my first surprise
at seeing a single plant of such rich growth flourishing luxuriantly
in a spot where only the harsh fern-canes seemed to thrive.

"The deer meanwhile were midway between me and the tree,
and looking at them I saw they were going to cross the glade. Exactly
opposite them was an opening in the forest, in which I should certainly have lost my supper; so I fired into the middle of the family
as they were filing before me. I hit a young fawn, and the rest of
the herd, wheeling round in their sudden terror, made off in the
direction of the tree, leaving the fawn struggling on the ground.
Otona, the boy, ran forward at my order to secure it, but the little
creature seeing him coming, attempted to follow its comrades, and
at a fair pace held on their course. The herd had meanwhile reached
the tree, but suddenly, instead of passing under it, swerved in their
career, and swept round it at some yards distance.

"*Was I mad, or did the plant really try to catch the deer?* On a
sudden I saw, or thought I saw, the tree violently agitated, and

while the ferns all round were standing motionless in the dead evening air, its boughs were swayed by some sudden gust towards the herd, and swept, in the force of their impulse, almost to the ground. I drew my hand across my eyes, closed them for a moment, and looked again. The tree was as motionless as myself!

"Towards it, and now close to it, the boy was running in excited pursuit of the fawn. He stretched out his hands to catch it. It bounded from his eager grasp. Again he reached forward, and again it escaped him. There was another rush forward, and the next instant boy and deer were beneath the tree.

"And now there was no mistaking what I saw.

"The tree was convulsed with motion, leaned forward; swept its thick foliaged boughs to the ground, and enveloped from my sight the pursuer and the pursued; I was within a hundred yards, and the cry of Otona from the midst of the tree came to me in all the clearness of its agony. There was then one stifled, strangling scream, and except for the agitation of the leaves where they had closed upon the boy, there was not a sign of life!

"I called out 'Otona!' No answer came. I tried to call out again, but my utterance was like that of some wild beast smitten at once with sudden terror and its death wound. I stood there, changed from all semblance of a human being. Not all the terrors of earth together could have made me take my eye from the awful plant, or my foot off the ground. I must have stood thus for at least an hour, for the shadows had crept out from the forest half across the glade before that hideous paroxysm of fear left me. My first impulse then was to creep stealthily away lest the tree should perceive me, but my returning reason bade me approach it. The boy might have fallen into the lair of some beast of prey, or perhaps the terrible life in the tree was that of some great serpent among its branches. Preparing to defend myself I approached the silent tree,—the harsh grass crisping beneath my feet with a strange loudness, the cicadas in the forest shrilling till the air seemed throbbing round me with waves of sound. The terrible truth was soon before me in all its awful novelty.

"The vegetable first discovered my presence at about fifty yards distance. I then became aware of a stealthy motion among the thick-lipped leaves, reminding me of some wild beast slowly gathering itself up from long sleep, a vast coil of snakes in restless motion. Have you ever seen bees hanging from a bough—a great cluster of bodies, bee clinging to bee—and by striking the bough, or agitating the air, caused that massed life to begin sulkily to disintegrate, each insect asserting its individual right to move? And do you remember how without one bee leaving the pensile cluster, the whole became gradually instinct with sullen life and horrid with a multitudinous motion?

"I came within twenty yards of it. The tree was quivering through every branch, muttering for blood, and, helpless with rooted feet, yearning with every branch towards me. It was that terror of the deep sea which the men of the northern fiords dread, and which, anchored upon some sunken rock, stretches into vain space its longing arms, pellucid as the sea itself, and as relentless—maimed Polypheme groping for his victims.

"Each separate leaf was agitated and hungry. Like hands they fumbled together, their fleshy palms curling upon themselves and again unfolding, closing on each other and falling apart again,—thick, helpless, fingerless hands (rather lips or tongues than hands) dimpled closely with little cup-like hollows. I approached nearer and nearer, step by step, till I saw that these soft horrors were all of them in motion, opening and closing incessantly.

"I was now within ten yards of the farthest reaching bough. Every part of it was hysterical with excitement. The agitation of its members was awful—sickening yet fascinating. In an ecstasy of eagerness for the food so near them, the leaves turned upon each other. Two meeting would suck together face to face, with a force that compressed their joint thickness to a half, thinning the two leaves into one, now grappling in a volute like a double shell, writhing like some green worm, and at last, faint with the violence of the paroxysm, would slowly separate, falling apart as leeches gorged drop off the limbs. A sticky dew glistened in the dimples, welled over, and trickled down the leaf. The sound of it dripping from leaf to leaf made it seem as if the tree was muttering to itself. The beautiful golden fruit as they swung here and there were clutched now by one leaf and now by another, held for a moment close enfolded from the sight, and then as suddenly released. Here a large leaf, vampire-like, had sucked out the juices of a smaller one. It hung limp and bloodless, like a carcass of which the weasel has tired.

"I watched the terrible struggle till my starting eyes, strained by intense attention, refused their office, and I can hardly say what I saw.

But the tree before me seemed to have become a live beast. Above me I felt conscious was a great limb, and each of its thousand clammy hands reached downwards towards me, fumbling. It strained, shivered, rocked, and heaved. It flung itself about in despair. The boughs, tantalized to madness with the presence of flesh, were tossed to this side and to that, in the agony of a frantic desire. The leaves were wrung together as the hands of one driven to madness by sudden misery. I felt the vile dew spurting from the tense veins fall upon me. My clothes began to give out a strange odor. The ground I stood on glistened with animal juices.

"Was I bewildered by terror? Had my senses abandoned me in my need? I know not—but the tree seemed to me to be alive. Leaning over towards me, it seemed to be pulling up its roots from the softened ground, and to be moving towards me. A mountainous monster, with myriad lips, mumbling together for my life, was upon me!

"Like one who desperately defends himself from imminent death, I made an effort for life, and fired my gun at the approaching horror. To my dizzied senses the sound seemed far off, but the shock of the recoil partially recalled me to myself, and starting back I reloaded. The shot had torn their way into the soft body of the great thing. The trunk as it received the wound shuddered, and the whole tree was struck with a sudden quiver. A fruit fell down—slipping from the leaves, now rigid with swollen veins, as from carven foliage. Then I saw a large arm slowly droop, and without a sound it was severed from the juice-fattened bole, and sank down softly, noiselessly, through the glistening leaves. I fired again, and another vile fragment was powerless—dead. At each discharge the terrible vegetable yielded a life. Piecemeal I attacked it, killing here a leaf and there a branch. My fury increased with the slaughter till, when my ammunition was exhausted, the splendid giant was left a wreck as if some hurricane had torn through it. On the ground lay heaped together the fragments, struggling, rising and falling, gasping. Over them drooped in dying languor a few stricken boughs, while upright in the midst stood, dripping at every joint, the glistening trunk.

"My continued firing had brought up one of my men on my mule. He dared not, so he told me, come near me, thinking me mad. I had now drawn my hunting-knife, and with this was fighting—with the leaves. Yes—but each leaf was instinct with a horrid life; and more than once I felt my hand entangled for a moment and seized as if by sharp lips. Ignorant of the presence of my companion I made a rush forward over the fallen foliage, and with a last paroxysm of frenzy drove my knife up to the handle into the soft bole, and, slipping on the fast congealing sap, fell exhausted and unconscious, among the still panting leaves.

"My companions carried me back to the camp, and after vainly searching for Otona awaited my return to consciousness. Two or three hours elapsed before I could speak, and several days before I could approach the terrible thing. My men would not go near it. It was quite dead; for as we came up a great-billed bird with gaudy plumage that had been securely feasting on the decaying fruit, flew up from the wreck. We removed the rotting foliage, and there among the dead leaves still limp with juices, and piled round the roots, we found the ghastly relics of many former meals, and—its last nourishment—the corpse of little Otona. To have removed the leaves would have taken too long, so we buried the body as it was with a hundred vampire leaves still clinging to it."

Such, as nearly as I remember it, was my uncle's story of the man-eating tree.

The Balloon Tree

Edward Page Mitchell

I

The colonel said:

We rode for several hours straight from the shore toward the heart of the island. The sun was low in the western sky when we left the ship. Neither on the water nor on the land had we felt a breath of air stirring. The glare was upon everything. Over the low range of hills miles away in the interior hung a few copper-colored clouds. "Wind," said Briery. Kilooa shook his head.

Vegetation of all kinds showed the effects of the long continued drought. The eye wandered without relief from the sickly russet of the undergrowth, so dry in places that leaves and stems crackled under the horses' feet, to the yellowish-brown of the thirsty trees that skirted the bridle path. No growing thing was green except the bell-top cactus, fit to flourish in the crater of a living volcano.

Kilooa leaned over in the saddle and tore from one of these plants its top, as big as a California pear and bloated with juice. He crushed the bell in his fist, and, turning, flung into our hot faces a few grateful drops of water.

Then the guide began to talk rapidly in his language of vowels and liquids. Briery translated for my benefit.

The god Lalala loved a woman of the island. He came in the form of fire. She, accustomed to the ordinary temperature of the clime, only shivered before his approaches. Then he wooed her as a shower of rain and won her heart. Kakal was a divinity much more powerful than Lalala, but malicious to the last degree. He also coveted this woman, who was very beautiful. Kakal's importunities

49

were in vain. In spite, he changed her to a cactus, and rooted her to the ground under the burning sun. The god Lalala was power- less to avert this vengeance; but he took up his abode with the cactus woman, still in the form of a rain shower, and never left her, even in the driest seasons. Thus it happens that the bell-top cactus is an unfailing reservoir of pure cool water.

Long after dark we reached the channel of a vanished stream, and Kilooa led us for several miles along its dry bed. We were exceed- ingly tired when the guide bade us dismount. He tethered the pant- ing horses and then dashed into the dense thicket on the bank. A hundred yards of scrambling, and we came to a poor thatched hut. The savage raised both hands above his head and uttered a musi- cal falsetto, not unlike the yodel peculiar to the Valais. This call brought out the occupant of the hut, upon whom Briery flashed the light of his lantern. It was an old woman, hideous beyond the imagination of a dyspeptic's dream.

"Omanana gelaãl!" exclaimed Kilooa.

"Hail, holy woman," translated Briery.

Between Kilooa and the holy hag there ensued a long colloquy, respectful on his part, sententious and impatient on hers, Briery listened with eager attention. Several times he clutched my arm, as if unable to repress his anxiety. The woman seemed to be per- suaded by Kilooa's arguments, or won by his entreaties. At last she pointed toward the southeast, slowly pronouncing a few words that apparently satisfied my companions.

The direction indicated by the holy woman was still toward the hills, but twenty or thirty degrees to the left of the general course which we had pursued since leaving the shore.

"Push on! Push on!" cried Briery. "We can afford to lose no time."

II

We rode all night. At sunrise there was a pause of hardly ten minutes for the scanty breakfast supplied by our haversacks. Then we were again in the saddle, making our way through a thicket that grew more and more difficult, and under a sun that grew hotter.

"Perhaps," I remarked finally to my taciturn friend, "you have no objection to telling me now why two civilized beings and one amiable savage should be plunging through this infernal jungle, as if they were on an errand of life or death?"

"Yes," said he, "it is best you should know."

Briery produced from an inner breast pocket a letter which had been read and reread until it was worn in the creases. "This," he went on, "is from Professor Quakversuch of the University of Upsala. It reached me at Valparaiso."

Glancing cautiously around, as if he feared that every tree fern in that tropical wilderness was an eavesdropper, or that the hood-like spathes of the giant caladiums overhead were ears waiting to drink in some mighty secret of science, Briery read in a low voice from the letter of the great Swedish botanist:

"You will have in these islands," wrote the professor, "a rare opportunity to investigate certain extraordinary accounts given me years ago by the Jesuit missionary Buteaux concerning the Migratory Tree, the cereus ragrans of Jansenius and other speculative physiologists.

"The explorer Spohr claims to have beheld it; but there is reason, as you know, for accepting all of Spohr's statements with caution.

"That is not the case with the assertions of my late valued correspondent, the Jesuit missionary. Father Buteaux was a learned botanist, an accurate observer, and a most pious and conscientious man. He never saw the Migratory Tree; but during the long period of his labors in that part of the world he accumulated, from widely different sources, a mass of testimony as to its existence and habits.

"Is it quite inconceivable, my dear Briery, that somewhere in the range of nature there is a vegetable organization as far above the cabbage, let us say, in complexity and potentiality as the ape is above the polyp? Nature is continuous. In all her schemes we find no chasms, no gaps. There may be missing links in our books and classifications and cabinets, but there are none in the organic world. Is not all of lower nature struggling upward to arrive at the point of self-consciousness and volition? In the unceasing process of evolution, differentiation, improvement in special functions, why may not a plant arrive at this point and feel, will, act, in short, possess and exercise the characteristics of the true animal?"

Briery's voice trembled with enthusiasm as he read this.

"I have no doubt," continued Professor Quakversuch, "that if it shall be your great good fortune to encounter a specimen of the Migratory Tree described by Buteaux, you will find that it possesses a well-defined system of real nerves and ganglia, constituting, in fact, the seat of vegetable intelligence. I conjure you to be very thorough in your dissections.

"According to the indications furnished me by the Jesuit, this extraordinary tree should belong to the order of Cactaceae. It should be developed only in conditions of extreme heat and dryness. Its roots should be hardly more than rudimentary, affording a precarious attachment to the earth. This attachment it should be able to sever at will, soaring up into the air and away to another place selected by itself, as a bird shifts its habitation. I infer that these migrations are accomplished by means of the property of secreting hydrogen gas, with which it inflates at pleasure a bladder-like organ of highly elastic tissue, thus lifting itself out of the ground and off to a new abode.

"Buteaux added that the Migratory Tree was invariably worshiped by the natives as a supernatural being, and that the mystery thrown by them around its cult was the greatest obstacle in the path of the investigator."

"There!" exclaimed Briery, folding up Professor Quakversuch's letter. "Is not that a quest worthy the risk or sacrifice of life itself!? To add to the recorded facts of vegetable morphology the proved existence of a tree that wanders, a tree that wills, a tree, perhaps, that thinks—this is glory to be won at any cost! The lamented Decandolle of Geneva—"

"Confound the lamented Decandolle of Geneva!" shouted I, for it was excessively hot, and I felt that we had come on a fool's errand.

III

It was near sunset on the second day of our journey, when Kilooa, who was riding several rods in advance of us, uttered a quick cry, leaped from his saddle, and stooped to the ground.

Briery was at his side in an instant. I followed with less agility; my joints were very stiff and I had no scientific enthusiasm to lubricate them. Briery was on his hands and knees, eagerly examining what seemed to be a recent disturbance of the soil. The savage was prostrate, rubbing his forehead in the dust, as if in a religious ecstasy, and warbling the same falsetto notes that we had heard at the holy woman's hut.

"What beast's trail have you struck?" I demanded.

"The trail of no beast," answered Briery, almost angrily. "Do you see this broad round abrasion of the surface, where a heavy weight has rested? Do you see these little troughs in the fresh earth, radiating from the center like the points of a star? They are the scars left by slender roots torn up from their shallow beds. Do you see Kilooa's hysterical performance? I tell you we are on the track of the Sacred Tree. It has been here, and not long ago."

Acting under Briery's excited instructions we continued the hunt on foot. Kilooa started toward the east, I toward the west, and Briery took the southward course.

To cover the ground thoroughly, we agreed to advance in gradually widening zigzags, communicating with each other at intervals by pistol shots. There could have been no more foolish arrangement. In a quarter of an hour I had lost my head and my bearings in a thicket. For another quarter of an hour I discharged my revolver repeatedly, without getting a single response from east or south. I spent the remainder of daylight in a blundering effort to make my way back to the place where the horses were; and then the sun went down, leaving me in sudden darkness, alone in a wilderness of, the extent and character of which I had not the faintest idea.

I will spare you the history of my sufferings during the whole of that night, and the next day, and the next night, and another day. When it was dark I wandered about in blind despair, longing for daylight, not daring to sleep or even to stop, and in continual terror of the unknown dangers that surrounded me. In the daytime I longed for night, for the sun scorched its way through the thickest roof that the luxuriant foliage afforded, and drove me nearly mad. The provisions in my haversack were exhausted. My canteen was on my saddle; I should have died of thirst had it not been for the bell-top cactus, which I found twice. But in that horrible experience neither the torture of hunger and thirst nor the torture of heat equalled the misery of the thought that my life was to be sacrificed to the delusion of a crazy botanist, who had dreamed of the impossible.

The impossible?

On the second afternoon, still staggering aimlessly on through the jungle, I lost my last strength and fell to the ground. Despair and indifference had long since given way to an eager desire for the end. I closed my eyes with indescribable relief; the hot sun seemed pleasant on my face as consciousness departed.

Did a beautiful and gentle woman come to me while I lay unconscious, and take my head in her lap, and put her arms around me? Did she press her face to mine and in a whisper bid me have courage? That was the belief that filled my mind when it struggled back for a moment into consciousness; I clutched at the warm, soft arms, and swooned again.

Do not look at each other and smile, gentlemen; in that cruel wilderness, in my helpless condition, I found pity and benignant tenderness. The next time my senses returned I saw that Something was bending over me—something majestic if not beautiful, humane if not human, gracious if not woman. The arms that held me and drew me up were moist, and they throbbed with the pulsation of life. There was a faint, sweet odor, like the smell of a woman's perfumed hair. The touch was a caress, the clasp an embrace.

Can I describe its form? No, not with the definiteness that would satisfy the Quakversuches and the Brierys. I saw that the trunk was massive. The branches that lifted me from the ground and held me carefully and gently were flexible and symmetrically disposed. Above my head there was a wreath of strange foliage, and in the midst of it a dazzling sphere of scarlet. The scarlet globe grew while I watched it but the effort of watching was too much for me.

Remember, if you please, that at this time, physical exhaustion and mental torture had brought me to the point where I passed to and fro between consciousness and unconsciousness as easily and as frequently as one fluctuates between slumber and wakefulness during a night of fever. It seemed the most natural thing in the world that in my extreme weakness I should be beloved and cared for by a cactus. I did not seek an explanation of this good fortune, or try to analyze it; I simply accepted it as a matter of course, as a child accepts a benefit from an unexpected quarter. The one idea that possessed me was that I had found an unknown friend, instinct with womanly sympathy and immeasurably kind.

And as night came on it seemed to me that the scarlet bulb overhead became enormously distended, so that it almost filled the sky. Was I gently rocked by the supple arms that still held me? Were we floating off together into the air? I did not know, or care. Now I fancied that I was in my berth on board ship, cradled by the swell of the sea; now, that I was sharing the flight of some great bird;

now, that I was borne on with prodigious speed through the darkness by my own volition. The sense of incessant motion affected all my dreams. Whenever I awoke I felt a cool breeze steadily beating against my face—the first breath of air since we had landed. I was vaguely happy, gentlemen. I had surrendered all responsibility for my own fate. I had gained the protection of a being of superior powers.

"The brandy flask, Kilooa!"

It was daylight. I lay upon the ground and Briery was supporting my shoulders. In his face was a look of bewilderment that I shall never forget.

"My God!" he cried, "and how did you get here? We gave up the search two days ago."

The brandy pulled me together. I staggered to my feet and looked around. The cause of Briery's extreme amazement was apparent at a glance. We were not in the wilderness. We were at the shore. There was the bay, and the ship at anchor, half a mile off. They were already lowering a boat to send for us.

And there to the south was a bright red spot on the horizon, hardly larger than the morning star—the Balloon Tree returning to the wilderness. I saw it, Briery saw it, the savage Kilooa saw it. We watched it till it vanished. We watched it with very different emotions, Kilooa with superstitious reverence, Briery with scientific interest and intense disappointment, I with a heart full of wonder and gratitude.

I clasped my forehead with both hands. It was no dream, then. The Tree, the caress, the embrace, the scarlet bulb, the night journey through the air, were not creations and incidents of delirium. Call it tree, or call it plant-animal—there it was! Let men of science quarrel over the question of its existence in nature; this I know: It had found me dying and had brought me more than a hundred miles straight to the ship where I belonged. Under Providence, gentlemen, that sentient and intelligent vegetable organism had saved my life.

At this point the colonel got up and left the club. He was very much moved. Pretty soon Briery came in, briskly as usual. He picked up an uncut copy of Lord Bragmuch's *Travels in Kerguellon's Land*, and settled himself in an easy chair at the corner of the fireplace.

Young Traddies timidly approached the veteran globetrotter. "Excuse me, Mr. Briery," said he, "but I should like to ask you a question about the Balloon Tree. Were there scientific reasons for believing that its sex was—"

"Ah," interrupted Briery, looking bored; "the colonel has been favoring you with that extraordinary narrative? Has he honored me again with a share in the adventure? Yes? Well, did we bag the game this time?"

"Why, no," said young Traddies. "You last saw the Tree as a scarlet spot against the horizon."

"By Jove, another miss!" said Briery, calmly beginning to cut the leaves of his book.

The Flowering of the Strange Orchid
H. G. Wells

The buying of orchids always has in it a certain speculative flavour. You have before you the brown shrivelled lump of tissue, and for the rest you must trust your judgment, or the auctioneer, or your good-luck, as your taste may incline. The plant may be moribund or dead, or it may be just a respectable purchase, fair value for your money, or perhaps—for the thing has happened again and again—there slowly unfolds before the delighted eyes of the happy purchaser, day after day, some new variety, some novel richness, a strange twist of the labellum, or some subtler colouration or unexpected mimicry. Pride, beauty, and profit blossom together on one delicate green spike, and, it may be, even immortality. For the new miracle of Nature may stand in need of a new specific name, and what so convenient as that of its discoverer? "Johnsmithia"! There have been worse names.

It was perhaps the hope of some such happy discovery that made Winter-Wedderburn such a frequent attendant at these sales—that hope, and also, maybe, the fact that he had nothing else of the slightest interest to do in the world. He was a shy, lonely, rather ineffectual man, provided with just enough income to keep off the spur of necessity, and not enough nervous energy to make him seek any exacting employments. He might have collected stamps or coins, or translated Horace, or bound books, or invented new species of diatoms. But, as it happened, he grew orchids, and had one ambitious little hothouse.

"I have a fancy," he said over his coffee, "that something is going to happen to me to-day." He spoke—as he moved and thought—slowly.

"Oh, don't say *that!*" said his housekeeper— who was also his remote cousin. For "something happening" was a euphemism that meant only one thing to her.

"You misunderstand me. I mean nothing unpleasant—though what I do mean I scarcely know.

"To-day," he continued after a pause, "Peters are going to sell a batch of plants from the Andamans and the Indies. I shall go up and see what they have. It may be I shall buy something good, un-awares. That may be it."

He passed his cup for his second cupful of coffee.

"Are these the things collected by that poor young fellow you told me of the other day?" asked his cousin as she filled his cup.

"Yes," he said, and became meditative over a piece of toast.

"Nothing ever does happen to me," he remarked presently, be-ginning to think aloud. "I wonder why? Things enough happen to other people. There is Harvey. Only the other week, on Monday he picked up sixpence, on Wednesday his chicks all had the staggers, on Friday his cousin came home from Australia, and on Saturday he broke his ankle. What a whirl of excitement!— compared to me."

"I think I would rather be without so much excitement," said his housekeeper. "It can't be good for you."

"I suppose it's troublesome. Still—you see, nothing ever hap-pens to me. When I was a little boy I never had accidents. I never fell in love as I grew up. Never married—I wonder how it feels to have something happen to you, something really remarkable.

"That orchid-collector was only thirty-six—twenty years younger than myself—when he died. And he had been married twice and divorced once; he had had malarial fever four times, and once he broke his thigh. He killed a Malay once, and once he was wounded by a poisoned dart. And in the end he was killed by jungle-leeches. It must have all been very troublesome, but then it must have been very interesting, you know—except, perhaps, the leeches."

"I am sure it was not good for him," said the lady, with convic-tion.

"Perhaps not." And then Wedderburn looked at his watch. "Twenty-three minutes past eight. I am going up by the quarter to twelve train, so that there is plenty of time. I think I shall wear my alpaca jacket—it is quite warm enough—and my grey felt hat and brown shoes. I suppose—"

He glanced out of the window at the serene sky and sunlit garden, and then nervously at his cousin's face.

"I think you had better take an umbrella if you are going to London," she said in a voice that admitted of no denial. "There's all between here and the station coming back."

When he returned he was in a state of mild excitement. He had made a purchase. It was rare that he could make up his mind quickly enough to buy, but this time he had done so.

"There are *Vandas*," he said, "and a *Dendrobe* and some *Palæonophis*." He surveyed his purchases lovingly as he consumed his soup. They were laid out on the spotless tablecloth before him, and he was telling his cousin all about them as he slowly meandered through his dinner. It was his custom to live all his visits to London over again in the evening for her and his own entertainment.

"I knew something would happen to-day. And I have bought all these. Some of them—some of them—I feel sure, do you know, that some of them will be remarkable. I don't know how it is, but I feel just as sure as if some one had told me that some of these will turn out remarkable.

"That one"—he pointed to a shrivelled rhizome— "was not identified. It may be a *Palæonophis*—or it may not. It may be a new species, or even a new genus. And it was the last that poor Batten ever collected."

"I don't like the look of it," said his housekeeper. "It's such an ugly shape."

"To me it scarcely seems to have a shape."

"I don't like those things that stick out," said his housekeeper.

"It shall be put away in a pot to-morrow."

"It looks," said the housekeeper, "like a spider shamming dead."

Wedderburn smiled and surveyed the root with his head on one side. "It is certainly not a pretty lump of stuff. But you can never judge of these things from their dry appearance. It may turn out to be a very beautiful orchid indeed. How busy I shall be to-morrow! I must see tonight just exactly what to do with these things, and to-morrow I shall set to work.

"They found poor Batten lying dead, or dying, in a mangrove swamp—I forget which," he began again presently, "with one of these very orchids crushed up under his body. He had been unwell for some days with some kind of native fever, and I suppose he fainted. These mangrove swamps are very unwholesome. Every drop of blood, they say, was taken out of him by the jungle-leeches. It may be that very plant that cost him his life to obtain."

"I think none the better of it for that."

"Men must work though women may weep," said Wedderburn, with profound gravity.

"Fancy dying away from every comfort in a nasty swamp! Fancy being ill of fever with nothing to take but chlorodyne and quinine—if men were left to themselves they would live on chlorodyne and quinine—and no one round you but horrible natives! They say the Andaman islanders are most disgusting wretches — and, anyhow, they can scarcely make good nurses, not having the necessary training. And just for people in England to have orchids!"

"I don't suppose it was comfortable, but some men seem to enjoy that kind of thing," said Wedderburn. " Anyhow, the natives of his party were sufficiently civilised to take care of all his collection until his colleague, who was an ornithologist, came back again from the interior; though they could not tell the species of the orchid, and had let it wither. And it makes these things more interesting."

"It makes them disgusting. I should be afraid of some of the malaria clinging to them. And just think, there has been a dead body lying across that ugly thing! I never thought of that before. There! I declare I cannot eat another mouthful of dinner."

"I will take them off the table if you like, and put them in the window-seat. I can see them just as well there."

The next few days he was indeed singularly busy in his steamy little hothouse, fussing about with charcoal, lumps of teak, moss, and all the other mysteries of the orchid cultivator. He considered he was having a wonderfully eventful time. In the evening he would talk about these new orchids to his friends, and over and over again he reverted to his expectation of something strange.

Several of the *Vandas* and the *Dendrobium* died under his care, but presently the strange orchid began to show signs of life. He was delighted, and took his housekeeper right away from jam-making to see it at once, directly he made the discovery.

"That is a bud," he said, "and presently there will be a lot of leaves there, and those little things coming out here are aerial rootlets."

"They look to me like little white fingers poking out of the brown. I don't like them," said his housekeeper.

"Why not?"

"I don't know. They look like fingers trying to get at you. I can't help my likes and dislikes."

"I don't know for certain, but I don't *think* there are any orchids I know that have aerial rootlets quite like that. It may be my fancy, of course. You see they are a little flattened at the ends."

"I don't like 'em," said his housekeeper, suddenly shivering and turning away. "I know it's very silly of me—and I'm very sorry, particularly as you like the thing so much. But I can't help thinking of that corpse."

"But it may not be that particular plant. That was merely a guess of mine."

His housekeeper shrugged her shoulders.

"Anyhow I don't like it," she said.

Wedderburn felt a little hurt at her dislike to the plant. But that did not prevent his talking to her about orchids generally, and this orchid in particular, whenever he felt inclined.

"There are such queer things about orchids," he said one day; "such possibilities of surprises. You know, Darwin studied their fertilisation, and showed that the whole structure of an ordinary orchid-flower was contrived in order that moths might carry the pollen from plant to plant. Well, it seems that there are lots of orchids known the flower of which cannot possibly be used for fertilisation in that way. Some of the Cypripediums, for instance; there are no insects known that can possibly fertilise them, and some of them have never been found with seed."

"But how do they form new plants?"

"By runners and tubers, and that kind of outgrowth. That is easily explained. The puzzle is, what are the flowers for?

"Very likely," he added, "*my* orchid may be something extraordinary in that way. If so, I shall study it. I have often thought of making researches as Darwin did. But hitherto I have not found the time, or something else has happened to prevent it. The leaves are beginning to unfold now. I do wish you would come and see them!"

But she said that the orchid-house was so hot it gave her the headache. She had seen the plant once again, and the aerial rootlets, which were now some of them more than a foot long, had unfortunately reminded her of tentacles reaching out after something; and they got into her dreams, growing after her with incredible rapidity. So that she had settled to her entire satisfaction that she would not see that plant again, and Wedderburn had to admire its leaves alone. They were of the ordinary broad form, and a deep glossy green, with splashes and dots of deep red towards the base. He knew of no other leaves quite like them. The plant was placed on a low bench near the thermometer, and close by was a simple arrangement by which a tap dripped on the hot-water pipes and kept the air steamy. And he spent his afternoons now with some regularity meditating on the approaching flowering of this strange plant.

And at last the great thing happened. Directly he entered the little glass house he knew that the spike had burst out, although his great *Palæonophis Lowii* hid the corner where his new darling stood. There was a new odour in the air, a rich, intensely sweet scent, that overpowered every other in that crowded, steaming little greenhouse.

Directly he noticed this he hurried down to the strange orchid. And, behold! the trailing green spikes bore now three great splashes of blossom, from which this overpowering sweetness proceeded. He stopped before them in an ecstasy of admiration.

The flowers were white, with streaks of golden orange upon the petals; the heavy labellum was coiled into an intricate projection, and a wonderful bluish purple mingled there with the gold. He could see at once that the genus was altogether a new one. And the insufferable scent! How hot the place was! The blossoms swam before his eyes.

He would see if the temperature was right. He made a step towards the thermometer. Suddenly everything appeared unsteady. The bricks on the floor were dancing up and down. Then the white blossoms, the green leaves behind them, the whole greenhouse, seemed to sweep sideways, and then in a curve upward.

· · · · ·

At half-past four his cousin made the tea, according to their invariable custom. But Wedderburn did not come in for his tea.

"He is worshipping that horrid orchid," she told herself, and waited ten minutes. "His watch must have stopped. I will go and call him."

She went straight to the hothouse, and, opening the door, called his name. There was no reply. She noticed that the air was very

close, and loaded with an intense perfume. Then she saw something lying on the bricks between the hot-water pipes.

For a minute, perhaps, she stood motionless.

He was lying, face upward, at the foot of the strange orchid.
The tentacle-like aerial rootlets no longer swayed freely in the air,
but were crowded together, a tangle of grey ropes, and stretched
tight with their ends closely applied to his chin and neck and hands.

She did not understand. Then she saw from under one of the
exultant tentacles upon his cheek there trickled a little thread of
blood.

With an inarticulate cry she ran towards him, and tried to pull
him away from the leech-like suckers. She snapped two of these
tentacles, and their sap dripped red.

Then the overpowering scent of the blossom began to make her
head reel. How they clung to him! She tore at the tough ropes, and
he and the white inflorescence swam about her. She felt she was
fainting, knew she must not. She left him and hastily opened the
nearest door, and, after she had panted for a moment in the fresh
air, she had a brilliant inspiration. She caught up a flower-pot and
smashed in the windows at the end of the greenhouse. Then she
re-entered. She tugged now with renewed strength at Wedderburn's
motionless body, and brought the strange orchid crashing to the
floor. It still clung with the grimmest tenacity to its victim. In a
frenzy, she lugged it and him into the open air.

Then she thought of tearing through the sucker rootlets one by
one, and in another minute she had released him and was dragging him away from the horror.

He was white and bleeding from a dozen circular patches.

The odd-job man was coming up the garden, amazed at the
smashing of glass, and saw her emerge, hauling the inanimate body
with red-stained hands. For a moment he thought impossible
things.

"Bring some water!" she cried, and her voice dispelled his fancies. When, with unnatural alacrity, he returned with the water,
he found her weeping with excitement, and with Wedderburn's
head upon her knee, wiping the blood from his face.

"What's the matter?" said Wedderburn, opening his eyes feebly,
and closing them again at once.

"Go and tell Annie to come out here to me, and then go for Dr.
Haddon at once," she said to the odd-job man so soon as he brought

the water; and added, seeing he hesitated, "I will tell you all about it when you come back."

Presently Wedderburn opened his eyes again, and, seeing that he was troubled by the puzzle of his position, she explained to him, "You fainted in the hothouse."

"And the orchid?"

"I will see to that," she said.

Wedderburn had lost a good deal of blood, but beyond that he had suffered no very great injury. They gave him brandy mixed with some pink extract of meat, and carried him upstairs to bed. His housekeeper told her incredible story in fragments to Dr. Haddon. "Come to the orchid-house and see," she said.

The cold outer air was blowing in through the open door, and the sickly perfume was almost dispelled. Most of the torn aerial rootlets lay already withered amidst a number of dark stains upon the bricks. The stem of the inflorescence was broken by the fall of the plant, and the flowers were growing limp and brown at the edges of the petals. The doctor stooped towards it, then saw that one of the aerial rootlets still stirred feebly, and hesitated.

The next morning the strange orchid still lay there, black now and putrescent. The door banged intermittingly in the morning breeze, and all the array of Wedderburn's orchids was shrivelled and prostrate. But Wedderburn himself was bright and garrulous upstairs in the story of his strange adventure.

The Treasure in the Forest

H. G. Wells

The canoe was now approaching the land. The bay opened out, and a gap in the white surf of the reef marked where the little river ran out to the sea; the thicker and deeper green of the virgin forest showed its course down the distant hill-slope. The forest here came close to the beach. Far beyond, dim and almost cloudlike in texture, rose the mountains, like suddenly frozen waves. The sea was still save for an almost imperceptible swell. The sky blazed.

The man with the carved paddle stopped. "It should be somewhere here," he said. He shipped the paddle and held his arms out straight before him.

The other man had been in the fore part of the canoe, closely scrutinising the land. He had a sheet of yellow paper on his knee.

"Come and look at this, Evans," he said.

Both men spoke in low tones, and their lips were hard and dry.

The man called Evans came swaying along the canoe until he could look over his companion's shoulder.

The paper had the appearance of a rough map. By much folding it was creased and worn to the pitch of separation, and the second man held the discoloured fragments together where they had parted. On it one could dimly make out, in almost obliterated pencil, the outline of the bay.

"Here," said Evans, "is the reef and here is the gap." He ran his thumb-nail over the chart.

"This curved and twisting line is the river—I could do with a drink now!—and this star is the place."

"You see this dotted line," said the man with the map; "it is a straight line, and runs from the opening of the reef to a clump of

65

palm-trees. The star comes just where it cuts the river. We must mark the place as we go into the lagoon."

"It's queer," said Evans, after a pause, "what these little marks down here are for. It looks like the plan of a house or something; but what all these little dashes, pointing this way and that, may mean I can't get a notion. And what's the writing?"

"Chinese," said the man with the map.

"Of course! *He* was a Chinee," said Evans.

"They all were," said the man with the map.

They both sat for some minutes staring at the land, while the canoe drifted slowly. Then Evans looked towards the paddle.

"Your turn with the paddle now, Hooker," said he.

And his companion quietly folded up his map, put it in his pocket, passed Evans carefully, and began to paddle. His movements were languid, like those of a man whose strength was nearly exhausted.

Evans sat with his eyes half closed, watching the frothy breakwater of the coral creep nearer and nearer. The sky was like a furnace now, for the sun was near the zenith. Though they were so near the Treasure he did not feel the exaltation he had anticipated. The intense excitement of the struggle for the plan, and the long night voyage from the mainland in the unprovisioned canoe had, to use his own expression, "taken it out of him." He tried to arouse himself by directing his mind to the ingots the Chinamen had spoken of, but it would not rest there; it came back headlong to the thought of sweet water rippling in the river, and to the almost unendurable dryness of his lips and throat. The rhythmic wash of the sea upon the reef was becoming audible now, and it had a pleasant sound in his ears; the water washed along the side of the canoe, and the paddle dripped between each stroke. Presently he began to doze.

He was still dimly conscious of the island, but a queer dream texture interwove with his sensations. Once again it was the night when he and Hooker had hit upon the Chinamen's secret; he saw the moonlit trees, the little fire burning, and the black figures of the three Chinamen—silvered on one side by moonlight, and on the other glowing from the firelight—and heard them talking together in pigeon-English—for they came from different provinces. Hooker had caught the drift of their talk first, and had motioned to him to listen. Fragments of the conversation were inaudible and fragments incomprehensible. A Spanish galleon from the Philippines hopelessly aground, and its treasure buried against the day of return, lay in the background of the story; a shipwrecked crew thinned by disease, a quarrel or so, and the needs of discipline, and at last taking to their boats never to be heard of again. Then Chang-hi, only a year since, wandering ashore, had happened upon the ingots hidden for two hundred years, had deserted his junk, and reburied them with infinite toil, single-handed but very safe. He laid great stress on the safety—it was a secret of his. Now he wanted help to return and exhume them. Presently the little map fluttered and the voices sank. A fine story for two stranded British wastrels to hear! Evans' dream shifted to the moment when he had Chang-hi's pigtail in his hand. The life of a Chinaman is scarcely sacred like a European's. The cunning little face of Chang-hi, first keen and furious like a startled snake, and then fearful, treacherous, and pitiful, became overwhelmingly prominent in the dream. At the end Chang-hi had grinned, a most incomprehensible and startling grin. Abruptly things became very unpleasant, as they will do at times in dreams. Chang-hi gibbered and threatened him. He saw in his dream heaps and heaps of gold, and Chang-hi intervening and struggling to hold him back from it. He took Chang-hi by the pigtail—how big the yellow brute was, and how he struggled and grinned! He kept growing bigger, too. Then the bright heaps of gold turned to a roaring furnace, and a vast devil, surprisingly like Chang-hi, but with a huge black tail, began to feed him with coals. They burnt his mouth horribly. Another devil was shouting his name: "Evans, Evans, you sleepy fool!"—or was it Hooker?

He woke up. They were in the mouth of the lagoon.

"There are the three palm-trees. It must be in a line with that clump of bushes," said his companion. "Mark that. If we go to those bushes and then strike into the bush in a straight line from here, we shall come to it when we come to the stream."

They could see now where the mouth of the stream opened out. At the sight of it Evans revived. "Hurry up, man," he said, "or, by heaven, I shall have to drink sea-water! "He gnawed his hand and stared at the gleam of silver among the rocks and green tangle.

Presently he turned almost fiercely upon Hooker. "Give *me* the paddle," he said.

So they reached the river mouth. A little way up Hooker took some water in the hollow of his hand, tasted it, and spat it out. A little further he tried again. "This will do," he said, and they began drinking eagerly.

"Curse this!" said Evans, suddenly. "It's too slow." And, leaning dangerously over the fore part of the canoe, he began to suck up the water with his lips.

Presently they made an end of drinking, and, running the canoe into a little creek, were about to land among the thick growth that overhung the water.

"We shall have to scramble through this to the beach to find our bushes and get the line to the place," said Evans.

"We had better paddle round," said Hooker.

So they pushed out again into the river and paddled back down it to the sea, and along the shore to the place where the clump of bushes grew. Here they landed, pulled the light canoe far up the beach, and then went up towards the edge of the jungle until they could see the opening of the reef and the bushes in a straight line. Evans had taken a native implement out of the canoe. It was L-shaped, and the transverse piece was armed with polished stone. Hooker carried the paddle. "It is straight now in this direction," said he; "we must push through this till we strike the stream. Then we must prospect."

They pushed through a close tangle of reeds, broad fronds, and young trees, and at first it was toilsome going; but very speedily the trees became larger and the ground beneath them opened out. The blaze of the sunlight was replaced by insensible degrees by cool shadow. The trees became at last vast pillars that rose up to a canopy of greenery far overhead. Dim white flowers hung from their stems, and ropy creepers swung from tree to tree. The shadow deepened. On the ground, blotched fungi and a red-brown incrustation became frequent.

Evans shivered. "It seems almost cold here after the blaze outside."

"I hope we are keeping to the straight," said Hooker.

Presently they saw, far ahead, a gap in the sombre darkness where white shafts of hot sunlight smote into the forest. There also was brilliant green undergrowth, and coloured flowers. Then they heard the rush of water.

"Here is the river. We should be close to it now," said Hooker.

The vegetation was thick by the river bank. Great plants, as yet unnamed, grew among the roots of the big trees, and spread rosettes of huge green fans towards the strip of sky. Many flowers and a creeper with shiny foliage clung to the exposed stems. On the water of the broad, quiet pool which the treasure-seekers now overlooked there floated big, oval leaves and a waxen, pinkish-white flower not unlike a water-lily. Further, as the river bent away from them, the water suddenly frothed and became noisy in a rapid.

"Well?" said Evans.

"We have swerved a little from the straight," said Hooker. " That was to be expected."

He turned and looked into the dim, cool shadows of the silent forest behind them. "If we beat a little way up and down the stream we should come to something."

"You said—" began Evans.

"*He* said there was a heap of stones," said Hooker.

The two men looked at each other for a moment.

"Let us try a little down-stream first," said Evans.

They advanced slowly, looking curiously about them. Suddenly Evans stopped. "What the devil's that?" he said.

Hooker followed his finger. "Something blue," he said. It had come into view as they topped a gentle swell of the. ground. Then he began to distinguish what it was.

He advanced suddenly with hasty steps, until the body that belonged to the limp hand and arm had become visible. His grip tightened on the implement he carried. The thing was the figure of a Chinaman lying on his face. The *abandon* of the pose was unmistakable.

The two men drew closer together, and stood staring silently at this ominous dead body. It lay in a clear space among the trees. Near by was a spade after the Chinese pattern, and further off lay a scattered heap of stones, close to a freshly dug hole.

"Somebody has been here before," said Hooker, clearing his throat.

Then suddenly Evans began to swear and rave, and stamp upon the ground.

Hooker turned white but said nothing. He advanced towards the prostrate body. He saw the neck was puffed and purple, and the hands and ankles swollen. "Pah!" he said, and suddenly turned away and went towards the excavation. He gave a cry of surprise. He shouted to Evans, who was following him slowly.

"You fool! It's all right. It's here still." Then he turned again and looked at the dead Chinaman, and then again at the hole.

Evans hurried to the hole. Already half exposed by the ill-fated wretch beside them lay a number of dull yellow bars. He bent down in the hole, and, clearing off the soil with his bare hands, hastily pulled one of the heavy masses out. As he did so a little thorn pricked his hand. He pulled the delicate spike out with his fingers and lifted the ingot.

"Only gold or lead could weigh like this," he said exultantly.

Hooker was still looking at the dead Chinaman. He was puzzled.

"He stole a march on his friends," he said at last. "He came here alone, and some poisonous snake has killed him— I wonder how he found the place."

Evans stood with the ingot in his hands. What did a dead Chinaman signify? "We shall have to take this stuff to the mainland piecemeal, and bury it there for a while. How shall we get it to the canoe?"

He took his jacket off and spread it on the ground, and flung two or three ingots into it. Presently he found that another little thorn had punctured his skin.

"This is as much as we can carry," said he. Then suddenly, with a queer rush of irritation, "What are you staring at?"

Hooker turned to him. "I can't stand—him." He nodded towards the corpse. "It's so like—"

"Rubbish!" said Evans. "All Chinamen are alike."

Hooker looked into his face. "I'm going to bury *that*, anyhow, before I lend a hand with this stuff."

"Don't be a fool, Hooker," said Evans. "Let that mass of corruption bide."

Hooker hesitated, and then his eye went carefully over the brown soil about them. "It scares me somehow," he said.

"The thing is," said Evans, "what to do with these ingots. Shall we re-bury them over here, or take them across the strait in the canoe?"

Hooker thought. His puzzled gaze wandered among the tall tree-trunks, and up into the remote sunlit greenery overhead. He shivered again as his eye rested upon the blue figure of the Chinaman. He stared searchingly among the grey depths between the trees.

"What s come to you, Hooker?" said Evans. "Have you lost your wits?"

"Let's get the gold out of this place, anyhow," said Hooker.

He took the ends of the collar of the coat in his hands, and Evans took the opposite corners, and they lifted the mass. "Which way?" said Evans. "To the canoe?"

"It's queer," said Evans, when they had advanced only a few steps, " but my arms ache still with that paddling.

"Curse it!" he said. "But they ache! I must rest."

They let the coat down. Evans' face was white, and little drops of sweat stood out upon his forehead. "It's stuffy, somehow, in this forest."

Then with an abrupt transition to unreasonable anger: "What is the good of waiting here all the day? Lend a hand, I say! You have done nothing but moon since we saw the dead Chinaman."

Hooker was looking steadfastly at his companion's face. He helped raise the coat bearing the ingots, and they went forward perhaps a hundred yards in silence. Evans began to breathe heavily. "Can't you speak?" he said.

"What's the matter with you?" said Hooker.

Evans stumbled, and then with a sudden curse flung the coat from him. He stood for a moment staring at Hooker, and then with a groan clutched at his own throat.

"Don't come near me," he said, and went and leant against a tree. Then in a steadier voice, "I'll be better in a minute."

Presently his grip upon the trunk loosened, and he slipped slowly down the stem of the tree until he was a crumpled heap at its foot. His hands were clenched convulsively. His face became distorted with pain. Hooker approached him.

"Don't touch me! Don't touch me!" said Evans, in a stifled voice. "Put the gold back on the coat."

"Can't I do anything for you?" said Hooker.

"Put the gold back on the coat."

As Hooker handled the ingots he felt a little prick on the ball of his thumb. He looked at his hand and saw a slender thorn, per-haps two inches in length.

Evans gave an inarticulate cry and rolled over.

Hooker's jaw dropped. He stared at the thorn for a moment with dilated eyes. Then he looked at Evans, who was now crumpled together on the ground, his back bending and straitening spasmodi-cally. Then he looked through the pillars of the trees and net-work of creeper stems, to where in the dim grey shadow the blue-clad body of the Chinaman was still indistinctly visible. He thought of the little dashes in the corner of the plan, and in a moment he understood.

"God help me!" he said. For the thorns were similar to those the Dyaks poison and use in their blowing-tubes. He understood now what Chang-hi's assurance of the safety of his treasure meant. He understood that grin now.

"Evans!" he cried

But Evans was silent and motionless now, save for a horrible spasmodic twitching of his limbs. A profound silence brooded over the forest.

Then, Hooker began to suck furiously at the little pink spot on the ball of his thumb—sucking for dear life. Presently he felt a strange aching pain in his arms and shoulders, and his fingers seemed difficult to bend. Then he knew that sucking was no good.

Abruptly he stopped, and sitting down by the pile of ingots, and resting his chin upon his hands and his elbows upon his knees, stared at the distorted but still stirring body of his companion. Chang-hi's grin came in his mind again. The dull pain spread towards his throat and grew slowly in intensity. Far above him a faint breeze stirred the greenery, and the white petals of some unknown flower came floating down through the gloom.

The Purple Pileus
H. G. Wells

Mr. Coombes was sick of life. He walked away from his unhappy home, and, sick not only of his own existence but of everybody else's, turned aside down Gaswork Lane to avoid the town, and, crossing the wooden bridge that goes over the canal to Starling's Cottages, was presently alone in the damp pine woods and out of sight and sound of human habitation. He would stand it no longer. He repeated aloud with blasphemies unusual to him that he would stand it no longer.

He was a pale-faced little man, with dark eyes and a fine and very black moustache. He had a very stiff, upright collar slightly frayed, that gave him an illusory double chin, and his overcoat (albeit shabby) was trimmed with astrachan. His gloves were a bright brown with black stripes over the knuckles, and split at the finger ends. His appearance, his wife had said once in the dear, dead days beyond recall—before he married her, that is—was military. But now she called him—it seems a dreadful thing to tell of between husband and wife, but she called him "a little grub." It wasn't the only thing she had called him, either.

The row had arisen about that beastly Jennie again. Jennie was his wife's friend, and, by no invitation of Mr. Coombes, she came in every blessed Sunday to dinner, and made a shindy all the afternoon. She was a big, noisy girl, with a taste for loud colours and a strident laugh; and this Sunday she had outdone all her previous intrusions by bringing in a fellow with her, a chap as showy as herself. And Mr. Coombes, in a starchy, clean collar and his Sunday frock-coat, had sat dumb and wrathful at his own table, while his wife and her guests talked foolishly and undesirably, and laughed aloud. Well, he stood that, and after dinner (which, "as usual," was late), what must Miss Jennie do but go to the piano and play banjo tunes, for all the world as if it were a week-day! Flesh and blood could not endure such goings on. They would hear next door, they would hear in the road, it was a public announcement of their disrepute. He had to speak.

He had felt himself go pale, and a kind of rigour had affected his respiration as he delivered himself. He had been sitting on one of the chairs by the window—the new guest had taken possession of the arm-chair. He turned his head. "Sun Day!" he said over the collar, in the voice of one who warns. "Sun Day!" What people call a "nasty" tone, it was.

Jennie had kept on playing, but his wife, who was looking through some music that was piled on the top of the piano, had stared at him. "What's wrong now?" she said; "can't people enjoy themselves?"

"I don't mind rational 'njoyment, at all," said little Coombes, "but I ain't a-going to have week-day tunes playing on a Sunday in this house."

"What's wrong with my playing now?" said Jennie, stopping and twirling round on the music-stool with a monstrous rustle of flounces.

Coombes saw it was going to be a row, and opened too vigorously, as is common with your timid, nervous men all the world over. "Steady on with that music-stool!" said he; "it ain't made for 'eavy-weights."

"Never you mind about weights," said Jennie, incensed. "What was you saying behind my back about my playing?"

"Surely you don't 'old with not having a bit of music on a Sunday, Mr. Coombes?" said the new guest, leaning back in the arm-chair, blowing a cloud of cigarette smoke and smiling in a kind of pitying way. And simultaneously his wife said something to Jennie about "Never mind 'im. You go on, Jinny."

"I do," said Mr. Coombes, addressing the new guest.

"May I arst why?" said the new guest, evidently enjoying both his cigarette and the prospect of an argument. He was, by-the-by, a lank young man, very stylishly dressed in bright drab, with a white cravat and a pearl and silver pin. It had been better taste to come in a black coat, Mr. Coombes thought.

"Because," began Mr. Coombes, "it don't suit me. I'm a business man. I 'ave to study my connection. Rational 'njoyment—"

"His connection!" said Mrs. Coombes scornfully. "That's what he's always a-saying. We got to do this, and we got to do that—"

"If you don't mean to study my connection," said Mr. Coombes, "what did you marry me for?"

"I wonder," said Jennie, and turned back to the piano.

"I never saw such a man as you," said Mrs. Coombes. "You've altered all round since we were married. Before—"

Then Jennie began at the turn, turn, turn again.

"Look here!" said Mr. Coombes, driven at last to revolt, standing up and raising his voice. "I tell you I won't have that." The frock-coat heaved with his indignation.

"No vi'lence, now," said the long young man in drab, sitting up.

"Who the juice are you?" said Mr. Coombes fiercely.

Whereupon they all began talking at once. The new guest said he was Jennie's "intended," and meant to protect her, and Mr. Coombes said he was welcome to do so anywhere but in his (Mr. Coombes') house; and Mrs. Coombes said he ought to be ashamed of insulting his guests, and (as I have already mentioned) that he was getting a regular little grub; and the end was, that Mr. Coombes ordered his visitors out of the house, and they wouldn't go, and so he said he would go himself. With his face burning and tears of excitement in his eyes, he went into the passage, and as he struggled with his overcoat—his frock-coat sleeves got concertinaed up his arm—and gave a brush at his silk hat, Jennie began again at the piano, and strummed him insultingly out of the house. Turn, turn, turn. He slammed the shop door so that the house quivered. That, briefly, was the immediate making of his mood. You will perhaps begin to understand his disgust with existence.

As he walked along the muddy path under the firs,—it was late October, and the ditches and heaps of fir needles were gorgeous with clumps of fungi,—he recapitulated the melancholy history of his marriage. It was brief and commonplace enough. He now perceived with sufficient clearness that his wife had married him out of a natural curiosity and in order to escape from her worrying, laborious, and uncertain life in the workroom; and, like the majority of her class, she was far too stupid to realise that it was her duty to co-operate with him in his business. She was greedy of enjoyment, loquacious, and socially-minded, and evidently disappointed to find the restraints of poverty still hanging about her.

His worries exasperated her, and the slightest attempt to control her proceedings resulted in a charge of "grumbling." Why couldn't he be nice—as he used to be? And Coombes was such a harmless little man, too, nourished mentally on *Self-Help*, and with a meagre ambition of self-denial and competition, that was to end in a "sufficiency." Then Jennie came in as a female Mephistopheles, a gabbling chronicle of "fellers," and was always wanting his wife to go to theatres, and "all that." And in addition were aunts of his wife, and cousins (male and female) to eat up capital, insult him personally, upset business arrangements, annoy good customers, and generally blight his life. It was not the first occasion by many that Mr. Coombes had fled his home in wrath and indignation, and something like fear, vowing furiously and even aloud that he wouldn't stand it, and so frothing away his energy along the line of least resistance. But never before had he been quite so sick of life as on this particular Sunday afternoon. The Sunday dinner may have had its share in his despair—and the greyness of the sky. Perhaps, too, he was beginning to realise his unendurable frustration as a business man as the consequence of his marriage. Presently bankruptcy, and after that——

Perhaps she might have reason to repent when it was too late. And destiny, as I have already intimated, had planted the path through the wood with evil-smelling fungi, thickly and variously planted it, not only on the right side, but on the left.

A small shopman is in such a melancholy position, if his wife turns out a disloyal partner. His capital is all tied up in his business, and to leave her means to join the unemployed in some strange part of the earth. The luxuries of divorce are beyond him altogether. So that the good old tradition of marriage for better or worse holds inexorably for him, and things work up to tragic culminations. Bricklayers kick their wives to death, and dukes betray theirs; but it is among the small clerks and shopkeepers nowadays that it comes most often to a cutting of throats. Under the circumstances it is not so very remarkable—and you must take it as charitably as you can—that the mind of Mr. Coombes ran for a while on some such glorious close to his disappointed hopes, and that he thought of razors, pistols, bread-knives, and touching letters to the coroner denouncing his enemies by name, and praying piously for forgiveness. After a time his fierceness gave way to melancholia. He had been married in this very overcoat, in his first and only frock-coat that was buttoned up beneath it. He began to recall their courting along this very walk, his years of penurious saving to get capital, and the bright hopefulness of his marrying days. For it all to work out like this! Was there no sympathetic ruler anywhere in the world? He reverted to death as a topic.

He thought of the canal he had just crossed, and doubted whether he shouldn't stand with his head out, even in the middle, and it was while drowning was in his mind that the purple pileus caught his eye. He looked at it mechanically for a moment, and stopped and stooped towards it to pick it up, under the impression that it was some such small leather object as a purse. Then he saw that it was the purple top of a fungus, a peculiarly poisonous-looking purple: slimy, shiny, and emitting a sour odour. He hesitated with his hand an inch or so from it, and the thought of poison crossed his mind. With that he picked the thing, and stood up again with it in his hand.

The odour was certainly strong—acrid, but by no means disgusting. He broke off a piece, and the fresh surface was a creamy white, that changed like magic in the space of ten seconds to a yellowish-green colour. It was even an inviting-looking change. He broke off two other pieces to see it repeated. They were wonderful things these fungi, thought Mr. Coombes, and all of them the deadliest poisons, as his father had often told him. Deadly poisons!

There is no time like the present for a rash resolve. Why not here and now? thought Mr. Coombes. He tasted a little piece, a very little piece indeed—a mere crumb. It was so pungent that he almost spat it out again, then merely hot and full-flavoured: a kind of German mustard with a touch of horse-radish and—well, mushroom. He swallowed it in the excitement of the moment. Did he like it or did he not? His mind was curiously careless. He would try another bit. It really wasn't bad—it was good. He forgot his troubles in the interest of the immediate moment. Playing with death it was. He took another bite, and then deliberately finished a mouthful. A curious, tingling sensation began in his finger-tips and toes. His pulse began to move faster. The blood in his ears sounded like a mill-race. "Try bi' more," said Mr. Coombes. He turned and looked about him, and found his feet unsteady. He saw, and struggled towards, a little patch of purple a dozen yards away. "Jol' goo' stuff," said Mr. Coombes. "E—lomore ye'." He pitched forward and fell on his face, his hands outstretched towards the cluster of pilei. But he did not eat any more of them. He forgot forthwith.

He rolled over and sat up with a look of astonishment on his face. His carefully brushed silk hat had rolled away towards the ditch. He pressed his hand to his brow. Something had happened, but he could not rightly determine what it was. Anyhow, he was no longer dull—he felt bright, cheerful. And his throat was afire. He laughed in the sudden gaiety of his heart. Had he been dull? He did not know; but at any rate he would be dull no longer. He got up and stood unsteadily, regarding the universe with an agreeable smile. He began to remember. He could not remember very well, because of a steam roundabout that was beginning in his head. And he knew he had been disagreeable at home, just because they wanted to be happy. They were quite right; life should be as gay as possible. He would go home and make it up, and reassure them. And why not take some of this delightful toadstool with him, for them to eat? A hatful, no less. Some of those red ones with white spots as well, and a few yellow. He had been a dull dog, an enemy to merriment; he would make up for it. It would be gay to turn his coat-sleeves inside out, and stick some yellow gorse into his waist-coat pockets. Then home—singing—for a jolly evening.

After the departure of Mr. Coombes, Jennie discontinued play-ing, and turned round on the music-stool again. "What a fuss about nothing!" said Jennie.

"You see, Mr. Clarence, what I've got to put up with," said Mrs. Coombes.

"He is a bit hasty," said Mr. Clarence judicially.

"He ain't got the slightest sense of our position," said Mrs. Coombes; "that's what I complain of. He cares for nothing but his old shop; and if I have a bit of company, or buy anything to keep myself decent, or get any little thing I want out of the housekeep-ing money, there's disagreeables. 'Economy' he says; 'struggle for life,' and all that. He lies awake of nights about it, worrying how he can screw me out of a shilling. He wanted us to eat Dorset but-ter once. If once I was to give in to him—there!"

"Of course," said Jennie.

"If a man values a woman," said Mr. Clarence, lounging back in the arm-chair, "he must be prepared to make sacrifices for her. For my own part," said Mr. Clarence, with his eye on Jennie, "I shouldn't think of marrying till I was in a position to do the thing in style. It's downright selfishness. A man ought to go through the rough-and-tumble by himself, and not drag her—"

"I don't agree altogether with that," said Jennie. "I don't see why a man shouldn't have a woman's help, provided he doesn't treat her meanly, you know. It's meanness—"

"You wouldn't believe," said Mrs. Coombes. "But I was a fool to 'ave 'im. I might 'ave known. If it 'adn't been for my father, we shouldn't 'ave 'ad not a carriage to our wedding."

"Lord! he didn't stick out at that?" said Mr. Clarence, quite shocked.

"Said he wanted the money for his stock, or some such rubbish. Why, he wouldn't have a woman in to help me once a week if it wasn't for my standing out plucky. And the fusses he makes about money—comes to me, well, pretty near crying, with sheets of paper and figgers. 'If only we can tide over this year,' he says, 'the business is bound to go.' 'If only we can tide over this year,' I says; 'then it'll be, if only we can tide over next year. I know you,' I says. 'And you don't catch me screwing myself lean and ugly. Why didn't you marry a slavey?' I says, 'if you wanted one—instead of a respectable girl,' I says."

So Mrs. Coombes. But we will not follow this unedifying conversation further. Suffice it that Mr. Coombes was very satisfactorily disposed of, and they had a snug little time round the fire. Then Mrs. Coombes went to get the tea, and Jennie sat coquettishly on the arm of Mr. Clarence's chair until the tea-things clattered outside. "What was that I heard?" asked Mrs. Coombes playfully, as she entered, and there was badinage about kissing. They were just sitting down to the little circular table when the first intimation of Mr. Coombes' return was heard.

This was a fumbling at the latch of the front door.

"'Ere's my lord," said Mrs. Coombes. "Went out like a lion and comes back like a lamb, I'll lay."

Something fell over in the shop: a chair, it sounded like. Then there was a sound as of some complicated step exercise in the passage. Then the door opened and Coombes appeared. But it was Coombes transfigured. The immaculate collar had been torn carelessly from his throat. His carefully-brushed silk hat, half-full of a crush of fungi, was under one arm; his coat was inside out, and his waistcoat adorned with bunches of yellow-blossomed furze. These little eccentricities of Sunday costume, however, were quite overshadowed by the change in his face; it was livid white, his eyes were unnaturally large and bright, and his pale blue lips were drawn back in a cheerless grin. "Merry!" he said. He had stopped dancing to open the door. "Rational 'njoyment. Dance." He made three fantastic steps into the room, and stood bowing.

"Jim!" shrieked Mrs. Coombes, and Mr. Clarence sat petrified, with a dropping lower jaw.

"Tea," said Mr. Coombes. "Jol' thing, tea. Tose-stools, too. Brosher."

"He's drunk," said Jennie in a weak voice. Never before had she seen this intense pallor in a drunken man, or such shining, dilated eyes.

Mr. Coombes held out a handful of scarlet agaric to Mr. Clarence. "Jo' stuff," said he; "ta' some."

At that moment he was genial. Then at the sight of their startled faces he changed, with the swift transition of insanity, into overbearing fury. And it seemed as if he had suddenly recalled the quarrel of his departure. In such a huge voice as Mrs. Coombes had never heard before, he shouted, "My house. I'm master 'ere. Eat what I give yer!" He bawled this, as it seemed, without an effort, without a violent gesture, standing there as motionless as one who whispers, holding out a handful of fungus.

Clarence approved himself a coward. He could not meet the mad fury in Coombes' eyes; he rose to his feet, pushing back his chair, and turned, stooping. At that Coombes rushed at him. Jennie saw her opportunity, and, with the ghost of a shriek, made for the door.

Mrs. Coombes followed her. Clarence tried to dodge. Over went the tea-table with a smash as Coombes clutched him by the collar and tried to thrust the fungus into his mouth. Clarence was content to leave his collar behind him, and shot out into the passage with red patches of fly agaric still adherent to his face. "Shut 'im in!" cried Mrs. Coombes, and would have closed the door, but her supports deserted her; Jennie saw the shop door open, and vanished thereby, locking it behind her, while Clarence went on hastily into the kitchen. Mr. Coombes came heavily against the door, and Mrs. Coombes, finding the key was inside, fled upstairs and locked herself in the spare bedroom.

So the new convert to *joie de vivre* emerged upon the passage, his decorations a little scattered, but that respectable hatful of fungi still under his arm. He hesitated at the three ways, and decided on the kitchen. Whereupon Clarence, who was fumbling with the key, gave up the attempt to imprison his host, and fled into the scullery, only to be captured before he could open the door into the yard. Mr. Clarence is singularly reticent of the details of what occurred. It seems that Mr. Coombes' transitory irritation had vanished again, and he was once more a genial playfellow. And as there were knives and meat choppers about, Clarence very generously resolved to humour him and so avoid anything tragic. It is beyond dispute that Mr. Coombes played with Mr. Clarence to his heart's content; they could not have been more playful and familiar if they had known each other for years. He insisted gaily on Clarence trying the fungi, and, after a friendly tussle, was smitten with remorse at the mess he was making of his guest's face. It also appears that Clarence was dragged under the sink and his face scrubbed with the blacking brush—he being still resolved to humour the lunatic at any cost—and that finally, in a somewhat dishevelled, chipped, and discoloured condition, he was assisted to his coat and shown out by the back door, the shopway being barred by Jennie. Mr. Coombes' wandering thoughts then turned to Jennie. Jennie had been unable to unfasten the shop door, but she shot the bolts against Mr. Coombes' latch-key, and remained in possession of the shop for the rest of the evening.

It would appear that Mr. Coombes then returned to the kitchen, still in pursuit of gaiety, and, albeit a strict Good Templar, drank (or spilt down the front of the first and only frock-coat) no less than five bottles of the stout Mrs. Coombes insisted upon having for her health's sake. He made cheerful noises by breaking off the necks of the bottles with several of his wife's wedding-present dinner-plates, and during the earlier part of this great drunk he sang divers merry ballads. He cut his finger rather badly with one of the bottles—the only bloodshed in this story—and what with that, and the systematic convulsion of his inexperienced physiology by the liquorish brand of Mrs. Coombes' stout, it may be the evil of the fungus poison was somehow allayed. But we prefer to draw a veil over the concluding incidents of this Sunday afternoon. They ended in the coal cellar, in a deep and healing sleep.

An interval of five years elapsed. Again it was a Sunday afternoon in October, and again Mr. Coombes walked through the pine wood beyond the canal. He was still the same dark-eyed, black-moustached

little man that he was at the outset of the story, but his double
chin was now scarcely so illusory as it had been. His overcoat was new,
with a velvet lapel, and a stylish collar with turn-down corners,
free of any coarse starchiness, had replaced the original all-round
article. His hat was glossy, his gloves newish—though one finger
had split and been carefully mended. And a casual observer would
have noticed about him a certain rectitude of bearing, a certain
erectness of head that marks the man who thinks well of himself.
He was a master now, with three assistants. Beside him walked a
larger sunburnt parody of himself, his brother Tom, just back from
Australia. They were recapitulating their early struggles, and Mr.
Coombes had just been making a financial statement.

"It's a very nice little business, Jim," said brother Tom. "In
these days of competition you're jolly lucky to have worked it up
so. And you're jolly lucky, too, to have a wife who's willing to help
like yours does."

"Between ourselves," said Mr. Coombes, "it wasn't always so.
It wasn't always like this. To begin with, the missus was a bit giddy.
Girls are funny creatures."

"Dear me!"

"Yes. You'd hardly think it, but she was downright extravagant,
and always having slaps at me. I was a bit too easy and loving, and
all that, and she thought the whole blessed show was run for her.
Turned the 'ouse into a regular caravansery, always having her relations and girls from business in, and their chaps. Comic songs a'
Sunday, it was getting to, and driving trade away. And she was
making eyes at the chaps, too! I tell you, Tom, the place wasn't my
own."

"Shouldn't a' thought it."

"It was so. Well—I reasoned with her. I said, 'I ain't a duke, to
keep a wife like a pet animal. I married you for 'elp and company.'
I said, 'You got to 'elp and pull the business through.' She wouldn't
'ear of it. 'Very well,' I says?? 'I'm a mild man till I'm roused,' I
says, 'and it's getting to that.' But she wouldn't 'ear of no warnings."

"Well?"

"It's the way with women. She didn't think I 'ad it in me to be
roused. Women of her sort (between ourselves, Tom) don't respect
a man until they're a bit afraid of him. So I just broke out to show
her. In comes a girl named Jennie, that used to work with her, and

her chap. We 'ad a bit of a row, and I came out 'ere—it was just such another day as this—and I thought it all out. Then I went back and pitched into them."

"You did?"

"I did. I was mad, I can tell you. I wasn't going to 'it 'er if I could 'elp it, so I went back and licked into this chap, just to show 'er what I could do. 'E was a big chap, too. Well, I chucked him, and smashed things about, and gave 'er a scaring, and she ran up and locked 'erself into the spare room."

"Well?"

"That's all. I says to 'er the next morning, 'Now you know,' I says, 'what I'm like when I'm roused.' And I didn't have to say anything more."

"And you've been happy ever after, eh?"

"So to speak. There's nothing like putting your foot down with them. If it 'adn't been for that afternoon I should 'a' been tramping the roads now, and she'd 'a' been grumbling at me, and all her family grumbling for bringing her to poverty—I know their little ways. But we're all right now. And it's a very decent little business, as you say."

They proceeded on their way meditatively. "Women are funny creatures," said Brother Tom.

"They want a firm hand," says Coombes.

"What a lot of these funguses there are about here!" remarked Brother Tom presently. "I can't see what use they are in the world."

Mr. Coombes looked. "I dessay they're sent for some wise purpose," said Mr. Coombes.

And that was as much thanks as the purple pileus ever got for maddening this absurd little man to the pitch of decisive action, and so altering the whole course of his life.

The Purple Terror

Fred M. White

I

Lieutenant Will Scarlett's instructions were devoid of problems, physical or otherwise. To convey a letter from Captain Driver of the *Yankee Doodle*, in Porto Rico Bay, to Admiral Lake on the other side of the isthmus, was an apparently simple matter.

"All you have to do," the captain remarked, "is to take three or four men with you in case of accidents, cross the isthmus on foot, and simply give this letter into the hands of Admiral Lake. By so doing we shall save at least four days, and the aborigines are presumedly friendly."

The aborigines aforesaid were Cuban insurgents. Little or no strife had taken place along the neck lying between Porto Rico and the north bay where Lake's flagship lay, though the belt was known to be given over to the disaffected Cubans.

"It is a matter of fifty miles through practically unexplored country," Scarlett replied; "and there's a good deal of the family quarrel in this business, sir. If the Spaniards hate us, the Cubans are not exactly enamoured of our flag."

Captain Driver roundly denounced the whole pack of them.

"Treacherous thieves to a man," he said. "I don't suppose your progress will have any brass bands and floral arches to it. And they tell me the forest is pretty thick. But you'll get there all the same. There is the letter, and you can start as soon as you like."

"I may pick my own men, sir?"

"My dear fellow, take whom you please. Take the mastiff, if you like."

"I'd like the mastiff," Scarlett replied; "as he is practically my own, I thought you would not object."

Will Scarlett began to glow as the prospect of adventure stimulated his imagination. He was rather a good specimen of West Point naval dandyism. He had brains at the back of his smartness, and his geological and botanical knowledge were going to prove of considerable service to a grateful country when said grateful country should have passed beyond the rudimentary stages of colonization. And there was some disposition to envy Scarlett on the part of others floating for the past month on the liquid prison of the sapphire sea.

A warrant officer, Tarrer by name, *plus* two A.B.'s of thews and sinews, to say nothing of the dog, completed the exploring party. By the time that the sun kissed the tip of the feathery hills they had covered some six miles of their journey. From the first Scarlett had been struck by the absolute absence of the desolation and horror of civil strife. Evidently the fiery cross had not been carried here; huts and houses were intact; the villagers stood under sloping eaves, and regarded the Americans with a certain sullen curiosity.

"We'd better stop for the night here," said Scarlett.

They had come at length to a village that boasted some pretensions. An adobe chapel at one end of the straggling street was faced by a wine-house at the other. A padre, with hands folded over a bulbous, greasy gabardine, bowed gravely to Scarlett's salutation. The latter had what Tarrer called "considerable Spanish."

"We seek quarters for the night," said Scarlett. "Of course, we are prepared to pay for them."

The sleepy padre nodded towards the wine-house.

"You will find fair accommodations there," he said. "We are friends of the Americanos."

Scarlett doubted the fact, and passed on with florid thanks. So far, little signs of friendliness had been encountered on the march. Coldness, suspicion, a suggestion of fear, but no friendliness to be embarrassing.

The keeper of the wine-shop had his doubts. He feared his poor accommodation for guests so distinguished. A score or more of picturesque, cut-throat-looking rascals with cigarettes in their mouths lounged sullenly in the bar. The display of a brace of gold dollars enlarged mine host's opinion of his household capacity.

"I will do my best, señors," he said. "Come this way."

So it came to pass that an hour after twilight Tarrer and Scarlett were seated in the open amongst the oleanders and the trailing gleam of the fire-flies, discussing cigars of average merit and a native wine that was not without virtues. The long bar of the wine-house was brilliantly illuminated; from within came shouts of laughter mingled with the ting, tang of the guitar and the rollick-ing clack of the castanets.

"They seem to be happy in there," Tarrer remarked. "It isn't all daggers and ball in this distressful country."

A certain curiosity came over Scarlett.

"It is the duty of a good officer," he said, "to lose no opportunity of acquiring useful information. Let us join the giddy throng, Tarrer."

Tarrer expressed himself with enthusiasm in favour of any amusement that might be going. A month's idleness on shipboard increases the appetite for that kind of thing wonderfully. The long bar was comfortable, and filled with Cubans who took absolutely no notice of the intruders. Their eyes were turned towards a rude stage at the far end of the bar, whereon a girl was gyrating in a dance with a celerity and grace that caused the wreath of flowers around her shoulders to resemble a trembling zone of purple flame.

"A wonderfully pretty girl and a wonderfully pretty dance," Scarlett murmured, when the motions ceased and the girl leapt gracefully to the ground. "Largesse, I expect. I thought so. Well, I'm good for a quarter."

The girl came forward, extending a shell prettily. She curtsied before Scarlett and fixed her dark, liquid eyes on his. As he smiled and dropped his quarter-dollar into the shell a coquettish gleam came into the velvety eyes. An ominous growl came from the lips of a bearded ruffian close by.

"Othello's jealous," said Tarrer. "Look at his face."

"I am better employed," Scarlett laughed. "That was a graceful dance, pretty one. I hope you are going to give us another one pres-ently—"

Scarlett paused suddenly. His eyes had fallen on the purple band of flowers the girl had twined round her shoulder. Scarlett was an enthusiastic botanist; he knew most of the gems in Flora's crown, but he had never looked upon such a vivid wealth of blossom before.

The flowers were orchids, and orchids of a kind unknown to collectors anywhere. On this point Scarlett felt certain. And yet this part of the world was by no means a difficult one to explore in comparison with New Guinea and Sumatra, where the rarer varieties had their homes.

The blooms were immensely large, far larger than any flower of the kind known to Europe or America, of a deep pure purple, with a blood-red centre. As Scarlett gazed upon them he noticed a certain cruel expression on the flower. Most orchids have a kind of face of their own; the purple blooms had a positive expression of ferocity and cunning. They exhumed, too, a queer, sickly fragrance. Scarlett had smelt something like it before, after the Battle of Manila. The perfume was the perfume of a corpse.

"And yet they are magnificent flowers," said Scarlett. "Won't you tell me where you got them from, pretty one?"

The girl was evidently flattered by the attention bestowed upon her by the smart young American. The bearded Othello alluded to edged up to her side.

"The señor had best leave the girl alone," he said, insolently.

Scarlett's fist clenched as he measured the Cuban with his eyes. The Admiral's letter crackled in his breast-pocket, and discretion got the best of valour.

"You are paying yourself a poor compliment, my good fellow," he said, "though I certainly admire your good taste. Those flowers interested me."

The man appeared to be mollified. His features corrugated in a smile.

"The señor would like some of those blooms?" he asked. "It was I who procured them for little Zara here. I can show you where they grow."

Every eye in the room was turned in Scarlett's direction. It seemed to him that a kind of diabolical malice glistened on every dark face there, save that of the girl, whose features paled under her healthy tan.

"If the señor is wise," she began, "he will not—"

"Listen to the tales of a silly girl," Othello put in menacingly. He grasped the girl by the arm, and she winced in positive pain. "Pshaw, there is no harm where the flowers grow, if one is only careful. I will take you there, and I will be your guide to Port Anna, where you are going, for a gold dollar."

All Scarlett's scientific enthusiasm was aroused. It is not given to every man to present a new orchid to the horticultural world. And this one would dwarf the finest plant hitherto discovered.

"Done with you," he said; "we start at daybreak. I shall look to you to be ready. Your name is Tito? Well, good-night, Tito."

As Scarlett and Tarrer withdrew the girl suddenly darted forward. A wild word or two fluttered from her lips. Then there was a sound as of a blow, followed by a little stifled cry of pain.

"No, no," Tarrer urged, as Scarlett half turned. "Better not. They are ten to one, and they are no friends of ours. It never pays to interfere in these family quarrels. I daresay, if you interfered, the girl would be just as ready to knife you as her jealous lover."

"But a blow like that, Tarrer!"

"It's a pity, but I don't see how we can help it. Your business is the quick dispatch of the Admiral's letter, not the squiring of dames."

Scarlett owned with a sigh that Tarrer was right.

II

It was quite a different Tito who presented himself at daybreak the following morning. His insolent manner had disappeared. He was cheerful, alert, and he had a manner full of the most winning politeness.

"You quite understand what we want," Scarlett said. "My desire is to reach Port Anna as soon as possible. You know the way?"

"Every inch of it, señor. I have made the journey scores of times. And I shall have the felicity of getting you there early on the third day from now."

"Is it so far as that?"

"The distance is not great, señor. It is the passage through the woods. There are parts where no white man has been before."

"And you will not forget the purple orchids?"

A queer gleam trembled like summer lightning in Tito's eyes. The next instant it had gone. A time was to come when Scarlett was to recall that look, but for the moment it was allowed to pass.

"The señor shall see the purple orchid," he said; "thousands of them. They have a bad name amongst our people, but that is all nonsense. They grow in the high trees, and their blossoms cling to long, green tendrils. These tendrils are poisonous to the flesh, and great care should be taken in handling them. And the flowers are quite harmless, though we call them the devil's poppies."

To all of this Scarlett listened eagerly. He was all-impatient to see and handle the mysterious flower for himself. The whole excursion was going to prove a wonderful piece of luck. At the same time he had to curb his impatience. There would be no chance of seeing the purple orchid to-day.

For hours they fought their way along through the dense tangle. A heat seemed to lie over all the land like a curse—a blistering, sweltering, moist heat with no puff of wind to temper its breathlessness. By the time that the sun was sliding down, most of the party had had enough of it.

They passed out of the underwood at length, and, striking upwards, approached a clump of huge forest trees on the brow of a ridge. All kinds of parasites hung from the branches; there were ropes and bands of green, and high up a fringe of purple glory that caused Scarlett's pulses to leap a little faster.

"Surely that is the purple orchid?" he cried.

Tito shrugged his shoulders contemptuously.

"A mere straggler or two," he said, "and out of reach in any case. The señor will have all he wants and more to-morrow."

"But it seems to me," said Scarlett, "that I could—"

Then he paused. The sun like a great glowing shield was shining full behind the tree with its crown of purple, and showing up every green rope and thread clinging to the branches with the clearness of liquid crystal. Scarlett saw a network of green cords like a huge spider's web, and in the centre of it was not a fly, but a human skeleton!

The arms and legs were stretched apart as if the victim had been crucified. The wrists and ankles were bound in the cruel web. Fragments of tattered clothing fluttered in the faint breath of the evening breeze.

"Horrible," Scarlett cried, "absolutely horrible!"

"You may well say that," Tarrer exclaimed, with a shudder. "Like the fly in the amber or the apple in the dumpling, the mystery is how he got there."

"Perhaps Tito can explain the mystery," Scarlett suggested.

Tito appeared to be uneasy and disturbed. He looked furtively from one to the other of his employers as a culprit might who feels he has been found out. But his courage returned as he noted the absence of suspicion in the faces turned upon him.

"I can explain," he exclaimed, with teeth that chattered from some unknown terror or guilt. "It is not the first time that I have seen the skeleton. Some plant-hunter doubtless who came here alone. He climbed into the tree without a knife, and those green ropes got twisted round his limbs, as a swimmer gets entangled in the weeds. The more he struggled, the more the cords bound him. He would call in vain for anyone to assist him here. And so he must have died."

The explanation was a plausible one, but by no means detracted from the horror of the discovery. For some time the party pushed their way on in the twilight, till the darkness descended suddenly like a curtain.

"We will camp here," Tito said; "it is high, dry ground, and we have this belt of trees above us. There is no better place than this for miles around. In the valley the miasma is dangerous."

As Tito spoke he struck a match, and soon a torch flamed up. The little party were on a small plateau, fringed by trees. The ground was dry and hard, and, as Scarlett and his party saw to their astonishment, littered with bones. There were skulls of animals and skulls of human beings, the skeletons of birds, the frames of beasts both great and small. It was a weird, shuddering sight.

"We can't possibly stay here," Scarlett exclaimed.

Tito shrugged his shoulders.

"There is nowhere else," he replied. "Down in the valley there are many dangers. Further in the woods are the snakes and jaguars. Bones are nothing. Peuf, they can be easily cleared away."

They had to be cleared away, and there was an end of the matter. For the most part the skeletons were white and dry as air and sun could make them. Over the dry, calcined mass the huge fringe of trees nodded mournfully. With the rest, Scarlett was busy scattering the mocking frames aside. A perfect human skeleton lay at his feet. On one finger something glittered—a signet ring. As Scarlett took it in his hand he started.

"I know this ring!" he exclaimed; "it belonged to Pierre Anton, perhaps the most skilled and intrepid plant-hunter the *Jardin des Plantes* ever employed. The poor fellow was by way of being a friend of mine. He met the fate that he always anticipated."

"There must have been a rare holocaust here," said Tarrer.

"It beats me," Scarlett responded. By this time a large circle had been shifted clear of human and other remains. By the light of the fire loathsome insects could be seen scudding and straddling away. "It beats me entirely. Tito, can you offer any explanation? If the bones were all human I could get some grip of the problem. But when one comes to birds and animals as well! Do you see that the skeletons lie in a perfect circle, starting from the centre of the clump of trees above us? What does it mean?"

Tito professed utter ignorance of the subject. Some years before a small tribe of natives invaded the peninsula for religious rites. They came from a long way off in canoes, and wild stories were told concerning them. They burnt sacrifices, no doubt.

Scarlett turned his back contemptuously on this transparent tale. His curiosity was aroused. There must be some explanation, for Pierre Anton had been seen of men within the last ten years.

"There's something uncanny about this," he said, to Tarrer. "I mean to get to the bottom of it, or know why."

"As for me," said Tarrer, with a cavernous yawn, "I have but one ambition, and that is my supper, followed by my bed."

III

Scarlett lay in the light of the fire looking about him. He felt restless and uneasy, though he would have found it difficult to explain the reason. For one thing, the air trembled to strange noises. There seemed to be something moving, writhing in the forest trees above his head. More than once it seemed to his distorted fancy that he could see a squirming knot of green snakes in motion.

Outside the circle, in a grotto of bones, Tito lay sleeping. A few moments before his dark, sleek head had been furtively raised, and his eyes seemed to gleam in the flickering firelight with malignant cunning. As he met Scarlett's glance he gave a deprecatory gesture and subsided.

"What the deuce does it all mean?" Scarlett muttered. "I feel certain yonder rascal is up to some mischief. Jealous still because I paid his girl a little attention. But he can't do us any real harm. Quiet, there!"

The big mastiff growled and then whined uneasily. Even the dog seemed to be conscious of some unseen danger. He lay down again, cowed by the stern command, but he still whimpered in his dreams.

"I fancy I'll keep awake for a spell," Scarlett told himself.

For a time he did so. Presently he began to slide away into the land of poppies. He was walking amongst a garden of bones which bore masses of purple blossoms. Then Pierre Anton came on the scene, pale and resolute as Scarlett had always known him; then the big mastiff seemed in some way to be mixed up with the phantasm of the dream, barking as if in pain, and Scarlett came to his senses.

He was breathing short, a beady perspiration stood on his forehead, his heart hammered in quick thuds—all the horrors of nightmare were still upon him. In a vague way as yet he heard the mastiff howl, a real howl of real terror, and Scarlett knew that he was awake.

Then a strange thing happened. In the none too certain light of the fire, Scarlett saw the mastiff snatched up by some invisible hand, carried far on high towards the trees, and finally flung to the earth with a crash. The big dog lay still as a log.

A sense of fear born of the knowledge of impotence came over Scarlett; what in the name of evil did it all mean? The smart scientist had no faith in the occult, and yet what *did* it all mean?

Nobody stirred. Scarlett's companions were soaked and soddened with fatigue; the rolling thunder of artillery would have scarce disturbed them. With teeth set and limbs that trembled, Scarlett crawled over to the dog.

The great, black-muzzled creature was quite dead. The full chest was stained and soaked in blood; the throat had been cut apparently with some jagged, saw-like instrument away to the bone. And, strangest thing of all, scattered all about the body was a score or more of the great purple orchid flowers broken off close to the head. A hot, pricking sensation travelled slowly up Scarlett's spine and seemed to pass out at the tip of his skull. He felt his hair rising.

He was frightened. As a matter of honest fact, he had never been so horribly scared in his life before. The whole thing was so mysterious, so cruel, so bloodthirsty.

Still, there must be some rational explanation. In some way the matter had to do with the purple orchid. The flower had an evil reputation. Was it not known to these Cubans as the devil's poppy?

Scarlett recollected vividly now Zara's white, scared face when Tito had volunteered to show the way to the resplendent bloom; he remembered the cry of the girl and the blow that followed. He could see it all now. The girl had meant to warn him against some nameless horror to which Tito was leading the small party. This was the jealous Cuban's revenge.

A wild desire to pay this debt to the uttermost fraction filled Scarlett, and shook him with a trembling passion. He crept along in the drenching dew to where Tito lay, and touched his forehead with the chill blue rim of a revolver barrel. Tito stirred slightly.

"You dog!" Scarlett cried. "I am going to shoot you."

Tito did not move again. His breathing was soft and regular. Beyond a doubt the man was sleeping peacefully. After all he might be innocent; and yet, on the other hand, he might be so sure of his quarry that he could afford to slumber without anxiety as to his vengeance.

In favour of the latter theory was the fact that the Cuban lay beyond the limit of what had previously been the circle of dry bones. It was just possible that there was no danger outside that pale. In that case it would be easy to arouse the rest, and so save them from the horrible death which had befallen the mastiff. No doubt these were a form of upas tree, but that would not account for the ghastly spectacle in mid-air.

"I'll let this chap sleep for the present," Scarlett muttered.

He crawled back, not without misgivings, into the ring of death. He meant to wake the others and then wait for further developments. By now his senses were more alert and vigorous than they had ever been before. A preternatural clearness of brain and vision possessed him. As he advanced he saw suddenly falling a green bunch of cord that straightened into a long, emerald line. It was triangular in shape, fine at the apex, and furnished with hooked spines. The rope appeared to dangle from the tree overhead; the broad, sucker-like termination was evidently soaking up moisture.

A natural phenomenon evidently, Scarlett thought. This was some plant new to him, a parasite living amongst the tree-tops and drawing life and vigour by means of these green, rope-like antennae designed by Nature to soak and absorb the heavy dews of night.

For a moment the logic of this theory was soothing to Scarlett's distracted nerves, but only for a moment, for then he saw at regular intervals along the green rope the big purple blossoms of the devil's poppy.

He stood gasping there, utterly taken aback for the moment. There must be some infernal juggling behind all this business. He saw the rope slacken and quiver, he saw it swing forward like a pendulum, and the next minute it had passed across the shoulders of a sleeping seaman.

Then the green root became as the arm of an octopus. The line shook from end to end like the web of an angry spider when invaded by a wasp. It seemed to grip the sailor and tighten, and then, before Scarlett's afrighted eyes, the sleeping man was raised gently from the ground.

Scarlett jumped forward with a desire to scream hysterically. Now that a comrade was in danger he was no longer afraid. He whipped a jack-knife from his pocket and slashed at the cruel cord. He half expected to meet with the stoutness of a steel strand, but to his surprise the feeler snapped like a carrot, bumping the sailor heavily on the ground.

He sat up, rubbing his eyes vigorously.

"That you, sir?" he asked. "What is the matter?"

"For the love of God, get up at once and help me to arouse the others," Scarlett said, hoarsely. "We have come across the devil's workshop. All the horrors of the inferno are invented here."

The bluejacket struggled to his feet. As he did so, the clothing from his waist downwards slipped about his feet, clean cut through by the teeth of the green parasite. All around the body of the sailor blood oozed from a zone of teeth-marks.

Two-o'clock-in-the-morning courage is a virtue vouchsafed to few. The tar, who would have faced an ironclad cheerfully, fairly shivered with fright and dismay.

"What does it mean, sir?" he cried. "I've been—"

"Wake the others," Scarlett screamed; "wake the others."

Two or three more green tangles of rope came tumbling to the ground, straightening and quivering instantly. The purple blossoms stood out like a frill upon them. Like a madman, Scarlett shouted, kicking his companions without mercy.

They were all awake at last, grumbling and moaning for their lost slumbers. All this time Tito had never stirred.

"I don't understand it at all," said Tarrer.

"Come from under those trees," said Scarlett, "and I will endeavour to explain. Not that you will believe me for a moment. No man can be expected to believe the awful nightmare I am going to tell you."

Scarlett proceeded to explain. As he expected, his story was followed with marked incredulity, save by the wounded sailor, who had strong evidence to stimulate his otherwise defective imagination.

"I can't believe it," Tarrer said, at length. They were whispering together beyond earshot of Tito, whom they had no desire to arouse for obvious reasons. "This is some diabolical juggling of yonder rascally Cuban. It seems impossible that those slender green cords could—"

Scarlett pointed to the centre of the circle.

"Call the dog," he said grimly, "and see if he will come."

"I admit the point as far as the poor old mastiff is concerned. But at the same time I don't—however, I'll see for myself."

By this time a dozen or more of the slender cords were hanging pendent from the trees. They moved from spot to spot as if jerked up by some unseen hand and deposited a foot or two farther. With the great purple bloom fringing the stem, the effect was not unlovely save to Scarlett, who could see only the dark side of it. As Tarrer spoke he advanced in the direction of the trees.

"What are you going to do?" Scarlett asked.

"Exactly what I told you. I am going to investigate this business for myself."

Without wasting further words Scarlett sprang forward. It was no time for the niceties of an effete civilization. Force was the only logical argument to be used in a case like this, and Scarlett was the more powerful man of the two.

Tarrer saw and appreciated the situation.

"No, no," he cried; "none of that. Anyway, you're too late."

He darted forward and threaded his way between the slender emerald columns. As they moved slowly and with a certain stately deliberation there was no great danger to an alert and vigorous individual. As Scarlett entered the avenue he could hear the soak and suck as the dew was absorbed.

"For Heaven's sake, come out of it," he cried.

The warning came too late. A whip-like trail of green touched Tarrer from behind, and in a lightning flash he was in the toils. The tendency to draw up anything and everything gave the cords a terrible power. Tarrer evidently felt it, for his breath came in great gasps.

"Cut me free," he said, hoarsely; "cut me free. I am being carried off my feet."

He seemed to be doomed for a moment, for all the cords there were apparently converging in his direction. This, as a matter of fact, was a solution of the whole sickening, horrible sensation. Pulled here and there, thrust in one direction and another, Tarrer contrived to keep his feet.

Heedless of possible danger to himself Scarlett darted forward, calling to his companions to come to the rescue. In less time than it takes to tell, four knives were at work ripping and slashing in all directions.

"Not all of you," Scarlett whispered. So tense was the situation that no voice was raised above a murmur. "You two keep your eyes open for fresh cords, and cut them as they fall, instantly. Now then."

The horrible green spines were round Tarrer's body like snakes. His face was white, his breath came painfully, for the pressure was terrible. It seemed to Scarlett to be one horrible dissolving view of green, slimy cords and great weltering, purple blossoms. The whole of the circle was strewn with them. They were wet and slimy underfoot.

Tarrer had fallen forward half unconscious. He was supported now by but two cords above his head. The cruel pressure had been relieved. With one savage sweep of his knife Scarlett cut the last of the lines, and Tarrer fell like a log unconscious to the ground. A feeling of nausea, a yellow dizziness, came over Scarlett as he staggered beyond the dread circle. He saw Tarrer carried to a place of safety, and then the world seemed to wither and leave him in the dark.

"I feel a bit groggy and weak," said Tarrer an hour or so later: "but beyond that this idiot of a Richard is himself again. So far as I am concerned, I should like to get even with our friend Tito for this."

"Something with boiling oil in it," Scarlett suggested, grimly. "The callous scoundrel has slept soundly through the whole of this business. I suppose he felt absolutely certain that he had finished with us."

"Upon my word, we ought to shoot the beggar," Tarrer exclaimed.

"I have a little plan of my own," said Scarlett, "which I am going to put in force later on. Meanwhile we had better get on with breakfast. When Tito wakes a pleasant little surprise will await him."

Tito roused from his slumbers in due course and looked around him. His glance was curious, disappointed, then full of a white and yellow fear. A thousand conflicting emotions streamed across his dark face. Scarlett read them at a glance as he called the Cuban over to him.

"I am not going into any unnecessary details with you," he said. "It has come to my knowledge that you are playing traitor to us. Therefore we prefer to complete our journey alone. We can easily find the way now."

"The señor may do as he pleases," he replied. "Give me my dollar and let me go."

Scarlett replied grimly that he had no intention of doing anything of the kind. He did not propose to place the lives of himself and his comrades in the power of a rascally Cuban who had played false.

"We are going to leave you here till we return," he said. "You will have plenty of food, you will be perfectly safe under the shelter of these trees, and there is no chance of anybody disturbing you. We are going to tie you up to one of these trees for the next four-and-twenty hours."

All the insolence died out of Tito's face. His knees bowed, a cold dew came out over the ghastly green of his features. From the shaking of his limbs he might have fared disastrously with ague.

"The trees," he stammered, "the trees, señor! There is danger from snakes, and—and from many things. There are other places—"

"If this place was safe last night it is safe to-day," Scarlett said, grimly. "I have quite made up my mind."

Tito fought no longer. He fell forward on his knees, he howled for mercy, till Scarlett fairly kicked him up again.

"Make a clean breast of it," he said, "or take the consequences. You know perfectly well that we have found you out, scoundrel."

Tito's story came in gasps. He wanted to get rid of the Americans. He was jealous. Besides, under the Americanos would Cuba be any better off? By no means and assuredly not. Therefore it was the duty of every good Cuban to destroy the Americanos where possible.

"A nice lot to fight for," Scarlett muttered. "Get to the point."

Hastened to the point by a liberal application of stout shoe-leather, Tito made plenary confession. The señor himself had suggested death by medium of the devil's poppies. More than one predatory plant-hunter had been lured to his destruction in the same way. The skeleton hung on the tree was a Dutchman who had walked into the clutch of the purple terror innocently. And Pierre Anton had done the same. The suckers of the devil's poppy only came down at night to gather moisture; in the day they were coiled up like a spring. And anything that they touched they killed. Tito had watched more than one bird or small beast crushed and mauled by these cruel spines with their fringe of purple blossoms.

"How do you get the blooms?" Scarlett asked.

"That is easy," Tito replied. "In the daytime I moisten the ground under the trees. Then the suckers unfold, drawn by the water. Once the suckers unfold one cuts several of them off with long knives. There is danger, of course, but not if one is careful."

"I'll not trouble the devil's poppy any further at present," said Scarlett, "but I shall trouble you to accompany me to my destination as a prisoner."

Tito's eyes dilated.

"They will not shoot me?" he asked, hoarsely.

"I don't know," Scarlett replied. "They may hang you instead. At any rate, I shall be bitterly disappointed if they don't end you one way or the other. Whichever operation it is, I can look forward to it with perfect equanimity."

A Vine on a House
Ambrose Bierce

About three miles from the little town of Norton, in Missouri, on the road leading to Maysville, stands an old house that was last occupied by a family named Harding. Since 1886 no one has lived in it, nor is anyone likely to live in it again. Time and the disfavor of persons dwelling thereabout are converting it into a rather picturesque ruin. An observer unacquainted with its history would hardly put it into the category of "haunted houses," yet in all the region round such is its evil reputation. Its windows are without glass, its doorways without doors; there are wide breaches in the shingle roof, and for lack of paint the weatherboarding is a dun gray. But these unfailing signs of the supernatural are partly concealed and greatly softened by the abundant foliage of a large vine overrunning the entire structure. This vine—of a species which no botanist has ever been able to name—has an important part in the story of the house.

The Harding family consisted of Robert Harding, his wife Matilda, Miss Julia Went, who was her sister, and two young children. Robert Harding was a silent, cold-mannered man who made no friends in the neighborhood and apparently cared to make none. He was about forty years old, frugal and industrious, and made a living from the little farm which is now overgrown with brush and brambles. He and his sister-in-law were rather tabooed by their neighbors, who seemed to think that they were seen too frequently together—not entirely their fault, for at these times they evidently did not challenge observation. The moral code of rural Missouri is stern and exacting.

Mrs. Harding was a gentle, sad-eyed woman, lacking a left foot.

At some time in 1884 it became known that she had gone to visit her mother in Iowa. That was what her husband said in reply to inquiries, and his manner of saying it did not encourage further questioning. She never came back, and two years later, without selling his farm or anything that was his, or appointing an agent to look after his interests, or removing his household goods, Harding, with the rest of the family, left the country. Nobody knew whither he went; nobody at that time cared. Naturally, whatever was movable about the place soon disappeared and the deserted house became "haunted" in the manner of its kind.

One summer evening, four or five years later, the Rev. J. Gruber, of Norton, and a Maysville attorney named Hyatt met on horseback in front of the Harding place. Having business matters to discuss, they hitched their animals and going to the house sat on the porch to talk. Some humorous reference to the somber reputation of the place was made and forgotten as soon as uttered, and they talked of their business affairs until it grew almost dark. The evening was oppressively warm, the air stagnant.

Presently both men started from their seats in surprise: a long vine that covered half the front of the house and dangled its branches from the edge of the porch above them was visibly and audibly agitated, shaking violently in every stem and leaf.

"We shall have a storm," Hyatt exclaimed.

Gruber said nothing, but silently directed the other's attention to the foliage of adjacent trees, which showed no movement; even the delicate tips of the boughs silhouetted against the clear sky were motionless. They hastily passed down the steps to what had been a lawn and looked upward at the vine, whose entire length was now visible. It continued in violent agitation, yet they could discern no disturbing cause.

"Let us leave," said the minister.

And leave they did. Forgetting that they had been traveling in opposite directions, they rode away together. They went to Norton, where they related their strange experience to several discreet friends. The next evening, at about the same hour, accompanied by two others whose names are not recalled, they were again on the porch of the Harding house, and again the mysterious phenomenon occurred: the vine was violently agitated while under the closest scrutiny from root to tip, nor did their combined strength applied to the trunk serve to still it. After an hour's observation they retreated, no less wise, it is thought, than when they had come.

No great time was required for these singular facts to rouse the curiosity of the entire neighborhood. By day and by night crowds of persons assembled at the Harding house "seeking a sign." It does not appear that any found it, yet so credible were the witnesses mentioned that none doubted the reality of the "manifestations" to which they testified.

By either a happy inspiration or some destructive design, it was one day proposed—nobody appeared to know from whom the suggestion came—to dig up the vine, and after a good deal of debate this was done. Nothing was found but the root, yet nothing could have been more strange!

For five or six feet from the trunk, which had at the surface of the ground a diameter of several inches, it ran downward, single and straight, into a loose, friable earth; then it divided and subdivided into rootlets, fibers and filaments, most curiously interwoven. When carefully freed from soil they showed a singular formation. In their ramifications and doublings back upon themselves they made a compact network, having in size and shape an amazing resemblance to the human figure. Head, trunk and limbs were there; even the fingers and toes were distinctly defined; and many professed to see in the distribution and arrangement of the fibers in the globular mass representing the head a grotesque suggestion of a face. The figure was horizontal; the smaller roots had begun to unite at the breast.

In point of resemblance to the human form this image was imperfect. At about ten inches from one of the knees, the cilia forming that leg had abruptly doubled backward and inward upon their course of growth. The figure lacked the left foot.

There was but one inference—the obvious one; but in the ensuing excitement as many courses of action were proposed as there were incapable counselors. The matter was settled by the sheriff of the county, who as the lawful custodian of the abandoned estate ordered the root replaced and the excavation filled with the earth that had been removed.

Later inquiry brought out only one fact of relevancy and significance: Mrs. Harding had never visited her relatives in Iowa, nor did they know that she was supposed to have done so.

Of Robert Harding and the rest of his family nothing is known. The house retains its evil reputation, but the replanted vine is as orderly and well-behaved a vegetable as a nervous person could wish to sit under of a pleasant night, when the katydids grate out their immemorial revelation and the distant whippoorwill signifies his notion of what ought to be done about it.

Professor Jonkin's Cannibal Plant

Howard R. Garis

After Professor Jeptha Jonkin had, by skillful grafting and care, succeeded in raising a single tree that produced, at different seasons, apples, oranges, pineapples, figs, coconuts, and peaches, it might have been supposed he would rest from his scientific labors. But Professor Jonkin was not that kind of a man.

He was continually striving to grow something new in the plant world. So it was no surprise to Bradley Adams, when calling on his friend the professor one afternoon, to find that scientist busy in his large conservatory.

"What are you up to now?" asked Adams. "Trying to make a rosebush produce violets, or a honeysuckle vine bring forth pumpkins?"

"Neither," replied Professor Jonkin a little stiffly, for he resented Adams' playful tone. "Not that either of those things would be difficult. But look at that."

He pointed to a small plant with bright, glossy green leaves mottled with red spots. The thing was growing in a large earthen pot.

It bore three flowers, about the size of morning glories, and not unlike that blossom in shape, save, near the top, there was a sort of lid similar to the flap observed on a jack-in-the-pulpit plant.

"Look down one of those flowers," went on the professor, and Adams, wondering what was to come, did so.

He saw within a small tube, lined with fine, hairlike filaments, which seemed to be in motion. And the shaft or tube went down to the bottom of the morning-glory-shaped part of the flower. At the lower extremity was a little clear liquid.

"Kind of a queer blossom. What is it?" asked Adams.

"That," said the professor with a note of pride in his voice, "is a specimen of the *Sarracenia nepenthis*."

"What's that? French for sunflower, or Latin for sweet pea?" asked Adams irreverently.

"It is Latin for pitcher plant," responded the professor, drawing himself up to his full height of five-feet-three. "One of the most interesting of the South American flora."

"The name fits it pretty well," observed Adams. "I see there's water at the bottom. I suppose this isn't the pitcher that went to the well too often."

"The Sarracenia nepenthis is a most wonderful plant," went on the professor in his lecture voice, not heeding Adams's joking remarks. "It belongs to what Darwin calls the carnivorous family of flowers, and other varieties of the same species are the *Dionaea muscipula*, or Venus Flytrap, the *Darlingtonia*, the *Pinguicula*, and *Aldrovandra*, as well as—"

"Hold on, professor," pleaded Adams. "I'll take the rest on faith. Tell me about this pitcher plant, sounds interesting."

"It is interesting," said Professor Jonkin. "It eats insects."

"Eats insects?"

"Certainly. Watch."

The professor opened a small wire cage lying on a shelf and took from it several flies. These he liberated close to the queer plant.

The insects buzzed about a few seconds, dazed with their sudden liberty.

Then they began slowly to circle in the vicinity of the strange flowers. Nearer and nearer the blossoms they came, attracted by some subtle perfume, as well as by a sweet syrup that was on the edge of the petals, put there by nature for the very purpose of drawing hapless insects into the trap.

The flies settled down, some on the petals of all three blooms. Then a curious thing happened.

The little hairlike filaments in the tube within the petals suddenly reached out and wound themselves about the insects feeding on the sweet stuff, which seemed to intoxicate them. In an instant the flies were pulled to the top of the flower shaft by a contraction of the hairs, and then they went tumbling down the tube into the miniature pond below, where they were drowned after a brief struggle. Their crawling back was prevented by spines growing with points down, as the wires in some rat traps are fastened.

Meanwhile the cover of the plant closed down.

"Why, it's a regular flytrap, isn't it?" remarked Adams, much surprised.

"It is," replied the professor. "The plant lives off the insects it captures. It absorbs them, digests them, and, when it is hungry again, catches more.

"Where'd you get such an uncanny thing?" asked Adams, moving away from the plant as if he feared it might take a sample bite out of him.

"A friend sent it to me from Brazil."

"But you're not going to keep it, I hope."

"I certainly am," rejoined Professor Jonkin.

"Maybe you're going to train it to come to the table and eat like a human being," suggested Adams, with a laugh that nettled the professor.

"I wouldn't have to train it much to induce it to be polite," snapped back the owner of the pitcher plant.

And then, seeing that his jokes were not relished, Adams assumed an interest he did not feel, and listened to a long dissertation on botany in general and carnivorous plants in particular.

He would much rather have been eating some of the queer hybrid fruits the professor raised. He pleaded an engagement when he saw an opening in the talk, and went away.

It was some months after that before he saw the professor again. The botanist was busy in his conservatory in the meantime, and the gardener he hired to do rough work noticed that his master spent much time in that part of the glass house where the pitcher plant was growing.

For Professor Jonkin had become so much interested in his latest acquisition that he seemed to think of nothing else. His plan for increasing strawberries to the size of peaches was abandoned for a time, as was his pet scheme of raising apples without any core.

The gardener wondered what there was about the South American blossoms to require such close attention.

One day he thought he would find out, and he started to enter that part of the conservatory where the pitcher plant was growing. Professor Jonkin halted him before he had stepped inside and sternly bade him never to appear there again.

As the gardener, crestfallen, moved away after a glimpse into the forbidden region he muttered:

"My, that plant has certainly grown! And I wonder what the professor was doing so close to it. Looked as if he was feeding the thing."

As the days went by the conduct of Professor Jonkin became more and more curious. He scarcely left the southern end of the conservatory, save at night, when he entered his house to sleep.

He was a bachelor, and had no family cares to trouble him, so he could spend all his time among his plants. But hitherto he had divided his attention among his many experiments in the floral kingdom.

Now he was always with his mysterious pitcher plant. He even had his meals sent into the greenhouse.

"Be you keepin' boarders?" asked the butcher boy of the gardener one day, passing on his return to the store, his empty basket on his arm.

"No. Why?"

"The professor is orderin' so much meat lately. I thought you had company."

"No, there's only us two. Mr. Adams used to come to dinner once in a while, but not lately."

"Then you an' the professor must have big appetites."

"What makes you think so?"

"The number of beefsteaks you eat."

"Number of beefsteaks? Why, my lad, the professor and I are both vegetarians."

"What's them?"

"We neither of us eat a bit of meat. We don't believe it's healthy."

"Then what becomes of the three big porterhouse steaks I deliver to the professor in the greenhouse every day?"

"Porterhouse steaks?" questioned the gardener, amazed.

"Do you feed 'em to the dog?"

"We don't keep a dog."

But the butcher boy questioned no further, for he saw a chum and hastened off to join him.

"Three porterhouse steaks a day!" mused the gardener, shaking his head. "I do hope the professor has not ceased to be a vegetarian. Yet it looks mighty suspicious. And he's doing it on the sly, too, for there's been no meat cooked in the house, of that I'm sure."

And the gardener, sorely puzzled over the mystery, went off, shaking his head more solemnly than before.

He resolved to have a look in the place the professor guarded so carefully. He tried the door when he was sure his master was in another part of the Conservatory, but it was locked, and no key the gardener had would unfasten it.

A month after the gardener had heard of the porterhouse steaks, Adams happened to drop in to see the professor again.

"He's in with the *Sarracenia nepenthis*, " said the gardener in answer to the visitor's inquiry. "But I doubt if he will let you enter."

"Why won't he?"

"Because he's become mighty close-mouthed of late over that pitcher plant. "

"Oh, I guess he'll see me," remarked Adams confidently, and he knocked on the door that shut off the locked section of the greenhouse from the main portion.

"Who's there?" called the professor.

"Adams."

"Oh," in a more conciliatory tone. "I was just wishing you'd come along. I have something to show you."

Professor Jonkin opened the door, and the sight that met Adams' gaze startled him.

The only plant in that part of the conservatory was a single specimen of the *Sarracenia nepenthis*. Yet it had attained such enormous proportions that at first Adams thought he must be dreaming.

"What do you think of that for an achievement in science?" asked the professor proudly.

"Do you mean to say that is the small, fly-catching plant your friend sent you from Brazil?"

"The same."

"But—but—"

"But how it's grown. That's what you want to say, isn't it?"

"It is. How did you do it?"

"By dieting the blossoms."

"You mean—?"

"I mean feeding them. Listen. I reasoned that if a small blossom of the plant would thrive on a few insects, by giving it larger meals I might get a bigger plant. So I made my plans.

"First I cut off all but one blossom, so that the strength of the plant would nourish that alone. Then I made out a bill of fare. I began feeding it on chopped beef. The plant took to it like a puppy.

It seemed to beg for more. From chopped meat I went to small pieces, cut up. I could fairly see the blossom increase in size. From that I went to choice mutton chops, and, after a week of them, with the plant becoming more gigantic all the while, I increased its meals to a porterhouse steak a day. And now—"

The professor paused to contemplate his botanical work.

"Well, now?" questioned Adams.

"Now," went on the professor proudly, "my pitcher plant takes three big beefsteaks every day—one for breakfast, one for dinner, and one for supper. And see the result."

Adams gazed at the immense plant. From a growth about as big as an Easter lily it had increased until the top was near the roof of the greenhouse, twenty-five feet above.

About fifteen feet up, or ten feet from the top, there branched out a great flower, about eight feet long and three feet across the bell-shaped mouth, which except for the cap or cover, was not unlike the opening of an immense morning glory.

The flower was heavy, and the stalk on which it grew was not strong enough to support it upright. So a rude scaffolding had been constructed of wood and boards, and on a frame the flower was held upright.

In order to see it to better advantage, and also that he might feed it, the professor had a ladder by which he could ascend to a small platform in front of the bell-shaped mouth of the blossom.

"It is time to give my pet its meal," he announced, as if he were speaking of some favorite horse. "Want to come up and watch it eat?"

"No, thank you," responded Adams. "It's too uncanny."

The professor took a large steak, one of the three the butcher boy had left that day. Holding it in his hand, he climbed up the ladder and was soon on the platform in front of the plant.

Adams watched him curiously. The professor leaned over to toss the steak into the yawning mouth of the flower.

Suddenly Adams saw him totter, throw his arms wildly in the air, and then, as if drawn by some overpowering force, he fell forward, lost his balance, and toppled into the maw of the pitcher plant!

There was a jar to the stalk and blossom as the professor fell within. He went head first into the tube, or eating apparatus of the strange plant, his legs sticking out for an instant, kicking wildly. Then he disappeared entirely.

Adams didn't know whether to laugh or be alarmed.

He mounted the ladder, and stood in amazement before the result of the professor's work as he looked down into the depth of the gigantic flower, increased a hundred times in size.

He was aware of a strange, sickish-sweet odor that seemed to steal over his senses. It was lulling him to sleep, and he fought against it. Then he looked down and saw that the huge hairs or filaments with which the tube was lined were in violent motion.

He could just discern the professor's feet about three feet below the rim of the flower. They were kicking, but with a force growing less very second. The filaments seemed to be winding about the professor's legs, holding him in a deadly embrace.

Then the top cover, or flap of the plant, closed down suddenly. The professor was a prisoner inside.

The plant had turned cannibal and eaten the man who had grown it!

For an instant, fear deprived Adams of reason. He did not know what to do. Then the awful plight of his friend brought back his senses.

"Professor!" he shouted. "Are you alive? Can you hear me?"

"Yes," came back in faint and muffled tones. "This beast has me, all right."

Then followed a series of violent struggles that shook the plant.

"I'll get you out. Where's an ax? I'll chop the cursed plant to pieces!" cried Adams.

"Don't! Don't" came in almost pleading tones from the imprisoned professor.

"Don't what?"

"Don't hurt my pet!"

"Your pet!" snorted Adams angrily. "Nice kind of a pet you have! One that tries to eat you alive! But I've got to do something if I want to save you. Where's the ax?"

"No! No!" begged the professor, his voice becoming more and more muffled. "Use chloroform."

"Use what?"

"Chloroform! You'll find some in the closet."

Then Adams saw what the professor's idea was. The plant could be made insensible, and the imprisoned man released with no harm to the blossom.

He raced down the ladder, ran to a closet where he had seen the professor's stock of drugs and chemicals stowed away on the occasion of former visits, and grabbed a big bottle of chloroform. He caught up a towel and ran back up the ladder.

Not a sign of the professor could be seen. The plant had swallowed him up, but by the motion and swaying of the flower Adams knew his friend was yet alive.

He was in some doubt as to the success of this method, and would rather have taken an ax and chopped a hole in the side of the blossom, thus releasing the captive. But he decided to obey the professor.

Saturating the towel well with the chloroform, and holding his nose away from it, he pressed the wet cloth over the top of the blossom where the lid touched the edge of the bloom.

There was a slight opening at one point, and Adams poured some of the chloroform down this. He feared lest the fumes of the anesthetic might overpower the professor also, but he knew they would soon pass away if this happened.

For several minutes he waited anxiously. Would the plan succeed? Would the plant be overcome before it had killed the professor inside?

Adams was in a fever of terror. Again and again he saturated the towel with the powerful drug. Then he had the satisfaction of seeing the lid of the pitcher plant relax.

It slowly lifted and fell over to one side, making a good-sized opening. The strong filaments, not unlike the arms of a devil fish, Adams thought, were no longer in uneasy motion. They had released their grip on the professor's legs and body.

The spines that had pointed downward, holding the plant's prey, now became limber.

Adams leaned over. He reached down, grasped the professor by the feet, and, being a strong man, while his friend was small and light, he pulled him from the tube of the flower, a little dazed from the fumes of the chloroform the plant had breathed in, but otherwise not much the worse for his adventure.

He had not reached the water at the bottom of the tube, which fact saved him from drowning.

"Well, you certainly had a narrow squeak," observed Adams as he helped the professor down the ladder.

"I did," admitted the botanist. "If you had not been on hand I don't know what would have happened. I suppose I would have been eaten alive."

"Unless you could have cut yourself out of the side of the flower with your knife," observed Adams.

"What! And killed the plant I raised with such pains?" ejaculated the professor. "Spoil the largest *Sarracenia nepenthis* in the world? I guess not. I would rather have let it eat me."

"I think you ought to call it the cannibal plant instead of the pitcher plant," suggested Adams.

"Oh, no," responded the professor dreamily, examining the flower from a distance to see if any harm had come to it. "But to punish it, I will not give it any supper or breakfast. That's what it gets for being naughty," he added as if the plant were a child.

"And I suggest that when you feed it hereafter," said Adams, "you pass the beefsteaks in on a pitch fork. You won't run so much danger then."

"That's a good idea. I'll do it," answered the professor heartily.

And he has followed that plan ever since.

The Willows
Algernon Blackwood

After leaving Vienna, and long before you come to Budapesth, the Danube enters a region of singular loneliness and desolation, where its waters spread away on all sides regardless of a main channel, and the country becomes a swamp for miles upon miles, covered by a vast sea of low willow-bushes. On the big maps this deserted area is painted in a fluffy blue, growing fainter in colour as it leaves the banks, and across it may be seen in large straggling letters the word Sumpfe, meaning marshes.

In high flood this great acreage of sand, shingle-beds, and willow-grown islands is almost topped by the water, but in normal seasons the bushes bend and rustle in the free winds, showing their silver leaves to the sunshine in an ever-moving plain of bewildering beauty. These willows never attain to the dignity of trees; they have no rigid trunks; they remain humble bushes, with rounded tops and soft outline, swaying on slender stems that answer to the least pressure of the wind; supple as grasses, and so continually shifting that they somehow give the impression that the entire plain is moving and alive. For the wind sends waves rising and falling over the whole surface, waves of leaves instead of waves of water, green swells like the sea, too, until the branches turn and lift, and then silvery white as their under-side turns to the sun.

Happy to slip beyond the control of the stern banks, the Danube here wanders about at will among the intricate network of channels intersecting the islands everywhere with broad avenues down which the waters pour with a shouting sound; making whirlpools, eddies, and foaming rapids; tearing at the sandy banks; carrying away masses of shore and willow-clumps; and forming new islands innumerably which shift daily in size and shape and possess at best an impermanent life, since the flood-time obliterates their very existence.

Properly speaking, this fascinating part of the river's life begins soon after leaving Pressburg, and we, in our Canadian canoe, with gipsy tent and frying-pan on board, reached it on the crest of a rising flood about mid-July. That very same morning, when the sky was reddening before sunrise, we had slipped swiftly through still-sleeping Vienna, leaving it a couple of hours later a mere patch of smoke against the blue hills of the Wienerwald on the horizon; we had breakfasted below Fischeramend under a grove of birch trees roaring in the wind; and had then swept on the tearing current past Orth, Hainburg, Petronell (the old Roman Carnuntum of Marcus Aurelius), and so under the frowning heights of Thelsen on a spur of the Carpathians, where the March steals in quietly from the left and the frontier is crossed between Austria and Hungary.

Racing along at twelve kilometres an hour soon took us well into Hungary, and the muddy waters—sure sign of flood—sent us aground on many a shingle-bed, and twisted us like a cork in many a sudden belching whirlpool before the towers of Pressburg (Hungarian, Poszony) showed against the sky; and then the canoe, leaping like a spirited horse, flew at top speed under the grey walls, negotiated safely the sunken chain of the Fliegende Brucke ferry, turned the corner sharply to the left, and plunged on yellow foam into the wilderness of islands, sand-banks, and swamp-land beyond—the land of the willows.

The change came suddenly, as when a series of bioscope pictures snaps down on the streets of a town and shifts without warning into the scenery of lake and forest. We entered the land of desolation on wings, and in less than half an hour there was neither boat nor fishing-hut nor red roof, nor any single sign of human habitation and civilisation within sight. The sense of remoteness from the world of human kind, the utter isolation, the fascination of this singular world of willows, winds, and waters, instantly laid its spell upon us both, so that we allowed laughingly to one another that we ought by rights to have held some special kind of passport to admit us, and that we had, somewhat audaciously, come without asking leave into a separate little kingdom of wonder and magic—a kingdom that was reserved for the use of others who had a right to it, with everywhere unwritten warnings to trespassers for those who had the imagination to discover them.

Though still early in the afternoon, the ceaseless buffetings of a most tempestuous wind made us feel weary, and we at once began casting about for a suitable camping-ground for the night. But the bewildering character of the islands made landing difficult; the swirling flood carried us in shore and then swept us out again; the willow branches tore our hands as we seized them to stop the canoe, and we pulled many a yard of sandy bank into the water before at length we shot with a great sideways blow from the wind into a backwater and managed to beach the bows in a cloud of spray. Then we lay panting and laughing after our exertions on the hot yellow sand, sheltered from the wind, and in the full blaze of a scorching sun, a cloudless blue sky above, and an immense army of dancing, shouting willow bushes, closing in from all sides, shining with spray and clapping their thousand little hands as though to applaud the success of our efforts.

"What a river!" I said to my companion, thinking of all the way we had travelled from the source in the Black Forest, and how he had often been obliged to wade and push in the upper shallows at the beginning of June.

"Won't stand much nonsense now, will it?" he said, pulling the canoe a little farther into safety up the sand, and then composing himself for a nap.

I lay by his side, happy and peaceful in the bath of the elements—water, wind, sand, and the great fire of the sun—thinking of the long journey that lay behind us, and of the great stretch before us to the Black Sea, and how lucky I was to have such a delightful and charming travelling companion as my friend, the Swede.

We had made many similar journeys together, but the Danube, more than any other river I knew, impressed us from the very beginning with its aliveness. From its tiny bubbling entry into the world among the pinewood gardens of Donaueschingen, until this moment when it began to play the great river-game of losing itself among the deserted swamps, unobserved, unrestrained, it had seemed to us like following the grown of some living creature. Sleepy at first, but later developing violent desires as it became conscious of its deep soul, it rolled, like some huge fluid being, through all the countries we had passed, holding our little craft on its mighty shoulders, playing roughly with us sometimes, yet always friendly and well-meaning, till at length we had come inevitably to regard it as a Great Personage.

How, indeed, could it be otherwise, since it told us so much of its secret life? At night we heard it singing to the moon as we lay in our tent, uttering that odd sibilant note peculiar to itself and said to be caused by the rapid tearing of the pebbles along its bed, so great is its hurrying speed. We knew, too, the voice of its gurgling whirlpools, suddenly bubbling up on a surface previously quite calm; the roar of its shallows and swift rapids; its constant steady thundering below all mere surface sounds; and that ceaseless tearing of its icy waters at the banks. How it stood up and shouted when the rains fell flat upon its face! And how its laughter roared out when the wind blew upstream and tried to stop its growing speed! We knew all its sounds and voices, its tumblings and foamings, its unnecessary splashing against the bridges; that self-conscious chatter when there were hills to look on; the affected dignity of its speech when it passed through the little towns, far too important to laugh; and all these faint, sweet whisperings when the sun caught it fairly in some slow curve and poured down upon it till the steam rose.

It was full of tricks, too, in its early life before the great world knew it. There were places in the upper reaches among the Swabian forests, when yet the first whispers of its destiny had not reached it, where it elected to disappear through holes in the ground, to appear again on the other side of the porous limestone hills and start a new river with another name; leaving, too, so little water in its own bed that we had to climb out and wade and push the canoe through miles of shallows.

And a chief pleasure, in those early days of its irresponsible youth, was to lie low, like Brer Fox, just before the little turbulent tributaries came to join it from the Alps, and to refuse to acknowledge them when in, but to run for miles side by side, the dividing line well marked, the very levels different, the Danube utterly declining to recognize the newcomer. Below Passau, however, it gave up this particular trick, for there the Inn comes in with a thundering power impossible to ignore, and so pushes and incommodes the parent river that there is hardly room for them in the long twisting gorge that follows, and the Danube is shoved this way and that against the cliffs, and forced to hurry itself with great waves and much dashing to and fro in order to get through in time. And during the fight our canoe slipped down from its shoulder to its breast, and had the time of its life among the struggling waves. But the Inn taught the old river a lesson, and after Passau it no longer pretended to ignore new arrivals.

This was many days back, of course, and since then we had come to know other aspects of the great creature, and across the Bavarian wheat plain of Straubing she wandered so slowly under the blazing June sun that we could well imagine only the surface inches were water, while below there moved, concealed as by a silken mantle, a whole army of Undines, passing silently and unseen down to the sea, and very leisurely too, lest they be discovered.

Much, too, we forgave her because of her friendliness to the birds and animals that haunted the shores. Cormorants lined the banks in lonely places in rows like short black palings; grey crows crowded the shingle-beds; storks stood fishing in the vistas of shallower water that opened up between the islands, and hawks, swans, and marsh birds of all sorts filled the air with glinting wings and singing, petulant cries. It was impossible to feel annoyed with the river's vagaries after seeing a deer leap with a splash into the water at sunrise and swim past the bows of the canoe; and often we saw fawns peering at us from the underbrush, or looked straight into the brown eyes of a stag as we charged full tilt round a corner and entered another reach of the river. Foxes, too, everywhere haunted the banks, tripping daintily among the driftwood and disappearing so suddenly that it was impossible to see how they managed it.

But now, after leaving Pressburg, everything changed a little, and the Danube became more serious. It ceased trifling. It was halfway to the Black Sea, within seeming distance almost of other, stranger countries where no tricks would be permitted or understood. It became suddenly grown-up, and claimed our respect and even our awe. It broke out into three arms, for one thing, that only met again a hundred kilometres farther down, and for a canoe there were no indications which one was intended to be followed.

"If you take a side channel," said the Hungarian officer we met in the Pressburg shop while buying provisions, "you may find yourselves, when the flood subsides, forty miles from anywhere, high and dry, and you may easily starve. There are no people, no farms, no fishermen. I warn you not to continue. The river, too, is still rising, and this wind will increase."

The rising river did not alarm us in the least, but the matter of being left high and dry by a sudden subsidence of the waters might be serious, and we had consequently laid in an extra stock of provisions. For the rest, the officer's prophecy held true, and the wind, blowing down a perfectly clear sky, increased steadily till it reached the dignity of a westerly gale.

It was earlier than usual when we camped, for the sun was a good hour or two from the horizon, and leaving my friend still asleep on the hot sand, I wandered about in desultory examination of our hotel. The island, I found, was less than an acre in extent, a mere sandy bank standing some two or three feet above the level of the river. The far end, pointing into the sunset, was covered with flying spray which the tremendous wind drove off the crests of the broken waves. It was triangular in shape, with the apex up stream.

I stood there for several minutes, watching the impetuous crimson flood bearing down with a shouting roar, dashing in waves against the bank as though to sweep it bodily away, and then swirling by in two foaming streams on either side. The ground seemed to shake with the shock and rush, while the furious movement of the willow bushes as the wind poured over them increased the curious illusion that the island itself actually moved. Above, for a mile or two, I could see the great river descending upon me; it was like looking up the slope of a sliding hill, white with foam, and leaping up everywhere to show itself to the sun.

The rest of the island was too thickly grown with willows to make walking pleasant, but I made the tour, nevertheless. From the lower end the light, of course, changed, and the river looked dark and angry. Only the backs of the flying waves were visible, streaked with foam, and pushed forcibly by the great puffs of wind that fell upon them from behind. For a short mile it was visible, pouring in and out among the islands, and then disappearing with a huge sweep into the willows, which closed about it like a herd of monstrous antediluvian creatures crowding down to drink. They made me think of gigantic sponge-like growths that sucked the river up into themselves. They caused it to vanish from sight. They herded there together in such overpowering numbers.

Altogether it was an impressive scene, with its utter loneliness, its bizarre suggestion; and as I gazed, long and curiously, a singular emotion began to stir somewhere in the depths of me. Midway in my delight of the wild beauty, there crept, unbidden and unex-plained, a curious feeling of disquietude, almost of alarm.

A rising river, perhaps, always suggests something of the omi-nous; many of the little islands I saw before me would probably have been swept away by the morning; this resistless, thundering flood of water touched the sense of awe. Yet I was aware that my uneasiness lay deeper far than the emotions of awe and wonder. It was not that I felt. Nor had it directly to do with the power of the driving wind—this shouting hurricane that might almost carry up a few acres of willows into the air and scatter them like so much chaff over the landscape. The wind was simply enjoying itself, for nothing rose out of the flat landscape to stop it, and I was conscious of sharing its great game with a kind of pleasurable excitement. Yet this novel emotion had nothing to do with the wind. Indeed, so vague was the sense of distress I experienced, that it was impos-sible to trace it to its source and deal with it accordingly, though I was aware somehow that it had to do with my realisation of our utter insignificance before this unrestrained power of the elements about me. The huge-grown river had something to do with it too— a vague, unpleasant idea that we had somehow trifled with these great elemental forces in whose power we lay helpless every hour of the day and night. For here, indeed, they were gigantically at play together, and the sight appealed to the imagination.

But my emotion, so far as I could understand it, seemed to attach itself more particularly to the willow bushes, to these acres and acres of willows, crowding, so thickly growing there, swarming everywhere the eye could reach, pressing upon the river as though to suffocate it, standing in dense array mile after mile beneath the sky, watching, waiting, listening. And, apart quite from the elements, the willows connected themselves subtly with my malaise, attacking the mind insidiously somehow by reason of their vast numbers, and contriving in some way or other to represent to the imagination a new and mighty power, a power, moreover, not altogether friendly to us.

Great revelations of nature, of course, never fail to impress in one way or another, and I was no stranger to moods of the kind. Mountains overawe and oceans terrify, while the mystery of great forests exercises a spell peculiarly its own. But all these, at one point or another, somewhere link on intimately with human life and human experience. They stir comprehensible, even if alarming, emotions. They tend on the whole to exalt.

With this multitude of willows, however, it was something far different, I felt. Some essence emanated from them that besieged the heart. A sense of awe awakened, true, but of awe touched somewhere by a vague terror. Their serried ranks, growing everywhere darker about me as the shadows deepened, moving furiously yet softly in the wind, woke in me the curious and unwelcome suggestion that we had trespassed here upon the borders of an alien world, a world where we were intruders, a world where we were not wanted or invited to remain—where we ran grave risks perhaps!

The feeling, however, though it refused to yield its meaning entirely to analysis, did not at the time trouble me by passing into menace. Yet it never left me quite, even during the very practical business of putting up the tent in a hurricane of wind and building a fire for the stew-pot. It remained, just enough to bother and perplex, and to rob a most delightful camping-ground of a good portion of its charm. To my companion, however, I said nothing, for he was a man I considered devoid of imagination. In the first place, I could never have explained to him what I meant, and in the second, he would have laughed stupidly at me if I had.

There was a slight depression in the centre of the island, and here we pitched the tent. The surrounding willows broke the wind a bit.

"A poor camp," observed the imperturbable Swede when at last the tent stood upright, "no stones and precious little firewood. I'm for moving on early to-morrow—eh? This sand won't hold anything."

But the experience of a collapsing tent at midnight had taught us many devices, and we made the cosy gipsy house as safe as possible, and then set about collecting a store of wood to last till bedtime. Willow bushes drop no branches, and driftwood was our only source of supply. We hunted the shores pretty thoroughly. Everywhere the banks were crumbling as the rising flood tore at them and carried away great portions with a splash and a gurgle.

"The island's much smaller than when we landed," said the accurate Swede. "It won't last long at this rate. We'd better drag the canoe close to the tent, and be ready to start at a moment's notice. I shall sleep in my clothes."

He was a little distance off, climbing along the bank, and I heard his rather jolly laugh as he spoke.

"By Jove!" I heard him call, a moment later, and turned to see what had caused his exclamation. But for the moment he was hidden by the willows, and I could not find him.

"What in the world's this?" I heard him cry again, and this time his voice had become serious.

I ran up quickly and joined him on the bank. He was looking over the river, pointing at something in the water.

"Good heavens, it's a man's body!" he cried excitedly. "Look!"

A black thing, turning over and over in the foaming waves, swept rapidly past. It kept disappearing and coming up to the surface again. It was about twenty feet from the shore, and just as it was opposite to where we stood it lurched round and looked straight at us. We saw its eyes reflecting the sunset, and gleaming an odd yellow as the body turned over. Then it gave a swift, gulping plunge, and dived out of sight in a flash.

"An otter, by gad!" we exclaimed in the same breath, laughing.

It was an otter, alive, and out on the hunt; yet it had looked exactly like the body of a drowned man turning helplessly in the current. Far below it came to the surface once again, and we saw its black skin, wet and shining in the sunlight.

Then, too, just as we turned back, our arms full of driftwood, another thing happened to recall us to the river bank. This time it really was a man, and what was more, a man in a boat. Now a small boat on the Danube was an unusual sight at any time, but here in this deserted region, and at flood time, it was so unexpected as to constitute a real event. We stood and stared.

Whether it was due to the slanting sunlight, or the refraction from the wonderfully illumined water, I cannot say, but, whatever the cause, I found it difficult to focus my sight properly upon the flying apparition. It seemed, however, to be a man standing upright in a sort of flat-bottomed boat, steering with a long oar, and being carried down the opposite shore at a tremendous pace. He apparently was looking across in our direction, but the distance was too great and the light too uncertain for us to make out very plainly what he was about. It seemed to me that he was gesticulating and making signs at us. His voice came across the water to us shouting something furiously, but the wind drowned it so that no single word was audible. There was something curious about the whole appearance—man, boat, signs, voice—that made an impression on me out of all proportion to its cause.

"He's crossing himself!" I cried. "Look, he's making the sign of the Cross!"

"I believe you're right," the Swede said, shading his eyes with his hand and watching the man out of sight. He seemed to be gone in a moment, melting away down there into the sea of willows where the sun caught them in the bend of the river and turned them into a great crimson wall of beauty. Mist, too, had begun to ruse, so that the air was hazy.

"But what in the world is he doing at nightfall on this flooded river?" I said, half to myself. "Where is he going at such a time, and what did he mean by his signs and shouting? D'you think he wished to warn us about something?"

"He saw our smoke, and thought we were spirits probably," laughed my companion. "These Hungarians believe in all sorts of rubbish; you remember the shopwoman at Pressburg warning us that no one ever landed here because it belonged to some sort of beings outside man's world! I suppose they believe in fairies and elementals, possibly demons, too. That peasant in the boat saw people on the islands for the first time in his life," he added, after a slight pause, "and it scared him, that's all."

The Swede's tone of voice was not convincing, and his manner lacked something that was usually there. I noted the change instantly while he talked, though without being able to label it precisely.

"If they had enough imagination," I laughed loudly—I remember trying to make as much noise as I could— "they might well people a place like this with the old gods of antiquity. The Romans must have haunted all this region more or less with their shrines and sacred groves and elemental deities."

The subject dropped and we returned to our stew-pot, for my friend was not given to imaginative conversation as a rule. Moreover, just then I remember feeling distinctly glad that he was not imaginative; his stolid, practical nature suddenly seemed to me welcome and comforting. It was an admirable temperament, I felt; he could steer down rapids like a red Indian, shoot dangerous bridges and whirlpools better than any white man I ever saw in a canoe. He was a grand fellow for an adventurous trip, a tower of strength when untoward things happened. I looked at his strong face and light curly hair as he staggered along under his pile of driftwood (twice the size of mine!), and I experienced a feeling of relief. Yes, I was distinctly glad just then that the Swede was—what he was, and that he never made remarks that suggested more than they said.

"The river's still rising, though," he added, as if following out some thoughts of his own, and dropping his load with a gasp. "This island will be under water in two days if it goes on."

"I wish the wind would go down," I said. "I don't care a fig for the river."

The flood, indeed, had no terrors for us; we could get off at ten minute's notice, and the more water the better we liked it. It meant an increasing current and the obliteration of the treacherous shingle-beds that so often threatened to tear the bottom out of our canoe.

Contrary to our expectations, the wind did not go down with the sun. It seemed to increase with the darkness, howling overhead and shaking the willows round us like straws. Curious sounds accompanied it sometimes, like the explosion of heavy guns, and it fell upon the water and the island in great flat blows of immense power. It made me think of the sounds a planet must make, could we only hear it, driving along through space.

But the sky kept wholly clear of clouds, and soon after supper the full moon rose up in the east and covered the river and the plain of shouting willows with a light like the day.

We lay on the sandy patch beside the fire, smoking, listening to the noises of the night round us, and talking happily of the journey we had already made, and of our plans ahead. The map lay spread in the door of the tent, but the high wind made it hard to study, and presently we lowered the curtain and extinguished the lantern. The firelight was enough to smoke and see each other's faces by, and the sparks flew about overhead like fireworks. A few yards beyond, the river gurgled and hissed, and from time to time a heavy splash announced the falling away of further portions of the bank.

Our talk, I noticed, had to do with the far-away scenes and incidents of our first camps in the Black Forest, or of other subjects altogether remote from the present setting, for neither of us spoke of the actual moment more than was necessary—almost as though we had agreed tacitly to avoid discussion of the camp and its incidents. Neither the otter nor the boatman, for instance, received the honour of a single mention, though ordinarily these would have furnished discussion for the greater part of the evening. They were, of course, distinct events in such a place.

The scarcity of wood made it a business to keep the fire going, for the wind, that drove the smoke in our faces wherever we sat, helped at the same time to make a forced draught. We took it in turn to make some foraging expeditions into the darkness, and the

quantity the Swede brought back always made me feel that he took
an absurdly long time finding it; for the fact was I did not care
much about being left alone, and yet it always seemed to be my
turn to grub about among the bushes or scramble along the slippery banks in the moonlight. The long day's battle with wind and
water—such wind and such water!—had tired us both, and an early
bed was the obvious programme. Yet neither of us made the move
for the tent. We lay there, tending the fire, talking in desultory
fashion, peering about us into the dense willow bushes, and listening to the thunder of wind and river. The loneliness of the place
had entered our very bones, and silence seemed natural, for after
a bit the sound of our voices became a trifle unreal and forced;
whispering would have been the fitting mode of communication, I
felt, and the human voice, always rather absurd amid the roar of
the elements, now carried with it something almost illegitimate. It
was like talking out loud in church, or in some place where it was
not lawful, perhaps not quite safe, to be overheard.

The eeriness of this lonely island, set among a million willows,
swept by a hurricane, and surrounded by hurrying deep waters,
touched us both, I fancy. Untrodden by man, almost unknown to
man, it lay there beneath he moon, remote from human influence,
on the frontier of another world, an alien world, a world tenanted
by willows only and the souls of willows. And we, in our rashness,
had dared to invade it, even to make use of it! Something more
than the power of its mystery stirred in me as I lay on the sand,
feet to fire, and peered up through the leaves at the stars. For the
last time I rose to get firewood.

"When this has burnt up," I said firmly, "I shall turn in," and
my companion watched me lazily as I moved off into the surrounding shadows.

For an unimaginative man I thought he seemed unusually receptive that night, unusually open to suggestion of things other than
sensory. He too was touched by the beauty and loneliness of the
place. I was not altogether pleased, I remember, to recognise this
slight change in him, and instead of immediately collecting sticks,
I made my way to the far point of the island where the moonlight
on plain and river could be seen to better advantage. The desire to
be alone had come suddenly upon me; my former dread returned
in force; there was a vague feeling in me I wished to face and probe
to the bottom.

When I reached the point of sand jutting out among the waves, the spell of the place descended upon me with a positive shock. No mere "scenery" could have produced such an effect. There was something more here, something to alarm.

I gazed across the waste of wild waters; I watched the whispering willows; I heard the ceaseless beating of the tireless wind; and, one and all, each in its own way, stirred in me this sensation of a strange distress. But the willows especially; for ever they went on chattering and talking among themselves, laughing a little, shrilly crying out, sometimes sighing—but what it was they made so much to-do about belonged to the secret life of the great plain they inhabited. And it was utterly alien to the world I knew, or to that of the wild yet kindly elements. They made me think of a host of beings from another plane of life, another evolution altogether, perhaps, all discussing a mystery known only to themselves. I watched them moving busily together, oddly shaking their big bushy heads, twirling their myriad leaves even when there was no wind. They moved of their own will as though alive, and they touched, by some incalculable method, my own keen sense of the horrible.

There they stood in the moonlight, like a vast army surrounding our camp, shaking their innumerable silver spears defiantly, formed all ready for an attack.

The psychology of places, for some imaginations at least, is very vivid; for the wanderer, especially, camps have their "note" either of welcome or rejection. At first it may not always be apparent, because the busy preparations of tent and cooking prevent, but with the first pause—after supper usually—it comes and announces itself. And the note of this willow-camp now became unmistakably plain to me; we were interlopers, trespassers; we were not welcomed. The sense of unfamiliarity grew upon me as I stood there watching. We touched the frontier of a region where our presence was resented. For a night's lodging we might perhaps be tolerated; but for a prolonged and inquisitive stay—No! by all the gods of the trees and wilderness, no! We were the first human influences upon this island, and we were not wanted. The willows were against us.

Strange thoughts like these, bizarre fancies, borne I know not whence, found lodgment in my mind as I stood listening. What, I thought, if, after all, these crouching willows proved to be alive; if suddenly they should rise up, like a swarm of living creatures, marshalled by the gods whose territory we had invaded, sweep towards us off

the vast swamps, booming overhead in the night—and then settle
down! As I looked it was so easy to imagine they actually moved,
crept nearer, retreated a little, huddled together in masses, hostile,
waiting for the great wind that should finally start them a-run-
ning. I could have sworn their aspect changed a little, and their
ranks deepened and pressed more closely together.

The melancholy shrill cry of a night-bird sounded overhead,
and suddenly I nearly lost my balance as the piece of bank I stood
upon fell with a great splash into the river, undermined by the
flood. I stepped back just in time, and went on hunting for firewood again, half laughing at the odd fancies that crowded so thickly
into my mind and cast their spell upon me. I recalled the Swede's
remark about moving on next day, and I was just thinking that I
fully agreed with him, when I turned with a start and saw the subject of my thoughts standing immediately in front of me. He was
quite close. The roar of the elements had covered his approach.

"You've been gone so long," he shouted above the wind, "I
thought something must have happened to you."

But there was that in his tone, and a certain look in his face as
well, that conveyed to me more than his usual words, and in a flash
I understood the real reason for his coming. It was because the
spell of the place had entered his soul too, and he did not like being
alone.

"River still rising," he cried, pointing to the flood in the moonlight, "and the wind's simply awful."

He always said the same things, but it was the cry for companionship that gave the real importance to his words.

"Lucky," I cried back, "our tent's in the hollow. I think it'll hold
all right." I added something about the difficulty of finding wood,
in order to explain my absence, but the wind caught my words and
flung them across the river, so that he did not hear, but just looked
at me through the branches, nodding his head.

"Lucky if we get away without disaster!" he shouted, or words
to that effect; and I remember feeling half angry with him for putting the thought into words, for it was exactly what I felt myself.
There was disaster impending somewhere, and the sense of presentiment lay unpleasantly upon me.

We went back to the fire and made a final blaze, poking it up
with our feet. We took a last look round. But for the wind the heat
would have been unpleasant. I put this thought into words, and I

remember my friend's reply struck me oddly: that he would rather have the heat, the ordinary July weather, than this "diabolical wind".

Everything was snug for the night; the canoe lying turned over beside the tent, with both yellow paddles beneath her; the provision sack hanging from a willow-stem, and the washed-up dishes removed to a safe distance from the fire, all ready for the morning meal.

We smothered the embers of the fire with sand, and then turned in. The flap of the tent door was up, and I saw the branches and the stars and the white moonlight. The shaking willows and the heavy buffetings of the wind against our taut little house were the last things I remembered as sleep came down and covered all with its soft and delicious forgetfulness.

Suddenly I found myself lying awake, peering from my sandy mattress through the door of the tent. I looked at my watch pinned against the canvas, and saw by the bright moonlight that it was past twelve o'clock—the threshold of a new day—and I had there-fore slept a couple of hours. The Swede was asleep still beside me; the wind howled as before; something plucked at my heart and made me feel afraid. There was a sense of disturbance in my immediate neighbourhood.

I sat up quickly and looked out. The trees were swaying vio-lently to and fro as the gusts smote them, but our little bit of green canvas lay snugly safe in the hollow, for the wind passed over it without meeting enough resistance to make it vicious. The feeling of disquietude did not pass, however, and I crawled quietly out of the tent to see if our belongings were safe. I moved carefully so as not to waken my companion. A curious excitement was on me.

I was half-way out, kneeling on all fours, when my eye first took in that the tops of the bushes opposite, with their moving tracery of leaves, made shapes against the sky. I sat back on my haunches and stared. It was incredible, surely, but there, opposite and slightly above me, were shapes of some indeterminate sort among the willows, and as the branches swayed in the wind they seemed to group themselves about these shapes, forming a series of monstrous outlines that shifted rapidly beneath the moon. Close, about fifty feet in front of me, I saw these things.

My first instinct was to waken my companion, that he too might see them, but something made me hesitate—the sudden realisation, probably, that I should not welcome corroboration; and meanwhile

I crouched there staring in amazement with smarting eyes. I was wide awake. I remember saying to myself that I was not dreaming.

They first became properly visible, these huge figures, just within the tops of the bushes—immense, bronze-coloured, moving, and wholly independent of the swaying of the branches. I saw them plainly and noted, now I came to examine them more calmly, that they were very much larger than human, and indeed that something in their appearance proclaimed them to be not human at all. Certainly they were not merely the moving tracery of the branches against the moonlight. They shifted independently. They rose upwards in a continuous stream from earth to sky, vanishing utterly as soon as they reached the dark of the sky. They were interlaced one with another, making a great column, and I saw their limbs and huge bodies melting in and out of each other, forming this serpentine line that bent and swayed and twisted spirally with the contortions of the wind-tossed trees. They were nude, fluid shapes, passing up the bushes, within the leaves almost—rising up in a living column into the heavens. Their faces I never could see. Unceasingly they poured upwards, swaying in great bending curves, with a hue of dull bronze upon their skins.

I stared, trying to force every atom of vision from my eyes. For a long time I thought they must every moment disappear and resolve themselves into the movements of the branches and prove to be an optical illusion. I searched everywhere for a proof of reality, when all the while I understood quite well that the standard of reality had changed. For the longer I looked the more certain I became that these figures were real and living, though perhaps not according to the standards that the camera and the biologist would insist upon.

Far from feeling fear, I was possessed with a sense of awe and wonder such as I have never known. I seemed to be gazing at the personified elemental forces of this haunted and primeval region. Our intrusion had stirred the powers of the place into activity. It was we who were the cause of the disturbance, and my brain filled to bursting with stories and legends of the spirits and deities of places that have been acknowledged and worshipped by men in all ages of the world's history. But, before I could arrive at any possible explanation, something impelled me to go farther out, and I crept forward on the sand and stood upright. I felt the ground still warm under my bare feet; the wind tore at my hair and face; and the sound of the river burst upon my ears with a sudden roar. These things, I knew, were real, and proved that my senses were acting normally. Yet the figures still rose from earth to heaven, silent, majestically, in a great spiral of grace and strength that over-whelmed me at length with a genuine deep emotion of worship. I felt that I must fall down and worship—absolutely worship.

Perhaps in another minute I might have done so, when a gust of wind swept against me with such force that it blew me sideways, and I nearly stumbled and fell. It seemed to shake the dream violently out of me. At least it gave me another point of view somehow. The figures still remained, still ascended into heaven from the heart of the night, but my reason at last began to assert itself. It must be a subjec-tive experience, I argued—none the less real for that, but still sub-jective. The moonlight and the branches combined to work out these pictures upon the mirror of my imagination, and for some reason I projected them outwards and made them appear objective. I knew this must be the case, of course. I took courage, and began to move forward across the open patches of sand. By Jove, though, was it all hallucination? Was it merely subjective? Did not my reason argue in the old futile way from the little standard of the known?

I only know that great column of figures ascended darkly into the sky for what seemed a very long period of time, and with a very complete measure of reality as most men are accustomed to gauge reality. Then suddenly they were gone!

And, once they were gone and the immediate wonder of their great presence had passed, fear came down upon me with a cold rush. The esoteric meaning of this lonely and haunted region sud-denly flamed up within me, and I began to tremble dreadfully. I took a quick look round—a look of horror that came near to panic—calculating vainly ways of escape; and then, realising how helpless I was to achieve anything really effective, I crept back silently into the tent and lay down again upon my sandy mattress, first lower-ing the door-curtain to shut out the sight of the willows in the moonlight, and then burying my head as deeply as possible be-neath the blankets to deaden the sound of the terrifying wind.

As though further to convince me that I had not been dream-ing, I remember that it was a long time before I fell again into a troubled and restless sleep; and even then only the upper crust of me slept, and underneath there was something that never quite lost consciousness, but lay alert and on the watch.

But this second time I jumped up with a genuine start of terror. It was neither the wind nor the river that woke me, but the slow approach of something that caused the sleeping portion of me to grow smaller and smaller till at last it vanished altogether, and I found myself sitting bolt upright—listening.

Outside there was a sound of multitudinous little patterings. They had been coming, I was aware, for a long time, and in my sleep they had first become audible. I sat there nervously wide awake as though I had not slept at all. It seemed to me that my breathing came with difficulty, and that there was a great weight upon the surface of my body. In spite of the hot night, I felt clammy with cold and shivered. Something surely was pressing steadily against the sides of the tent and weighing down upon it from above. Was it the body of the wind? Was this the pattering rain, the dripping of the leaves? The spray blown from the river by the wind and gathering in big drops? I thought quickly of a dozen things.

Then suddenly the explanation leaped into my mind: a bough from the poplar, the only large tree on the island, had fallen with the wind. Still half caught by the other branches, it would fall with the next gust and crush us, and meanwhile its leaves brushed and tapped upon the tight canvas surface of the tent. I raised a loose flap and rushed out, calling to the Swede to follow.

But when I got out and stood upright I saw that the tent was free. There was no hanging bough; there was no rain or spray; nothing approached.

A cold, grey light filtered down through the bushes and lay on the faintly gleaming sand. Stars still crowded the sky directly overhead, and the wind howled magnificently, but the fire no longer gave out any glow, and I saw the east reddening in streaks through the trees. Several hours must have passed since I stood there before watching the ascending figures, and the memory of it now came back to me horribly, like an evil dream. Oh, how tired it made me feel, that ceaseless raging wind! Yet, though the deep lassitude of a sleepless night was on me, my nerves were tingling with the activity of an equally tireless apprehension, and all idea of repose was out of the question. The river I saw had risen further. Its thunder filled the air, and a fine spray made itself felt through my thin sleeping shirt.

Yet nowhere did I discover the slightest evidence of anything to cause alarm. This deep, prolonged disturbance in my heart remained wholly unaccounted for.

My companion had not stirred when I called him, and there was no need to waken him now. I looked about me carefully, noting everything; the turned-over canoe; the yellow paddles—two of them, I'm certain; the provision sack and the extra lantern hanging together from the tree; and, crowding everywhere about me, enveloping all, the willows, those endless, shaking willows. A bird uttered its morning cry, and a string of duck passed with whirring flight overhead in the twilight. The sand whirled, dry and stinging, about my bare feet in the wind.

I walked round the tent and then went out a little way into the bush, so that I could see across the river to the farther landscape, and the same profound yet indefinable emotion of distress seized upon me again as I saw the interminable sea of bushes stretching to the horizon, looking ghostly and unreal in the wan light of dawn. I walked softly here and there, still puzzling over that odd sound of infinite pattering, and of that pressure upon the tent that had wakened me. It must have been the wind, I reflected—the wind bearing upon the loose, hot sand, driving the dry particles smartly against the taut canvas—the wind dropping heavily upon our fragile roof.

Yet all the time my nervousness and malaise increased appreciably.

I crossed over to the farther shore and noted how the coastline had altered in the night, and what masses of sand the river had torn away. I dipped my hands and feet into the cool current, and bathed my forehead. Already there was a glow of sunrise in the sky and the exquisite freshness of coming day. On my way back I passed purposely beneath the very bushes where I had seen the column of figures rising into the air, and midway among the clumps I suddenly found myself overtaken by a sense of vast terror. From the shadows a large figure went swiftly by. Someone passed me, as sure as ever man did. . . .

It was a great staggering blow from the wind that helped me forward again, and once out in the more open space, the sense of terror diminished strangely. The winds were about and walking, I remember saying to myself, for the winds often move like great presences under the trees. And altogether the fear that hovered about me was such an unknown and immense kind of fear, so unlike anything I had ever felt before, that it woke a sense of awe and wonder in me that did much to counteract its worst effects; and when I reached a high point in the middle of the island from which I could see the wide stretch of river, crimson in the sunrise, the whole magical beauty of it all was so overpowering that a sort of wild yearning woke in me and almost brought a cry up into the throat.

But this cry found no expression, for as my eyes wandered from the plain beyond to the island round me and noted our little tent half hidden among the willows, a dreadful discovery leaped out at me, compared to which my terror of the walking winds seemed as nothing at all.

For a change, I thought, had somehow come about in the arrangement of the landscape. It was not that my point of vantage gave me a different view, but that an alteration had apparently been effected in the relation of the tent to the willows, and of the willows to the tent. Surely the bushes now crowded much closer—unnecessarily, unpleasantly close. They had moved nearer.

Creeping with silent feet over the shifting sands, drawing imperceptibly nearer by soft, unhurried movements, the willows had come closer during the night. But had the wind moved them, or had they moved of themselves? I recalled the sound of infinite small patterings and the pressure upon the tent and upon my own heart that caused me to wake in terror. I swayed for a moment in the wind like a tree, finding it hard to keep my upright position on the sandy hillock. There was a suggestion here of personal agency, of deliberate intention, of aggressive hostility, and it terrified me into a sort of rigidity.

Then the reaction followed quickly. The idea was so bizarre, so absurd, that I felt inclined to laugh. But the laughter came no more readily than the cry, for the knowledge that my mind was so receptive to such dangerous imaginings brought the additional terror that it was through our minds and not through our physical bodies that the attack would come, and was coming.

The wind buffeted me about, and, very quickly it seemed, the sun came up over the horizon, for it was after four o'clock, and I must have stood on that little pinnacle of sand longer than I knew, afraid to come down to close quarters with the willows. I returned quietly, creepily, to the tent, first taking another exhaustive look round and—yes, I confess it—making a few measurements. I paced out on the warm sand the distances between the willows and the tent, making a note of the shortest distance particularly.

I crawled stealthily into my blankets. My companion, to all appearances, still slept soundly, and I was glad that this was so. Provided my experiences were not corroborated, I could find strength somehow to deny them, perhaps. With the daylight I could persuade myself that it was all a subjective hallucination, a fantasy of the night, a projection of the excited imagination.

Nothing further came in to disturb me, and I fell asleep almost at once, utterly exhausted, yet still in dread of hearing again that weird sound of multitudinous pattering, or of feeling the pressure upon my heart that had made it difficult to breathe.

The sun was high in the heavens when my companion woke me from a heavy sleep and announced that the porridge was cooked and there was just time to bathe. The grateful smell of frizzling bacon entered the tent door.

"River still rising," he said, "and several islands out in midstream have disappeared altogether. Our own island's much smaller."

"Any wood left?" I asked sleepily.

"The wood and the island will finish to-morrow in a dead heat," he laughed, "but there's enough to last us till then."

I plunged in from the point of the island, which had indeed altered a lot in size and shape during the night, and was swept down in a moment to the landing-place opposite the tent. The water was icy, and the banks flew by like the country from an express train. Bathing under such conditions was an exhilarating operation, and the terror of the night seemed cleansed out of me by a process of evaporation in the brain. The sun was blazing hot; not a cloud showed itself anywhere; the wind, however, had not abated one little jot.

Quite suddenly then the implied meaning of the Swede's words flashed across me, showing that he no longer wished to leave post-haste, and had changed his mind. "Enough to last till to-morrow"— he assumed we should stay on the island another night. It struck me as odd. The night before he was so positive the other way. How had the change come about?

Great crumblings of the banks occurred at breakfast, with heavy splashings and clouds of spray which the wind brought into our frying-pan, and my fellow-traveller talked incessantly about the difficulty the Vienna-Pesth steamers must have to find the channel in flood. But the state of his mind interested and impressed

me far more than the state of the river or the difficulties of the
steamers. He had changed somehow since the evening before. His
manner was different—a trifle excited, a trifle shy, with a sort of
suspicion about his voice and gestures. I hardly know how to describe it now in cold blood, but at the time I remember being quite
certain of one thing—that he had become frightened?

He ate very little breakfast, and for once omitted to smoke his
pipe. He had the map spread open beside him, and kept studying
its markings.

"We'd better get off sharp in an hour," I said presently, feeling
for an opening that must bring him indirectly to a partial confession at any rate. And his answer puzzled me uncomfortably:
"Rather! If they'll let us."

"Who'll let us? The elements?" I asked quickly, with affected
indifference.

"The powers of this awful place, whoever they are," he replied,
keeping his eyes on the map. "The gods are here, if they are anywhere at all in the world."

"The elements are always the true immortals," I replied, laughing as naturally as I could manage, yet knowing quite well that my
face reflected my true feelings when he looked up gravely at me
and spoke across the smoke:

"We shall be fortunate if we get away without further disaster."

This was exactly what I had dreaded, and I screwed myself up
to the point of the direct question. It was like agreeing to allow the
dentist to extract the tooth; it had to come anyhow in the long run,
and the rest was all pretence.

"Further disaster! Why, what's happened?"

"For one thing—the steering paddle's gone," he said quietly.

"The steering paddle gone!" I repeated, greatly excited, for this
was our rudder, and the Danube in flood without a rudder was suicide. "But what —"

"And there's a tear in the bottom of the canoe," he added, with
a genuine little tremor in his voice.

I continued staring at him, able only to repeat the words in his
face somewhat foolishly. There, in the heat of the sun, and on this
burning sand, I was aware of a freezing atmosphere descending
round us. I got up to follow him, for he merely nodded his head
gravely and led the way towards the tent a few yards on the other
side of the fireplace. The canoe still lay there as I had last seen her

in the night, ribs uppermost, the paddles, or rather, the paddle, on the sand beside her.

"There's only one," he said, stooping to pick it up. "And here's the rent in the base-board."

It was on the tip of my tongue to tell him that I had clearly noticed two paddles a few hours before, but a second impulse made me think better of it, and I said nothing. I approached to see.

There was a long, finely made tear in the bottom of the canoe where a little slither of wood had been neatly taken clean out; it looked as if the tooth of a sharp rock or snag had eaten down her length, and investigation showed that the hole went through. Had we launched out in her without observing it we must inevitably have foundered. At first the water would have made the wood swell so as to close the hole, but once out in mid-stream the water must have poured in, and the canoe, never more than two inches above the surface, would have filled and sunk very rapidly.

"There, you see an attempt to prepare a victim for the sacrifice," I heard him saying, more to himself than to me, "two victims rather," he added as he bent over and ran his fingers along the slit.

I began to whistle—a thing I always do unconsciously when utterly nonplussed—and purposely paid no attention to his words. I was determined to consider them foolish.

"It wasn't there last night," he said presently, straightening up from his examination and looking anywhere but at me.

"We must have scratched her in landing, of course," I stopped whistling to say. "The stones are very sharp."

I stopped abruptly, for at that moment he turned round and met my eye squarely. I knew just as well as he did how impossible my explanation was. There were no stones, to begin with.

"And then there's this to explain too," he added quietly, handing me the paddle and pointing to the blade.

A new and curious emotion spread freezingly over me as I took and examined it. The blade was scraped down all over, beautifully scraped, as though someone had sand-papered it with care, making it so thin that the first vigorous stroke must have snapped it off at the elbow.

"One of us walked in his sleep and did this thing," I said feebly, "or—or it has been filed by the constant stream of sand particles blown against it by the wind, perhaps."

"Ah," said the Swede, turning away, laughing a little, "you can explain everything."

"The same wind that caught the steering paddle and flung it so near the bank that it fell in with the next lump that crumbled," I called out after him, absolutely determined to find an explanation for everything he showed me.

"I see," he shouted back, turning his head to look at me before disappearing among the willow bushes.

Once alone with these perplexing evidences of personal agency, I think my first thoughts took the form of "One of us must have done this thing, and it certainly was not I." But my second thought decided how impossible it was to suppose, under all the circumstances, that either of us had done it. That my companion, the trusted friend of a dozen similar expeditions, could have knowingly had a hand in it, was a suggestion not to be entertained for a moment. Equally absurd seemed the explanation that this imperturbable and densely practical nature had suddenly become insane and was busied with insane purposes.

Yet the fact remained that what disturbed me most, and kept my fear actively alive even in this blaze of sunshine and wild beauty, was the clear certainty that some curious alteration had come about in his mind—that the was nervous, timid, suspicious, aware of goings on he did not speak about, watching a series of secret and hitherto unmentionable events—waiting, in a word, for a climax that he expected, and, I thought, expected very soon. This grew up in my mind intuitively—I hardly knew how.

I made a hurried examination of the tent and its surroundings, but the measurements of the night remained the same. There were deep hollows formed in the sand I now noticed for the first time, basin-shaped and of various depths and sizes, varying from that of a tea-cup to a large bowl. The wind, no doubt, was responsible for these miniature craters, just as it was for lifting the paddle and tossing it towards the water. The rent in the canoe was the only thing that seemed quite inexplicable; and, after all, it was conceivable that a sharp point had caught it when we landed. The examination I made of the shore did not assist this theory, but all the same I clung to it with that diminishing portion of my intelligence which I called my "reason." An explanation of some kind was an absolute necessity, just as some working explanation of the universe is necessary—however absurd—to the happiness of every individual who seeks to do his duty in the world and face the problems of life. The simile seemed to me at the time an exact parallel.

I at once set the pitch melting, and presently the Swede joined me at the work, though under the best conditions in the world the canoe could not be safe for travelling till the following day. I drew his attention casually to the hollows in the sand.

"Yes," he said, "I know. They're all over the island. But you can explain them, no doubt!"

"Wind, of course," I answered without hesitation. "Have you never watched those little whirlwinds in the street that twist and twirl everything into a circle? This sand's loose enough to yield, that's all."

He made no reply, and we worked on in silence for a bit. I watched him surreptitiously all the time, and I had an idea he was watching me. He seemed, too, to be always listening attentively to something I could not hear, or perhaps for something that he expected to hear, for he kept turning about and staring into the bushes, and up into the sky, and out across the water where it was visible through the openings among the willows. Sometimes he even put his hand to his ear and held it there for several minutes. He said nothing to me, however, about it, and I asked no questions. And meanwhile, as he mended that torn canoe with the skill and address of a red Indian, I was glad to notice his absorption in the work, for there was a vague dread in my heart that he would speak of the changed aspect of the willows. And, if he had noticed that, my imagination could no longer be held a sufficient explanation of it.

At length, after a long pause, he began to talk.

"Queer thing," he added in a hurried sort of voice, as though he wanted to say something and get it over. "Queer thing. I mean, about that otter last night."

I had expected something so totally different that he caught me with surprise, and I looked up sharply.

"Shows how lonely this place is. Otters are awfully shy things —"

"I don't mean that, of course," he interrupted. "I mean—do you think—did you think it really was an otter?"

"What else, in the name of Heaven, what else?"

"You know, I saw it before you did, and at first it seemed—so much bigger than an otter."

"The sunset as you looked up-stream magnified it, or something," I replied.

He looked at me absently a moment, as though his mind were busy with other thoughts.

"It had such extraordinary yellow eyes," he went on half to himself.

"That was the sun too," I laughed, a trifle boisterously. "I suppose you'll wonder next if that fellow in the boat —"

I suddenly decided not to finish the sentence. He was in the act again of listening, turning his head to the wind, and something in the expression of his face made me halt. The subject dropped, and we went on with our caulking. Apparently he had not noticed my unfinished sentence. Five minutes later, however, he looked at me across the canoe, the smoking pitch in his hand, his face exceedingly grave.

"I did rather wonder, if you want to know," he said slowly, "what that thing in the boat was. I remember thinking at the time it was not a man. The whole business seemed to rise quite suddenly out of the water."

I laughed again boisterously in his face, but this time there was impatience, and a strain of anger too, in my feeling.

"Look here now," I cried, "this place is quite queer enough without going out of our way to imagine things! That boat was an ordinary boat, and the man in it was an ordinary man, and they were both going down-stream as fast as they could lick. And that otter was an otter, so don't let's play the fool about it!"

He looked steadily at me with the same grave expression. He was not in the least annoyed. I took courage from his silence.

"And, for Heaven's sake," I went on, "don't keep pretending you hear things, because it only gives me the jumps, and there's nothing to hear but the river and this cursed old thundering wind."

"You fool!" he answered in a low, shocked voice, "you utter fool. That's just the way all victims talk. As if you didn't understand just as well as I do!" he sneered with scorn in his voice, and a sort of resignation. "The best thing you can do is to keep quiet and try to hold your mind as firm as possible. This feeble attempt at self-deception only makes the truth harder when you're forced to meet it."

My little effort was over, and I found nothing more to say, for I knew quite well his words were true, and that I was the fool, not he. Up to a certain stage in the adventure he kept ahead of me easily, and I think I felt annoyed to be out of it, to be thus proved less psychic, less sensitive than himself to these extraordinary happenings, and half ignorant all the time of what was going on under my very nose. He knew from the very beginning, apparently. But at the moment I wholly missed the point of his words about the necessity of there being a victim, and that we ourselves were destined to satisfy the want. I dropped all pretence thenceforward, but thenceforward likewise my fear increased steadily to the climax.

"But you're quite right about one thing," he added, before the subject passed, "and that is that we're wiser not to talk about it, or even to think about it, because what one thinks finds expression in words, and what one says, happens."

That afternoon, while the canoe dried and hardened, we spent trying to fish, testing the leak, collecting wood, and watching the enormous flood of rising water. Masses of driftwood swept near our shores sometimes, and we fished for them with long willow branches. The island grew perceptibly smaller as the banks were torn away with great gulps and splashes. The weather kept brilliantly fine till about four o'clock, and then for the first time for three days the wind showed signs of abating. Clouds began to gather in the south-west, spreading thence slowly over the sky.

This lessening of the wind came as a great relief, for the incessant roaring, banging, and thundering had irritated our nerves. Yet the silence that came about five o'clock with its sudden cessation was in a manner quite as oppressive. The booming of the river had everything in its own way then; it filled the air with deep murmurs, more musical than the wind noises, but infinitely more monotonous. The wind held many notes, rising, falling always beating out some sort of great elemental tune; whereas the river's song lay between three notes at most—dull pedal notes, that held a lugubrious quality foreign to the wind, and somehow seemed to me, in my then nervous state, to sound wonderfully well the music of doom.

It was extraordinary, too, how the withdrawal suddenly of bright sunlight took everything out of the landscape that made for cheerfulness; and since this particular landscape had already managed to convey the suggestion of something sinister, the change of course was all the more unwelcome and noticeable. For me, I know, the darkening outlook became distinctly more alarming, and I found myself more than once calculating how soon after sunset the full moon would get up in the east, and whether the gathering clouds would greatly interfere with her lighting of the little island.

With this general hush of the wind—though it still indulged in occasional brief gusts—the river seemed to me to grow blacker, the willows to stand more densely together. The latter, too, kept up a

sort of independent movement of their own, rustling among themselves when no wind stirred, and shaking oddly from the roots
upwards. When common objects in this way be come charged with
the suggestion of horror, they stimulate the imagination far more
than things of unusual appearance; and these bushes, crowding
huddled about us, assumed for me in the darkness a bizarre gro-
tesquerie of appearance that lent to them somehow the aspect of
purposeful and living creatures. Their very ordinariness, I felt,
masked what was malignant and hostile to us. The forces of the
region drew nearer with the coming of night. They were focusing
upon our island, and more particularly upon ourselves. For thus,
somehow, in the terms of the imagination, did my really indescribable sensations in this extraordinary place present themselves.

I had slept a good deal in the early afternoon, and had thus
recovered somewhat from the exhaustion of a disturbed night, but
this only served apparently to render me more susceptible than
before to the obsessing spell of the haunting. I fought against it,
laughing at my feelings as absurd and childish, with very obvious
physiological explanations, yet, in spite of every effort, they gained
in strength upon me so that I dreaded the night as a child lost in a
forest must dread the approach of darkness.

The canoe we had carefully covered with a waterproof sheet
during the day, and the one remaining paddle had been securely
tied by the Swede to the base of a tree, lest the wind should rob us
of that too. From five o'clock onwards I busied myself with the
stew-pot and preparations for dinner, it being my turn to cook that
night. We had potatoes, onions, bits of bacon fat to add flavour,
and a general thick residue from former stews at the bottom of the
pot; with black bread broken up into it the result was most excellent, and it was followed by a stew of plums with sugar and a brew
of strong tea with dried milk. A good pile of wood lay close at hand,
and the absence of wind made my duties easy. My companion sat
lazily watching me, dividing his attentions between cleaning his
pipe and giving useless advice—an admitted privilege of the off-
duty man. He had been very quiet all the afternoon, engaged in re-
caulking the canoe, strengthening the tent ropes, and fishing for
driftwood while I slept. No more talk about undesirable things had
passed between us, and I think his only remarks had to do with
the gradual destruction of the island, which he declared was not
fully a third smaller than when we first landed.

The pot had just begun to bubble when I heard his voice calling to me from the bank, where he had wandered away without my noticing. I ran up.

"Come and listen," he said, "and see what you make of it." He held his hand cupwise to his ear, as so often before.

"Now do you hear anything?" he asked, watching me curiously.

We stood there, listening attentively together. At first I heard only the deep note of the water and the hissings rising from its turbulent surface. The willows, for once, were motionless and silent. Then a sound began to reach my ears faintly, a peculiar sound— something like the humming of a distant gong. It seemed to come across to us in the darkness from the waste of swamps and willows opposite. It was repeated at regular intervals, but it was certainly neither the sound of a bell nor the hooting of a distant steamer. I can liken it to nothing so much as to the sound of an immense gong, suspended far up in the sky, repeating incessantly its muffled metallic note, soft and musical, as it was repeatedly struck. My heart quickened as I listened.

"I've heard it all day," said my companion. "While you slept this afternoon it came all round the island. I hunted it down, but could never get near enough to see—to localise it correctly. Sometimes it was overhead, and sometimes it seemed under the water. Once or twice, too, I could have sword it was not outside at all, but within myself—you know—the way a sound in the fourth dimension is supposed to come."

I was too much puzzled to pay much attention to his words. I listened carefully, striving to associate it with any known familiar sound I could think of, but without success. It changed in the direction, too, coming nearer, and then sinking utterly away into remote distance. I cannot say that it was ominous in quality, because to me it seemed distinctly musical, yet I must admit it set going a distressing feeling that made me wish I had never heard it.

"The wind blowing in those sand-funnels," I said determined to find an explanation, "or the bushes rubbing together after the storm perhaps."

"It comes off the whole swamp," my friend answered. "It comes from everywhere at once." He ignored my explanations. "It comes from the willow bushes somehow—"

"But now the wind has dropped," I objected. "The willows can hardly make a noise by themselves, can they?"

His answer frightened me, first because I had dreaded it, and secondly, because I knew intuitively it was true.

"It is because the wind has dropped we now hear it. It was drowned before. It is the cry, I believe, of the—"

I dashed back to my fire, warned by the sound of bubbling that the stew was in danger, but determined at the same time to escape further conversation. I was resolute, if possible, to avoid the exchanging of views. I dreaded, too, that he would begin about the gods, or the elemental forces, or something else disquieting, and I wanted to keep myself well in hand for what might happen later. There was another night to be faced before we escaped from this distressing place, and there was no knowing yet what it might bring forth.

"Come and cut up bread for the pot," I called to him, vigorously stirring the appetising mixture. That stew-pot held sanity for us both, and the thought made me laugh.

He came over slowly and took the provision sack from the tree, fumbling in its mysterious depths, and then emptying the entire contents upon the ground-sheet at his feet.

"Hurry up!" I cried; "it's boiling."

The Swede burst out into a roar of laughter that startled me. It was forced laughter, not artificial exactly, but mirthless.

"There's nothing here!" he shouted, holding his sides.

"Bread, I mean."

"It's gone. There is no bread. They've taken it!"

I dropped the long spoon and ran up. Everything the sack had contained lay upon the ground-sheet, but there was no loaf.

The whole dead weight of my growing fear fell upon me and shook me. Then I burst out laughing too. It was the only thing to do: and the sound of my laughter also made me understand his. The stain of psychical pressure caused it—this explosion of unnatural laughter in both of us; it was an effort of repressed forces to seek relief; it was a temporary safety-valve. And with both of us it ceased quite suddenly.

"How criminally stupid of me!" I cried, still determined to be consistent and find an explanation. "I clean forgot to buy a loaf at Pressburg. That chattering woman put everything out of my head, and I must have left it lying on the counter or—"

"The oatmeal, too, is much less than it was this morning," the Swede interrupted.

Why in the world need he draw attention to it? I thought angrily.

"There's enough for to-morrow," I said, stirring vigorously, "and we can get lots more at Komorn or Gran. In twenty-four hours we shall be miles from here."

"I hope so—to God," he muttered, putting the things back into the sack, "unless we're claimed first as victims for the sacrifice," he added with a foolish laugh. He dragged the sack into the tent, for safety's sake, I suppose, and I heard him mumbling to himself, but so indistinctly that it seemed quite natural for me to ignore his words.

Our meal was beyond question a gloomy one, and we ate it almost in silence, avoiding one another's eyes, and keeping the fire bright. Then we washed up and prepared for the night, and, once smoking, our minds unoccupied with any definite duties, the apprehension I had felt all day long became more and more acute. It was not then active fear, I think, but the very vagueness of its origin distressed me far more that if I had been able to ticket and face it squarely. The curious sound I have likened to the note of a gong became now almost incessant, and filled the stillness of the night with a faint, continuous ringing rather than a series of distinct notes. At one time it was behind and at another time in front of us. Sometimes I fancied it came from the bushes on our left, and then again from the clumps on our right. More often it hovered directly overhead like the whirring of wings. It was really everywhere at once, behind, in front, at our sides and over our heads, completely surrounding us. The sound really defies description. But nothing within my knowledge is like that ceaseless muffled humming rising off the deserted world of swamps and willows.

We sat smoking in comparative silence, the strain growing every minute greater. The worst feature of the situation seemed to me that we did not know what to expect, and could therefore make no sort of preparation by way of defence. We could anticipate nothing. My explanations made in the sunshine, moreover, now came to haunt me with their foolish and wholly unsatisfactory nature, and it was more and more clear to us that some kind of plain talk with my companion was inevitable, whether I liked it or not. After all, we had to spend the night together, and to sleep in the same tent side by side. I saw that I could not get along much longer without the support of his mind, and for that, of course, plain talk was imperative. As long as possible, however, I postponed this little climax, and tried to ignore or laugh at the occasional sentences he flung into the emptiness.

Some of these sentences, moreover, were confoundedly disquieting to me, coming as they did to corroborate much that I felt myself; corroboration, too—which made it so much more convincing—from a totally different point of view. He composed such curious sentences, and hurled them at me in such an inconsequential sort of way, as though his main line of thought was secret to himself, and these fragments were mere bits he found it impossible to digest. He got rid of them by uttering them. Speech relieved him. It was like being sick.

"There are things about us, I'm sure, that make for disorder, disintegration, destruction, our destruction," he said once, while the fire blazed between us. "We've strayed out of a safe line somewhere."

And, another time, when the gong sounds had come nearer, ringing much louder than before, and directly over our heads, he said as though talking to himself:

"I don't think a gramophone would show any record of that. The sound doesn't come to me by the ears at all. The vibrations reach me in another manner altogether, and seem to be within me, which is precisely how a fourth dimensional sound might be supposed to make itself heard."

I purposely made no reply to this, but I sat up a little closer to the fire and peered about me into the darkness. The clouds were massed all over the sky, and no trace of moonlight came through. Very still, too, everything was, so that the river and the frogs had things all their own way.

"It has that about it," he went on, "which is utterly out of common experience. It is unknown. Only one thing describes it really; it is a non-human sound; I mean a sound outside humanity."

Having rid himself of this indigestible morsel, he lay quiet for a time, but he had so admirably expressed my own feeling that it was a relief to have the though out, and to have confined it by the limitation of words from dangerous wandering to and fro in the mind.

The solitude of that Danube camping-place, can I ever forget it? The feeling of being utterly alone on an empty planet! My thoughts ran incessantly upon cities and the haunts of men. I would have given my soul, as the saying is, for the "feel" of those Bavarian

villages we had passed through by the score; for the normal, human
commonplaces; peasants drinking beer, tables beneath the trees,
hot sunshine, and a ruined castle on the rocks behind the red-
roofed church. Even the tourists would have been welcome.

Yet what I felt of dread was no ordinary ghostly fear. It was
infinitely greater, stranger, and seemed to arise from some dim
ancestral sense of terror more profoundly disturbing than anything
I had known or dreamed of. We had "strayed", as the Swede put it,
into some region or some set of conditions where the risks were
great, yet unintelligible to us; where the frontiers of some unknown
world lay close about us. It was a spot held by the dwellers in some
outer space, a sort of peep-hole whence they could spy upon the
earth, themselves unseen, a point where the veil between had worn
a little thin. As the final result of too long a sojourn here, we should
be carried over the border and deprived of what we called "our
lives", yet by mental, not physical, processes. In that sense, as he
said, we should be the victims of our adventure—a sacrifice.

It took us in different fashion, each according to the measure
of his sensitiveness and powers of resistance. I translated it vaguely
into a personification of the mightily disturbed elements, investing
them with the horror of a deliberate and malefic purpose, resentful of our audacious intrusion into their breeding-place; whereas
my friend threw it into the unoriginal form at first of a trespass on
some ancient shrine, some place where the old gods still held sway,
where the emotional forces of former worshippers still clung, and
the ancestral portion of him yielded to the old pagan spell.

At any rate, here was a place unpolluted by men, kept clean by
the winds from coarsening human influences, a place where spiritual agencies were within reach and aggressive. Never, before or
since, have I been so attacked by indescribable suggestions of a
"beyond region", of another scheme of life, another revolution not
parallel to the human. And in the end our minds would succumb
under the weight of the awful spell, and we should be drawn across
the frontier into their world.

Small things testified to the amazing influence of the place, and
now in the silence round the fire they allowed themselves to be
noted by the mind. The very atmosphere had proved itself a mag-
nifying medium to distort every indication: the otter rolling in the
current, the hurrying boatman making signs, the shifting willows,
one and all had been robbed of its natural character, and revealed

in something of its other aspect—as it existed across the border to that other region. And this changed aspect I felt was now not merely to me, but to the race. The whole experience whose verge we touched was unknown to humanity at all. It was a new order of experience, and in the true sense of the word unearthly.

"It's the deliberate, calculating purpose that reduces one's courage to zero," the Swede said suddenly, as if he had been actually following my thoughts. "Otherwise imagination might count for much. But the paddle, the canoe, the lessening food—"

"Haven't I explained all that once?" I interrupted viciously.

"You have," he answered dryly; "you have indeed."

He made other remarks too, as usual, about what he called the "plain determination to provide a victim"; but, having now arranged my thoughts better, I recognised that this was simply the cry of his frightened soul against the knowledge that he was being attacked in a vital part, and that he would be somehow taken or destroyed. The situation called for a courage and calmness of reasoning that neither of us could compass, and I have never before been so clearly conscious of two persons in me—the one that explained everything, and the other that laughed at such foolish explanations, yet was horribly afraid.

Meanwhile, in the pitchy night the fire died down and the wood pile grew small. Neither of us moved to replenish the stock, and the darkness consequently came up very close to our faces. A few feet beyond the circle of firelight it was inky black. Occasionally a stray puff of wind set the willows shivering about us, but apart from this not very welcome sound a deep and depressing silence reigned, broken only by the gurgling of the river and the humming in the air overhead.

We both missed, I think, the shouting company of the winds.

At length, at a moment when a stray puff prolonged itself as though the wind were about to rise again, I reached the point for me of saturation, the point where it was absolutely necessary to find relief in plain speech, or else to betray myself by some hysterical extravagance that must have been far worse in its effect upon both of us. I kicked the fire into a blaze, and turned to my companion abruptly. He looked up with a start.

"I can't disguise it any longer," I said; "I don't like this place, and the darkness, and the noises, and the awful feelings I get. There's something here that beats me utterly. I'm in a blue funk, and that's the plain truth. If the other shore was—different, I swear I'd be inclined to swim for it!"

The Swede's face turned very white beneath the deep tan of sun and wind. He stared straight at me and answered quietly, but his voice betrayed his huge excitement by its unnatural calmness. For the moment, at any rate, he was the strong man of the two. He was more phlegmatic, for one thing.

"It's not a physical condition we can escape from by running away," he replied, in the tone of a doctor diagnosing some grave disease; "we must sit tight and wait. There are forces close here that could kill a herd of elephants in a second as easily as you or I could squash a fly. Our only chance is to keep perfectly still. Our insignificance perhaps may save us."

I put a dozen questions into my expression of face, but found no words. It was precisely like listening to an accurate description of a disease whose symptoms had puzzled me.

"I mean that so far, although aware of our disturbing presence, they have not found us—not 'located' us, as the Americans say," he went on. "They're blundering about like men hunting for a leak of gas. The paddle and canoe and provisions prove that. I think they feel us, but cannot actually see us. We must keep our minds quiet— it's our minds they feel. We must control our thoughts, or it's all up with us."

"Death, you mean?" I stammered, icy with the horror of his suggestion.

"Worse—by far," he said. "Death, according to one's belief, means either annihilation or release from the limitations of the senses, but it involves no change of character. You don't suddenly alter just because the body's gone. But this means a radical alter-ation, a complete change, a horrible loss of oneself by substitu-tion—far worse than death, and not even annihilation. We happen to have camped in a spot where their region touches ours, where the veil between has worn thin"—horrors! he was using my very own phrase, my actual words— "so that they are aware of our being in their neighbourhood."

"But who are aware?" I asked.

I forgot the shaking of the willows in the windless calm, the humming overhead, everything except that I was waiting for an answer that I dreaded more than I can possibly explain.

He lowered his voice at once to reply, leaning forward a little over the fire, an indefinable change in his face that made me avoid his eyes and look down upon the ground.

"All my life," he said, "I have been strangely, vividly conscious of another region—not far removed from our own world in one sense, yet wholly different in kind—where great things go on unceasingly, where immense and terrible personalities hurry by, intent on vast purposes compared to which earthly affairs, the rise and fall of nations, the destinies of empires, the fate of armies and continents, are all as dust in the balance; vast purposes, I mean, that deal directly with the soul, and not indirectly with more expressions of the soul—"

"I suggest just now—" I began, seeking to stop him, feeling as though I was face to face with a madman. But he instantly overbore me with his torrent that had to come.

"You think," he said, "it is the spirit of the elements, and I thought perhaps it was the old gods. But I tell you now it is—neither. These would be comprehensible entities, for they have relations with men, depending upon them for worship or sacrifice, whereas these beings who are now about us have absolutely nothing to do with mankind, and it is mere chance that their space happens just at this spot to touch our own."

The mere conception, which his words somehow made so convincing, as I listened to them there in the dark stillness of that lonely island, set me shaking a little all over. I found it impossible to control my movements.

"And what do you propose?" I began again.

"A sacrifice, a victim, might save us by distracting them until we could get away," he went on, "just as the wolves stop to devour the dogs and give the sleigh another start. But—I see no chance of any other victim now."

I stared blankly at him. The gleam in his eye was dreadful. Presently he continued.

"It's the willows, of course. The willows mask the others, but the others are feeling about for us. If we let our minds betray our fear, we're lost, lost utterly." He looked at me with an expression so calm, so determined, so sincere, that I no longer had any doubts as to his sanity. He was as sane as any man ever was. "If we can hold out through the night," he added, "we may get off in the daylight unnoticed, or rather, undiscovered."

"But you really think a sacrifice would—"

That gong-like humming came down very close over our heads as I spoke, but it was my friend's scared face that really stopped my mouth.

"Hush!" he whispered, holding up his hand. "Do not mention them more than you can help. Do not refer to them by name. To name is to reveal; it is the inevitable clue, and our only hope lies in ignoring them, in order that they may ignore us."

"Even in thought?" He was extraordinarily agitated.

"Especially in thought. Our thoughts make spirals in their world. We must keep them out of our minds at all costs if possible."

I raked the fire together to prevent the darkness having everything its own way. I never longed for the sun as I longed for it then in the awful blackness of that summer night.

"Were you awake all last night?" he went on suddenly.

"I slept badly a little after dawn," I replied evasively, trying to follow his instructions, which I knew instinctively were true, "but the wind, of course—"

"I know. But the wind won't account for all the noises."

"Then you heard it too?"

"The multiplying countless little footsteps I heard," he said, adding, after a moment's hesitation, "and that other sound—"

"You mean above the tent, and the pressing down upon us of something tremendous, gigantic?"

He nodded significantly.

"It was like the beginning of a sort of inner suffocation?" I said.

"Partly, yes. It seemed to me that the weight of the atmosphere had been altered—had increased enormously, so that we should have been crushed."

"And that," I went on, determined to have it all out, pointing upwards where the gong-like note hummed ceaselessly, rising and falling like wind. "What do you make of that?"

"It's their sound," he whispered gravely. "It's the sound of their world, the humming in their region. The division here is so thin that it leaks through somehow. But, if you listen carefully, you'll find it's not above so much as around us. It's in the willows. It's the willows themselves humming, because here the willows have been made symbols of the forces that are against us."

I could not follow exactly what he meant by this, yet the thought and idea in my mind were beyond question the thought an idea in his. I realised what he realised, only with less power of analysis than his. It was on the tip of my tongue to tell him at last about my hallucination of the ascending figures and the moving bushes, when he suddenly thrust his face again close into mine across the fire-light and began to speak in a very earnest whisper. He amazed me by his calmness and pluck, his apparent control of the situation. This man I had for years deemed unimaginative, stolid!

"Now listen," he said. "The only thing for us to do is to go on as though nothing had happened, follow our usual habits, go to bed, and so forth; pretend we feel nothing and notice nothing. It is a question wholly of the mind, and the less we think about them the better our chance of escape. Above all, don't think, for what you think happens!"

"All right," I managed to reply, simply breathless with his words and the strangeness of it all; "all right, I'll try, but tell me one more thing first. Tell me what you make of those hollows in the ground all about us, those sand-funnels?"

"No!" he cried, forgetting to whisper in his excitement. "I dare not, simply dare not, put the thought into words. If you have not guessed I am glad. Don't try to. They have put it into my mind; try your hardest to prevent their putting it into yours."

He sank his voice again to a whisper before he finished, and I did not press him to explain. There was already just about as much horror in me as I could hold. The conversation came to an end, and we smoked our pipes busily in silence.

Then something happened, something unimportant apparently, as the way is when the nerves are in a very great state of tension, and this small thing for a brief space gave me an entirely different point of view. I chanced to look down at my sand-shoe—the sort we used for the canoe—and something to do with the hole at the toe suddenly recalled to me the London shop where I had bought them, the difficulty the man had in fitting me, and other details of the uninteresting but practical operation. At once, in its train, followed a wholesome view of the modern sceptical world I was accustomed to move in at home. I thought of roast beef, and ale, motor-cars, policemen, brass bands, and a dozen other things that proclaimed the soul of ordinariness or utility. The effect was immediate and astonishing even to myself. Psychologically, I suppose, it was simply a sudden and violent reaction after the strain of living in an atmosphere of things that to the normal consciousness must seem impossible and incredible. But, whatever the cause, it momentarily lifted the spell from my heart, and left me for the short space of a minute feeling free and utterly unafraid. I looked up at my friend opposite.

"You damned old pagan!" I cried, laughing aloud in his face. "You imaginative idiot! You superstitious idolator! You—"

I stopped in the middle, seized anew by the old horror. I tried to smother the sound of my voice as something sacrilegious. The Swede, of course, heard it too—the strange cry overhead in the darkness—and that sudden drop in the air as though something had come nearer.

He had turned ashen white under the tan. He stood bolt upright in front of the fire, stiff as a rod, staring at me.

"After that," he said in a sort of helpless, frantic way, "we must go! We can't stay now; we must strike camp this very instant and go on—down the river."

He was talking, I saw, quite wildly, his words dictated by abject terror—the terror he had resisted so long, but which had caught him at last.

"In the dark?" I exclaimed, shaking with fear after my hysterical outburst, but still realising our position better than he did. "Sheer madness! The river's in flood, and we've only got a single paddle. Besides, we only go deeper into their country! There's nothing ahead for fifty miles but willows, willows, willows!"

He sat down again in a state of semi-collapse. The positions, by one of those kaleidoscopic changes nature loves, were suddenly reversed, and the control of our forces passed over into my hands. His mind at last had reached the point where it was beginning to weaken.

"What on earth possessed you to do such a thing?" he whispered with the awe of genuine terror in his voice and face.

I crossed round to his side of the fire. I took both his hands in mine, kneeling down beside him and looking straight into his frightened eyes.

"We'll make one more blaze," I said firmly, "and then turn in for the night. At sunrise we'll be off full speed for Komorn. Now, pull yourself together a bit, and remember your own advice about not thinking fear!"

He said no more, and I saw that he would agree and obey. In some measure, too, it was a sort of relief to get up and make an excursion into the darkness for more wood. We kept close together, almost touching, groping among the bushes and along the bank. The humming overhead never ceased, but seemed to me to grow louder as we increased our distance from the fire. It was shivery work!

We were grubbing away in the middle of a thickish clump of willows where some driftwood from a former flood had caught high among the branches, when my body was seized in a grip that made me half drop upon the sand. It was the Swede. He had fallen against me, and was clutching me for support. I heard his breath coming and going in short gasps.

"Look! By my soul!" he whispered, and for the first time in my experience I knew what it was to hear tears of terror in a human voice. He was pointing to the fire, some fifty feet away. I followed the direction of his finger, and I swear my heart missed a beat.

There, in front of the dim glow, something was moving.

I saw it through a veil that hung before my eyes like the gauze drop-curtain used at the back of a theatre—hazily a little. It was neither a human figure nor an animal. To me it gave the strange impression of being as large as several animals grouped together, like horses, two or three, moving slowly. The Swede, too, got a similar result, though expressing it differently, for he thought it was shaped and sized like a clump of willow bushes, rounded at the top, and moving all over upon its surface— "coiling upon itself like smoke," he said afterwards.

"I watched it settle downwards through the bushes," he sobbed at me. "Look, by God! It's coming this way! Oh, oh!"—he gave a kind of whistling cry. "They've found us."

I gave one terrified glance, which just enabled me to see that the shadowy form was swinging towards us through the bushes, and then I collapsed backwards with a crash into the branches. These failed, of course, to support my weight, so that with the Swede on top of me we fell in a struggling heap upon the sand. I really hardly knew what was happening. I was conscious only of a sort of enveloping sensation of icy fear that plucked the nerves out of their fleshly covering, twisted them this way and that, and replaced them quivering. My eyes were tightly shut; something in my throat choked me; a feeling that my consciousness was expanding, extending out into space, swiftly gave way to another feeling that I was losing it altogether, and about to die.

An acute spasm of pain passed through me, and I was aware that the Swede had hold of me in such a way that he hurt me abominably. It was the way he caught at me in falling.

But it was the pain, he declared afterwards, that saved me; it caused me to forget them and think of something else at the very instant when they were about to find me. It concealed my mind from them at the moment of discovery, yet just in time to evade their terrible seizing of me. He himself, he says, actually swooned at the same moment, and that was what saved him.

I only know that at a later date, how long or short is impossible to say, I found myself scrambling up out of the slippery network of willow branches, and saw my companion standing in front of me holding out a hand to assist me. I stared at him in a dazed way, rubbing the arm he had twisted for me. Nothing came to me to say, somehow.

"I lost consciousness for a moment or two," I heard him say. "That's what saved me. It made me stop thinking about them."

"You nearly broke my arm in two," I said, uttering my only connected thought at the moment. A numbness came over me.

"That's what saved you!" he replied. "Between us, we've managed to set them off on a false tack somewhere. The humming has ceased. It's gone—for the moment at any rate!"

A wave of hysterical laughter seized me again, and this time spread to my friend too—great healing gusts of shaking laughter that brought a tremendous sense of relief in their train. We made our way back to the fire and put the wood on so that it blazed at once. Then we saw that the tent had fallen over and lay in a tangled heap upon the ground.

We picked it up, and during the process tripped more than once and caught our feet in sand.

"It's those sand-funnels," exclaimed the Swede, when the tent was up again and the firelight lit up the ground for several yards about us. "And look at the size of them!"

All round the tent and about the fireplace where we had seen the moving shadows there were deep funnel-shaped hollows in the sand, exactly similar to the ones we had already found over the island, only far bigger and deeper, beautifully formed, and wide enough in some instances to admit the whole of my foot and leg.

Neither of us said a word. We both knew that sleep was the safest thing we could do, and to bed we went accordingly without further delay, having first thrown sand on the fire and taken the provision sack and the paddle inside the tent with us. The canoe, too, we propped in such a way at the end of the tent that our feet touched it, and the least motion would disturb and wake us.

In case of emergency, too, we again went to bed in our clothes, ready for a sudden start.

It was my firm intention to lie awake all night and watch, but the exhaustion of nerves and body decreed otherwise, and sleep after a while came over me with a welcome blanket of oblivion. The fact that my companion also slept quickened its approach. At first he fidgeted and constantly sat up, asking me if I "heard this" or "heard that." He tossed about on his cork mattress, and said the tent was moving and the river had risen over the point of the island, but each time I went out to look I returned with the report that all was well, and finally he grew calmer and lay still. Then at length his breathing became regular and I heard unmistakable sounds of snoring—the first and only time in my life when snoring has been a welcome and calming influence.

This, I remember, was the last thought in my mind before dozing off.

A difficulty in breathing woke me, and I found the blanket over my face. But something else besides the blanket was pressing upon me, and my first thought was that my companion had rolled off his mattress on to my own in his sleep. I called to him and sat up, and at the same moment it came to me that the tent was surrounded. That sound of multitudinous soft pattering was again audible outside, filling the night with horror.

I called again to him, louder than before. He did not answer, but I missed the sound of his snoring, and also noticed that the flap of the tent was down. This was the unpardonable sin. I crawled out in the darkness to hook it back securely, and it was then for the first time I realised positively that the Swede was not here. He had gone.

I dashed out in a mad run, seized by a dreadful agitation, and the moment I was out I plunged into a sort of torrent of humming that surrounded me completely and came out of every quarter of the heavens at once. It was that same familiar humming—gone mad! A swarm of great invisible bees might have been about me in the air. The sound seemed to thicken the very atmosphere, and I felt that my lungs worked with difficulty.

But my friend was in danger, and I could not hesitate.

The dawn was just about to break, and a faint whitish light spread upwards over the clouds from a thin strip of clear horizon. No wind stirred. I could just make out the bushes and river beyond, and the pale sandy patches. In my excitement I ran frantically to and fro about the island, calling him by name, shouting at the top

of my voice the first words that came into my head. But the willows
smothered my voice, and the humming muffled it, so that the sound
only travelled a few feet round me. I plunged among the bushes,
tripping headlong, tumbling over roots, and scraping my face as I
tore this way and that among the preventing branches.

Then, quite unexpectedly, I came out upon the island's point
and saw a dark figure outlined between the water and the sky. It was
the Swede. And already he had one foot in the river! A moment
more and he would have taken the plunge.

I threw myself upon him, flinging my arms about his waist and
dragging him shorewards with all my strength. Of course he
struggled furiously, making a noise all the time just like that cursed
humming, and using the most outlandish phrases in his anger
about "going inside to Them", and "taking the way of the water
and the wind", and God only knows what more besides, that I tried
in vain to recall afterwards, but which turned me sick with horror
and amazement as I listened. But in the end I managed to get him
into the comparative safety of the tent, and flung him breathless
and cursing upon the mattress where I held him until the fit had
passed.

I think the suddenness with which it all went and he grew calm,
coinciding as it did with the equally abrupt cessation of the humming and pattering outside—I think this was almost the strangest
part of the whole business perhaps. For he had just opened his
eyes and turned his tired face up to me so that the dawn threw a
pale light upon it through the doorway, and said, for all the world
just like a frightened child:

"My life, old man—it's my life I owe you. But it's all over now
anyhow. They've found a victim in our place!"

Then he dropped back upon his blankets and went to sleep literally under my eyes. He simply collapsed, and began to snore again
as healthily as though nothing had happened and he had never tried
to offer his own life as a sacrifice by drowning. And when the sunlight woke him three hours later—hours of ceaseless vigil for me—
it became so clear to me that he remembered absolutely nothing
of what he had attempted to do, that I deemed it wise to hold my
peace and ask no dangerous questions.

He woke naturally and easily, as I have said, when the sun was
already high in a windless hot sky, and he at once got up and set about
the preparation of the fire for breakfast. I followed him anxiously at

bathing, but he did not attempt to plunge in, merely dipping his head and making some remark about the extra coldness of the water.

"River's falling at last," he said, "and I'm glad of it."

"The humming has stopped too," I said.

He looked up at me quietly with his normal expression. Evidently he remembered everything except his own attempt at suicide.

"Everything has stopped," he said, "because—"

He hesitated. But I knew some reference to that remark he had made just before he fainted was in his mind, and I was determined to know it.

"Because 'They've found another victim'?" I said, forcing a little laugh.

"Exactly," he answered, "exactly! I feel as positive of it as though—as though—I feel quite safe again, I mean," he finished.

He began to look curiously about him. The sunlight lay in hot patches on the sand. There was no wind. The willows were motionless. He slowly rose to feet.

"Come," he said; "I think if we look, we shall find it."

He started off on a run, and I followed him. He kept to the banks, poking with a stick among the sandy bays and caves and little back- waters, myself always close on his heels.

"Ah!" he exclaimed presently, "ah!"

The tone of his voice somehow brought back to me a vivid sense of the horror of the last twenty-four hours, and I hurried up to join him. He was pointing with his stick at a large black object that lay half in the water and half on the sand. It appeared to be caught by some twisted willow roots so that the river could not sweep it away. A few hours before the spot must have been under water.

"See," he said quietly, "the victim that made our escape possible!"

And when I peered across his shoulder I saw that his stick rested on the body of a man. He turned it over. It was the corpse of a peasant, and the face was hidden in the sand. Clearly the man had been drowned, but a few hours before, and his body must have been swept down upon our island somewhere about the hour of the dawn—at the very time the fit had passed.

"We must give it a decent burial, you know."

"I suppose so," I replied. I shuddered a little in spite of myself, for there was something about the appearance of that poor drowned man that turned me cold.

The Swede glanced up sharply at me, an undecipherable expression on his face, and began clambering down the bank. I followed him

more leisurely. The current, I noticed, had torn away much of the clothing from the body, so that the neck and part of the chest lay bare.

Half-way down the bank my companion suddenly stopped and
held up his hand in warning; but either my foot slipped, or I had
gained too much momentum to bring myself quickly to a halt, for I
bumped into him and sent him forward with a sort of leap to save
himself. We tumbled together on to the hard sand so that our feet
splashed into the water. And, before anything could be done, we
had collided a little heavily against the corpse.

The Swede uttered a sharp cry. And I sprang back as if I had
been shot.

At the moment we touched the body there rose from its surface
the loud sound of humming—the sound of several hummings—which
passed with a vast commotion as of winged things in the air about us
and disappeared upwards into the sky, growing fainter and fainter
till they finally ceased in the distance. It was exactly as though we
had disturbed some living yet invisible creatures at work.

My companion clutched me, and I think I clutched him, but
before either of us had time properly to recover from the unexpected shock, we saw that a movement of the current was turning
the corpse round so that it became released from the grip of the
willow roots. A moment later it had turned completely over, the
dead face uppermost, staring at the sky. It lay on the edge of the
main stream. In another moment it would be swept away.

The Swede started to save it, shouting again something I did
not catch about a "proper burial"—and then abruptly dropped upon
his knees on the sand and covered his eyes with his hands. I was
beside him in an instant.

I saw what he had seen.

For just as the body swung round to the current the face and
the exposed chest turned full towards us, and showed plainly how
the skin and flesh were indented with small hollows, beautifully
formed, and exactly similar in shape and kind to the sand-funnels
that we had found all over the island.

"Their mark!" I heard my companion mutter under his breath.
"Their awful mark!"

And when I turned my eyes again from his ghastly face to the
river, the current had done its work, and the body had been swept
away into mid-stream and was already beyond our reach and almost out of sight, turning over and over on the waves like an otter.

The Voice in the Night
William Hope Hodgson

It was a dark, starless night. We were becalmed in the Northern Pacific. Our exact position I do not know; for the sun had been hidden during the course of a weary, breathless week, by a thin haze which had seemed to float above us, about the height of our mast-heads, at whiles descending and shrouding the surrounding sea.

With there being no wind, we had steadied the tiller, and I was the only man on deck. The crew, consisting of two men and a boy, were sleeping forrard in their den; while Will — my friend, and the master of our little craft — was aft in his bunk on the port side of the little cabin.

Suddenly, from out of the surrounding darkness, there came a hail: "Schooner, ahoy!"

The cry was so unexpected that I gave no immediate answer, because of my surprise.

It came again — a voice curiously throaty and inhuman, calling from somewhere upon the dark sea away on our port broadside: "Schooner, ahoy!"

"Hullo!" I sung out, having gathered my wits somewhat. "What are you? What do you want?"

"You need not be afraid," answered the queer voice, having probably noticed some trace of confusion in my tone. "I am only an old man."

The pause sounded oddly; but it was only afterwards that it came back to me with any significance.

"Why don't you come alongside, then?" I queried somewhat snappishly; for I liked not his hinting at my having been a trifle shaken.

"I — I — can't. It wouldn't be safe. I —" The voice broke off, and there was silence.

"What do you mean?" I asked, growing more and more astonished. "Why not safe? Where are you?"

I listened for a moment; but there came no answer. And then, a sudden indefinite suspicion, of I knew not what, coming to me, I stepped swiftly to the binnacle, and took out the lighted lamp. At the same time, I knocked on the deck with my heel to waken Will. Then I was back at the side, throwing the yellow funnel of light out into the silent immensity beyond our rail. As I did so, I heard a slight, muffled cry, and then the sound of a splash as though someone had dipped oars abruptly. Yet I cannot say that I saw anything with certainty; save, it seemed to me, that with the first flash of the light, there had been something upon the waters, where now there was nothing.

"Hullo, there!" I called. "What foolery is this!"

But there came only the indistinct sounds of a boat being pulled away into the night.

Then I heard Will's voice, from the direction of the after scuttle: "What's up, George?"

"Come here, Will!" I said.

"What is it?" he asked, coming across the deck.

I told him the queer thing which had happened. He put several questions; then, after a moment's silence, he raised his hands to his lips, and hailed: "Boat, ahoy!"

From a long distance away there came back to us a faint reply, and my companion repeated his call. Presently, after a short period of silence, there grew on our hearing the muffled sound of oars; at which Will hailed again.

This time there was a reply: "Put away the light."

"I'm damned if I will," I muttered; but Will told me to do as the voice bade, and I shoved it down under the bulwarks.

"Come nearer," he said, and the oar-strokes continued. Then, when apparently some half-dozen fathoms distant, they again ceased.

"Come alongside," exclaimed Will. "There's nothing to be frightened of aboard here!"

"Promise that you will not show the light?"

"What's to do with you," I burst out, "that you're so infernally afraid of the light?"

"Because —" began the voice, and stopped short.

"Because what?" I asked quickly.

Will put his hand on my shoulder.

"Shut up a minute, old man," he said, in a low voice. "Let me tackle him."

He leant more over the rail.

"See here, Mister," he said, "this is a pretty queer business, you coming upon us like this, right out in the middle of the blessed Pacific. How are we to know what sort of a hanky-panky trick you're up to? You say there's only one of you. How are we to know, unless we get a squint at you — eh? What's your objection to the light, anyway?"

As he finished, I heard the noise of the oars again, and then the voice came; but now from a greater distance, and sounding extremely hopeless and pathetic.

"I am sorry — sorry! I would not have troubled you, only I am hungry, and — so is she."

The voice died away, and the sound of the oars, dipping irregularly, was borne to us.

"Stop!" sung out Will. "I don't want to drive you away. Come back! We'll keep the light hidden, if you don't like it."

He turned to me: "It's a damned queer rig, this; but I think there's nothing to be afraid of?"

There was a question in his tone, and I replied.

"No, I think the poor devil's been wrecked around here, and gone crazy."

The sound of the oars drew nearer.

"Shove that lamp back in the binnacle," said Will; then he leaned over the rail and listened. I replaced the lamp, and came back to his side. The dipping of the oars ceased some dozen yards distant.

"Won't you come alongside now?" asked Will in an even voice. "I have had the lamp put back in the binnacle."

"I — I cannot," replied the voice. "I dare not come nearer. I dare not even pay you for the — the provisions."

"That's all right," said Will, and hesitated. "You're welcome to as much grub as you can take —" Again he hesitated.

"You are very good," exclaimed the voice. "May God, Who understands everything, reward you —" It broke off huskily.

"The — the lady?" said Will abruptly. "Is she —"

"I have left her behind upon the island," came the voice.

"What island?" I cut in.

"I know not its name," returned the voice. "I would to God —!" it began, and checked itself as suddenly.

"Could we not send a boat for her?" asked Will at this point.

"No!" said the voice, with extraordinary emphasis. "My God! No!" There was a moment's pause; then it added, in a tone which seemed a merited reproach: "It was because of our want I ventured — because her agony tortured me."

"I am a forgetful brute," exclaimed Will. "Just wait a minute, whoever you are, and I will bring you up something at once."

In a couple of minutes he was back again, and his arms were full of various edibles. He paused at the rail.

"Can't you come alongside for them?" he asked.

"No — I DARE NOT," replied the voice, and it seemed to me that in its tones I detected a note of stifled craving — as though the owner hushed a mortal desire. It came to me then in a flash, that the poor old creature out there in the darkness, was SUFFERING for actual need of that which Will held in his arms; and yet, because of some unintelligible dread, refraining from dashing to the side of our little schooner, and receiving it. And with the lightning-like conviction, there came the knowledge that the Invisible was not mad; but sanely facing some intolerable horror.

"Damn it, Will!" I said, full of many feelings, over which pre-dominated a vast sympathy. "Get a box. We must float off the stuff to him in it."

This we did — propelling it away from the vessel, out into the darkness, by means of a boathook. In a minute, a slight cry from the Invisible came to us, and we knew that he had secured the box.

A little later, he called out a farewell to us, and so heartful a blessing, that I am sure we were the better for it. Then, without more ado, we heard the ply of oars across the darkness.

"Pretty soon off," remarked Will, with perhaps just a little sense of injury.

"Wait," I replied. "I think somehow he'll come back. He must have been badly needing that food."

"And the lady," said Will. For a moment he was silent; then he continued: "It's the queerest thing ever I've tumbled across, since I've been fishing."

"Yes," I said, and fell to pondering.

And so the time slipped away — an hour, another, and still Will stayed with me; for the queer adventure had knocked all desire for sleep out of him.

The third hour was three parts through, when we heard again the sound of oars across the silent ocean.

"Listen!" said Will, a low note of excitement in his voice.

"He's coming, just as I thought," I muttered.

The dipping of the oars grew nearer, and I noted that the strokes were firmer and longer. The food had been needed.

They came to a stop a little distance off the broadside, and the queer voice came again to us through the darkness: "Schooner, ahoy!"

"That you?" asked Will.

"Yes," replied the voice. "I left you suddenly; but — but there was great need."

"The lady?" questioned Will.

"The — lady is grateful now on earth. She will be more grateful soon in — in heaven."

Will began to make some reply, in a puzzled voice; but became confused, and broke off short. I said nothing. I was wondering at the curious pauses, and, apart from my wonder, I was full of a great sympathy.

The voice continued: "We — she and I, have talked, as we shared the result of God's tenderness and yours —"

Will interposed; but without coherence.

"I beg of you not to — to belittle your deed of Christian charity this night," said the voice. "Be sure that it has not escaped His notice."

It stopped, and there was a full minute's silence. Then it came again: "We have spoken together upon that which — which has befallen us. We had thought to go out, without telling any, of the terror which has come into our — lives. She is with me in believing that to-night's happenings are under a special ruling, and that it is God's wish that we should tell to you all that we have suffered since — since —"

"Yes?" said Will softly.

"Since the sinking of the *Albatross*."

"Ah!" I exclaimed involuntarily. "She left Newcastle for 'Frisco some six months ago, and hasn't been heard of since."

"Yes," answered the voice. "But some few degrees to the North of the line she was caught in a terrible storm, and dismasted. When

the day came, it was found that she was leaking badly, and, presently, it falling to a calm, the sailors took to the boats, leaving —
leaving a young lady — my fiancée — and myself upon the wreck.

"We were below, gathering together a few of our belongings,
when they left. They were entirely callous, through fear, and when
we came up upon the deck, we saw them only as small shapes afar
off upon the horizon. Yet we did not despair, but set to work and
constructed a small raft. Upon this we put such few matters as it
would hold including a quantity of water and some ship's biscuit.
Then, the vessel being very deep in the water, we got ourselves on
to the raft, and pushed off.

"It was later, when I observed that we seemed to be in the way
of some tide or current, which bore us from the ship at an angle;
so that in the course of three hours, by my watch, her hull became
invisible to our sight, her broken masts remaining in view for a
somewhat longer period. Then, towards evening, it grew misty,
and so through the night. The next day we were still encompassed
by the mist, the weather remaining quiet.

"For four days we drifted through this strange haze, until, on
the evening of the fourth day, there grew upon our ears the murmur of breakers at a distance. Gradually it became plainer, and,
somewhat after midnight, it appeared to sound upon either hand
at no very great space. The raft was raised upon a swell several
times, and then we were in smooth water, and the noise of the
breakers was behind.

"When the morning came, we found that we were in a sort of
great lagoon; but of this we noticed little at the time; for close
before us, through the enshrouding mist, loomed the hull of a large
sailing-vessel. With one accord, we fell upon our knees and
thanked God; for we thought that here was an end to our perils.
We had much to learn.

"The raft drew near to the ship, and we shouted on them to
take us aboard; but none answered. Presently the raft touched
against the side of the vessel, and, seeing a rope hanging downwards, I seized it and began to climb. Yet I had much ado to make
my way up, because of a kind of grey, lichenous fungus which had
seized upon the rope, and which blotched the side of the ship
lividly.

"I reached the rail and clambered over it, on to the deck. Here
I saw that the decks were covered, in great patches, with grey

masses, some of them rising into nodules several feet in height; but at the time I thought less of this matter than of the possibility of there being people aboard the ship. I shouted; but none answered. Then I went to the door below the poop deck. I opened it, and peered in. There was a great smell of staleness, so that I knew in a moment that nothing living was within, and with the knowledge, I shut the door quickly; for I felt suddenly lonely.

"I went back to the side where I had scrambled up. My — my sweetheart was still sitting quietly upon the raft. Seeing me look down she called up to know whether there were any aboard of the ship. I replied that the vessel had the appearance of having been long deserted; but that if she would wait a little I would see whether there was anything in the shape of a ladder by which she could ascend to the deck. Then we would make a search through the vessel together. A little later, on the opposite side of the decks, I found a rope side-ladder. This I carried across, and a minute afterwards she was beside me.

"Together we explored the cabins and apartments in the after part of the ship; but nowhere was there any sign of life. Here and there within the cabins themselves, we came across odd patches of that queer fungus; but this, as my sweetheart said, could be cleansed away.

"In the end, having assured ourselves that the after portion of the vessel was empty, we picked our ways to the bows, between the ugly grey nodules of that strange growth; and here we made a further search which told us that there was indeed none aboard but ourselves.

"This being now beyond any doubt, we returned to the stern of the ship and proceeded to make ourselves as comfortable as possible. Together we cleared out and cleaned two of the cabins: and after that I made examination whether there was anything eatable in the ship. This I soon found was so, and thanked God in my heart for His goodness. In addition to this I discovered the whereabouts of the fresh-water pump, and having fixed it I found the water drinkable, though somewhat unpleasant to the taste.

"For several days we stayed aboard the ship, without attempting to get to the shore. We were busily engaged in making the place habitable. Yet even thus early we became aware that our lot was even less to be desired than might have been imagined; for though, as a first step, we scraped away the odd patches of growth that studded the floors and walls of the cabins and saloon, yet they returned almost to their original size within the space of twenty-four hours, which not only discouraged us, but gave us a feeling of vague unease.

"Still we would not admit ourselves beaten, so set to work afresh, and not only scraped away the fungus, but soaked the places where it had been, with carbolic, a can-full of which I had found in the pantry. Yet, by the end of the week the growth had returned in full strength, and, in addition, it had spread to other places, as though our touching it had allowed germs from it to travel elsewhere.

"On the seventh morning, my sweetheart woke to find a small patch of it growing on her pillow, close to her face. At that, she came to me, so soon as she could get her garments upon her. I was in the galley at the time lighting the fire for breakfast.

"Come here, John," she said, and led me aft. When I saw the thing upon her pillow I shuddered, and then and there we agreed to go right out of the ship and see whether we could not fare to make ourselves more comfortable ashore.

"Hurriedly we gathered together our few belongings, and even among these I found that the fungus had been at work; for one of her shawls had a little lump of it growing near one edge. I threw the whole thing over the side, without saying anything to her.

"The raft was still alongside, but it was too clumsy to guide, and I lowered down a small boat that hung across the stern, and in this we made our way to the shore. Yet, as we drew near to it, I became gradually aware that here the vile fungus, which had driven us from the ship, was growing riot. In places it rose into horrible, fantastic mounds, which seemed almost to quiver, as with a quiet life, when the wind blew across them. Here and there it took on the forms of vast fingers, and in others it just spread out flat and smooth and treacherous. Odd places, it appeared as grotesque stunted trees, seeming extraordinarily kinked and gnarled — the whole quaking vilely at times.

"At first, it seemed to us that there was no single portion of the surrounding shore which was not hidden beneath the masses of the hideous lichen; yet, in this, I found we were mistaken; for somewhat later, coasting along the shore at a little distance, we descried a smooth white patch of what appeared to be fine sand, and there we landed. It was not sand. What it was I do not know. All that I have observed is that upon it the fungus will not grow;

while everywhere else, save where the sand-like earth wanders oddly, path-wise, amid the grey desolation of the lichen, there is nothing but that loathsome greyness.

"It is difficult to make you understand how cheered we were to find one place that was absolutely free from the growth, and here we deposited our belongings. Then we went back to the ship for such things as it seemed to us we should need. Among other matters, I managed to bring ashore with me one of the ship's sails, with which I constructed two small tents, which, though exceedingly rough-shaped, served the purpose for which they were intended. In these we lived and stored our various necessities, and thus for a matter of some four weeks all went smoothly and without particular un-happiness. Indeed, I may say with much of happiness — for — for we were together.

"It was on the thumb of her right hand that the growth first showed. It was only a small circular spot, much like a little grey mole. My God! how the fear leapt to my heart when she showed me the place. We cleansed it, between us, washing it with carbolic and water. In the morning of the following day she showed her hand to me again. The grey warty thing had returned. For a little while, we looked at one another in silence. Then, still wordless, we started again to remove it. In the midst of the operation she spoke suddenly.

"'What's that on the side of your face, dear?' Her voice was sharp with anxiety. I put my hand up to feel.

"'There! Under the hair by your ear. A little to the front a bit.' My finger rested upon the place, and then I knew.

"'Let us get your thumb done first,' I said. And she submitted, only because she was afraid to touch me until it was cleansed. I finished washing and disinfecting her thumb, and then she turned to my face. After it was finished we sat together and talked awhile of many things for there had come into our lives sudden, very terrible thoughts. We were, all at once, afraid of something worse than death. We spoke of loading the boat with provisions and water and making our way out on to the sea; yet we were helpless, for many causes, and — and the growth had attacked us already. We decided to stay. God would do with us what was His will. We would wait.

"A month, two months, three months passed and the places grew somewhat, and there had come others. Yet we fought so

strenuously with the fear that its headway was but slow, comparatively speaking.

"Occasionally we ventured off to the ship for such stores as we
needed. There we found that the fungus grew persistently. One of
the nodules on the maindeck became soon as high as my head.

"We had now given up all thought or hope of leaving the island.
We had realized that it would be unallowable to go among healthy
humans, with the things from which we were suffering.

"With this determination and knowledge in our minds we knew
that we should have to husband our food and water; for we did not
know, at that time, but that we should possibly live for many years.

"This reminds me that I have told you that I am an old man.
Judged by the years this is not so. But — but —"

He broke off; then continued somewhat abruptly: "As I was
saying, we knew that we should have to use care in the matter of
food. But we had no idea then how little food there was left of
which to take care. It was a week later that I made the discovery
that all the other bread tanks — which I had supposed full — were
empty, and that (beyond odd tins of vegetables and meat, and some
other matters) we had nothing on which to depend, but the bread
in the tank which I had already opened.

"After learning this I bestirred myself to do what I could, and
set to work at fishing in the lagoon; but with no success. At this I
was somewhat inclined to feel desperate until the thought came to
me to try outside the lagoon, in the open sea.

"Here, at times, I caught odd fish; but so infrequently that they
proved of but little help in keeping us from the hunger which
threatened.

"It seemed to me that our deaths were likely to come by hunger,
and not by the growth of the thing which had seized upon our bodies.

"We were in this state of mind when the fourth month wore
out. When I made a very horrible discovery. One morning, a little
before midday. I came off from the ship with a portion of the biscuits which were left. In the mouth of her tent I saw my sweetheart sitting, eating something.

"'What is it, my dear?' I called out as I leapt ashore. Yet, on
hearing my voice, she seemed confused, and, turning, slyly threw
something towards the edge of the little clearing. It fell short, and
a vague suspicion having arisen within me, I walked across and
picked it up. It was a piece of the grey fungus.

"As I went to her with it in my hand, she turned deadly pale; then rose red.

"I felt strangely dazed and frightened.

"'My dear! My dear!' I said, and could say no more. Yet at words she broke down and cried bitterly. Gradually, as she calmed, I got from her the news that she had tried it the preceding day, and — and liked it. I got her to promise on her knees not to touch it again, however great our hunger. After she had promised she told me that the desire for it had come suddenly, and that, until the moment of desire, she had experienced nothing towards it but the most extreme repulsion.

"Later in the day, feeling strangely restless, and much shaken with the thing which I had discovered, I made my way along one of the twisted paths — formed by the white, sand-like substance — which led among the fungoid growth. I had, once before, ventured along there; but not to any great distance. This time, being involved in perplexing thought, I went much further than hitherto.

"Suddenly I was called to myself by a queer hoarse sound on my left. Turning quickly I saw that there was movement among an extraordinarily shaped mass of fungus, close to my elbow. It was swaying uneasily, as though it possessed life of its own. Abruptly, as I stared, the thought came to me that the thing had a grotesque resemblance to the figure of a distorted human creature. Even as the fancy flashed into my brain, there was a slight, sickening noise of tearing, and I saw that one of the branch-like arms was detaching itself from the surrounding grey masses, and coming towards me. The head of the thing — a shapeless grey ball, inclined in my direction. I stood stupidly, and the vile arm brushed across my face. I gave out a frightened cry, and ran back a few paces. There was a sweetish taste upon my lips where the thing had touched me. I licked them, and was immediately filled with an inhuman desire. I turned and seized a mass of the fungus. Then more and — more. I was insatiable. In the midst of devouring, the remembrance of the morning's discovery swept into my mazed brain. It was sent by God. I dashed the fragment I held to the ground. Then, utterly wretched and feeling a dreadful guiltiness, I made my way back to the little encampment.

"I think she knew, by some marvellous intuition which love must have given, so soon as she set eyes on me. Her quiet sympathy made it easier for me, and I told her of my sudden weakness;

yet omitted to mention the extraordinary thing which had gone before. I desired to spare her all unnecessary terror.

"But, for myself, I had added an intolerable knowledge, to breed an incessant terror in my brain; for I doubted not but that I had seen the end of one of those men who had come to the island in the ship in the lagoon; and in that monstrous ending I had seen our own.

"Thereafter we kept from the abominable food, though the desire for it had entered into our blood. Yet our drear punishment was upon us; for, day by day, with monstrous rapidity, the fungoid growth took hold of our poor bodies. Nothing we could do would check it materially, and so — and so — we who had been human, became — Well, it matters less each day. Only — only we had been man and maid!

"And day by day the fight is more dreadful, to withstand the hungerlust for the terrible lichen.

"A week ago we ate the last of the biscuit, and since that time I have caught three fish. I was out here fishing tonight when your schooner drifted upon me out of the mist. I hailed you. You know the rest, and may God, out of His great heart, bless you for your goodness to a — a couple of poor outcast souls."

There was the dip of an oar — another. Then the voice came again, and for the last time, sounding through the slight surrounding mist, ghostly and mournful.

"God bless you! Good-bye!"

"Good-bye," we shouted together, hoarsely, our hearts full of many emotions.

I glanced about me. I became aware that the dawn was upon us.

The sun flung a stray beam across the hidden sea; pierced the mist dully, and lit up the receding boat with a gloomy fire. Indistinctly I saw something nodding between the oars. I thought of a sponge — a great, grey nodding sponge — The oars continued to ply. They were grey — as was the boat — and my eyes searched a moment vainly for the conjunction of hand and oar. My gaze flashed back to the — head. It nodded forward as the oars went backward for the stroke. Then the oars were dipped, the boat shot out of the patch of light, and the — the thing went nodding into the mist.

The Orchid Horror
John Blunt

So the four of us, Helen Chadwick, Dufresne, who was our host, Loring, and I, went into the conservatory. The argument, begun at dinner, as to whether the sensitive plant is responsive to the breath as well as to the touch, had to be settled. Dufresne, laughing, promised that we should soon see how wrong we were—how little we really knew.

The warm damp of the place was a trifle disagreeable to me. I would much rather have kept my seat at table, where the port and cigarettes were, than to have made one of this pseudo-scientific investigating party. But, idly drawn into the discussion at first, nothing would do save that I come along and have my chance-expressed opinions beaten to earth under the demonstrated truth of Dufresne's assertions.

He and the girl had paused near the door of the hot-house to admire a rhododendron in full bloom; I was loitering a little way behind them on the brick-paved walk—when it happened. Nothing more thoroughly unexpected could have been imagined. Loring, who had wandered a bit farther along, suddenly turned and came hurtling toward us, his jaw hanging, eyes a-bulge, the light of stark madness on his face!

I took a step forward.

"What, in the name—"

And then he was upon the two beside the pink-blossomed bush. Dufresne, knocked clean off his feet, with a stifled cry and a wild upflinging of his arms, sank from view in a whirlpool of swishing leaves into the foliage beside the path. Miss Chadwick, sent spinning to the opposite edge of the walk by a glancing blow from the

Loring's shoulder, staggered a moment, strove ineffectually to regain her balance by clutching at the near-by shrubbery, then toppled ungracefully to her knees in the moist loam.

"Loring!" I cried out. "In pity's name, man—"

Side-stepping quickly, I reached out and tried to hold him. As well try to detain a runaway express-train. My grip on his shoulder was off in a twinkling, and on he plowed, with huge, swift strides toward the conservatory door.

Another moment and he had gone.

Dazed, I stared at the aperture through which he had fled. Behind me I heard fat Dufresne struggling to get out of the branches into which he had fallen; vaguely gathered that he had at last extricated himself and approached the girl, inquiring with wheezing solicitude as to her state.

Loring was sane when he came into the green-house. Sane up to thirty seconds ago. And then—mad.

What in the world—

Then I came to myself with a start. Loring was my friend. I had brought him to this house to-night. In a way, I was responsible for his actions. Curse the fellow! Yet he hadn't cut up as he had because he wanted to be eccentric. Something had happened to him. Something back there along the walk had given him a bad scare. Something, terrifying enough to unbalance his reason.

Great Heaven, he was at large now in the crowded drawing-rooms beyond! What might he not be up to? I was his friend, accountable to my host and hostess.

Swiftly I turned and went out of the door. No trace of him, or of any freakish action of which he might have been guilty, appearing among the gay party in the ground-floor rooms, I mounted the stairs to the chamber set apart for the men's hats and coats, and there found Loring's things. Evidently he had not left the house.

"Beg pardon, sir?" the servant at the front door met me at the foot of the stairway. "The gentleman who came in with you this evening, sir. I thought I ought to say something to you. Left without a thing on his head, just the way you are now, Mr. Murdock, not ten minutes ago. First I thought he was going after something he'd left behind in the motor you came in. But he ain't come back. I thought—"

I had run up-stairs, got into my overcoat and hat, and was descending the steps of the stoop in another two minutes. The fellow *was* mad! Whatever had upset him in the conservatory had driven him in a panic of fright from the very house itself, bare-headed, coatless.

I was frightfully worried. Unconsciously my steps were taking me in the direction of our club, where, I suppose, I had an unformed idea be might have run. As I entered the place, the first man I saw was—Loring!

He sat at a table nearest the open door of the café. His dress-coat had been exchanged for a dinner-jacket; there was something liquid in a glass before him. I crossed to his side. He did not look up. To all outward appearance, he was as cool and collected as ever I had seen him.

"Well?"

I let a pent breath escape me, and dropped into the opposite chair. I stared, speechless, at the man. And what a man he was! Six feet three, huge in proportion, with a bronze-skinned, smooth-shaven face. A man to look at with an involuntary straightening of the shoulders, inflation of the chest, and general attempt at "bigening"—if I may coin the word—in instinctive imitation of his splendid physique. Indeed, a man!

And he had been thrown into a paroxysm of fear so great that heedlessly he had knocked down his host of the evening and a frail woman, then bolted from the house to flee through the streets without stopping for proper covering, temporarily a lunatic through excessive fright—*this* near-giant, as badly scared as that?

"Well?" I repeated eagerly after him. "What's it all about?"

He said nothing.

"Don't you mean to talk?" I blurted, amazed. "Am I entitled to an explanation—or not?"

His eyes had not yet met mine.

"Can't you see," he said through his set teeth, "that I've had a shock, and a bad one? I'm trying to hold myself together. It isn't easy. I'd be obliged to you if you wouldn't ask questions. Not just now, anyway."

I sat back, gnawing my mustache. Could any but a strong man have held himself even thus well in check after the way he had gone to pieces not a half-hour before? Yet, if he was strong-willed enough for that, what could have shaken him so completely at Dufresne's house? Curiosity such as mine could not be concealed under even the wettest blanket.

"Will you tell me this?" I said after a while. "What threw you into such a funk?"

In silence he tore the bar-check between his fingers into tiny bits.

"You didn't see a reptile in the greenhouse?" I hazarded. "There wasn't a tarantula hidden on some transplanted bush? Nothing like that?"

He gave a scornfully negative gesture.

"Well, what the deuce was it?" I rapped out. "Dufresne, the girl, and myself were the only living human beings besides yourself in the place. We didn't do anything to alarm you surely. Did you go stark, staring mad on account of the silly flowers themselves?"

At last he looked full at me.

"What would you say," he almost whispered in his intensity, "if I told you it *was* the flowers? A little cluster of exotic plants that you didn't see in the far corner of the room, and that I didn't see either, but that I smelled? That those drove me clear out of my mind for a minute and more—eh?"

He leaned back.

"What would you say?" he went on. "You'd have nothing to say, because you don't understand. You don't know the past. It won't make pleasant telling, I promise you. But you must know. Very well. Listen to me.

"Nine years ago I sat in this very club. Thirty at the time, I had realized every ambition in life but one. I had money, plenty of it, all earned by myself. Thirty, you understand, and with a fortune means hard work. I had worked hard. harder than most men ever do, I guess; but I was built for doing hard things.

"The one attainment I lacked was a wife. No woman so far had pleased me. If that sounds egotistical, remember that my financial success had convinced me that I was the sort of a man capable of entertaining for a woman that thing known as a 'grand passion'; that I must pick and choose the girl upon whom to lavish a powerful love with care. Hence I had been waiting all these years, waiting for the one woman.

"But I was tired of waiting. And that night a man came and sat in the next lounge-chair to mine in the billiard-room and gave me hope that perhaps my waiting was over. A new member of the club, I believe. A corpse was what he would have reminded you of; his yellow skin was drawn tight over his cheek-bones; there was far too little flesh on his limbs to make him an attractive figure to contemplate;

and his eyes—I don't like to think of those burned holes in a sheep-skin even now.

"His talk was full of a wonderful collection of exotic plants he had seen in a house near Washington Square. To my monosyllables of polite interest he brought forth an invitation to visit the place and look at the collection. I protested myself ignorant in such matters. That made no difference, said he; I would enjoy seeing this botanical display, he was sure. Besides, the collector had a daughter. I would surely like to see *her*.

"And then, for a solid hour, the emaciated stranger poured into my ear a description of a woman such as no one ever listened to, I'll take oath upon, since the world began. Impassioned, inspired of his theme, he set my brain on fire with the picture of his friend, the daughter of the floramaniac.

"I jumped to my feet.

"'Take me there!' I exclaimed, 'I want to see—these wonderful plants.'

"We went straight to the house, a large brown stone dwelling of the old-fashioned type. The conservatory was in the rear of the building. My breath caught in my throat as I entered the heated room. Orchids, nothing but orchids, thousands, tens of thousands of the flowing, multi-shaded flowers, hung from the walls and ceiling of the place. Having seen nobody but the servant at the door, my corpse-like acquaintance told me that doubtless the collector was too busy at the moment to welcome me; however, he assured me that it was all right; I might stay there as long as I chose; then he left me.

"As I stood gazing around the room I felt my senses swaying within me in time to the languorous nodding of the rows upon rows of trailing blossoms everywhere in view. What was this feeling? I looked down at my outstretched hand. Steady as a rock. Yet all inside my arm, the nerves, the tissue, the blood, the muscle, were in motion, in swaying motion.

"How long I stood entranced, deliciously thrilled by that movement within me which the rhythmical moving of the flowers inspired, I cannot say. Perhaps it was five, ten minutes—perhaps an hour, two—that I stood spellbound, hypnotized, incapable of any other sensation but that one of inner motion. And then—

"Before my eyes the rows of orchids bent apart. Slowly, with exquisite grace, it was like the waving open of a lane in a wheat field caused by the wind. Yet there was no wind, not the faintest breeze, in the room. Wider became the opening of that aisle in the blossoms' close ranks. Suddenly at its end I saw—the collector's daughter.

"How the man who had brought me here had lied. She was a million times more perfect than he had pictured her. Beautiful, she transcended beauty. A tall woman, lithe, well-rounded as to figure, black-haired and with eyes and lips which were the only 'rememberable' features of her face for me at the moment, I felt love at first sight—a stirring of my grand passion at last!—at my first glimpse of her, this goddess of the orchids.

"Slowly, with the languid grace of the swaying flowers, she advanced toward me through the lane they had made, as though by her royal command. She put out her hand. I took it in mine. The words I would have said to explain my presence there did not pass my lips. What use were words—between us? Eye to eye, hand clasped in hand, it was as if all the words in the world had already been spoken to perform our introduction.

"After a while we talked. What of is no matter. Hours later I left the house—alone. The next afternoon I returned. The day following found me there as well. Days sped into weeks, the weeks into a month, and we were engaged. I did not declare my love. I had no need to do so. It was plain without speech—as was her regard for me.

"'When will you marry me, my Goddess of the Orchids?' I whispered.

"At first she hesitated. She could not leave her father; he was very old; she was all he had, and he would be unhappy without her. I remarked that his unhappiness could not be of long standing, surely, if she came with me, since he had never manifested enough interest in her welfare even to see me from the first time I came into the house.

"'You do not understand,' she told me gently. 'My father's way is strange, perhaps, but he loves me. Next to his flowers I come only second in his heart. If he lost me he would grieve. I cannot cause him pain. There is only one way—'

"She stopped.

"'What is the one way?' I asked.

"'There's an orchid,' said she, 'that he would give his life to possess if he could. So rare is it that not one has ever been seen by a white man; only rumors of its existence have come through the natives in the region of its growth. If my father could own one of that rare species, a single specimen—well, don't you see that he would be so happy, so completely absorbed in its possession, that he would not mind the shock of giving me up—not till long after you had brought the *Cattleyea Trixsemptia* back and we were married, at all events.'

"'I am to bring him this orchid, am I?' I smiled.

"'You love me?' she asked, anxiously.

"We were sitting on the ledge of a splashing fountain in the center of the conservatory. I rose and took her hands.

"'You shall see,' I said. 'Tell me where this flower grows. I will get it. Not till I have proved my love for you will I look into your eyes again.'

"We parted. That night I made one at a dinner given in honor of a celebrated Englishman who was a professional orchid-hunter. Bound for South America next day, to the section of the country, indeed, near which I had been told the plant I sought was to be found, I decided that I would be in luck if I could persuade this experienced traveler to let me accompany him into that strange land. Of course, after we arrived in Venezuela our ways would part; he was after a type of orchid different from the species I desired, and in hunting his quarry, he would go along one route inland, I another.

"He was sincerely glad of my offer to join him. I explained that I wanted to go on an orchid hunt 'just for the adventure.' Next morning we took steamer together; in a week had reached South America, and then—a queer thing fell out.

"An Indian came to the Englishman with word of an orchid field that lay behind the Orinoco. It was the same spot toward which I had been directed to go. According to the native's story, it was perilous work getting to the place, and would take at least a month of the hardest kind of journeying. But the orchids there were very fine, very rare. If the professional cared to make the attempt—

"'Look here,' said he to me, 'I'm going to have a try for some of those flowers.'

"Here was a second stroke of luck. Since there was an entire field of these plants, I could come out with the truth at last that this, I felt certain, was the species of orchid I was hunting on my own hook. There was no longer any danger that the Englishman would hunt the same flower that I wanted if he knew my purpose, and would perhaps be lucky enough to 'nose me out' in the search. Plainly, there were enough orchids of this description for all. So, together with this expert huntsman, I could journey to the spot with much less difficulty than alone.

"'But I won't take you with me,' he went on. 'You heard what his nibs the native chief said just now. The trip's mighty dangerous. You couldn't stand it. Sorry, old man, but you've got to be left our of this.'

"'Just the same,' I informed him. 'I'm coming.' And I told him the business that had brought me from home. 'That's all—I'm coming,' I added.

"'No, you aren't,' said he firmly. 'That's all right about your hunting this kind of an orchid. Don't know where you ever heard of it, or what put the notion of finding one in your head. But you've got to give it up. You don't know what you're about. A green hand at the business, and take a journey like this—man, you'd die!'

"'Will you?' I asked.

"That I can't say,' and he shrugged his shoulders. 'I'll stand a better chance of getting to the place than you, though. I'm inured, rather, to this sort of thing. Though I don't mind saying that I'd rather not go on this particular journey. From maps and hearsay of the trail it's going to be a little bit of a crosscut through Hades.'

"'Then why go?' I pursued.

"'There's an incentive in my case. A group of collectors is behind me, money-coffers open to pay a prize for whatever I get. My reason's clear. But, blame me if I can see yours in wanting to come along with me so headstrong and keen.'

"This time I shrugged.

"'Oh,' said he, 'so it's a girl? Been thrown over by some woman, have you, and want to go into danger to forget?'

"'On the contrary,' I smiled. 'I'm doing it to please the girl I've won.'

"'Good Lord!' he blurted out, gaping at me. 'Good Lord—you mean to tell me a girl, a girl who cares about you, has let you come down here to hunt a trophy in the spot you want to go? Does she know anything about the way orchids are found? Oh, her father's a collector? Then she does know.'

"He continued to stare at me.

"'Look here, Loring,' he said suddenly. 'Don't mind if I ask you a question. But weren't you introduced to the lady of your choice by a rack-boned skeleton of a man with yellow skin, deep-burning eyes—sort of an upheaval-from-the-crypt sort of chap?'

"'Yes,' I exclaimed, my eyes widening.

"'I thought so,' he said. And after a moment: 'I see,' he added. 'The same old game. I know the woman who sent you down here. Everybody in the orchid-collecting business knows her, more or less. She's a plant fiend. Same sort of mania as attacks people by way of drugs, the drink, and so on, you know. Seen her collection? It's the finest in the world; pretty nearly every orchid known is there. Shall I tell you how she got them?' He leaned toward me. 'Through just such fools as you, Loring.'

"I stumbled to my feet, furious.

"'Steady on!' he cried. 'Hear me out. I want to do you a friendly turn, old fellow; upon my soul I do. Listen. That woman, I tell you, is a fiend. We all know her well. See if this isn't the way she's hood-winked you. Told you, didn't she, that her father would never be happy if she married and left him; that just one thing might be counted on to take his mind off losing her—a certain rare orchid? Any-way, that's what she's told other men time and again. All of them have started out to bring here the plant, too. Some succeeded. And the re-ward? She laughs at them, and then tells the truth. There is no doting father. The orchids she wanted for herself. It's all she cares for—orchids. Men are nothing. Orchids—they cost men—she wants orchids.

"'That's the fate of the men who succeed. But those who fail? Loring, the bones of a dozen, a score of the men who have tried to perform her mission lie bleaching now in the swamps and along the roots of jungle-trees the world over. Only one man failed to bring back the orchid for which he was sent and still lives. Do you know who he is? The man who brought you and the orchid queen together.

"'You remember his looks. She put that brand on him down this very way three years ago. Since then he's been trying to win her in the only way that seems possible—through her passion for the flow-ers. Men like you, big and strong, he seeks out, brings to her so that she can send them forth to complete her collection. When she has a specimen of every orchid ever known, he hopes that she will marry him. That's the living, disgusting truth, old man, as I breathe here before you.

"'Believe me, you're designed for a victim like all the rest. I'm telling you the truth. And I'm warning you to turn back before it's too late. Will you take my word—will you go home?'

"'No!' I roared. 'You lying hound—'

"I think I meant to kill him with my own hands. But suddenly reason came to my aid. Evidently it was going to be no easy matter for an untoughened white man to penetrate alone to the spot where the orchids I was after were to be found; I must bring what I had vowed I would back to my affianced. With this man's aid, I might better be able to do so. What if he had dared to traduce the woman who was to be my wife? I could gloss even that over for the time, for the sake of getting what I sought. Afterward the lies he had told me—the lies, built up on some rumor of the girl's existence which he had come upon, and retailed to me for the purpose of causing me to abandon the field, with the glory of being first to find a new plant, to him—I could cram these down his throat with my fists.

"'I beg your pardon,' I said, appearing to be cool. 'You'll have to overlook what I've just said. I'm a good deal upset over what you've told me. I—I've no doubt you mean to be decent to me.'

"'And you'll quit this idea of hunting the orchid?' he asked eagerly.

"'No,' I replied, and the sneer with which I glanced him over must have been plain. 'I'm going with you.'

"His face reddened.

"'As you like,' he said curtly.

"Followed a week of busiest activity. Our outfit was purchased, porters hired, guides engaged. At length, when everything was in readiness, we assembled, a small army with enough supplies for quite that body, to start the march into the solitude. One month it took us to reach the head of the Orinoco. Then began the real hardships of the journey into the unbroken jungle.

"No such strain could be imagined as was put upon our party in the next fortnight. A bare chronicle of the events that befell us could not convey a tithe of what the suffering really meant. Menaced by reptiles, crawling creatures of every revolting description; attacked by the wild men of that forest region with their deadly blowguns; racked by swamp fevers, and always pressing on—on into the unknown—in a silence that daily grew more and more oppressive—the memory of that trip will be with me always in its harrowing details.

"And now our chief guide died. Before him had dropped a third of our original number of porters and choppers. Without the leadership of the native, who knew the general direction in which lay the orchids, we were helpless. A party of Indians were encountered three days later, and, in response to our question, they waved their hands toward the sun as the course we must follow before the 'poison plants' were in reach. On we fought.

"And in another week a perceptible odor was in the air; an odor which the Englishman said meant that we were nearing the orchids. Each day, as we progressed, this odor became more clearly defined. Finally it was distinctly unpleasant, then disagreeable, lastly uncomfortable. Another day and the scent grew positively menacing. Each breath one drew into the lungs seemed charged with fumes of a poisonous sickish-sweet drug. Five porters fell senseless on the fifth day as we drew nearer to the source of the noxious aroma.

"And yet the orchids were not yet in sight, seemingly no nearer than when we started. Another day, and the odor in the air was insupportable. The natives refused to go farther. My white companion, the professional hunter, lay senseless in his tracks. I was near swooning myself. With the wind in our faces, blowing that poison off the orchid-field somewhere in advance of us, it was useless to think of keeping on any further.

"Then, and then only, did I believe the truth of what I had heard of the woman who had sent me on this wild-goose chase. Indeed, she must have known something of the perils into which I had gone at her bidding. And she had let me go. I was to have been another victim.

"I cursed her to high heaven, there in the middle of that black, silent forest, with the spirals of the invisible poison-odor coiling around me in the air. And I swore that I would have revenge—the revenge of bringing her what she had driven me out to get!

"Alone, I essayed one final dash forward in the endeavor to reach the flowers which seemed so near, yet were ever so far from my touch. Surely, we could not have halted many miles distant from the field. Perhaps by running, with body bent close to the ground— but it was useless. The wind brought the deadly fumes full in my face, cramming them down throat and nostrils. Reeling, half dead, I returned to the others.

"At once we began the homeward march. More than half our corps were dead by the time we had progressed a quarter way back along our trail. Half-way to the coast, and only a miserable handful of our original party remained. How those of us who survived managed to do so is a mystery. But at last four shattered ghosts of human beings, two Indian porters, the Englishman and myself, returned to the civilization of Venezuela.

"But I was not through. A month's rest, and I was trying to organize another party to start back toward our abandoned goal. Not in the same way we had gone before. I had worked out a plan. By approaching that unseen field of orchids from the opposite side, the wind blowing the other way, a chance might hold good that the flowers could be reached by circumventing the full effect of the poisoned perfume.

"No one would attempt the journey with me. The Englishman was finished—forever, he said, with all orchid-hunting. His motive was now not so strong as mine, I thought with a smile. Money could not tempt him to keep up the search for the *Cattleyea Trixsemptia*. My revenge, though, kept me in full enthusiasm for the hunt; it was all I thought of, waking or sleeping.

"When I was satisfied that nobody would accompany me, I set back toward the head of the Orinoco myself alone. This time, traveling swiftly because lightly burdened and unaccompanied by any laggards, I made the edge of the jungle in a little over two weeks. The plunge through the forest, however, took longer alone than when I had expert choppers to clear a trail before me. But I made progress somehow.

"Often as I fought my way through the tangle of rank underbrush, waist-high and almost inextricable, I muttered aloud: 'So they picked you for a strong man, eh? A strong, robust man? A good one to send on a difficult mission, yes. Well, I'll show them yet—I'll bring back that flower!'

"And—how I do not know—I reached the orchid field at last! For two days previously the same old noxious odor had been in the air, but not nearly so perceptibly as before, because I had figured well in keeping the wind in my back. Inside an hour all the gathering force of the perfume which had turned our party back on the first attempt was compressed; dizzy, almost stupefied, drugged into partially insensibility, I parted the leaves in the foliage before me—and gazed upon the end of my journey!

"There were the flowers—blue, blue orchids! The only ones ever looked upon by white man's eyes. A thrill ran through me; almost I had the feeling then of the collector, the scientist in untrod fields, the primal discoverer of the miraculous.

"And then—drowsiness, languid heaviness, an overwhelming desire to cast myself down to sleep then and there, came to replace the momentary feeding of elation. I must pick my blossom, and be quick. The fumes of those waving, ultramarine flowers before my eyes were stealing over me more powerfully than ever before. Quick! I must be quick!

"I advanced. Step by step I drew near the largest cluster of the nodding, swaying poisoned cups of light, dark, dappled blue. Another dozen paces forward. My sensations were those of the opium smoker yielding himself gradually to the influence of the drug, yet withholding full surrender to prolong the delicious agony of complete capitulation. Could I reach an orchid, pluck it, get away, before—before it was—too—late—

"Heavens, I must fly! I could not hold out against that overpowering odor. I wheeled drunkenly. Blindly I lurched forward. Something swept my face. My eyes flew open—it was a cluster of orchids behind me which had been drawn across my cheek. With a scream of fright, I bounded sidewise, tripped over a vine, fell—

"And for that interval I knew no more.

"When I awoke it was to find that the breeze which blew over the tiny clearing where the poison plants were had shifted. Their perfume was no longer in the air. I staggered up. My head ached, and my eyeballs burned. What had I been doing, lying there on the ground?

"It came back to me. I had been overcome by the odor of the flowers. Only for the changing of the wind, preventing more of the fumes entering my lungs as I slept that drugged sleep—I shook myself together. Now was my chance to get away.

"Not for any price on earth would I have sought once again to pluck one of those blossoms so near to me. My plan of revenge against the woman who had sent me into this Gehenna was completely driven from my head. Now—while I yet could—was my chance to get away. Facing about, I started running.

"On and on I sped. Gradually, though, my speed was diminishing. Not from weariness, not from fatigue. Something else. I slackened to a walk. I stopped short in my tracks. Turning about, I sniffed the air. No trace of that odor—no trace—

"Wildly I dashed back toward the clearing and its orchids. *I must have that scent in my nostrils again! I must go to sleep under its spell once more.* I could no more resist the impulse that brought me back toward the poisonous blossoms than I could voluntarily stop breathing. I burst into the clearing. On tiptoe, I reached up to the nearest cluster of the blue buds, drank deep of the awful, sickish odor—once—twice—

"In my tracks I fell, overcome, a smile on my lips.

"I ought never to have walked again, I know. Yet I did. How long after it was, I have no means of telling. It was still daylight—or was it another day? I was heavy, sluggish, deeply depressed. I felt suddenly so frightened there alone in the clearing with those hideous, mocking plants swaying around me, that I hurled myself upon the ground, screaming, beating the moss with my hands and feet, frantic with hear of my loneliness, my dreadful plight.

"Then that feeling passed. I would get out of here. I would break and run now, and never stop running till I had put the length and breadth of the jungle between me and those ghastly plants. I sprang up. With a wild yell—a sort of farewell to the fearful spot—I leaped away into the neighboring forest.

"This time I did run until I was physically exhausted. I dropped down on a fallen moss-hung log to gather breath. An hour or more I sat there. And when I rose—it was to hobble off in the direction of the *Cattleyea Trixsemptia* again, the lustful light in my eyes of the opium fiend returning to his den, the drunkard to his dive!

"I was caught. Useless to try to break away from the spell now. That poisonous perfume of the blue orchids had enchained me to the spot forever. I spent the next interval of the time—three days, as near as I could judge—in the heart of the clearing, drugging myself with the scent of the flowers, waking, drugging myself again.

"Why didn't I die? I prayed for death, a release from my agonizing dilemma. Weak, now, to the point of prostration, yet I continued to live. I knew that I had wasted away to a mere skeleton of skin and bones—by no effort could I make my lips meet over my teeth—that I was emaciated by lack of food as well as the injurious effects of the poison I was inhaling, to the point almost of bloodlessness in all my veins—and yet I lived on.

"What was to be the end? I felt only a mild curiosity as to this, so it be soon. Another day went by. I was weaker now. Sixteen hours of the twenty-four, at a guess, had been spent in drugged sleep on my back in the middle of the clearing.

"With glazed eyes I looked around me. And looked again.

"Was I mad at last?

"There before my eyes stood my Goddess of the Orchids—she who had brought me to this plight!

"Slowly she approached across the noiseless moss. She stretched out her hand. I tottered to my feet. The claw at the end of my broomstick arm went out, encountered her fingers—*real flesh and blood!*

"'Drink this,' she whispered in my ear.

"A flask was held to my chattering teeth. Something scalding hot ran down my parched throat.

"'Now lean on me'—again her voice, wondrous soft.

"And slowly, carefully she began to lead me out of the clearing, through the jungle. A little way and we meet her train of porters and guides. While a rough litter was being made for me I sat upon the ground, leaning against her knees as she stood. Strangely, now that I was with this party I felt no craving for the drugged breath of the blue orchid to which I had been the slave.

"The journey back to the coast I do not remember. Something of my days of convalescence in Venezuela, though, I can recall. There it was that I heard the story of her search for me from the woman who had saved my life.

"Her passion for orchids was really so powerful that she had served men very much as the Englishmen had told me for years. I was to have been treated no better nor worse than the rest. Only—me of all the others she really loved. After she had sent me forth on her mission, she recalled the fate of so many of her suitors who had gone into the wildernesses before; she realized then that she could not let me die or suffer as she knew I would.

"That was the strange point. You see, she knew the dangers that would beset any one upon that trail into the jungle. And, knowing the perils of such a journey, she took it upon herself to save me if she could. Much as she had always loved orchids never once had she sought a rare plant herself. With me, though—she thought me worth seeking after, it seems."

"So I suppose," I remarked, "you married her and lived happily ever after?"

He looked at me, wild-eyed. "*Married her?*" And he shuddered.

The Man Whom the Trees Loved
Algernon Blackwood

I

He painted trees as by some special divining instinct of their essential qualities. He understood them. He knew why in an oak forest, for instance, each individual was utterly distinct from its fellows, and why no two beeches in the whole world were alike. People asked him down to paint a favorite lime or silver birch, for he caught the individuality of a tree as some catch the individuality of a horse. How he managed it was something of a puzzle, for he never had painting lessons, his drawing was often wildly inaccurate, and, while his perception of a Tree Personality was true and vivid, his rendering of it might almost approach the ludicrous. Yet the character and personality of that particular tree stood there alive beneath his brush—shining, frowning, dreaming, as the case might be, friendly or hostile, good or evil. It emerged.

There was nothing else in the wide world that he could paint; flowers and landscapes he only muddled away into a smudge; with people he was helpless and hopeless; also with animals. Skies he could sometimes manage, or effects of wind in foliage, but as a rule he left these all severely alone. He kept to trees, wisely following an instinct that was guided by love. It was quite arresting, this way he had of making a tree look almost like a being—alive. It approached the uncanny. "Yes, Sanderson knows what he's doing when he paints a tree!" thought old David Bittacy, C.B., late of the Woods and Forests. "Why, you can almost hear it rustle. You can smell the thing. You can hear the rain drip through its leaves. You can almost see the branches move. It grows." For in this way somewhat he expressed his satisfaction, half to persuade himself that the twenty guineas were well spent (since his wife thought otherwise), and half to explain this uncanny reality of life that lay in the fine old cedar framed above his study table.

Yet in the general view the mind of Mr. Bittacy was held to be austere, not to say morose. Few divined in him the secretly tenacious love of nature that had been fostered by years spent in the forests and jungles of the eastern world. It was odd for an Englishman, due possibly to that Eurasian ancestor. Surreptitiously, as though half ashamed of it, he had kept alive a sense of beauty that hardly belonged to his type, and was unusual for its vitality. Trees, in particular, nourished it. He, also, understood trees, felt a subtle sense of communion with them, born perhaps of those years he had lived in caring for them, guarding, protecting, nursing, years of solitude among their great shadowy presences. He kept it largely to himself, of course, because he knew the world he lived in. He also kept it from his wife—to some extent. He knew it came between them, knew that she feared it, was opposed. But what he did not know, or realize at any rate, was the extent to which she grasped the power which they wielded over his life. Her fear, he judged, was simply due to those years in India, when for weeks at a time his calling took him away from her into the jungle forests, while she remained at home dreading all manner of evils that might befall him. This, of course, explained her instinctive opposition to the passion for woods that still influenced and clung to him. It was a natural survival of those anxious days of waiting in solitude for his safe return.

For Mrs. Bittacy, daughter of an evangelical clergy-man, was a self-sacrificing woman, who in most things found a happy duty in sharing her husband's joys and sorrows to the point of self-obliteration. Only in this matter of the trees she was less successful than in others. It remained a problem difficult of compromise.

He knew, for instance, that what she objected to in this portrait of the cedar on their lawn was really not the price he had given for it, but the unpleasant way in which the transaction emphasized this breach between their common interests—the only one they had, but deep.

Sanderson, the artist, earned little enough money by his strange talent; such checks were few and far between. The owners of fine or interesting trees who cared to have them painted singly were rare indeed, and the "studies" that he made for his own delight he also kept for his own delight. Even were there buyers, he would not sell them. Only a few, and these peculiarly intimate friends, might even see them, for he disliked to hear the undiscerning criticisms of those who did not understand. Not that he minded laughter at his craftsmanship—he admitted it with scorn—but that remarks about the personality of the tree itself could easily wound or anger him. He resented slighting observations concerning them, as though insults offered to personal friends who could not answer for themselves. He was instantly up in arms.

"It really is extraordinary," said a Woman who Understood, "that you can make that cypress seem an individual, when in reality all cypresses are so *exactly* alike."

And though the bit of calculated flattery had come so near to saying the right, true, thing, Sanderson flushed as though she had slighted a friend beneath his very nose. Abruptly he passed in front of her and turned the picture to the wall.

"Almost as queer," he answered rudely, copying her silly emphasis, "as that *you* should have imagined individuality in your husband, Madame, when in reality all men are so *exactly* alike!"

Since the only thing that differentiated her husband from the mob was the money for which she had married him, Sanderson's relations with that particular family terminated on the spot, chance of prospective orders with it. His sensitiveness, perhaps, was morbid. At any rate the way to reach his heart lay through his trees. He might be said to love trees. He certainly drew a splendid inspiration from them, and the source of a man's inspiration, be it music, religion, or a woman, is never a safe thing to criticize.

"I do think, perhaps, it was just a little extravagant, dear," said Mrs. Bittacy, referring to the cedar check, "when we want a lawnmower so badly too. But, as it gives you such pleasure—"

"It reminds me of a certain day, Sophia," replied the old gentleman, looking first proudly at herself, then fondly at the picture, "now long gone by. It reminds me of another tree—that Kentish lawn in the spring, birds singing in the lilacs, and some one in a muslin frock waiting patiently beneath a certain cedar—not the one in the picture, I know, but—"

"I was not waiting," she said indignantly, "I was picking fir-cones for the schoolroom fire—"

"Fir-cones, my dear, do not grow on cedars, and schoolroom fires were not made in June in my young days."

"And anyhow it isn't the same cedar."

"It has made me fond of all cedars for its sake," he answered, "and it reminds me that you are the same young girl still—"

She crossed the room to his side, and together they looked out of the window where, upon the lawn of their Hampshire cottage, a ragged Lebanon stood in a solitary state.

"You're as full of dreams as ever," she said gently, "and I don't regret the check a bit—really. Only it would have been more real if it had been the original tree, wouldn't it?"

"That was blown down years ago. I passed the place last year, and there's not a sign of it left," he replied tenderly. And presently, when he released her from his side, she went up to the wall and carefully dusted the picture Sanderson had made of the cedar on their present lawn. She went all round the frame with her tiny handkerchief, standing on tiptoe to reach the top rim.

"What I like about it," said the old fellow to himself when his wife had left the room, "is the way he has made it live. All trees have it, of course, but a cedar taught it to me first—the 'something' trees possess that make them know I'm there when I stand close and watch. I suppose I felt it then because I was in love, and love reveals life everywhere." He glanced a moment at the Lebanon looming gaunt and somber through the gathering dusk. A curious wistful expression danced a moment through his eyes. "Yes, Sanderson has seen it as it is," he murmured, "solemnly dreaming there its dim hidden life against the Forest edge, and as different from that other tree in Kent as I am from—from the vicar, say. It's quite a stranger, too. I don't know anything about it really. That other cedar I loved; this old fellow I respect. Friendly though— yes, on the whole quite friendly. He's painted the friendliness right enough. He saw that. I'd like to know that man better," he added. "I'd like to ask him how he saw so clearly that it stands there between this cottage and the Forest—yet somehow more in sympathy with us than with the mass of woods behind—a sort of go-between. *That* I never noticed before. I see it now—through his eyes. It stands there like a sentinel—protective rather."

He turned away abruptly to look through the window. He saw the great encircling mass of gloom that was the Forest, fringing their little lawn. It pressed up closer in the darkness. The prim garden with its formal beds of flowers seemed an impertinence almost—some little colored insect that sought to settle on a sleeping

monster—some gaudy fly that danced impudently down the edge
of a great river that could engulf it with a toss of its smallest wave.
That Forest with its thousand years of growth and its deep spreading being was some such slumbering monster, yes. Their cottage
and garden stood too near its running lip. When the winds were
strong and lifted its shadowy skirts of black and purple.... He loved
this feeling of the Forest Personality; he had always loved it.

"Queer," he reflected, "awfully queer, that trees should bring
me such a sense of dim, vast living! I used to feel it particularly, I
remember, in India; in Canadian woods as well; but never in little
English woods till here. And Sanderson's the only man I ever knew
who felt it too. He's never said so, but there's the proof," and he
turned again to the picture that he loved. A thrill of unaccustomed
life ran through him as he looked. "I wonder; by Jove, I wonder,"
his thoughts ran on, "whether a tree—er—in any lawful meaning of
the term can be—alive. I remember some writing fellow telling me
long ago that trees had once been moving things, animal organ-
isms of some sort, that had stood so long feeding, sleeping, dreaming, or something, in the same place, that they had lost the power
to get away...!"

Fancies flew pell-mell about his mind, and, lighting a cheroot,
he dropped into an armchair beside the open window and let them
play. Outside the blackbirds whistled in the shrubberies across the
lawn. He smelt the earth and trees and flowers, the perfume of
mown grass, and the bits of open heath-land far away in the heart
of the woods. The summer wind stirred very faintly through the
leaves. But the great New Forest hardly raised her sweeping skirts
of black and purple shadow.

Mr. Bittacy, however, knew intimately every detail of that wilderness of trees within. He knew all the purple coombs splashed with
yellow waves of gorse; sweet with juniper and myrtle, and gleaming with clear and dark-eyed pools that watched the sky. There
hawks hovered, circling hour by hour, and the flicker of the peewit's
flight with its melancholy, petulant cry, deepened the sense of stillness. He knew the solitary pines, dwarfed, tufted, vigorous, that
sang to every lost wind, travelers like the gypsies who pitched their
bush-like tents beneath them; he knew the shaggy ponies, with
foals like baby centaurs; the chattering jays, the milky call of the
cuckoos in the spring, and the boom of the bittern from the lonely
marshes. The undergrowth of watching hollies, he knew too,

strange and mysterious, with their dark, suggestive beauty, and the yellow shimmer of their pale dropped leaves.

Here all the Forest lived and breathed in safety, secure from mutilation. No terror of the axe could haunt the peace of its vast subconscious life, no terror of devastating Man afflict it with the dread of premature death. It knew itself supreme; it spread and preened itself without concealment. It set no spires to carry warnings, for no wind brought messages of alarm as it bulged outwards to the sun and stars.

But, once its leafy portals left behind, the trees of the countryside were otherwise. The houses threatened them; they knew themselves in danger. The roads were no longer glades of silent turf, but noisy, cruel ways by which men came to attack them. They were civilized, cared for—but cared for in order that some day they might be put to death. Even in the villages, where the solemn and immemorial repose of giant chestnuts aped security, the tossing of a silver birch against their mass, impatient in the littlest wind, brought warning. Dust clogged their leaves. The inner humming of their quiet life became inaudible beneath the scream and shriek of clattering traffic. They longed and prayed to enter the great Peace of the Forest yonder, but they could not move. They knew, moreover, that the Forest with its august, deep splendor despised and pitied them. They were a thing of artificial gardens, and belonged to beds of flowers all forced to grow one way....

"I'd like to know that artist fellow better," was the thought upon which he returned at length to the things of practical life. "I wonder if Sophia would mind him for a bit—?" He rose with the sound of the gong, brushing the ashes from his speckled waistcoat. He pulled the waistcoat down. He was slim and spare in figure, active in his movements. In the dim light, but for that silvery moustache, he might easily have passed for a man of forty. "I'll suggest it to her anyhow," he decided on his way upstairs to dress. His thought really was that Sanderson could probably explain his world of things he had always felt about—trees. A man who could paint the soul of a cedar in that way must know it all.

"Why not?" she gave her verdict later over the bread-and-butter pudding; "unless you think he'd find it dull without companions."

"He would paint all day in the Forest, dear. I'd like to pick his brains a bit, too, if I could manage it."

"You can manage anything, David," was what she answered, for this elderly childless couple used an affectionate politeness long since deemed old-fashioned. The remark, however, displeased her, making her feel uneasy, and she did not notice his rejoinder, smiling his pleasure and content— "Except yourself and our bank account, my dear." This passion of his for trees was of old a bone of contention, though very mild contention. It frightened her. That was the truth. The Bible, her Baedeker for earth and heaven, did not mention it. Her husband, while humoring her, could never alter that instinctive dread she had. He soothed, but never changed her. She liked the woods, perhaps as spots for shade and picnics, but she could not, as he did, love them.

And after dinner, with a lamp beside the open window, he read aloud from *The Times* the evening post had brought, such fragments as he thought might interest her. The custom was invariable, except on Sundays, when, to please his wife, he dozed over Tennyson or Farrar as their mood might be. She knitted while he read, asked gentle questions, told him his voice was a "lovely reading voice," and enjoyed the little discussions that occasions prompted because he always let her with them with "Ah, Sophia, I had never thought of it quite in *that* way before; but now you mention it I must say I think there's something in it...."

For David Bittacy was wise. It was long after marriage, during his months of loneliness spent with trees and forests in India, his wife waiting at home in the Bungalow, that his other, deeper side had developed the strange passion that she could not understand. And after one or two serious attempts to let her share it with him, he had given up and learned to hide it from her. He learned, that is, to speak of it only casually, for since she knew it was there, to keep silence altogether would only increase her pain. So from time to time he skimmed the surface just to let her show him where he was wrong and think she won the day. It remained a debatable land of compromise. He listened with patience to her criticisms, her excursions and alarms, knowing that while it gave her satisfaction, it could not change himself. The thing lay in him too deep and true for change. But, for peace' sake, some meeting-place was desirable, and he found it thus.

It was her one fault in his eyes, this religious mania carried over from her upbringing, and it did no serious harm. Great emotion could shake it sometimes out of her. She clung to it because her father taught it her and not because she had thought it out for herself. Indeed, like many women, she never really *thought* at all, but merely reflected the images of others' thinking which she had learned to see. So, wise in his knowledge of human nature, old David Bittacy accepted the pain of being obliged to keep a portion of his inner life shut off from the woman he deeply loved. He regarded her little biblical phrases as oddities that still clung to a rather fine, big soul—like horns and little useless things some animals have not yet lost in the course of evolution while they have outgrown their use.

"My dear, what is it? You frightened me!" She asked it suddenly, sitting up so abruptly that her cap dropped sideways almost to her ear. For David Bittacy behind his crackling paper had uttered a sharp exclamation of surprise. He had lowered the sheet and was staring at her over the tops of his gold glasses.

"Listen to this, if you please," he said, a note of eagerness in his voice, "listen to this, my dear Sophia. It's from an address by Francis Darwin before the Royal Society. He is president, you know, and son of the great Darwin. Listen carefully, I beg you. It is *most* significant."

"I *am* listening, David," she said with some astonishment, looking up. She stopped her knitting. For a second she glanced behind her. Something had suddenly changed in the room, and it made her feel wide awake, though before she had been almost dozing. Her husband's voice and manner had introduced this new thing. Her instincts rose in warning. "*Do* read it, dear." He took a deep breath, looking first again over the rims of his glasses to make quite sure of her attention. He had evidently come across something of genuine interest, although herself she often found the passages from these "Addresses" somewhat heavy.

In a deep, emphatic voice he read aloud:

"'It is impossible to know whether or not plants are conscious; but it is consistent with the doctrine of continuity that in all living things there is something psychic, and if we accept this point of view—'"

"*If*," she interrupted, scenting danger.

He ignored the interruption as a thing of slight value he was accustomed to.

"'If we accept this point of view,'" he continued, "'we must believe that in plants there exists a faint copy of *what we know as consciousness in ourselves.*'"

He laid the paper down and steadily stared at her. Their eyes met. He had italicized the last phrase.

For a minute or two his wife made no reply or comment. They stared at one another in silence. He waited for the meaning of the words to reach her understanding with full import. Then he turned and read them again in part, while she, released from that curious driving look in his eyes, instinctively again glanced over her shoulder round the room. It was almost as if she felt some one had come in to them unnoticed.

"We must believe that in plants there exists a faint copy of what we know as consciousness in ourselves."

"*If*," she repeated lamely, feeling before the stare of those questioning eyes she must say something, but not yet having gathered her wits together quite.

"*Consciousness*," he rejoined. And then he added gravely: "That, my dear, is the statement of a scientific man of the Twentieth Century."

Mrs. Bittacy sat forward in her chair so that her silk flounces crackled louder than the newspaper. She made a characteristic little sound between sniffling and snorting. She put her shoes closely together, with her hands upon her knees.

"David," she said quietly, "I think these scientific men are simply losing their heads. There is nothing in the Bible that I can remember about any such thing whatsoever."

"Nothing, Sophia, that I can remember either," he answered patiently. Then, after a pause, he added, half to himself perhaps more than to her: "And, now that I come to think about it, it seems that Sanderson once said something to me that was similar.

"Then Mr. Sanderson is a wise and thoughtful man, and a safe man," she quickly took up, "if he said that."

For she thought her husband referred to her remark about the Bible, and not to her judgment of the scientific men. And he did not correct her mistake.

"And plants, you see, dear, are not the same as trees," she drove her advantage home, "not quite, that is."

"I agree," said David quietly; "but both belong to the great vegetable kingdom."

There was a moment's pause before she answered.

"Pah! the vegetable kingdom, indeed!" She tossed her pretty old head. And into the words she put a degree of contempt that, could the vegetable kingdom have heard it, might have made it feel ashamed for covering a third of the world with its wonderful tangled network of roots and branches, delicate shaking leaves, and its millions of spires that caught the sun and wind and rain. Its very right to existence seemed in question.

II

Sanderson accordingly came down, and on the whole his short visit was a success. Why he came at all was a mystery to those who heard of it, for he never paid visits and was certainly not the kind of man to court a customer. There must have been something in Bittacy he liked.

Mrs. Bittacy was glad when he left. He brought no dress-suit for one thing, not even a dinner-jacket, and he wore very low collars with big balloon ties like a Frenchman, and let his hair grow longer than was nice, she felt. Not that these things were important, but that she considered them symptoms of something a little disordered. The ties were unnecessarily flowing.

For all that he was an interesting man, and, in spite of his eccentricities of dress and so forth, a gentleman. "Perhaps," she reflected in her genuinely charitable heart, "he had other uses for the twenty guineas, an invalid sister or an old mother to support!" She had no notion of the cost of brushes, frames, paints, and canvases. Also she forgave him much for the sake of his beautiful eyes and his eager enthusiasm of manner. So many men of thirty were already blasé.

Still, when the visit was over, she felt relieved. She said nothing about his coming a second time, and her husband, she was glad to notice, had likewise made no suggestion. For, truth to tell, the way the younger man engrossed the older, keeping him out for hours in the Forest, talking on the lawn in the blazing sun, and in the evenings when the damp of dusk came creeping out from the surrounding woods, all regardless of his age and usual habits, was not quite to her taste. Of course, Mr. Sanderson did not know how easily those attacks of Indian fever came back, but David surely might have told him.

They talked trees from morning to night. It stirred in her the old subconscious trail of dread, a trail that led ever into the darkness of big woods; and such feelings, as her early evangelical training taught her, were temptings. To regard them in any other way was to play with danger.

Her mind, as she watched these two, was charged with curious thoughts of dread she could not understand, yet feared the more on that account. The way they studied that old mangy cedar was a trifle unnecessary, unwise, she felt. It was disregarding the sense of proportion which deity had set upon the world for men's safe guidance.

Even after dinner they smoked their cigars upon the low branches that swept down and touched the lawn, until at length she insisted on their coming in. Cedars, she had somewhere heard, were not safe after sundown; it was not wholesome to be too near them; to sleep beneath them was even dangerous, though what the precise danger was she had forgotten. The upas was the tree she really meant.

At any rate she summoned David in, and Sanderson came presently after him.

For a long time, before deciding on this peremptory step, she had watched them surreptitiously from the drawing-room window—her husband and her guest. The dusk enveloped them with its damp veil of gauze. She saw the glowing tips of their cigars, and heard the drone of voices. Bats flitted overhead, and big, silent moths whirred softly over the rhododendron blossoms. And it came suddenly to her, while she watched, that her husband had somehow altered these last few days—since Mr. Sanderson's arrival in fact. A change had come over him, though what it was she could not say. She hesitated, indeed, to search. That was the instinctive dread operating in her. Provided it passed she would rather not know. Small things, of course, she noticed; small outward signs. He had neglected *The Times* for one thing, left off his speckled waistcoats for another. He was absent-minded sometimes; showed vagueness in practical details where hitherto he showed decision. And—he had begun to talk in his sleep again.

These and a dozen other small peculiarities came suddenly upon her with the rush of a combined attack. They brought with them a faint distress that made her shiver. Momentarily her mind was startled, then confused, as her eyes picked out the shadowy figures in the dusk, the cedar covering them, the Forest close at their backs. And then, before she could think, or seek internal guidance as her habit was, this whisper, muffled and very hurried, ran across her brain: "It's Mr. Sanderson. Call David in at once!"

And she had done so. Her shrill voice crossed the lawn and died away into the Forest, quickly smothered. No echo followed it. The sound fell dead against the rampart of a thousand listening trees.

"The damp is so very penetrating, even in summer," she murmured when they came obediently. She was half surprised at her open audacity, half repentant. They came so meekly at her call. "And my husband is sensitive to fever from the East. No, *please do not throw away your cigars. We can sit by the open window and enjoy the evening while you smoke.*"

She was very talkative for a moment; subconscious excitement was the cause.

"It is so still—so wonderfully still," she went on, as no one spoke; "so peaceful, and the air so very sweet ... and God is always near to those who need His aid." The words slipped out before she realized quite what she was saying, yet fortunately, in time to lower her voice, for no one heard them. They were, perhaps, an instinctive expression of relief. It flustered her that she could have said the thing at all.

Sanderson brought her shawl and helped to arrange the chairs; she thanked him in her old-fashioned, gentle way, declining the lamps which he had offered to light. "They attract the moths and insects so, I think!"

The three of them sat there in the gloaming. Mr. Bittacy's white moustache and his wife's yellow shawl gleaming at either end of the little horseshoe, Sanderson with his wild black hair and shining eyes midway between them. The painter went on talking softly, continuing evidently the conversation begun with his host beneath the cedar. Mrs. Bittacy, on her guard, listened—uneasily.

"For trees, you see, rather conceal themselves in daylight. They reveal themselves fully only after sunset. I never *know* a tree," he bowed here slightly towards the lady as though to apologize for something he felt she would not quite understand or like, "until I've seen it in the night. Your cedar, for instance," looking towards her husband again so that Mrs. Bittacy caught the gleaming of his turned eyes, "I failed with badly at first, because I did it in the morning. You shall see to-morrow what I mean—that first sketch is upstairs in my portfolio; it's quite another tree to the one you bought. That view"—he leaned forward, lowering his voice— "I caught one morning about two o'clock in very faint moonlight and the stars. I saw the naked being of the thing—"

"You mean that you went out, Mr. Sanderson, at that hour?" the old lady asked with astonishment and mild rebuke. She did not care particularly for his choice of adjectives either.

"I fear it was rather a liberty to take in another's house, perhaps," he answered courteously. "But, having chanced to wake, I saw the tree from my window, and made my way downstairs."

"It's a wonder Boxer didn't bit you; he sleeps loose in the hall," she said.

"On the contrary. The dog came out with me. I hope," he added, "the noise didn't disturb you, though it's rather late to say so. I feel quite guilty." His white teeth showed in the dusk as he smiled. A smell of earth and flowers stole in through the window on a breath of wandering air.

Mrs. Bittacy said nothing at the moment. "We both sleep like tops," put in her husband, laughing. "You're a courageous man, though, Sanderson, and, by Jove, the picture justifies you. Few artist would have taken so much trouble, though I read once that Holman Hunt, Rossetti, or some one of that lot, painted all night in his orchard to get an effect of moonlight that he wanted."

He chattered on. His wife was glad to hear his voice; it made her feel more easy in her mind. But presently the other held the floor again, and her thoughts grew darkened and afraid. Instinctively she feared the influence on her husband. The mystery and wonder that lie in woods, in forests, in great gatherings of trees everywhere, seemed so real and present while he talked.

"The Night transfigures all things in a way," he was saying; "but nothing so searchingly as trees. From behind a veil that sunlight hangs before them in the day they emerge and show themselves. Even buildings do that—in a measure—but trees particularly. In the daytime they sleep; at night they wake, they manifest, turn active—live. You remember," turning politely again in the direction of his hostess, "how clearly Henley understood that?"

"That socialist person, you mean?" asked the lady. Her tone and accent made the substantive sound criminal. It almost hissed, the way she uttered it.

"The poet, yes," replied the artist tactfully, "the friend of Stevenson, you remember, Stevenson who wrote those charming children's verses."

He quoted in a low voice the lines he meant. It was, for once, the time, the place, and the setting all together. The words floated out across the lawn towards the wall of blue darkness where the big Forest swept the little garden with its league-long curve that was like the shore-line of a sea. A wave of distant sound that was like surf accompanied his voice, as though the wind was fain to listen too:

> Not to the staring Day,
> For all the importunate questionings he pursues
> In his big, violent voice,
> Shall those mild things of bulk and multitude,
> The trees—God's sentinels ...
> Yield of their huge, unutterable selves
> But at the word
> Of the ancient, sacerdotal Night,
> Night of many secrets, whose effect—
> Transfiguring, hierophantic, dread—
> Themselves alone may fully apprehend,
> They tremble and are changed:
> In each the uncouth, individual soul
> Looms forth and glooms
> Essential, and, their bodily presences
> Touched with inordinate significance,
> Wearing the darkness like a livery
> Of some mysterious and tremendous guild,
> They brood—they menace—they appall.

The voice of Mrs. Bittacy presently broke the silence that followed.

"I like that part about God's sentinels," she murmured. There was no sharpness in her tone; it was hushed and quiet. The truth, so musically uttered, muted her shrill objections though it had not lessened her alarm. Her husband made no comment; his cigar, she noticed, had gone out.

"And old trees in particular," continued the artist, as though to himself, "have very definite personalities. You can offend, wound, please them; the moment you stand within their shade you feel whether they come out to you, or whether they withdraw." He turned abruptly towards his host. "You know that singular essay of Prentice Mulford's, no doubt— 'God in the Trees'—extravagant perhaps, but yet with a fine true beauty in it? You've never read it, no?" he asked.

But it was Mrs. Bittacy who answered; her husband keeping his curious deep silence.

"I never did!" It fell like a drip of cold water from the face muffled in the yellow shawl; even a child could have supplied the remainder of the unspoken thought.

"Ah," said Sanderson gently, "but there *is* 'God' in the trees. God in a very subtle aspect and sometimes—I have known the trees express it too—that which is *not* God—dark and terrible. Have you ever noticed, too, how clearly trees show what they want—choose their companions, at least? How beeches, for instance, allow no life too near them—birds or squirrels in their boughs, nor any growth beneath? The silence in the beech wood is quite terrifying often! And how pines like bilberry bushes at their feet and sometimes little oaks—all trees making a clear, deliberate choice, and holding firmly to it? Some trees obviously—it's very strange and marked—seem to prefer the human."

The old lady sat up crackling, for this was more than she could permit. Her stiff silk dress emitted little sharp reports.

"We know," she answered, "that He was said to have walked in the garden in the cool of the evening"—the gulp betrayed the effort that it cost her— "but we are nowhere told that He hid in the trees, or anything like that. Trees, after all, we must remember, are only large vegetables."

"True," was the soft answer, "but in everything that grows, has life, that is, there's mystery past all finding out. The wonder that lies hidden in our own souls lies also hidden, I venture to assert, in the stupidity and silence of a mere potato."

The observation was not meant to be amusing. It was not amusing. No one laughed. On the contrary, the words conveyed in too literal a sense the feeling that haunted all that conversation. Each one in his own way realized—with beauty, with wonder, with alarm—that the talk had somehow brought the whole vegetable kingdom nearer to that of man. Some link had been established between the two. It was not wise, with that great Forest listening at their very doors, to speak so plainly. The forest edged up closer while they did so.

And Mrs. Bittacy, anxious to interrupt the horrid spell, broke suddenly in upon it with a matter-of-fact suggestion. She did not like her husband's prolonged silence, stillness. He seemed so negative—so changed.

"David," she said, raising her voice, "I think you're feeling the dampness. It's grown chilly. The fever comes so suddenly, you know, and it might be wide to take the tincture. I'll go and get it, dear, at once. It's better." And before he could object she had left the room to bring the homeopathic dose that she believed in, and that, to please her, he swallowed by the tumbler-full from week to week.

And the moment the door closed behind her, Sanderson began again, though now in quite a different tone. Mr. Bittacy sat up in his chair. The two men obviously resumed the conversation—the real conversation interrupted beneath the cedar—and left aside the sham one which was so much dust merely thrown in the old lady's eyes.

"Trees love you, that's the fact," he said earnestly. "Your service to them all these years abroad has made them know you."

"Know me?"

"Made them, yes,"—he paused a moment, then added,— "made them *aware of your presence*; aware of a force outside themselves that deliberately seeks their welfare, don't you see?"

"By Jove, Sanderson—!" This put into plain language actual sensations he had felt, yet had never dared to phrase in words before. "They get into touch with me, as it were?" he ventured, laughing at his own sentence, yet laughing only with his lips.

"Exactly," was the quick, emphatic reply. "They seek to blend with something they feel instinctively to be good for them, helpful to their essential beings, encouraging to their best expression— their life."

"Good Lord, Sir!" Bittacy heard himself saying, "but you're putting my own thoughts into words. D'you know, I've felt something like that for years. As though—" he looked round to make sure his wife was not there, then finished the sentence— "as though the trees were after me!"

"'Amalgamate' seems the best word, perhaps," said Sanderson slowly. "They would draw you to themselves. Good forces, you see, always seek to merge; evil to separate; that's why Good in the end must always win the day—everywhere. The accumulation in the long run becomes overwhelming. Evil tends to separation, dissolution, death. The comradeship of trees, their instinct to run together, is a vital symbol. Trees in a mass are good; alone, you may take it generally, are—well, dangerous. Look at a monkey-puzzler, or better still, a holly. Look at it, watch it, understand it. Did you ever see more plainly an evil thought made visible? They're wicked.

Beautiful too, oh yes! There's a strange, miscalculated beauty often in evil—"

"That cedar, then—?"

"Not evil, no; but alien, rather. Cedars grow in forests all together. The poor thing has drifted, that is all."

They were getting rather deep. Sanderson, talking against time, spoke so fast. It was too condensed. Bittacy hardly followed that last bit. His mind floundered among his own less definite, less sorted thoughts, till presently another sentence from the artist startled him into attention again.

"That cedar will protect you here, though, because you both have humanized it by your thinking so lovingly of its presence. The others can't get past it, as it were."

"Protect me!" he exclaimed. "Protect me from their love?"

Sanderson laughed. "We're getting rather mixed," he said; "we're talking of one thing in the terms of another really. But what I mean is—you see—that their love for you, their 'awareness' of your personality and presence involves the idea of winning you—across the border—into themselves—into their world of living. It means, in a way, taking you over."

The ideas the artist started in his mind ran furious wild races to and fro. It was like a maze sprung suddenly into movement. The whirling of the intricate lines bewildered him. They went so fast, leaving but half an explanation of their goal. He followed first one, then another, but a new one always dashed across to intercept before he could get anywhere.

"But India," he said, presently in a lower voice, "India is so far away—from this little English forest. The trees, too, are utterly different for one thing?"

The rustle of skirts warned of Mrs. Bittacy's approach. This was a sentence he could turn round another way in case she came up and pressed for explanation.

"There is communion among trees all the world over," was the strange quick reply. "They always know."

"They always know! You think then—?"

"The winds, you see—the great, swift carriers! They have their ancient rights of way about the world. An easterly wind, for instance, carrying on stage by stage as it were—linking dropped messages and meanings from land to land like the birds—an easterly wind—"

Mrs. Bittacy swept in upon them with the tumbler—

"There, David," she said, "that will ward off any beginnings of attack. Just a spoonful, dear. Oh, oh! not *all!*" for he had swallowed half the contents at a single gulp as usual; "another dose before you go to bed, and the balance in the morning, first thing when you wake."

She turned to her guest, who put the tumbler down for her upon a table at his elbow. She had heard them speak of the east wind. She emphasized the warning she had misinterpreted. The private part of the conversation came to an abrupt end.

"It is the one thing that upsets him more than any other—an east wind," she said, "and I am glad, Mr. Sanderson, to hear you think so too."

III

A deep hush followed, in the middle of which an owl was heard calling its muffled note in the forest. A big moth whirred with a soft collision against one of the windows. Mrs. Bittacy started slightly, but no one spoke. Above the trees the stars were faintly visible. From the distance came the barking of a dog.

Bittacy, relighting his cigar, broke the little spell of silence that had caught all three.

"It's rather a comforting thought," he said, throwing the match out of the window, "that life is about us everywhere, and that there is really no dividing line between what we call organic and inorganic."

"The universe, yes," said Sanderson, "is all one, really. We're puzzled by the gaps we cannot see across, but as a fact, I suppose, there are no gaps at all."

Mrs. Bittacy rustled ominously, holding her peace meanwhile. She feared long words she did not understand. Beelzebub lay hid among too many syllables.

"In trees and plants especially, there dreams an exquisite life that no one yet has proved unconscious."

"Or conscious either, Mr. Sanderson," she neatly interjected. "It's only man that was made after His image, not shrubberies and things...."

Her husband interposed without delay.

"It is not necessary," he explained suavely, "to say that they're alive in the sense that we are alive. At the same time," with an eye to his wife, "I see no harm in holding, dear, that all created things contain some measure of His life Who made them. It's only beautiful to hold that He created nothing dead. We are not pantheists for all that!" he added soothingly.

"Oh, no! Not that, I hope!" The word alarmed her. It was worse than pope. Through her puzzled mind stole a stealthy, dangerous thing ... like a panther.

"I like to think that even in decay there's life," the painter murmured. "The falling apart of rotten wood breeds sentiency, there's force and motion in the falling of a dying leaf, in the breaking up and crumbling of everything indeed. And take an inert stone: it's crammed with heat and weight and potencies of all sorts. What holds its particles together indeed? We understand it as little as gravity or why a needle always turns to the 'North.' Both things may be a mode of life...."

"You think a compass has a soul, Mr. Sanderson?" exclaimed the lady with a crackling of her silk flounces that conveyed a sense of outrage even more plainly than her tone. The artist smiled to himself in the darkness, but it was Bittacy who hastened to reply.

"Our friend merely suggests that these mysterious agencies," he said quietly, "may be due to some kind of life we cannot understand. Why should water only run downhill? Why should trees grow at right angles to the surface of the ground and towards the sun? Why should the worlds spin for ever on their axes? Why should fire change the form of everything it touches without really destroying them? To say these things follow the law of their being explains nothing. Mr. Sanderson merely suggests—poetically, my dear, of course—that these may be manifestations of life, though life at a different stage to ours."

"The '*breath* of life,' we read, 'He breathed into them. These things do not breathe." She said it with triumph.

Then Sanderson put in a word. But he spoke rather to himself or to his host than by way of serious rejoinder to the ruffled lady.

"But plants do breathe too, you know," he said. "They breathe, they eat, they digest, they move about, and they adapt themselves to their environment as men and animals do. They have a nervous system too... at least a complex system of nuclei which have some of the qualities of nerve cells. They may have memory too. Certainly, they know definite action in response to stimulus. And though this may be physiological, no one has proved that it is only that, and not—psychological."

He did not notice, apparently, the little gasp that was audible behind the yellow shawl. Bittacy cleared his throat, threw his extinguished cigar upon the lawn, crossed and recrossed his legs.

"And in trees," continued the other, "behind a great forest, for instance," pointing towards the woods, "may stand a rather splendid Entity that manifests through all the thousand individual trees—some huge collective life, quite as minutely and delicately organized as our own. It might merge and blend with ours under certain conditions, so that we could understand it by *being* it, for a time at least. It might even engulf human vitality into the immense whirlpool of its own vast dreaming life. The pull of a big forest on a man can be tremendous and utterly overwhelming."

The mouth of Mrs. Bittacy was heard to close with a snap. Her shawl, and particularly her crackling dress, exhaled the protest that burned within her like a pain. She was too distressed to be over-awed, but at the same time too confused 'mid the litter of words and meanings half understood, to find immediate phrases she could use. Whatever the actual meaning of his language might be, however, and whatever subtle dangers lay concealed behind them meanwhile, they certainly wove a kind of gentle spell with the glimmering darkness that held all three delicately enmeshed there by that open window. The odors of dewy lawn, flowers, trees, and earth formed part of it.

"The moods," he continued, "that people waken in us are due to their hidden life affecting our own. Deep calls to sleep. A person, for instance, joins you in an empty room: you both instantly change. The new arrival, though in silence, has caused a change of mood. May not the moods of Nature touch and stir us in virtue of a similar prerogative? The sea, the hills, the desert, wake passion, joy, terror, as the case may be; for a few, perhaps," he glanced significantly at his host so that Mrs. Bittacy again caught the turning of his eyes, "emotions of a curious, flaming splendor that are quite nameless. Well ... whence come these powers? Surely from nothing that is ... dead! Does not the influence of a forest, its sway and strange ascendancy over certain minds, betray a direct manifestation of life? It lies otherwise beyond all explanation, this mysterious emanation of big woods. Some natures, of course, deliberately invite it.

The authority of a host of trees,"—his voice grew almost solemn as he said the words— "is something not to be denied. One feels it here, I think, particularly."

There was considerable tension in the air as he ceased speaking. Mr. Bittacy had not intended that the talk should go so far. They had drifted. He did not wish to see his wife unhappy or afraid, and he was aware—acutely so—that her feelings were stirred to a point he did not care about. Something in her, as he put it, was "working up" towards explosion.

He sought to generalize the conversation, diluting this accumulated emotion by spreading it.

"The sea is His and He made it," he suggested vaguely, hoping Sanderson would take the hint, "and with the trees it is the same...."

"The whole gigantic vegetable kingdom, yes," the artist took him up, "all at the service of man, for food, for shelter and for a thousand purposes of his daily life. Is it not striking what a lot of the globe they cover ... exquisitely organized life, yet stationary, always ready to our had when we want them, never running away? But the taking them, for all that, not so easy. One man shrinks from picking flowers, another from cutting down trees. And, it's curious that most of the forest tales and legends are dark, mysterious, and somewhat ill-omened. The forest-beings are rarely gay and harmless. The forest life was felt as terrible. Tree-worship still survives to-day. Wood-cutters... those who take the life of trees... you see a race of haunted men...."

He stopped abruptly, a singular catch in his voice. Bittacy felt something even before the sentences were over. His wife, he knew, felt it still more strongly. For it was in the middle of the heavy silence following upon these last remarks, that Mrs. Bittacy, rising with a violent abruptness from her chair, drew the attention of the others to something moving towards them across the lawn. It came silently. In outline it was large and curiously spread. It rose high, too, for the sky above the shrubberies, still pale gold from the sunset, was dimmed by its passage. She declared afterwards that it move in "looping circles," but what she perhaps meant to convey was "spirals."

She screamed faintly. "It's come at last! And it's you that brought it!"

She turned excitedly, half afraid, half angry, to Sanderson. With a breathless sort of gasp she said it, politeness all forgotten. "I knew it ... if you went on. I knew it. Oh! Oh!" And she cried again, "Your talking has brought it out!" The terror that shook her voice was rather dreadful.

But the confusion of her vehement words passed unnoticed in the first surprise they caused. For a moment nothing happened.

"What is it you think you see, my dear?" asked her husband, startled. Sanderson said nothing. All three leaned forward, the men still sitting, but Mrs. Bittacy had rushed hurriedly to the window, placing herself of a purpose, as it seemed, between her husband and the lawn. She pointed. Her little hand made a silhouette against the sky, the yellow shawl hanging from the arm like a cloud.

"Beyond the cedar—between it and the lilacs." The voice had lost its shrillness; it was thin and hushed. "There ... now you see it going round upon itself again—going back, thank God!... going back to the Forest." It sank to a whisper, shaking. She repeated, with a great dropping sigh of relief— "Thank God! I thought ... at first ... it was coming here ... to us!... David ... to *you!*"

She stepped back from the window, her movements confused, feeling in the darkness for the support of a chair, and finding her husband's outstretched hand instead. "Hold me, dear, hold me, please ... tight. Do not let me go." She was in what he called afterwards "a regular state." He drew her firmly down upon her chair again.

"Smoke, Sophie, my dear," he said quickly, trying to make his voice calm and natural. "I see it, yes. It's smoke blowing over from the gardener's cottage...."

"But, David,"—and there was a new horror in her whisper now— "it made a noise. It makes it still. I hear it swishing." Some such word she used—swishing, sishing, rushing, or something of the kind. "David, I'm very frightened. It's something awful! That man has called it out...!"

"Hush, hush," whispered her husband. He stroked her trembling hand beside him.

"It is in the wind," said Sanderson, speaking for the first time, very quietly. The expression on his face was not visible in the gloom, but his voice was soft and unafraid. At the sound of it, Mrs. Bittacy started violently again. Bittacy drew his chair a little forward to obstruct her view of him. He felt bewildered himself, a little, hardly knowing quite what to say or do. It was all so very curious and sudden.

But Mrs. Bittacy was badly frightened. It seemed to her that what she saw came from the enveloping forest just beyond their little garden. It emerged in a sort of secret way, moving towards them as with a purpose, stealthily, difficultly. Then something stopped it. It could not advance beyond the cedar. The cedar—this impression remained with her afterwards too—prevented, kept it back. Like a rising sea the Forest had surged a moment in their direction through the covering darkness, and this visible movement was its first wave. Thus to her mind it seemed... like that mysterious turn of the tide that used to frighten and mystify her in childhood on the sands. The outward surge of some enormous Power was what she felt... something to which every instinct in her being rose in opposition because it threatened her and hers. In that moment she realized the Personality of the Forest... menacing.

In the stumbling movement that she made away from the window and towards the bell she barely caught the sentence Sanderson—or was it her husband?—murmured to himself: "It came because we talked of it; our thinking made it aware of us and brought it out. But the cedar stops it. It cannot cross the lawn, you see...."

All three were standing now, and her husband's voice broke in with authority while his wife's fingers touched the bell.

"My dear, I should *not* say anything to Thompson." The anxiety he felt was manifest in his voice, but his outward composure had returned. "The gardener can go...."

Then Sanderson cut him short. "Allow me," he said quickly. "I'll see if anything's wrong." And before either of them could answer or object, he was gone, leaping out by the open window. They saw his figure vanish with a run across the lawn into the darkness.

A moment later the maid entered, in answer to the bell, and with her came the loud barking of the terrier from the hall.

"The lamps," said her master shortly, and as she softly closed the door behind her, they heard the wind pass with a mournful sound of singing round the outer walls. A rustle of foliage from the distance passed within it.

"You see, the wind *is* rising. It *was* the wind!" He put a comforting arm about her, distressed to feel that she was trembling. But he knew that he was trembling too, though with a kind of odd elation rather than alarm. "And it *was* smoke that you saw coming from Stride's cottage, or from the rubbish heaps he's been burning in the kitchen garden. The noise we heard was the branches rustling in the wind. Why should you be so nervous?"

A thin whispering voice answered him:

"I was afraid for *you*, dear. Something frightened me for *you*. That man makes me feel so uneasy and uncomfortable for his influence upon you. It's very foolish, I know. I think... I'm tired; I feel so overwrought and restless." The words poured out in a hurried jumble and she kept turning to the window while she spoke.

"The strain of having a visitor," he said soothingly, "has taxed you. We're so unused to having people in the house. He goes to-morrow." He warmed her cold hands between his own, stroking them tenderly. More, for the life of him, he could not say or do. The joy of a strange, internal excitement made his heart beat faster. He knew not what it was. He knew only, perhaps, whence it came.

She peered close into his face through the gloom, and said a curious thing. "I thought, David, for a moment... you seemed... different. My nerves are all on edge to-night." She made no further reference to her husband's visitor.

A sound of footsteps from the lawn warned of Sanderson's return, as he answered quickly in a lowered tone— "There's no need to be afraid on my account, dear girl. There's nothing wrong with me. I assure you; I never felt so well and happy in my life."

Thompson came in with the lamps and brightness, and scarcely had she gone again when Sanderson in turn was seen climbing through the window.

"There's nothing," he said lightly, as he closed it behind him. "Somebody's been burning leaves, and the smoke is drifting a little through the trees. The wind," he added, glancing at his host a moment significantly, but in so discreet a way that Mrs. Bittacy did not observe it, "the wind, too, has begun to roar... in the Forest... further out."

But Mrs. Bittacy noticed about him two things which increased her uneasiness. She noticed the shining of his eyes, because a similar light had suddenly come into her husband's; and she noticed, too, the apparent depth of meaning he put into those simple words that "the wind had begun to roar in the Forest ...further out." Her mind retained the disagreeable impression that he meant more than he said. In his tone lay quite another implication. It was not actually "wind" he spoke of, and it would not remain "further out"...rather, it was coming in. Another impression she got too—

still more unwelcome—was that her husband understood his hidden meaning.

IV

"David, dear," she observed gently as soon as they were alone
upstairs, "I have a horrible uneasy feeling about that man. I cannot get rid of it." The tremor in per voice caught all his tenderness.

He turned to look at her. "Of what kind, my dear? You're so
imaginative sometimes, aren't you?"

"I think," she hesitated, stammering a little, confused, still
frightened, "I mean—isn't he a hypnotist, or full of those theosophi-
cal ideas, or something of the sort? You know what I mean—"

He was too accustomed to her little confused alarms to explain
them away seriously as a rule, or to correct her verbal inaccura-
cies, but to-night he felt she needed careful, tender treatment. He
soothed her as best he could.

"But there's no harm in that, even if he is," he answered quietly.
"Those are only new names for very old ideas, you know, dear."
There was no trace of impatience in his voice.

"That's what I mean," she replied, the texts he dreaded rising
in an unuttered crowd behind the words. "He's one of those things
that we are warned would come—one of those Latter-Day things."
For her mind still bristled with the bogeys of the Antichrist and
Prophecy, and she had only escaped the Number of the Beast, as it
were, by the skin of her teeth. The Pope drew most of her fire usually, because she could understand him; the target was plain and
she could shoot. But this tree-and-forest business was so vague
and horrible. It terrified her. "He makes me think," she went on,
"of Principalities and Powers in high places, and of things that walk
in the darkness. I did *not* like the way he spoke of trees getting
alive in the night, and all that; it made me think of wolves in sheep's
clothing. And when I saw that awful thing in the sky above the
lawn—"

But he interrupted her at once, for that was something he had
decided it was best to leave unmentioned. Certainly it was better
not discussed.

"He only meant, I think, Sophie," he put in gravely, yet with a
little smile, "that trees may have a measure of conscious life—rather

a nice idea on the whole, surely,—something like that bit we read in the Times the other night, you remember—and that a big forest may possess a sort of Collective Personality. Remember, he's an artist, and poetical."

"It's dangerous," she said emphatically. "I feel it's playing with fire,unwise, unsafe—"

"Yet all to the glory of God," he urged gently. "We must not shut our ears and eyes to knowledge—of any kind, must we?"

"With you, David, the wish is always farther than the thought," she rejoined. For, like the child who thought that "suffered under Pontius Pilate" was "suffered under a bunch of violets," she heard her proverbs phonetically and reproduced them thus. She hoped to convey her warning in the quotation. "And we must always try the spirits whether they be of God," she added tentatively.

"Certainly, dear, we can always do that," he assented, getting into bed.

But, after a little pause, during which she blew the light out, David Bittacy settling down to sleep with an excitement in his blood that was new and bewilderingly delightful, realized that perhaps he had not said quite enough to comfort her. She was lying awake by his side, still frightened. He put his head up in the darkness.

"Sophie," he said softly, "you must remember, too, that in any case between us and—and all that sort of thing—there is a great gulf fixed, a gulf that cannot be crossed—er—while we are still in the body."

And hearing no reply, he satisfied himself that she was already asleep and happy. But Mrs. Bittacy was not asleep. She heard the sentence, only she said nothing because she felt her thought was better unexpressed. She was afraid to hear the words in the darkness. The Forest outside was listening and might hear them too—the Forest that was "roaring further out."

And the thought was this: That gulf, of course, existed, but Sanderson had somehow bridged it.

It was much later than night when she awoke out of troubled, uneasy dreams and heard a sound that twisted her very nerves with fear. It passed immediately with full waking, for, listen as she might, there was nothing audible but the inarticulate murmur of the night. It was in her dreams she heard it, and the dreams had vanished with it. But the sound was recognizable, for it was that rushing noise that had come across the lawn; only this time closer.

Just above her face while she slept had passed this murmur as of rustling branches in the very room, a sound of foliage whispering. "A going in the tops of the mulberry trees," ran through her mind. She had dreamed that she lay beneath a spreading tree somewhere, a tree that whispered with ten thousand soft lips of green; and the dream continued for a moment even after waking.

She sat up in bed and stared about her. The window was open at the top; she saw the stars; the door, she remembered, was locked as usual; the room, of course, was empty. The deep hush of the summer night lay over all, broken only by another sound that now issued from the shadows close beside the bed, a human sound, yet unnatural, a sound that seized the fear with which she had waked and instantly increased it. And, although it was one she recognized as familiar, at first she could not name it. Some seconds certainly passed—and, they were very long ones—before she understood that it was her husband talking in his sleep.

The direction of the voice confused and puzzled her, moreover, for it was not, as she first supposed, beside her. There was distance in it. The next minute, by the light of the sinking candle flame, she saw his white figure standing out in the middle of the room, half-way towards the window. The candle-light slowly grew. She saw him move then nearer to the window, with arms outstretched. His speech was low and mumbled, the words running together too much to be distinguishable.

And she shivered. To her, sleep-talking was uncanny to the point of horror; it was like the talking of the dead, mere parody of a living voice, unnatural.

"David!" she whispered, dreading the sound of her own voice, and half afraid to interrupt him and see his face. She could not bear the sight of the wide-opened eyes. "David, you're walking in your sleep. Do—come back to bed, dear, *please!*"

Her whisper seemed so dreadfully loud in the still darkness. At the sound of her voice he paused, then turned slowly round to face her. His widely-opened eyes stared into her own without recognition; they looked through her into something beyond; it was as though he knew the direction of the sound, yet cold not see her. They were shining, she noticed, as the eyes of Sanderson had shone several hours ago; and his face was flushed, distraught. Anxiety was written upon every feature. And, instantly, recognizing that the fever was upon him, she forgot her terror temporarily in practical considerations. He came back to bed without waking. She closed his eyelids. Presently he composed himself quietly to sleep, or rather to deeper sleep. She contrived to make him swallow something from the tumbler beside the bed.

Then she rose very quietly to close the window, feeling the night air blow in too fresh and keen. She put the candle where it could not reach him. The sight of the big Baxter Bible beside it comforted her a little, but all through her under-being ran the warnings of a curious alarm. And it was while in the act of fastening the catch with one hand and pulling the string of the blind with the other, that her husband sat up again in bed and spoke in words this time that were distinctly audible. The eyes had opened wide again. He pointed. She stood stock still and listened, her shadow distorted on the blind. He did not come out towards her as at first she feared.

The whispering voice was very clear, horrible, too, beyond all she had ever known.

"They are roaring in the Forest further out... and I... must go and see." He stared beyond her as he said it, to the woods. "They are needing me. They sent for me...." Then his eyes wandering back again to things within the room, he lay down, his purpose suddenly changed. And that change was horrible as well, more horrible, perhaps, because of its revelation of another detailed world he moved in far away from her.

The singular phrase chilled her blood, for a moment she was utterly terrified. That tone of the somnambulist, differing so slightly yet so distressingly from normal, waking speech, seemed to her somehow wicked. Evil and danger lay waiting thick behind it. She leaned against the window-sill, shaking in every limb. She had an awful feeling for a moment that something was coming in to fetch him.

"Not yet, then," she heard in a much lower voice from the bed, "but later. It will be better so... I shall go later...."

The words expressed some fringe of these alarms that had haunted her so long, and that the arrival and presence of Sanderson seemed to have brought to the very edge of a climax she could not even dare to think about. They gave it form; they brought it closer; they sent her thoughts to her Deity in a wild, deep prayer for help and guidance. For here was a direct, unconscious betrayal of a world of inner purposes and claims her husband recognized while he kept them almost wholly to himself.

By the time she reached his side and knew the comfort of his touch, the eyes had closed again, this time of their own accord, and the head lay calmly back upon the pillows. She gently straightened the bed clothes. She watched him for some minutes, shading the candle carefully with one hand. There was a smile of strangest peace upon the face.

Then, blowing out the candle, she knelt down and prayed before getting back into bed. But no sleep came to her. She lay awake all night thinking, wondering, praying, until at length with the chorus of the birds and the glimmer of the dawn upon the green blind, she fell into a slumber of complete exhaustion.

But while she slept the wind continued roaring in the Forest further out. The sound came closer—sometimes very close indeed.

V

With the departure of Sanderson the significance of the curious incidents waned, because the moods that had produced them passed away. Mrs. Bittacy soon afterwards came to regard them as some growth of disproportion that had been very largely, perhaps, in her own mind. It did not strike her that this change was sudden for it came about quite naturally. For one thing her husband never spoke of the matter, and for another she remembered how many things in life that had seemed inexplicable and singular at the time turned out later to have been quite commonplace.

Most of it, certainly, she put down to the presence of the artist and to his wild, suggestive talk. With his welcome removal, the world turned ordinary again and safe. The fever, though it lasted as usual a short time only, had not allowed of her husband's getting up to say good-bye, and she had conveyed his regrets and adieux. In the morning Mr. Sanderson had seemed ordinary enough. In his town hat and gloves, as she saw him go, he seemed tame and unalarming.

"After all," she thought as she watched the pony-cart bear him off, "he's only an artist!" What she had thought he might be otherwise her slim imagination did not venture to disclose. Her change of feeling was wholesome and refreshing. She felt a little ashamed of her behavior. She gave him a smile—genuine because the relief she felt was genuine—as he bent over her hand and kissed it, but she did not suggest a second visit, and her husband, she noted with satisfaction and relief, had said nothing either.

The little household fell again into the normal and sleepy routine to which it was accustomed. The name of Arthur Sanderson was rarely if ever mentioned. Nor, for her part, did she mention to her husband the incident of his walking in his sleep and the wild words he used. But to forget it was equally impossible. Thus it lay buried deep within her like a center of some unknown disease of which it was a mysterious symptom, waiting to spread at the first favorable opportunity. She prayed against it every night and morning: prayed that she might forget it—that God would keep her husband safe from harm.

For in spite of much surface foolishness that many might have read as weakness. Mrs. Bittacy had balance, sanity, and a fine deep faith. She was greater than she knew. Her love for her husband and her God were somehow one, an achievement only possible to a single-hearted nobility of soul.

There followed a summer of great violence and beauty; of beauty, because the refreshing rains at night prolonged the glory of the spring and spread it all across July, keeping the foliage young and sweet; of violence, because the winds that tore about the south of England brushed the whole country into dancing movement. They swept the woods magnificently, and kept them roaring with a perpetual grand voice. Their deepest notes seemed never to leave the sky. They sang and shouted, and torn leaves raced and fluttered through the air long before their usually appointed time. Many a tree, after days of roaring and dancing, fell exhausted to the ground. The cedar on the lawn gave up two limbs that fell upon successive days, at the same hour too—just before dusk. The wind often makes its most boisterous effort at that time, before it drops with the sun, and these two huge branches lay in dark ruin covering half the lawn. They spread across it and towards the house. They left an ugly gaping space upon the tree, so that the Lebanon looked unfinished, half destroyed, a monster shorn of its old-time comeliness and splendor. Far more of the Forest was now visible than before; it peered through the breach of the broken defenses. They could see from the windows of the house now—especially from the drawing-room and bedroom windows—straight out into the glades and depths beyond.

Mrs. Bittacy's niece and nephew, who were staying on a visit at the time, enjoyed themselves immensely helping the gardeners carry off the fragments. It took two days to do this, for Mr. Bittacy insisted on the branches being moved entire. He would not allow them to be chopped; also, he would not consent to their use as firewood. Under his superintendence the unwieldy masses were dragged to the edge of the garden and arranged upon the frontier line between the Forest and the lawn. The children were delighted with the scheme. They entered into it with enthusiasm. At all costs this defense against the inroads of the Forest must be made secure. They caught their uncle's earnestness, felt even something of a hidden motive that he had; and the visit, usually rather dreaded, became the visit of their lives instead. It was Aunt Sophia this time who seemed discouraging and dull.

"She's got so old and funny," opined Stephen.

But Alice, who felt in the silent displeasure of her aunt some secret thing that alarmed her, said:

"I think she's afraid of the woods. She never comes into them with us, you see."

"All the more reason then for making this wall impreg—all fat and thick and solid," he concluded, unable to manage the longer word. "Then nothing—simply *nothing*—can get through. Can't it, Uncle David?"

And Mr. Bittacy, jacket discarded and working in his speckled waistcoat, went puffing to their aid, arranging the massive limb of the cedar like a hedge.

"Come on," he said, "whatever happens, you know, we must finish before it's dark. Already the wind is roaring in the Forest further out." And Alice caught the phrase and instantly echoed it. "Stevie," she cried below her breath, "look sharp, you lazy lump. Didn't you hear what Uncle David said? It'll come in and catch us before we've done!"

They worked like Trojans, and, sitting beneath the wisteria tree that climbed the southern wall of the cottage, Mrs. Bittacy with her knitting watched them, calling from time to time insignificant messages of counsel and advice. The messages passed, of course, unheeded. Mostly, indeed, they were unheard, for the workers were too absorbed. She warned her husband not to get too hot, Alice not to tear her dress, Stephen not to strain his back with pulling. Her mind hovered between the homeopathic medicine-chest upstairs and her anxiety to see the business finished.

For this breaking up of the cedar had stirred again her slumbering alarms. It revived memories of the visit of Mr. Sanderson that had been sinking into oblivion; she recalled his queer and odious way of talking, and many things she hoped forgotten drew their heads up from that subconscious region to which all forgetting is impossible. They looked at her and nodded. They were full of life; they had no intention of being pushed aside and buried permanently. "Now look!" they whispered, "didn't we tell you so?" They had been merely waiting the right moment to assert their presence. And all her former vague distress crept over her. Anxiety, uneasiness returned. That dreadful sinking of the heart came too.

This incident of the cedar's breaking up was actually so unimportant, and yet her husband's attitude towards it made it so significant. There was nothing that he said in particular, or did, or left undone that frightened, her, but his general air of earnestness seemed so unwarranted. She felt that he deemed the thing important. He was so exercised about it. This evidence of sudden concern and interest, buried all the summer from her sight and knowledge, she realized now had been buried purposely, he had kept it intentionally concealed. Deeply submerged in him there ran this tide of other thoughts, desires, hopes. What were they? Whither did they lead? The accident to the tree betrayed it most unpleasantly, and, doubtless, more than he was aware.

She watched his grave and serious face as he worked there with the children, and as she watched she felt afraid. It vexed her that the children worked so eagerly. They unconsciously supported him. The thing she feared she would not even name. But it was waiting.

Moreover, as far as her puzzled mind could deal with a dread so vague and incoherent, the collapse of the cedar somehow brought it nearer. The fact that, all so ill-explained and formless, the thing yet lay in her consciousness, out of reach but moving and alive, filled her with a kind of puzzled, dreadful wonder. Its presence was so very real, its power so gripping, its partial concealment so abominable. Then, out of the dim confusion, she grasped one thought and saw it stand quite clear before her eyes. She found difficulty in clothing it in words, but its meaning perhaps was this: That cedar stood in their life for something friendly; its downfall meant disaster; a sense of some protective influence about the cottage, and about her husband in particular, was thereby weakened.

"Why do you fear the big winds so?" he had asked her several days before, after a particularly boisterous day; and the answer she gave surprised her while she gave it. One of those heads poked up unconsciously, and let slip the truth.

"Because, David, I feel they—bring the Forest with them," she faltered. "They blow something from the trees—into the mind—into the house."

He looked at her keenly for a moment.

"That must be why I love them then," he answered. "They blow the souls of the trees about the sky like clouds."

The conversation dropped. She had never heard him talk in quite that way before.

And another time, when he had coaxed her to go with him down one of the nearer glades, she asked why he took the small hand-axe with him, and what he wanted it for.

"To cut the ivy that clings to the trunks and takes their life away," he said.

"But can't the verdurers do that?" she asked. "That's what they're paid for, isn't it?"

Whereupon he explained that ivy was a parasite the trees knew not how to fight alone, and that the verdurers were careless and did not do it thoroughly. They gave a chop here and there, leaving the tree to do the rest for itself if it could.

"Besides, I like to do it for them. I love to help them and protect," he added, the foliage rustling all about his quiet words as they went.

And these stray remarks, as his attitude towards the broken cedar, betrayed this curious, subtle change that was going forward to his personality. Slowly and surely all the summer it had increased.

It was growing—the thought startled her horribly—just as a tree grows, the outer evidence from day to day so slight as to be unnoticeable, yet the rising tide so deep and irresistible. The alteration spread all through and over him, was in both mind and actions, sometimes almost in his face as well. Occasionally, thus, it stood up straight outside himself and frightened her. His life was somehow becoming linked so intimately with trees, and with all that trees signified. His interests became more and more their interests, his activity combined with theirs, his thoughts and feelings theirs, his purpose, hope, desire, his fate—

His fate! The darkness of some vague, enormous terror dropped its shadow on her when she thought of it. Some instinct in her heart she dreaded infinitely more than death—for death meant sweet translation for his soul—came gradually to associate the thought of him with the thought of trees, in particular with these Forest trees. Sometimes, before she could face the thing, argue it away, or pray it into silence, she found the thought of him running swiftly through her mind like a thought of the Forest itself, the two most intimately linked and joined together, each a part and complement of the other, one being.

The idea was too dim for her to see it face to face. Its mere possibility dissolved the instant she focused it to get the truth behind it. It was too utterly elusive, made, protæan. Under the attack of even a minute's concentration the very meaning of it vanished, melted away. The idea lay really behind any words that she could ever find, beyond the touch of definite thought.

Her mind was unable to grapple with it. But, while it vanished, the trail of its approach and disappearance flickered a moment before her shaking vision. The horror certainly remained.

Reduced to the simple human statement that her temperament sought instinctively, it stood perhaps at this: Her husband loved her, and he loved the trees as well; but the trees came first, claimed parts of him she did not know. *She* loved her God and him. *He* loved the trees and her.

Thus, in guise of some faint, distressing compromise, the matter shaped itself for her perplexed mind in the terms of conflict. A silent, hidden battle raged, but as yet raged far away. The breaking of the cedar was a visible outward fragment of a distant and mysterious encounter that was coming daily closer to them both. The wind, instead of roaring in the Forest further out, now cam nearer, booming in fitful gusts about its edge and frontiers.

Meanwhile the summer dimmed. The autumn winds went sighing through the woods, leaves turned to golden red, and the evenings were drawing in with cozy shadows before the first sign of anything seriously untoward made its appearance. It came then with a flat, decided kind of violence that indicated mature preparation beforehand. It was not impulsive nor ill-considered. In a fashion it seemed expected, and indeed inevitable. For within a fortnight of their annual change to the little village of Seillans above St. Raphael—a change so regular for the past ten years that it was not even discussed between them—David Bittacy abruptly refused to go.

Thompson had laid the tea-table, prepared the spirit lamp beneath the urn, pulled down the blinds in that swift and silent way she had, and left the room. The lamps were still unlit. The firelight shone on the chintz armchairs, and Boxer lay asleep on the black horse-hair rug. Upon the walls the gilt picture frames gleamed faintly, the pictures themselves indistinguishable. Mrs. Bittacy had warmed the teapot and was in the act of pouring the water in to heat the cups when her husband, looking up from his chair across the hearth, made the abrupt announcement:

"My dear," he said, as though following a train of thought of which she only heard this final phrase, "it's really quite impossible for me to go."

And so abrupt, inconsequent, it sounded that she at first misunderstood. She thought he meant to go out into the garden or the woods. But her heart leaped all the same. The tone of his voice was ominous.

"Of course not," she answered, "it would be *most* unwise. Why should you—?" She referred to the mist that always spread on autumn nights upon the lawn, but before she finished the sentence she knew that *he* referred to something else. And her heart then gave its second horrible leap.

"David! You mean abroad?" she gasped.

"I mean abroad, dear, yes."

It reminded her of the tone he used when saying good-bye years ago, before one of those jungle expeditions she dreaded. His voice then was so serious, so final. It was serious and final now. For several moments she could think of nothing to say. She busied herself with the teapot. She had filled one cup with hot water till it overflowed, and she emptied it slowly into the slop-basin, trying with all her might not to let him see the trembling of her hand. The firelight and the dimness of the room both helped her. But in any case he would hardly have noticed it. His thoughts were far away....

VI

Mrs. Bittacy had never liked their present home. She preferred a flat, more open country that left approaches clear. She liked to see things coming. This cottage on the very edge of the old hunting grounds of William the Conqueror had never satisfied her ideal of a safe and pleasant place to settle down in. The sea-coast, with treeless downs behind and a clear horizon in front, as at Eastbourne, say, was her ideal of a proper home.

It was curious, this instinctive aversion she felt to being shut in—by trees especially; a kind of claustrophobia almost; probably due, as has been said, to the days in India when the trees took her husband off and surrounded him with dangers. In those weeks of solitude the feeling had matured. She had fought it in her fashion, but never conquered it. Apparently routed, it had a way of creeping back in other forms. In this particular case, yielding to his strong desire, she thought the battle won, but the terror of the trees came back before the first month had passed. They laughed in her face.

She never lost knowledge of the fact that the leagues of forest lay about their cottage like a mighty wall, a crowding, watching, listening presence that shut them in from freedom and escape. Far from morbid naturally, she did her best to deny the thought, and so simple and unartificial was her type of mind that for weeks together she would wholly lose it. Then, suddenly it would return upon her with a rush of bleak reality. It was not only in her mind; it existed apart from any mere mood; a separate fear that walked alone; it came and went, yet when it went—went only to watch her from another point of view. It was in abeyance—hidden round the corner.

The Forest never let her go completely. It was ever ready to encroach. All the branches, she sometimes fancied, stretched one way—towards their tiny cottage and garden, as though it sought to draw them in and merge them in itself. Its great, deep-breathing soul resented the mockery, the insolence, the irritation of the prim garden at its very gates. It would absorb and smother them if it could. And every wind that blew its thundering message over the huge sounding-board of the million, shaking trees conveyed the purpose that it had. They had angered its great soul. At its heart was this deep, incessant roaring.

All this she never framed in words, the subtleties of language lay far beyond her reach. But instinctively she felt it; and more besides. It troubled her profoundly. Chiefly, moreover, for her husband. Merely for herself, the nightmare might have left her cold. It was David's peculiar interest in the trees that gave the special invitation. Jealousy, then, in its most subtle aspect came to strengthen this aversion and dislike, for it came in a form that no reasonable wife could possibly object to. Her husband's passion, she reflected, was natural and inborn. It had decided his vocation, fed his ambition, nourished his dreams, desires, hopes. All his best years of active life had been spent in the care and guardianship of trees. He knew them, understood their secret life and nature, "managed" them intuitively as other men "managed" dogs and horses. He could not live for long away from them without a strange, acute nostalgia that stole his peace of mind and consequently his strength of body. A forest made him happy and at peace; it nursed and fed and soothed his deepest moods. Trees influenced the sources of his life, lowered or raised the very heart-beat in him. Cut off from them he languished as a lover of the sea can droop inland, or a mountaineer may pine in the flat monotony of the plains.

This she could understand, in a fashion at least, and make allowances for. She had yielded gently, even sweetly, to his choice of their English home; for in the little island there is nothing that suggests the woods of wilder countries so nearly as the New Forest. It has the genuine air and mystery, the depth and splendor, the loneliness, and there and there the strong, untamable quality of old-time forests as Bittacy of the Department knew them.

In a single detail only had he yielded to her wishes. He consented to a cottage on the edge, instead of in the heart of it. And for a dozen years now they had dwelt in peace and happiness at the lips of this great spreading thing that covered so many leagues with its tangle of swamps and moors and splendid ancient trees.

Only with the last two years or so—with his own increasing age, and physical decline perhaps—had come this marked growth of passionate interest in the welfare of the Forest. She had watched it grow, at first had laughed at it, then talked sympathetically so far as sincerity permitted, then had argued mildly, and finally come to realize that its treatment lay altogether beyond her powers, and so had come to fear it with all her heart.

The six weeks they annually spent away from their English home, each regarded very differently, of course. For her husband it meant a painful exile that did his health no good; he yearned for his trees—the sight and sound and smell of them; but for herself it meant release from a haunting dread—escape. To renounce those six weeks by the sea on the sunny, shining coast of France, was almost more than this little woman, even with her unselfishness, could face.

After the first shock of the announcement, she reflected as deeply as her nature permitted, prayed, wept in secret—and made up her mind. Duty, she felt clearly, pointed to renouncement. The discipline would certainly be severe—she did not dream at the moment how severe!—but this fine, consistent little Christian saw it plain; she accepted it, too, without any sighing of the martyr, though the courage she showed was of the martyr order. Her husband should never know the cost. In all but this one passion his unselfishness was ever as great as her own. The love she had borne him all these years, like the love she bore her anthropomorphic deity, was deep and real. She loved to suffer for them both. Besides, the way her husband had put it to her was singular. It did not take the form of a mere selfish predilection. Something higher than two wills in conflict seeking compromise was in it from the beginning.

"I feel, Sophia, it would be really more than I could manage," he said slowly, gazing into the fire over the tops of his stretched-out muddy boots. "My duty and my happiness lie here with the Forest and with you. My life is deeply rooted in this place. Something I can't define connects my inner being with these trees, and separation would make me ill—might even kill me. My hold on life would weaken; here is my source of supply. I cannot explain it better than that." He looked up steadily into her face across the table so that she saw the gravity of his expression and the shining of his steady eyes.

"David, you feel it as strongly as that!" she said, forgetting the tea things altogether.

"Yes," he replied, "I do. And it's not of the body only, I feel it in my soul."

The reality of what he hinted at crept into that shadow-covered room like an actual Presence and stood beside them. It came not by the windows or the door, but it filled the entire space between the walls and ceiling. It took the heat from the fire before her face. She felt suddenly cold, confused a little, frightened. She almost felt the rush of foliage in the wind. It stood between them.

"There are things—some things," she faltered, "we are not intended to know, I think." The words expressed her general attitude to life, not alone to this particular incident.

And after a pause of several minutes, disregarding the criticism as though he had not heard it— "I cannot explain it better than that, you see," his grave voice answered. "There is this deep, tremendous link,—some secret power they emanate that keeps me well and happy and—alive. If you cannot understand, I feel at least you may be able to—forgive." His tone grew tender, gentle, soft. "My selfishness, I know, must seem quite unforgivable. I cannot help it somehow; these trees, this ancient Forest, both seem knitted into all that makes me live, and if I go—"

There was a little sound of collapse in his voice. He stopped abruptly, and sank back in his chair. And, at that, a distinct lump came up into her throat which she had great difficulty in managing while she went over and put her arms about him.

"My dear," she murmured, "God will direct. We will accept His guidance. He has always shown the way before."

"My selfishness afflicts me—" he began, but she would not let him finish.

"David, He will direct. Nothing shall harm you. You've never once been selfish, and I cannot bear to hear you say such things. The way will open that is best for you—for both of us." She kissed him, she would not let him speak; her heart was in her throat, and she felt for him far more than for herself.

And then he had suggested that she should go alone perhaps for a shorter time, and stay in her brother's villa with the children, Alice and Stephen. It was always open to her as she well knew.

"You need the change," he said, when the lamps had been lit and the servant had gone out again; "you need it as much as I dread it. I could manage somehow until you returned, and should feel happier that way if you went. I cannot leave this Forest that I love so well. I even feel, Sophie dear"—he sat up straight and faced her as he half whispered it— "that I can *never* leave it again. My life and happiness lie here together."

And eve while scorning the idea that she could leave him alone with the Influence of the Forest all about him to have its unimpeded way, she felt the pangs of that subtle jealousy bite keen and close. He loved the Forest better than herself, for he placed it first. Behind the words, moreover, hid the unuttered thought that made her so uneasy. The terror Sanderson had brought revived and shook its wings before her very eyes. For the whole conversation, of which this was a fragment, conveyed the unutterable implication that while he could not spare the trees, they equally could not spare him. The vividness with which he managed to conceal and yet betray

the fact brought a profound distress that crossed the border between presentiment and warning into positive alarm.

He clearly felt that the trees would miss him—the trees he
tended, guarded, watched over, loved.

"David, I shall stay here with you. I think you need me really,—
don't you?" Eagerly, with a touch of heart-felt passion, the words
poured out.

"Now more than ever, dear. God bless you for you sweet unselfishness. And your sacrifice," he added, "is all the greater because you cannot understand the thing that makes it necessary for
me to stay."

"Perhaps in the spring instead—" she said, with a tremor in the
voice.

"In the spring—perhaps," he answered gently, almost beneath his
breath. "For they will not need me then. All the world can love them
in the spring. It's in the winter that they're lonely and neglected. I
wish to stay with them particularly then. I even feel I ought to—
and I must."

And in this way, without further speech, the decision was made.
Mrs. Bittacy, at least, asked no more questions. Yet she could not
bring herself to show more sympathy than was necessary. She felt,
for one thing, that if she did, it might lead him to speak freely, and
to tell her things she could not possibly bear to know. And she dared
not take the risk of that.

VII

This was at the end of summer, but the autumn followed close.
The conversation really marked the threshold between the two seasons, and marked at the same time the line between her husband's
negative and aggressive state. She almost felt she had done wrong
to yield; he grew so bold, concealment all discarded. He went, that
is, quite openly to the woods, forgetting all his duties, all his former
occupations. He even sought to coax her to go with him. The hidden thing blazed out without disguise. And, while she trembled at
his energy, she admired the virile passion he displayed. Her jealousy had long ago retired before her fear, accepting the second
place. Her one desire now was to protect. The wife turned wholly
mother.

He said so little, but—he hated to come in. From morning to night he wandered in the Forest; often he went out after dinner; his mind was charged with trees—their foliage, growth, development; their wonder, beauty, strength; their loneliness in isolation, their power in a herded mass. He knew the effect of every wind upon them; the danger from the boisterous north, the glory from the west, the eastern dryness, and the soft, moist tenderness that a south wind left upon their thinning boughs. He spoke all day of their sensations: how they drank the fading sunshine, dreamed in the moonlight, thrilled to the kiss of stars. The dew could bring them half the passion of the night, but frost sent them plunging beneath the ground to dwell with hopes of a later coming softness in their roots. They nursed the life they carried—insects, larvae, chrysalis—and when the skies above them melted, he spoke of them standing "motionless in an ecstasy of rain," or in the noon of sunshine "self-poised upon their prodigy of shade."

And once in the middle of the night she woke at the sound of his voice, and heard him—wide awake, not talking in his sleep—but talking towards the window where the shadow of the cedar fell at noon:

O art thou sighing for Lebanon
In the long breeze that streams to thy delicious East?
Sighing for Lebanon,
Dark cedar;

and, when, half charmed, half terrified, she turned and called to him by name, he merely said—

"My dear, I felt the loneliness—suddenly realized it—the alien desolation of that tree, set here upon our little lawn in England when all her Eastern brothers call her in sleep." And the answer seemed so queer, so "un-evangelical," that she waited in silence till he slept again. The poetry passed her by. It seemed unnecessary and out of place. It made her ache with suspicion, fear, jealousy.

The fear, however, seemed somehow all lapped up and banished soon afterwards by her unwilling admiration of the rushing splendor of her husband's state. Her anxiety, at any rate, shifted from the religious to the medical. She thought he might be losing his steadiness of mind a little. How often in her prayers she offered thanks for the guidance that had made her stay with him to help and watch is impossible to say. It certainly was twice a day.

She even went so far once, when Mr. Mortimer, the vicar, called, and brought with him a more or less distinguished doctor—as to tell the professional man privately some symptoms of her husband's queerness. And his answer that there was "nothing he could prescribe for" added not a little to her sense of unholy bewilderment. No doubt Sir James had never been "consulted" under such unorthodox conditions before. His sense of what was becoming naturally overrode his acquired instincts as a skilled instrument that might help the race.

"No fever, you think?" she asked insistently with hurry, determined to get something from him.

"Nothing that *I* can deal with, as I told you, Madam," replied the offended allopathic Knight.

Evidently he did not care about being invited to examine patients in this surreptitious way before a teapot on the lawn, chance of a fee most problematical. He liked to see a tongue and feel a thumping pulse; to know the pedigree and bank account of his questioner as well. It was most unusual, in abominable taste besides. Of course it was. But the drowning woman seized the only straw she could.

For now the aggressive attitude of her husband overcame her to the point where she found it difficult even to question him. Yet in the house he was so kind and gentle, doing all he could to make her sacrifice as easy as possible.

"David, you really *are* unwise to go out now. The night is damp and very chilly. The ground is soaked in dew. You'll catch your death of cold."

His face lightened. "Won't you come with me, dear,—just for once? I'm only going to the corner of the hollies to see the beech that stands so lonely by itself."

She had been out with him in the short dark afternoon, and they had passed that evil group of hollies where the gypsies camped. Nothing else would grow there, but the hollies thrive upon the stony soil.

"David, the beech is all right and safe." She had learned his phraseology a little, made clever out of due season by her love. "There's no wind to-night."

"But it's rising," he answered, "rising in the east. I heard it in the bare and hungry larches. They need the sun and dew, and always cry out when the wind's upon them from the east."

She sent a short unspoken prayer most swiftly to her deity as she heard him say it. For every time now, when he spoke in this familiar, intimate way of the life of the trees, she felt a sheet of cold fasten tight against her very skin and flesh. She shivered. How could he possibly know such things?

Yet, in all else, and in the relations of his daily life, he was sane and reasonable, loving, kind and tender. It was only on the subject of the trees he seemed unhinged and queer. Most curiously it seemed that, since the collapse of the cedar they both loved, though in different fashion, his departure from the normal had increased. Why else did he watch them as a man might watch a sickly child? Why did he hunger especially in the dusk to catch their "mood of night" as he called it? Why think so carefully upon them when the frost was threatening or the wind appeared to rise?

As she put it so frequently now herself—How could he possibly *know* such things?

He went. As she closed the front door after him she heard the distant roaring in the Forest.

And then it suddenly struck her: How could she know them too?

It dropped upon her like a blow that she felt at once all over, upon body, heart and mind. The discovery rushed out from its ambush to overwhelm. The truth of it, making all arguing futile, numbed her faculties. But though at first it deadened her, she soon revived, and her being rose into aggressive opposition. A wild yet calculated courage like that which animates the leaders of splendid forlorn hopes flamed in her little person—flamed grandly, and invincible. While knowing herself insignificant and weak, she knew at the same time that power at her back which moves the worlds. The faith that filled her was the weapon in her hands, and the right by which she claimed it; but the spirit of utter, selfless sacrifice that characterized her life was the means by which she mastered its immediate use. For a kind of white and faultless intuition guided her to the attack. Behind her stood her Bible and her God.

How so magnificent a divination came to her at all may well be a matter for astonishment, though some clue of explanation lies, perhaps, in the very simpleness of her nature. At any rate, she saw quite clearly certain things; saw them in moments only—after prayer, in the still silence of the night, or when left alone those long hours in the house with her knitting and her thoughts—and the guidance which then flashed into her remained, even after the manner of its coming was forgotten.

They came to her, these things she saw, formless, wordless; she could not put them into any kind of language; but by the very fact of being uncaught in sentences they retained their original clear vigor.

Hours of patient waiting brought the first, and the others followed easily afterwards, by degrees, on subsequent days, a little and a little. Her husband had been gone since early morning, and had taken his luncheon with him. She was sitting by the tea things, the cups and teapot warmed, the muffins in the fender keeping hot, all ready for his return, when she realized quite abruptly that this thing which took him off, which kept him out so many hours day after day, this thing that was against her own little will and instincts—was enormous as the sea. It was no mere prettiness of single Trees, but something massed and mountainous. About her rose the wall of its huge opposition to the sky, its scale gigantic, its power utterly prodigious. What she knew of it hitherto as green and delicate forms waving and rustling in the winds was but, as it were the spray of foam that broke into sight upon the nearer edge of viewless depths far, far away. The trees, indeed, were sentinels set visibly about the limits of a camp that itself remained invisible. The awful hum and murmur of the main body in the distance passed into that still room about her with the firelight and hissing kettle. Out yonder—in the Forest further out—the thing that was ever roaring at the center was dreadfully increasing.

The sense of definite battle, too—battle between herself and the Forest for his soul—came with it. Its presentiment was as clear as though Thompson had come into the room and quietly told her that the cottage was surrounded. "Please, ma'am, there are trees come up about the house," she might have suddenly announced. And equally might have heard her own answer: "It's all right, Thompson. The main body is still far away."

Immediately upon its heels, then, came another truth, with a close reality that shocked her. She saw that jealousy was not confined to the human and animal world alone, but ran though all creation. The Vegetable Kingdom knew it too. So-called inanimate nature shared it with the rest. Trees felt it. This Forest just beyond the window—standing there in the silence of the autumn evening across the little lawn—this Forest understood it equally. The remorseless, branching power that sought to keep exclusively for itself the thing it loved and needed, spread like a running desire through all its million leaves and stems and roots. In humans, of course, it was consciously directed; in animals it acted with frank instinctiveness;

but in trees this jealousy rose in some blind tide of impersonal and unconscious wrath that would sweep opposition from its path as the wind sweeps powdered snow from the surface of the ice. Their number was a host with endless reinforcements, and once it realized its passion was returned the power increased.... Her husband loved the trees.... They had become aware of it.... They would take him from her in the end....

Then, while she heard his footsteps in the hall and the closing of the front door, she saw a third thing clearly;—realized the widening of the gap between herself and him. This other love had made it. All these weeks of the summer when she felt so close to him, now especially when she had made the biggest sacrifice of her life to stay by his side and help him, he had been slowly, surely—drawing away. The estrangement was here and now—a fact accomplished. It had been all this time maturing; there yawned this broad deep space between them. Across the empty distance she saw the change in merciless perspective. It revealed his face and figure, dearly-loved, once fondly worshipped, far on the other side in shadowy distance, small, the back turned from her, and moving while she watched—moving away from her.

They had their tea in silence then. She asked no questions, he volunteered no information of his day. The heart was big within her, and the terrible loneliness of age spread through her like a rising icy mist. She watched him, filling all his wants. His hair was untidy and his boots were caked with blackish mud. He moved with a restless, swaying motion that somehow blanched her cheek and sent a miserable shivering down her back. It reminded her of trees. His eyes were very bright.

He brought in with him an odor of the earth and forest that seemed to choke her and make it difficult to breathe; and—what she noticed with a climax of almost uncontrollable alarm—upon his face beneath the lamplight shone traces of a mild, faint glory that made her think of moonlight falling upon a wood through speckled shadows. It was his new-found happiness that shone there, a happiness uncaused by her and in which she had no part.

In his coat was a spray of faded yellow beech leaves. "I brought this from the Forest to you," he said, with all the air that belonged to his little acts of devotion long ago. And she took the spray of leaves mechanically with a smile and a murmured "thank you, dear," as though he had unknowingly put into her hands the weapon for her own destruction and she had accepted it.

And when the tea was over and he left the room, he did not go to his study, or to change his clothes. She heard the front door softly shut behind him as he again went out towards the Forest.

A moment later she was in her room upstairs, kneeling beside the bed—the side she slept on—and praying wildly through a flood of tears that God would save and keep him to her. Wind brushed the window panes behind her while she knelt.

VIII

One sunny November morning, when the strain had reached a pitch that made repression almost unmanageable, she came to an impulsive decision, and obeyed it. Her husband had again gone out with luncheon for the day. She took adventure in her hands and followed him. The power of seeing-clear was strong upon her, forcing her up to some unnatural level of understanding. To stay indoors and wait inactive for his return seemed suddenly impossible. She meant to know what he knew, feel what he felt, put herself in his place. She would dare the fascination of the Forest— share it with him. It was greatly daring; but it would give her greater understanding how to help and save him and therefore greater Power. She went upstairs a moment first to pray.

In a thick, warm skirt, and wearing heavy boots—those walking boots she used with him upon the mountains about Seillans— she left the cottage by the back way and turned towards the Forest. She could not actually follow him, for he had started off an hour before and she knew not exactly his direction. What was so urgent in her was the wish to be with him in the woods, to walk beneath leafless branches just as he did: to be there when he was there, even though not together. For it had come to her that she might thus share with him for once this horrible mighty life and breathing of the trees he loved. In winter, he had said, they needed him particularly, and winter now was coming. Her love must bring her something of what he felt himself—the huge attraction, the suction and the pull of all the trees. Thus, in some vicarious fashion, she might share, though unknown to himself, this very thing that was taking him away from her. She might thus even lessen its attack upon himself.

The impulse came to her clairvoyantly, and she obeyed without a sign of hesitation. Deeper comprehension would come to her of the whole awful puzzle. And come it did, yet not in the way she imagined and expected.

The air was very still, the sky a cold pale blue, but cloudless. The entire Forest stood silent, at attention. It knew perfectly well that she had come. It knew the moment when she entered; watched and followed her; and behind her something dropped without a sound and shut her in. Her feet upon the glades of mossy grass fell silently, as the oaks and beeches shifted past in rows and took up their positions at her back. It was not pleasant, this way they grew so dense behind her the instant she had passed. She realized that they gathered in an ever-growing army, massed, herded, trooped, between her and the cottage, shutting off escape. They let her pass so easily, but to get out again she would know them differently— thick, crowded, branches all drawn and hostile. Already their increasing numbers bewildered her. In front, they looked so sparse and scattered, with open spaces where the sunshine fell; but when she turned it seemed they stood so close together, a serried army, darkening the sunlight. They blocked the day, collected all the shadows, stood with their leafless and forbidding rampart like the night. They swallowed down into themselves the very glade by which she came. For when she glanced behind her—rarely—the way she had come was shadowy and lost.

Yet the morning sparkled overhead, and a glance of excitement ran quivering through the entire day. It was what she always knew as "children's weather," so clear and harmless, without a sign of danger, nothing ominous to threaten or alarm. Steadfast in her purpose, looking back as little as she dared, Sophia Bittacy marched slowly and deliberately into the heart of the silent woods, deeper, ever deeper.

And then, abruptly, in an open space where the sunshine fell unhindered, she stopped. It was one of the breathing places of the forest. Dead, withered bracken lay in patches of unsightly grey. There were bits of heather too. All round the trees stood looking on—oak, beech, holly, ash, pine, larch, with here and there small groups of juniper. On the lips of this breathing space of the woods she stopped to rest, disobeying her instinct for the first time. For the other instinct in her was to go on. She did not really want to rest.

This was the little act that brought it to her—the wireless message from a vast Emitter.

"I've been stopped," she thought to herself with a horrid qualm.

She looked about her in this quiet, ancient place. Nothing stirred. There was no life nor sign of life; no birds sang; no rabbits scuttled off at her approach. The stillness was bewildering, and gravity hung down upon it like a heavy curtain. It hushed the heart in her. Could this be part of what her husband felt—this sense of thick entanglement with stems, boughs, roots, and foliage?

"This has always been as it is now," she thought, yet not knowing why she thought it. "Ever since the Forest grew it has been still and secret here. It has never changed." The curtain of silence drew closer while she said it, thickening round her. "For a thousand years—I'm here with a thousand years. And behind this place stand all the forests of the world!"

So foreign to her temperament were such thoughts, and so alien to all she had been taught to look for in Nature, that she strove against them. She made an effort to oppose. But they clung and haunted just the same; they refused to be dispersed. The curtain hung dense and heavy as though its texture thickened. The air with difficulty came through.

And then she thought that curtain stirred. There was movement somewhere. That obscure dim thing which ever broods behind the visible appearances of trees came nearer to her. She caught her breath and stared about her, listening intently. The trees, perhaps because she saw them more in detail now, it seemed to her had changed. A vague, faint alteration spread over them, at first so slight she scarcely would admit it, then growing steadily, though still obscurely, outwards. "They tremble and are changed," flashed through her mind the horrid line that Sanderson had quoted. Yet the change was graceful for all the uncouthness attendant upon the size of so vast a movement. They had turned in her direction. That was it. *They saw her.* In this way the change expressed itself in her groping, terrified thought. Till now it had been otherwise: she had looked at them from her own point of view; now they looked at her from theirs. They stared her in the face and eyes; they stared at her all over. In some unkind, resentful, hostile way, they watched her. Hitherto in life she had watched them variously, in superficial ways, reading into them what her own mind suggested. Now they read into her the things they actually *were*, and not merely another's interpretations of them.

They seemed in their motionless silence there instinct with life, a life, moreover, that breathed about her a species of terrible soft enchantment that bewitched. It branched all through her, climbing to the brain. The Forest held her with its huge and giant fascination. In this secluded breathing spot that the centuries had left untouched, she had stepped close against the hidden pulse of the whole collective mass of them. They were aware of her and had turned to gaze with their myriad, vast sight upon the intruder. They shouted at her in the silence. For she wanted to look back at them, but it was like staring at a crowd, and her glance merely shifted from one tree to another, hurriedly, finding in none the one she sought. They saw her so easily, each and all. The rows that stood behind her also stared. But she could not return the gaze. Her husband, she realized, could. And their steady stare shocked her as though in some sense she knew that she was naked. They saw so much of her: she saw of them—so little.

Her efforts to return their gaze were pitiful. The constant shifting increased her bewilderment. Conscious of this awful and enormous sight all over her, she let her eyes first rest upon the ground, and then she closed them altogether. She kept the lids as tight together as ever they would go.

But the sight of the trees came even into that inner darkness behind the fastened lids, for there was no escaping it. Outside, in the light, she still knew that the leaves of the hollies glittered smoothly, that the dead foliage of the oaks hung crisp in the air about her, that the needles of the little junipers were pointing all one way. The spread perception of the Forest was focused on herself, and no mere shutting of the eyes could hide its scattered yet concentrated stare—the all-inclusive vision of great woods.

There was no wind, yet here and there a single leaf hanging by its dried-up stalk shook all alone with great rapidity—rattling. It was the sentry drawing attention to her presence. And then, again, as once long weeks before, she felt their Being as a tide about her. The tide had turned. That memory of her childhood sands came back, when the nurse said, "The tide has turned now; we must go in," and she saw the mass of piled-up waters, green and heaped to the horizon, and realized that it was slowly coming in. The gigantic mass of it, too vast for hurry, loaded with massive purpose, she used to feel, was moving towards herself. The fluid body of the sea was creeping along beneath the sky to the very spot upon the yellow sands where she stood and played. The sight and thought of it had always overwhelmed her with a sense of awe—as though her puny self were the object of the whole sea's advance. "The tide has turned; we had better now go in."

This was happening now about her—the same thing was happening in the woods—slow, sure, and steady, and its motion as little discernible as the sea's. The tide had turned. The small human presence that had ventured among its green and mountainous depths, moreover, was its objective.

That all was clear within her while she sat and waited with tight-shut lids. But the next moment she opened her eyes with a sudden realization of something more. The presence that it sought was after all not hers. It was the presence of some one other than herself. And then she understood. Her eyes had opened with a click, it seemed, but the sound, in reality, was outside herself.

Across the clearing where the sunshine lay so calm and still, she saw the figure of her husband moving among the trees—a man, like a tree, walking.

With hands behind his back, and head uplifted, he moved quite slowly, as though absorbed in his own thoughts. Hardly fifty paces separated them, but he had no inkling of her presence there so near. With mind intent and senses all turned inwards, he marched past her like a figure in a dream, and like a figure in a dream she saw him go. Love, yearning, pity rose in a storm within her, but as in nightmare she found no words or movement possible. She sat and watched him go—go from her—go into the deeper reaches of the green enveloping woods. Desire to save, to bid him stop and turn, ran in a passion through her being, but there was nothing she could do. She saw him go away from her, go of his own accord and willingly beyond her; she saw the branches drop about his steps and hid him. His figure faded out among the speckled shade and sunlight. The trees covered him. The tide just took him, all unresisting and content to go. Upon the bosom of the green soft sea he floated away beyond her reach of vision. Her eyes could follow him no longer. He was gone.

And then for the first time she realized, even at that distance, that the look upon his face was one of peace and happiness—rapt, and caught away in joy, a look of youth. That expression now he never showed to her. But she *had* known it. Years ago, in the early days of their married life, she had seen it on his face. Now it no longer obeyed the summons of her presence and her love. The woods alone could call it forth; it answered to the trees; the Forest had taken every part of him—from her—his very heart and soul.

Her sight that had plunged inwards to the fields of faded memory now came back to outer things again. She looked about her, and her love, returning empty-handed and unsatisfied, left her open to the invading of the bleakest terror she had ever known. That such things could be real and happen found her helpless utterly. Terror invaded the quietest corners of her heart, that had never yet known quailing. She could not—for moments at any rate—reach either her Bible or her God. Desolate in an empty world of fear she sat with eyes too dry and hot for tears, yet with a coldness as of ice upon her very flesh. She stared, unseeing, about her. That horror which stalks in the stillness of the noonday, when the glare of an artificial sunshine lights up the motionless trees, moved all about her. In front and behind she was aware of it. Beyond this stealthy silence, just within the edge of it, the things of another world were passing. But she could not know them. Her husband knew them, knew their beauty and their awe, yes, but for her they were out of reach. She might not share with him the very least of them. It seemed that behind and through the glare of this wintry noonday in the heart of the woods there brooded another universe of life and passion, for her all unexpressed. The silence veiled it, the stillness hid it; but he moved with it all and understood. His love interpreted it.

She rose to her feet, tottered feebly, and collapsed again upon the moss. Yet for herself she felt no terror; no little personal fear could touch her whose anguish and deep longing streamed all out to him whom she so bravely loved. In this time of utter self-forgetfulness, when she realized that the battle was hopeless, thinking she had lost even her God, she found Him again quite close beside her like a little Presence in this terrible heart of the hostile Forest. But at first she did not recognize that He was there; she did not know Him in that strangely unacceptable guise. For He stood so very close, so very intimate, so very sweet and comforting, and yet so hard to understand—as Resignation.

Once more she struggled to her feet, and this time turned successfully and slowly made her way along the mossy glade by which she came. And at first she marveled, though only for a moment, at the ease with which she found the path. For a moment only, because almost at once she saw the truth. The trees were glad that she should go. They helped her on her way. The Forest did not want her.

The tide was coming in, indeed, yet not for her.

And so, in another of those flashes of clear-vision that of late had lifted life above the normal level, she saw and understood the whole terrible thing complete.

Till now, though unexpressed in thought or language, her fear had been that the woods her husband loved would somehow take him from her—to merge his life in theirs—even to kill him on some mysterious way. This time she saw her deep mistake, and so seeing, let in upon herself the fuller agony of horror. For their jealousy was not the petty jealousy of animals or humans. They wanted him because they loved him, but they did *not* want him dead. Full charged with his splendid life and enthusiasm they wanted him. They wanted him—alive.

It was she who stood in their way, and it was she whom they intended to remove.

This was what brought the sense of abject helplessness. She stood upon the sands against an entire ocean slowly rolling in against her. For, as all the forces of a human being combine unconsciously to eject a grain of sand that has crept beneath the skin to cause discomfort, so the entire mass of what Sanderson had called the Collective Consciousness of the Forest strove to eject this human atom that stood across the path of its desire. Loving her husband, she had crept beneath its skin. It was her they would eject and take away; it was her they would destroy, not him. Him, whom they loved and needed, they would keep alive. They meant to take him living. She reached the house in safety, though she never remembered how she found her way. It was made all simple for her. The branches almost urged her out.

But behind her, as she left the shadowed precincts, she felt as though some towering Angel of the Woods let fall across the threshold the flaming sword of a countless multitude of leaves that formed behind her a barrier, green, shimmering, and impassable. Into the Forest she never walked again.

And she went about her daily duties with a calm and quietness that was a perpetual astonishment even to herself, for it hardly seemed of this world at all. She talked to her husband when he came in for tea—after dark. Resignation brings a curious large courage—when there is nothing more to lose. The soul takes risks, and dares. Is it a curious short-cut sometimes to the heights?

"David, I went into the Forest, too, this morning, soon after you I went. I saw you there."

"Wasn't it wonderful?" he answered simply, inclining his head a little. There was no surprise or annoyance in his look; a mild and gentle *ennui* rather. He asked no real question. She thought of some garden tree the wind attacks too suddenly, bending it over when it does not want to bend—the mild unwillingness with which it yields. She often saw him this way now, in the terms of trees.

"It was very wonderful indeed, dear, yes," she replied low, her voice not faltering though indistinct. "But for me it was too—too strange and big."

The passion of tears lay just below the quiet voice all unbetrayed. Somehow she kept them back.

There was a pause, and then he added:

"I find it more and more so every day." His voice passed through the lamp-lit room like a murmur of the wind in branches. The look of youth and happiness she had caught upon his face out there had wholly gone, and an expression of weariness was in its place, as of a man distressed vaguely at finding himself in uncongenial surroundings where he is slightly ill at ease. It was the house he hated—coming back to rooms and walls and furniture. The ceilings and closed windows confined him. Yet, in it, no suggestion that he found *her* irksome. Her presence seemed of no account at all; indeed, he hardly noticed her. For whole long periods he lost her, did not know that she was there. He had no need of her. He lived alone. Each lived alone.

The outward signs by which she recognized that the awful battle was against her and the terms of surrender accepted were pathetic. She put the medicine-chest away upon the shelf; she gave the orders for his pocket-luncheon before he asked; she went to bed alone and early, leaving the front door unlocked, with milk and bread and butter in the hall beside the lamp—all concessions that she felt impelled to make. Fore more and more, unless the weather was too violent, he went out after dinner even, staying for hours in the woods. But she never slept until she heard the front door close below, and knew soon afterwards his careful step come creeping up the stairs and into the room so softly. Until she heard his regular deep breathing close beside her, she lay awake. All strength or desire to resist had gone for good. The thing against her was too huge and powerful. Capitulation was complete, a fact accomplished. She dated it from the day she followed him to the Forest.

Moreover, the time for evacuation—her own evacuation—seemed approaching. It came stealthily ever nearer, surely and slowly as the

rising tide she used to dread. At the high-water mark she stood waiting calmly—waiting to be swept away. Across the lawn all those terrible days of early winter the encircling Forest watched it come, guid-
ing its silent swell and currents towards her feet. Only she never once
gave up her Bible or her praying. This complete resignation, moreover, had somehow brought to her a strange great understanding, and
if she could not share her husband's horrible abandonment to powers
outside himself, she could, and did, in some half-groping way grasp at
shadowy meanings that might make such abandonment—possible, yes,
but more than merely possible—in some extraordinary sense not evil.

Hitherto she had divided the beyond-world into two sharp
halves—spirits good or spirits evil. But thoughts came to her now,
on soft and very tentative feet, like the footsteps of the gods which
are on wool, that besides these definite classes, there might be other
Powers as well, belonging definitely to neither one nor other. Her
thought stopped dead at that. But the big idea found lodgment in
her little mind, and, owing to the largeness of her heart, remained
there unejected. It even brought a certain solace with it.

The failure—or unwillingness, as she preferred to state it—of her
God to interfere and help, that also she came in a measure to understand. For here, she found it more and more possible to imagine, was
perhaps no positive evil at work, but only something that usually stands
away from humankind, something alien and not commonly recognized.
There *was* a gulf fixed between the two, and Mr. Sanderson *had*
bridged it, by his talk, his explanations, his attitude of mind. Through
these her husband had found the way into it. His temperament and
natural passion for the woods had prepared the soul in him, and the
moment he saw the way to go he took it—the line of least resistance.
Life was, of course, open to all, and her husband had the right to choose
it where he would. He had chosen it—away from her, away from other
men, but not necessarily away from God. This was an enormous
concession that she skirted, never really faced; it was too revolu-
tionary to face. But its possibility peeped into her bewildered mind.
It might delay his progress, or it might advance it. Who could
know? And why should God, who ordered all things with such magnificent detail, from the pathway of a sun to the falling of a sparrow,
object to his free choice, or interfere to hinder him and stop?

She came to realize resignation, that is, in another aspect. It
gave her comfort, if not peace. She fought against all belittling of
her God. It was, perhaps, enough that He—knew.

"You are not alone, dear in the trees out there?" she ventured one night, as he crept on tiptoe into the room not far from midnight. "God is with you?"

"Magnificently," was the immediate answer, given with enthusiasm, "for He is everywhere. And I only wish that you—"

But she stuffed the clothes against her ears. That invitation on his lips was more than she could bear to hear. It seemed like asking her to hurry to her own execution. She buried her face among the sheets and blankets, shaking all over like a leaf.

IX

And so the thought that she was the one to go remained and grew. It was, perhaps, first sign of that weakening of the mind which indicated the singular manner of her going. For it was her mental opposition, the trees felt, that stood in their way. Once that was overcome, obliterated, her physical presence did not matter. She would be harmless.

Having accepted defeat, because she had come to feel that his obsession was not actually evil, she accepted at the same time the conditions of an atrocious loneliness. She stood now from her husband farther than from the moon. They had no visitors. Callers were few and far between, and less encouraged than before. The empty dark of winter was before them. Among the neighbors was none in whom, without disloyalty to her husband, she could confide. Mr. Mortimer, had he been single, might have helped her in this desert of solitude that preyed upon her mind, but his wife was there the obstacle; for Mrs. Mortimer wore sandals, believed that nuts were the complete food of man, and indulged in other idiosyncrasies that classed her inevitably among the "latter signs" which Mrs. Bittacy had been taught to dread as dangerous. She stood most desolately alone.

Solitude, therefore, in which the mind unhindered feeds upon its own delusions, was the assignable cause of her gradual mental disruption and collapse.

With the definite arrival of the colder weather her husband gave up his rambles after dark; evenings were spent together over the fire; he read *The Times*; they even talked about their postponed visit abroad in the coming spring. No restlessness was on him at

the change; he seemed content and easy in his mind; spoke little
of the trees and woods; enjoyed far better health than if there had
been change of scene, and to herself was tender, kind, solicitous
over trifles, as in the distant days of their first honeymoon.

But this deep calm could not deceive her; it meant, she fully
understood, that he felt sure of himself, sure of her, and sure of
the trees as well. It all lay buried in the depths of him, too secure
and deep, too intimately established in his central being to permit
of those surface fluctuations which betray disharmony within. His
life was hid with trees. Even the fever, so dreaded in the damp of
winter, left him free. She now knew why: the fever was due to their
efforts to obtain him, his efforts to respond and go—physical re-
sults of a fierce unrest he had never understood till Sanderson came
with his wicked explanations. Now it was otherwise. The bridge
was made. And—he had gone.

And she, brave, loyal, and consistent soul, found herself utterly
alone, even trying to make his passage easy. It seemed that she
stood at the bottom of some huge ravine that opened in her mind,
the walls whereof instead of rock were trees that reached enormous
to the sky, engulfing her. God alone knew that she was there. He
watched, permitted, even perhaps approved. At any rate—He knew.

During those quiet evenings in the house, moreover, while they
sat over the fire listening to the roaming winds about the house,
her husband knew continual access to the world his alien love had
furnished for him. Never for a single instant was he cut off from it.
She gazed at the newspaper spread before his face and knees, saw
the smoke of his cheroot curl up above the edge, noticed the little
hole in his evening socks, and listened to the paragraphs he read
aloud as of old. But this was all a veil he spread about himself of
purpose. Behind it—he escaped. It was the conjurer's trick to divert
the sight to unimportant details while the essential thing went forward unobserved. He managed wonderfully; she loved him for the
pains he took to spare her distress; but all the while she knew that
the body lolling in that armchair before her eyes contained the
merest fragment of his actual self. It was little better than a corpse.
It was an empty shell. The essential soul of him was out yonder
with the Forest—farther out near that ever-roaring heart of it.

And, with the dark, the Forest came up boldly and pressed
against the very walls and windows, peering in upon them, joining
hands above the slates and chimneys. The winds were always walking

on the lawn and gravel paths; steps came and went and came again; some one seemed always talking in the woods, some one was in the building too. She passed them on the stairs, or running soft and muffled, very large and gentle, down the passages and landings after dusk, as though loose fragments of the Day had broken off and stayed there caught among the shadows, trying to get out. They blundered silently all about the house. They waited till she passed, then made a run for it. And her husband always knew. She saw him more than once deliberately avoid them—because *she* was there. More than once, too, she saw him stand and listen when he thought she was not near, then heard herself the long bounding stride of their approach across the silent garden. Already *he* had heard them in the windy distance of the night, far, far away. They sped, she well knew, along that glade of mossy turf by which she last came out; it cushioned their tread exactly as it had cushioned her own.

It seemed to her the trees were always in the house with him, and in their very bedroom. He welcomed them, unaware that she also knew, and trembled.

One night in their bedroom it caught her unawares. She woke out of deep sleep and it came upon her before she could gather her forces for control.

The day had been wildly boisterous, but now the wind had dropped, only its rags went fluttering through the night. The rays of the full moon fell in a shower between the branches. Overhead still raced the scud and wrack, shaped like hurrying monsters; but below the earth was quiet. Still and dripping stood the hosts of trees. Their trunks gleamed wet and sparkling where the moon caught them. There was a strong smell of mould and fallen leaves. The air was sharp—heavy with odor.

And she knew all this the instant that she woke; for it seemed to her that she had been elsewhere—following her husband—as though she had been *out*! There was no dream at all, merely the definite, haunting certainty. It dived away, lost, buried in the night. She sat upright in bed. She had come back.

The room shone pale in the moonlight reflected through the windows, for the blinds were up, and she saw her husband's form beside her, motionless in deep sleep. But what caught her unawares was the horrid thing that by this fact of sudden, unexpected waking she had surprised these other things in the room, beside the very bed, gathered close about him while he slept. It was their dreadful boldness—herself of no account as it were—that terrified her into screaming before she could collect her powers to prevent. She screamed before she realized what she did—a long, high shriek of terror that filled the room, yet made so little actual sound. For wet and shimmering presences stood grouped all round that bed. She saw their outline underneath the ceiling, the green, spread bulk of them, their vague extension over walls and furniture. They shifted to and fro, massed yet translucent, mild yet thick, moving and turning within themselves to a hushed noise of multitudinous soft rustling. In their sound was something very sweet and sinning that fell into her with a spell of horrible enchantment. They were so mild, each one alone, yet so terrific in their combination. Cold seized her. The sheets against her body had turned to ice.

She screamed a second time, though the sound hardly issued from her throat. The spell sank deeper, reaching to the heart; for it softened all the currents of her blood and took life from her in a stream—towards themselves. Resistance in that moment seemed impossible.

Her husband then stirred in his sleep, and woke. And, instantly, the forms drew up, erect, and gathered themselves in some amazing way together. They lessened in extent—then scattered through the air like an effect of light when shadows seek to smother it. It was tremendous, yet most exquisite. A sheet of pale-green shadow that yet had form and substance filled the room. There was a rush of silent movement, as the Presences drew past her through the air,—and they were gone.

But, clearest of all, she saw the manner of their going; for she recognized in their tumult of escape by the window open at the top, the same wide "looping circles"—spirals as it seemed—that she had seen upon the lawn those weeks ago when Sanderson had talked. The room once more was empty.

In the collapse that followed, she heard her husband's voice, as though coming from some great distance. Her own replies she heard as well. Both were so strange and unlike their normal speech, the very words unnatural.

"What is it, dear? Why do you wake me *now*?" And his voice whispered it with a sighing sound, like wind in pine boughs.

"A moment since something went past me through the air of the room. Back to the night outside it went." Her voice, too, held the same note as of wind entangled among too many leaves.

"My dear, it *was* the wind."

"But it called, David. It was calling *you*—by name!"

"The air of the branches, dear, was what you heard. Now, sleep again, I beg you, sleep."

"It had a crowd of eyes all through and over it—before and be-hind—" Her voice grew louder. But his own in reply sank lower, far away, and oddly hushed.

"The moonlight, dear, upon the sea of twigs and boughs in the rain, was what you saw."

"But it frightened me. I've lost my God—and you—I'm cold as death!"

"My dear, it is the cold of the early morning hours. The whole world sleeps. Now sleep again yourself."

He whispered close to her ear. She felt his hand stroking her. His voice was soft and very soothing. But only a part of him was there; only a part of him was speaking; it was a half-emptied body that lay beside her and uttered these strange sentences, even forcing her own singular choice of words. The horrible, dim enchantment of the trees was close about them in the room—gnarled, ancient, lonely trees of winter, whispering round the human life they loved.

"And let me sleep again," she heard him murmur as he settled down among the clothes, "sleep back into that deep, delicious peace from which you called me."

His dreamy, happy tone, and that look of youth and joy she discerned upon his features even in the filtered moonlight, touched her again as with the spell of those shining, mild green presences. It sank down into her. She felt sleep grope for her. On the threshold of slumber one of those strange vagrant voices that loss of consciousness lets loose cried faintly in her heart—

"There is joy in the Forest over one sinner that—"

Then sleep took her before she had time to realize even that she was vilely parodying one of her most precious texts, and that the irreverence was ghastly.

And though she quickly slept again, her sleep was not as usual, dreamless. It was not woods and trees she dreamed of, but a small and curious dream that kept coming again and again upon her; that she stood upon a wee, bare rock I the sea, and that the tide was rising. The water first came to her feet, then to her knees, then to her waist. Each time the dream returned, the tide seemed higher. Once it rose to her neck, once even to her mouth, covering her lips for a moment so that she could not breathe. She did not wake between the dreams; a period of drab and dreamless slumber intervened. But, finally, the water rose above her eyes and face, completely covering her head.

And then came explanation—the sort of explanation dreams bring. She understood. For, beneath the water, she had seen the world of seaweed rising from the bottom of the sea like a forest of dense green-long, sinuous stems, immense thick branches, millions of feelers spreading through the darkened watery depths the power of their ocean foliage. The Vegetable Kingdom was even in the sea. It was everywhere. Earth, air, and water helped it, way of escape there was none.

And even underneath the sea she heard that terrible sound of roaring—was it surf or wind or voices?—further out, yet coming steadily towards her.

And so, in the loneliness of that drab English winter, the mind of Mrs. Bittacy, preying upon itself, and fed by constant dread, went lost in disproportion. Dreariness filled the weeks with dismal, sunless skies and a clinging moisture that knew no wholesome tonic of keen frosts. Alone with her thoughts, both her husband and her God withdrawn into distance, she counted the days to Spring. She groped her way, stumbling down the long dark tunnel. Through the arch at the far end lay a brilliant picture of the violet sea sparkling on the coast of France. There lay safety and escape for both of them, could she but hold on. Behind her the trees blocked up the other entrance. She never once looked back.

She drooped. Vitality passed from her, drawn out and away as by some steady suction. Immense and incessant was this sensation of her powers draining off. The taps were all turned on. Her personality, as it were, streamed steadily away, coaxed outwards by this Power that never wearied and seemed inexhaustible. It won her as the full moon wins the tide. She waned; she faded; she obeyed.

At first she watched the process, and recognized exactly what was going on. Her physical life, and that balance of mind which depends on physical well-being, were being slowly undermined. She saw that clearly. Only the soul, dwelling like a star apart from these and independent of them, lay safe somewhere—with her distant God. That she knew—tranquilly. The spiritual love that linked her to her husband was safe from all attack. Later, in His good

time, they would merge together again because of it. But meanwhile, all of her that had kinship with the earth was slowly going.
This separation was being remorselessly accomplished. Every part
of her the trees could touch was being steadily drained from her.
She was being—removed.

After a time, however, even this power of realization went, so
that she no longer "watched the process" or knew exactly what was
going on. The one satisfaction she had known—the feeling that it
was sweet to suffer for his sake—went with it. She stood utterly
alone with this terror of the trees ... mid the ruins of her broken
and disordered mind.

She slept badly; woke in the morning with hot and tired eyes;
her head ached dully; she grew confused in thought and lost the
clues of daily life in the most feeble fashion. At the same time she
lost sight, too, of that brilliant picture at the exist of the tunnel; it
faded away into a tiny semicircle of pale light, the violet sea and
the sunshine the merest point of white, remote as a star and equally
inaccessible. She knew now that she could never reach it. And
through the darkness that stretched behind, the power of the trees
came close and caught her, twining about her feet and arms, climbing to her very lips. She woke at night, finding it difficult to breathe.
There seemed wet leaves pressing against her mouth, and soft green
tendrils clinging to her neck. Her feet were heavy, half rooted, as
it were, in deep, thick earth. Huge creepers stretched along the
whole of that black tunnel, feeling about her person for points
where they might fasten well, as ivy or the giant parasites of the
Vegetable Kingdom settle down on the trees themselves to sap their
life and kill them.

Slowly and surely the morbid growth possessed her life and held
her. She feared those very winds that ran about the wintry forest.
They were in league with it. They helped it everywhere.

"Why don't you sleep, dear?" It was her husband now who
played the rôle of nurse, tending her little wants with an honest
care that at least aped the services of love. He was so utterly unconscious of the raging battle he had caused. "What is it keeps you
so wide awake and restless?"

"The winds," she whispered in the dark. For hours she had been
watching the tossing of the trees through the blindless windows.
"They go walking and talking everywhere to-night, keeping me
awake. And all the time they call so loudly to you."

And his strange whispered answer appalled her for a moment until the meaning of it faded and left her in a dark confusion of the mind that was now becoming almost permanent.

"The trees excite them in the night. The winds are the great swift carriers. Go with them, dear—and not against. You'll find sleep that way if you do."

"The storm is rising," she began, hardly knowing what she said.

"All the more then—go with them. Don't resist. They'll take you to the trees, that's all."

Resist! The word touched on the button of some text that once had helped her.

"Resist the devil and he will flee from you," she heard her whispered answer, and the same second had buried her face beneath the clothes in a flood of hysterical weeping.

But her husband did not seem disturbed. Perhaps he did not hear it, for the wind ran just then against the windows with a booming shout, and the roaring of the Forest farther out came behind the blow, surging into the room. Perhaps, too, he was already asleep again. She slowly regained a sort of dull composure. Her face emerged from the tangle of sheets and blankets. With a growing terror over her—she listened. The storm was rising. It came with a sudden and impetuous rush that made all further sleep for her impossible.

Alone in a shaking world, it seemed, she lay and listened. That storm interpreted for her mind the climax. The Forest bellowed out its victory to the winds; the winds in turn proclaimed it to the Night. The whole world knew of her complete defeat, her loss, her little human pain. This was the roar and shout of victory that she listened to.

For, unmistakably, the trees were shouting in the dark. These were sounds, too, like the flapping of great sails, a thousand at a time, and sometimes reports that resembled more than anything else the distant booming of enormous drums. The trees stood up— the whole beleaguering host of them stood up—and with the uproar of their million branches drummed the thundering message out across the night. It seemed as if they had all broken loose. Their roots swept trailing over field and hedge and roof. They tossed their bushy heads beneath the clouds with a wild, delighted shuffling of great boughs. With trunks upright they raced leaping through the sky. There was upheaval and adventure in the awful sound they made, and their cry was like the cry of a sea that has broken through its gates and poured loose upon the world....

Through it all her husband slept peacefully as though he heard it not. It was, as she well knew, the sleep of the semi-dead. For he was out with all that clamoring turmoil. The part of him that she had lost was there. The form that slept so calmly at her side was but the shell, half emptied.

And when the winter's morning stole upon the scene at length, with a pale, washed sunshine that followed the departing tempest, the first thing she saw, as she crept to the window and looked out, was the ruined cedar lying on the lawn. Only the gaunt and crippled trunk of it remained. The single giant bough that had been left to it lay dark upon the grass, sucked endways towards the Forest by a great wind eddy. It lay there like a mass of drift-wood from a wreck, left by the ebbing of a high spring-tide upon the sands—remnant of some friendly, splendid vessel that once sheltered men.

And in the distance she heard the roaring of the Forest further out. Her husband's voice was in it.

The Pavilion
E. Nesbit

There was never a moment's doubt in her own mind. So she
said afterwards. And everyone agreed that she had concealed her
feelings with true womanly discretion. Her friend and confidant,
Amelia Davenant, was at any rate completely deceived. Amelia was
one of those featureless blondes who seem born to be overlooked.
She adored her beautiful friend, and never, from first to last, could
see any fault in her, except, perhaps, on the evening when the real
things of the story happened. And even in that matter she owned
at the time that it was only that her darling Ernestine did not understand.

Ernestine was a prettyish girl with the airs, so irresistible and
misleading, of a beauty; most people said that she was beautiful,
and she certainly managed, with extraordinary success, to produce
the illusion of beauty. Quite a number of plainish girls achieve that
effect nowadays. The freedom of modern dress and coiffure and
the increasing confidence in herself which the modern girl experiences, aid her in fostering the illusion; but in the sixties, when
everyone wore much the same sort of bonnet, when your choice in
coiffure was limited to bandeaux or ringlets, and the crinoline was
your only wear, something very like genius was needed to deceive
the world in the matter of your personal charms. Ernestine had
that genius; hers was the smiling, ringleted, dark-haired, dark-
eyed, sparkling type.

Amelia had blonde bandeaux and kind appealing blue eyes,
rather too small and rather too dull; her hands and ears were beautiful, and she kept them out of sight as much as possible. In our
times the blonde hair would have been puffed out to make a frame

for the forehead, a little too high; a certain shade of blue and a certain shade of boldness would have made her eyes effective. And the beautiful hands would have learned that flowerlike droop of the wrist so justly and so universally admired. But as it was, Amelia was very nearly plain, and in her secret emotional self-communings told herself that she was ugly. It was she who, at the age of fourteen, composed the remarkable poem beginning:

I know that I am ugly: did I make
The face that is the laugh and jest of all?

and goes on, after disclaiming any personal responsibility for the face, to entreat the kind earth to "cover it away from mocking eyes," and to "let the daisies blossom where it lies."

Amelia did not want to die, and her face was not the laugh and jest, or indeed the special interest, of anyone. All that was poetic license. Amelia had read perhaps a little too much poetry of the type of '*Quand je suis morte, mes amies, plantez un saule au cimetière*'; but really life was a very good thing to Amelia, especially when she had a new dress and someone paid her a compliment. But she went on writing verses extolling the advantages of The Tomb, and grovelling metrically at the feet of One who was Another's until that summer, when she was nineteen, and went to stay with Ernestine at Doricourt. Then her Muse took flight, scared, perhaps, by the possibility, suddenly and threateningly presented, of being asked to inspire verse about the real things of life.

At any rate, Amelia ceased to write poetry about the time when she and Ernestine and Ernestine's aunt went on a visit to Doricourt, where Frederick Powell lived with his aunt. It was not one of those hurried motor-fed excursions which we have now, and call weekends, but a long leisurely visit, when all the friends of the static aunt called on the dynamic aunt, and both returned the calls with much state, a big barouche and a pair of fat horses. There were croquet parties and archery parties and little dances, all pleasant informal little gaieties arranged without ceremony among people who lived within driving distance of each other and knew each other's tastes and incomes and family history as well as they knew their own. The habit of importing huge droves of strangers from distant counties for brief harrying raids did not then obtain. There was instead a wide and constant circle of pleasant people with an unflagging stream of gaiety, mild indeed, but delightful to unjaded palates.

And at Doricourt life was delightful even on the days when there was no party. It was perhaps more delightful to Ernestine than to her friend, but even so, the one least pleased was Ernestine's aunt.

"I do think," she said to the other aunt whose name was Julia— "I daresay it is not so to you, being accustomed to Mr. W. Frederick, of course, from his childhood, but I always find gentlemen in the house so unsettling, especially young gentlemen, and when there are young ladies also. One is always on the *qui vive* for excitement."

"Of course," said Aunt Julia, with the air of a woman of the world; "living as you and dear Ernestine do, with only females in the house ..."

"We hang up an old coat and hat of my brother's on the hatstand in the hall," Aunt Emmeline protested.

"... The presence of gentlemen in the house must be a little unsettling. For myself, I am inured to it. Frederick has so many friends. Mr. Thesiger, perhaps, the greatest. I believe him to be a most worthy young man, but peculiar." She leaned forward across her bright-tinted Berlin woolwork and spoke impressively, the needle with its trailing red poised in air. "You know, I hope you will not think it indelicate of me to mention such a thing, but dear Frederick ... your dear Ernestine would have been in every way so suitable."

"Would have been?" Aunt Emmeline's tortoise-shell shuttle ceased its swift movement among the white loops and knots of her tatting.

"Well, my dear," said the other aunt, a little shortly, "you must surely have noticed ..."

"You don't mean to suggest that Amelia ... I thought Mr. Thesiger and Amelia ..."

"Amelia! I really must say! No, I was alluding to Mr. Thesiger's attentions to dear Ernestine. Most marked. In dear Frederick's place I should have found some excuse for shortening Mr. Thesiger's visit. But, of course, I cannot interfere. Gentlemen must manage these things for themselves. I only hope that there will be none of that trifling with the most holy affections of others which ..."

The less voluble aunt cut in hotly with: "Ernestine's incapable of anything so unladylike."

"Just what I was saying," the other rejoined blandly, got up and drew the blind a little lower, for the afternoon sun was glowing on the rosy wreaths of the drawing-room carpet.

Outside in the sunshine Frederick was doing his best to arrange his own affairs. He had managed to place himself beside Miss Ernestine Meutys on the stone steps of the pavilion; but then, Mr. Thesiger lay along the lower step at her feet, a very good position for looking up into her eyes. Amelia was beside him, but then it never seemed to matter whom Amelia sat beside.

They were talking about the pavilion on whose steps they sat, and Amelia who often asked uninteresting questions had wondered how old it was. It was Frederick's pavilion after all, and he felt this when his friend took the words out of his mouth and used them on his own account, even though he did give the answer in the form of an appeal.

"The foundations are Tudor, aren't they?" he said. "Wasn't it an observatory or laboratory or something of that sort in Fat Henry's time?"

"Yes," said Frederick, "there was some story about a wizard or an alchemist or something, and it was burned down, and then they rebuilt it in its present style."

"The Italian style, isn't it?" said Thesiger; "but you can hardly see what it is now, for the creeper."

"Virginia creeper, isn't it?" Amelia asked, and Frederick said; "Yes, Virginia creeper." Thesiger said it looked more like a South American plant, and Ernestine said Virginia was in South America and that was why. "I know, because of the war," she said modestly, and nobody smiled or answered. There were manners in those days.

"There's a ghost story about it surely," Thesiger began again, looking up at the dark closed doors of the pavilion.

"Not that I ever heard of," said the pavilion's owner. "I think the country people invented the tale because there have always been so many rabbits and weasels and things found dead near it. And once a dog, my uncle's favourite spaniel. But of course that's simply because they get entangled in the Virginia creeper—you see how fine and big it is—and can't get out, and die as they do in traps. But the villagers prefer to think it's ghosts."

"I thought there was a real ghost story," Thesiger persisted.

Ernestine said: "A ghost story. How delicious! Do tell it, Mr. Doricourt. This is just the place for a ghost story. Out of doors and the sun shining, so that we can't *really* be frightened."

Doricourt protested again that he knew no story.

"That's because you never read, dear boy," said Eugene Thesiger. "That library of yours. There's a delightful book—did you never notice it?—brown tree calf with your arms on it; the head of the house writes the history of the house as far as he knows it. There's a lot in that book. It began in Tudor times—1515 to be exact."

"Queen Elizabeth's time," Ernestine thought that made it so much more interesting. "And was the ghost story in that?"

"It isn't exactly a ghost story," said Thesiger. "It's only that the pavilion seems to be an unlucky place to sleep in."

"Haunted?" Frederick asked, and added that he must look up that book.

"Not haunted exactly. Only several people who have slept the night there went on sleeping."

"Dead, he means," said Ernestine, and it was left for Amelia to ask:

"Does the book tell anything particular about how the people died? What killed them, or anything?"

"There are suggestions," said Thesiger; "but there, it is a gloomy subject. I don't know why I started it. Should we have time for a game of croquet before tea, Doricourt?"

"I wish *you'd* read the book and tell me the stories," Ernestine said to Frederick, apart, over the croquet balls.

"I will," he answered fervently, "you've only to tell me what you want."

"Or perhaps Mr. Thesiger will tell us another time—in the twilight. Since people like twilight for ghosts. Will you, Mr. Thesiger?" She spoke over her blue muslin shoulder.

Frederick certainly meant to look up the book, but he delayed till after supper; the half-hour before bed when he and Thesiger put on their braided smoking-jackets and their braided smoking-caps with the long yellow tassels, and smoked the cigars which were, in those days still, more of a luxury than a necessity. Ordinarily, of course, these were smoked out of doors, or in the smoking-room, a stuffy little den littered with boots and guns and yellow-backed railway novels. But tonight Frederick left his friend in that dingy hutch, and went alone to the library, found the book and took it to the circle of light made by the colza lamp.

"I can skim through it in half an hour," he said, and wound up the lamp and lighted his second cigar. Then he opened the shutters and windows, so that the room should not smell of smoke in the morning. Those were the days of consideration for the ladies who had not yet learned that a cigarette is not exclusively a male accessory like a beard or a bass voice.

But when, his preparations completed, he opened the book, he was compelled to say "Pshaw!" Nothing short of this could relieve his feelings. (You know the expression I mean, though of course it isn't pronounced as it's spelt, any more than Featherstonehaugh or St. Maur are.)

"Pshaw!" said Frederick, fluttering the pages. His remark was justified. The earlier part of the book was written in the beautiful script of the early sixteenth century, that looks so plain and is so impossible to read, and the later pages, though the handwriting was clear and Italian enough, left Frederick helpless, for the language was Latin, and Frederick's Latin was limited to the particular passages he had "been through" at his private school. He recognized a word here and there, *mors*, for instance, and *pallidus* and *pavor* and *arcanum*, just as you or I might; but to read the complicated stuff and make sense of it ...! Frederick said something just a shade stronger than "Pshaw!"— "Botheration!" I think it was; replaced the book on the shelf, closed the shutters and turned out the lamp. He thought he would ask Thesiger to translate the thing, but then again he thought he wouldn't. So he went to bed wishing that he had happened to remember more of the Latin so painfully beaten into the best years of his boyhood.

And the story of the pavilion was, after all, told by Thesiger.

There was a little dance at Doricourt next evening, a carpet dance, they called it. The furniture was pushed back against the walls, and the tightly stretched Axminster carpet was not so bad to dance on as you might suppose. That, you see, was before the days of polished floors and large rugs with loose edges that you can catch your feet in. A carpet was a carpet in those days, well and truly laid, conscientiously exact to the last recess and fitting the floor like a skin. And on this quite tolerable surface the young people danced very happily, some ten or twelve couples. The old people did not dance in those days, except sometimes a quadrille of state to "open the ball." They played cards in a room provided for the purpose, and in the dancing-room three or four kindly middle-aged ladies were considered to provide ample chaperonage. You were not even expected to report yourself to your chaperone at the conclusion of a dance. It was not like a real ball. And even in those far-off days there were conservatories.

It was on the steps of the conservatory, not the steps leading from the dancing-room, but the steps leading to the garden, that the story was told. The four young people were sitting together, the girls' crinolined flounces spreading round them like huge pale roses, the young men correct in their high-shouldered coats and white cravats. Ernestine had been very kind to both the men—a little too kind, perhaps, who can tell? At any rate, there was in their eyes exactly that light which you may imagine in the eyes of rival stags in the mating season. It was Ernestine who asked Frederick for the story, and Thesiger who, at Amelia's suggestion, told it.

"It's quite a number of stories," he said, "and yet it's really all the same story. The first man to sleep in the pavilion slept there ten years after it was built. He was a friend of the alchemist or astrologer who built it. He was found dead in the morning. There seemed to have been a struggle. His arms bore the marks of cords. No; they never found any cords. He died from loss of blood. There were curious wounds. That was all the rude leeches of the day could report to the bereaved survivors of the deceased."

"How sunny you are, Mr. Thesiger," said Ernestine with that celebrated soft low laugh of hers. When Ernestine was elderly, many people thought her stupid. When she was young, no one seems to have been of this opinion.

"And the next?" asked Amelia.

"The next was sixty years later. It was a visitor that time, too. And he was found dead with just the same marks, and the doctors said the same thing. And so it went on. There have been eight deaths altogether—unexplained deaths. Nobody has slept in it now for over a hundred years. People seem to have a prejudice against the place as a sleeping apartment. I can't think why."

"Isn't he simply killing?" Ernestine asked Amelia, who said:

"And doesn't anyone know how it happened?" No one answered till Ernestine repeated the question in the form of: "I suppose it was just accident?"

"It was a curiously recurrent accident," said Thesiger, and Frederick, who throughout the conversation had said the right things at the right moment, remarked that it did not do to believe all these old legends. Most old families had them, he believed. Frederick had inherited Doricourt from an unknown great-uncle of whom in life he had not so much as heard, but he was very strong on the family tradition. "I don't attach any importance to these tales myself."

"Of course not. All the same," said Thesiger deliberately, "you wouldn't care to pass a night in that pavilion."

"No more would you," was all Frederick found on his lips.

"I admit that I shouldn't enjoy it," said Eugene, "but I'll bet you a hundred you don't *do* it."

"Done," said Frederick.

"Oh, Mr. Doricourt," breathed Ernestine, a little shocked at betting "before ladies."

"Don't!" said Amelia, to whom, of course, no one paid any attention, "don't do it."

You know how, in the midst of flower and leafage, a snake will suddenly, surprisingly rear a head that threatens? So, amid friendly talk and laughter, a sudden fierce antagonism sometimes looks out and vanishes again, surprising most of the antagonists. This antagonism spoke in the tones of both men, and after Amelia had said, "Don't," there was a curiously breathless little silence. Ernestine broke it. "Oh," she said, "I do wonder which of you will win. I should like them both to win, wouldn't you, Amelia? Only I suppose that's not always possible, is it?"

Both gentlemen assured her that in the case of bets it was very rarely possible.

"Then I wish you wouldn't," said Ernestine. "You could *both* pass the night there, couldn't you, and be company for each other? I don't think betting for such large sums is quite the thing, do you, Amelia?"

Amelia said No, she didn't, but Eugene had already begun to say:

"Let the bet be off then, if Miss Meutys doesn't like it. That suggestion was invaluable. But the thing itself needn't be off. Look here, Doricourt. I'll stay in the pavilion from one to three and you from three to five. Then honour will be satisfied. How will that do?"

The snake had disappeared.

"Agreed," said Frederick, "and we can compare impressions afterwards. That will be quite interesting."

Then someone came and asked where they had all got to, and they went in and danced some more dances. Ernestine danced twice with Frederick and drank iced sherry and water and they said goodnight and lighted their bedroom candles at the table in the hall.

"I do hope they won't," Amelia said as the girls sat brushing their hair at the two large white muslin frilled dressing-tables in the room they shared.

"Won't what?" said Ernestine, vigorous with the brush.

"Sleep in that hateful pavilion. I wish you'd ask them not to, Ernestine. They'd mind, if you asked them."

"Of course I will if you like, dear," said Ernestine cordially. She was always the soul of good nature. "But I don't think you ought to believe in ghost stories, not really."

"Why not?"

"Oh, because of the Bible and going to church and all that," said Ernestine. "Do you really think Rowland's Macassar has made any difference to my hair?"

"It is just as beautiful as it always was," said Amelia, twisting up her own little ashen-blonde handful. "What was that?"

That was a sound coming from the little dressing-room. There was no light in that room. Amelia went into the little room though Ernestine said: "Oh, don't! how can you? It might be a ghost or a rat or something," and as she went she whispered: "Hush!"

The window of the little room was open and she leaned out of it. The stone sill was cold to her elbows through her print dressing-jacket.

Ernestine went on brushing her hair. Amelia heard a movement below the window and listened. "Tonight will do," someone said.

"It's too late," said someone else.

"If you're afraid, it will always be too late or too early," said someone. And it was Thesiger.

"You know I'm not afraid," the other one, who was Doricourt, answered hotly.

"An hour for each of us will satisfy honour," said Thesiger carelessly. "The girls will expect it. I couldn't sleep. Let's do it now and get it over. Let's see. Oh, damn it!"

A faint click had sounded.

"Dropped my watch. I forgot the chain was loose. It's all right though; glass not broken even. Well, are you game?"

"Oh, yes, if you insist. Shall I go first, or you?"

"I will," said Thesiger. "That's only fair, because I suggested it. I'll stay till half-past one or a quarter to two, and then you come on. See?"

"Oh, all right. I think it's silly, though," said Frederick.

Then the voices ceased. Amelia went back to the other girl.

"They're going to do it tonight."

"Are they, dear?" Ernestine was placid as ever. "Do what?"

"Sleep in that horrible pavilion."

"How do you know?"

Amelia explained how she knew.

"Whatever can we do?" she added.

"Well, dear, suppose we go to bed," suggested Ernestine helpfully. "We shall hear all about it in the morning."

"But suppose anything happens?"

"What could happen?"

"Oh, *anything*," said Amelia. "Oh, I do wish they wouldn't! I shall go down and ask them not to."

"*Amelia!*" the other girl was at last aroused. "You *couldn't*. I shouldn't *let* you dream of doing anything so unladylike. What would the gentlemen think of you?"

The question silenced Amelia. But she began to put on her so lately discarded bodice.

"I won't go if you think I oughtn't," she said.

"Forward and fast, auntie would call it," said the other. "I am almost sure she would."

"But I'll keep dressed. I shan't disturb you. I'll sit in the dressing-room. I *can't* go to sleep while he's running into this awful danger."

"Which he?" Ernestine's voice was very sharp. "And there isn't any danger."

"Yes, there is," said Amelia sullenly, "and I mean *them*. Both of them."

Ernestine said her prayers and got into bed. She had put her hair in curl-papers which became her like a wreath of white roses.

"I don't think auntie will be pleased," she said, "when she hears that you sat up all night watching young gentlemen. Goodnight, dear!"

"Goodnight, darling," said Amelia. "I know you don't understand. It's all right."

She sat in the dark by the dressing-room window. There was no moon, but the starlight lay on the dew of the park, and the trees massed themselves in bunches of a darker grey, deepening to black at the roots of them. There was no sound to break the stillness, except the little cracklings of twigs and rustlings of leaves as birds or little night wandering beasts moved in the shadows of the garden, and the sudden creakings that furniture makes if you sit alone with it and listen in the night's silence.

Amelia sat on and listened, listened. The pavilion showed in broken streaks of pale grey against the wood, that seemed to be clinging to it in dark patches. But that, she reminded herself, was only the creeper. She sat there for a very long time, not knowing how long a time it was. For anxiety is a poor chronometer, and the first ten minutes had seemed an hour. She had no watch. Ernestine had—and slept with it under her pillow. The stable clock was out of order; the man had been sent for to see to it. There was nothing to measure time's flight by, and she sat there rigid, straining her ears for a footfall on the grass, straining her eyes to see a figure come out of the dark pavilion and across the dew-grey grass towards the house. And she heard nothing, saw nothing.

Slowly, imperceptibly, the grey of the sleeping trees took on faint dreams of colour. The sky turned faint above the trees, the moon perhaps was coming out. The pavilion grew more clearly visible. It seemed to Amelia that something moved along the leaves that surrounded it, and she looked to see him come out. But he did not come.

"I wish the moon would really shine," she told herself. And suddenly she knew that the sky was clear and that this growing light was not the moon's cold shiver, but the growing light of dawn.

She went quickly into the other room, put her hand under the pillow of Ernestine, and drew out the little watch with the diamond "E" on it.

"A quarter to three," she said aloud. Ernestine moved and grunted.

There was no hesitation about Amelia now. Without another thought for the ladylike and the really suitable, she lighted her candle and went quickly down the stairs, paused a moment in the hall, and so out through the front door. She passed along the terrace. The feet of Frederick protruded from the open French window of the smoking-room. She set down her candle on the terrace—it burned clearly enough in that clear air—went up to Frederick as he slept, his head between his shoulders and his hands loosely hanging, and shook him.

"Wake up," she said— "Wake up! Something's happened! It's a quarter to three and he's not come back."

"Who's not what?" Frederick asked sleepily.

"Mr. Thesiger. The pavilion."

"Thesiger!—the ... *You*, Miss Davenant? I beg your pardon. I must have dropped off."

He got up unsteadily, gazing dully at this white apparition still in evening dress with pale hair now no longer wreathed.

"What is it?" he said. "Is anybody ill?"

Briefly and very urgently Amelia told him what it was, implored him to go at once and see what had happened. If he had been fully awake, her voice and her eyes would have told him many things.

"He said he'd come back," he said. "Hadn't I better wait? You go back to bed, Miss Davenant. If he doesn't come in half an hour ..."

"If you don't go this minute," said Amelia tensely, "I shall."

"Oh, well, if you insist," Frederick said. "He has simply fallen asleep as I did. Dear Miss Davenant, return to your room, I beg. In the morning when we are all laughing at this false alarm, you will be glad to remember that Mr. Thesiger does not know of your anxiety."

"I hate you," said Amelia gently, "and I am going to see what has happened. Come or not, as you like."

She caught up the silver candlestick and he followed its wavering gleam down the terrace steps and across the grey dewy grass.

Half-way she paused, lifted the hand that had been hidden among her muslin flounces and held it out to him with a big Indian dagger in it.

"I got it out of the hall," she said. "If there's any *real* danger. Anything living. I mean. I thought ... But I know I couldn't use it. Will you take it?"

He took it, laughing kindly.

"How romantic you are," he said admiringly and looked at her standing there in the mingled gold and grey of dawn and candle-light. It was as though he had never seen her before.

They reached the steps of the pavilion and stumbled up them. The door was closed but not locked. And Amelia noticed that the trails of creeper had not been disturbed, they grew across the door-way, as thick as a man's finger, some of them.

"He must have got in by one of the windows," Frederick said. "Your dagger comes in handy, Miss Davenant."

He slashed at the wet sticky green stuff and put his shoulder to the door. It yielded at a touch and they went in.

The one candle lighted the pavilion hardly at all, and the dusky light that oozed in through the door and windows helped very little. And the silence was thick and heavy.

"Thesiger!" said Frederick, clearing his throat. "Thesiger! Hullo! Where are you?" Thesiger did not say where he was. And then they saw.

There were low seats to the windows, and between the windows low stone benches ran. On one of these something dark, something dark and in places white, confused the outline of the carved stone.

"Thesiger," said Frederick again in the tone a man uses to a room that he is almost sure is empty. "Thesiger!"

But Amelia was bending over the bench. She was holding the candle crookedly so that it flared and guttered.

"Is he there?" Frederick asked, following her; "is that him? Is he asleep?"

"Take the candle," said Amelia, and he took it obediently. Amelia was touching what lay on the bench. Suddenly she screamed. Just one scream, not very loud. But Frederick remembers just how it sounded. Sometimes he hears it in dreams and wakes moaning, though he is an old man now and his old wife says: "What is it, dear?" and he says: "Nothing, my Ernestine, nothing."

Directly she had screamed she said: "He's dead," and fell on her knees by the bench. Frederick saw that she held something in her arms.

"Perhaps he isn't," she said. "Fetch someone from the house, brandy—send for a doctor. Oh, go, go, go!"

"I can't leave you here," said Frederick with thoughtful propriety; "suppose he revives?"

"He will not revive," said Amelia dully, "go, go, go! Do as I tell you. Go! If you don't go," she added suddenly and amazingly, "I believe I shall kill you. It's all your doing."

The astounding sharp injustice of this stung Frederick into action.

"I believe he's only fainted or something," he said. "When I've roused the house and everyone has witnessed your emotion you will regret ..."

She sprang to her feet and caught the knife from him and raised it, awkwardly, clumsily, but with keen threatening, not to be mistaken or disregarded. Frederick went.

When Frederick came back, with the groom and the gardener (he hadn't thought it well to disturb the ladies), the pavilion was filled full of white revealing daylight. On the bench lay a dead man and kneeling by him a living woman on whose warm breast his cold and heavy head lay pillowed. The dead man's hands were full of the green crushed leaves, and thick twining tendrils were about his wrists and throat. A wave of green seemed to have swept from the open window to the bench where he lay.

The groom and the gardener and the dead man's friend looked and looked.

"Looks like as if he'd got himself entangled in the creeper and lost 'is 'ead," said the groom, scratching his own.

"How'd the creeper get in, though? That's what I says," it was the gardener who said it. "Through the window," said Doricourt, moistening his lips with his tongue.

"The window was shut, though, when I come by at five yesterday," said the gardener stubbornly. "'Ow did it get all that way since five?"

They looked at each other, voicing, silently, impossible things.

The woman never spoke. She sat there in the white ring of her crinolined dress like a broken white rose. But her arms were round Thesiger and she would not move them.

When the doctor came, he sent for Ernestine who came, flushed and sleepy-eyed and very frightened, and shocked.

"You're upset, dear," she said to her friend, "and no wonder. How brave of you to come out with Mr. Doricourt to see what happened. But you can't do anything now, dear. Come in and I'll tell them to get you some tea."

Amelia laughed, looked down at the face on her shoulder, laid the head back on the bench among the drooping green of the creeper, stooped over it, kissed it and said quite quietly and gently: "Goodbye, dear, goodbye!"—took Ernestine's arm and went away with her.

The doctor made an examination and gave a death-certificate. "Heart failure," was his original and brilliant diagnosis. The certificate said nothing, and Frederick said nothing, of the creeper that was wound about the dead man's neck, nor of the little white wounds, like little bloodless lips half-open, that they found about the dead man's neck.

"An imaginative or uneducated person," said the doctor, "might suppose that the creeper had something to do with his death. But we mustn't encourage superstition. I will assist my man to prepare the body for its last sleep. Then we need not have any chattering woman."

"Can you read Latin?" Frederick asked. The doctor could, and, later, did.

It was the Latin of that brown book with the Doricourt arms on it that Frederick wanted read. And when he and the doctor had been together with the book between them for three hours, they closed it, and looked at each other with shy and doubtful eyes.

"It can't be true," said Frederick.

"If it is," said the more cautious doctor, "you don't want it talked about. I should destroy that book if I were you. And I should root up that creeper and burn it. It is quite evident, from what you tell me, that your friend believed that this creeper was a man-eater, that it fed, just before its flowering time, as the book tells us, at dawn; and that he fully meant that the thing when it crawled into the pavilion seeking its prey should find you and not him. It would have been so, I understand, if his watch had not stopped at one o'clock."

"He dropped it, you know," said Doricourt like a man in a dream.

"All the cases in this book are the same," said the doctor, "the strangling, the white wounds. I have heard of such plants; I never believed." He shuddered. "Had your friend any spite against you? Any reason for wanting to get you out of the way?"

Frederick thought of Ernestine, of Thesiger's eyes on Ernestine, of her smile at him over her blue muslin shoulder.

"No," he said, "none. None whatever. It must have been an accident. I am sure he did not know. He could not read Latin." He lied, being, after all, a gentleman, and Ernestine's name being sacred.

"The creeper seems to have been brought here and planted in Henry the Eighth's time. And then the thing began. It seems to have been at its flowering season that it needed the ... that, in short, it was dangerous. The little animals and birds found dead near the pavilion ... But to move itself all that way, across the floor! The thing must have been almost conscient," he said with a sincere shudder. "One would think," he corrected himself at once, "that it knew what it was doing, if such a thing were not plainly contrary to the laws of nature."

"Yes," said Frederick, "one would. I think if I can't do anything more I'll go and rest. Somehow all this has given me a turn. Poor Thesiger!"

His last thought before he went to sleep was one of pity.

"Poor Thesiger," he said, "how violent and wicked! And what an escape for me! I must never tell Ernestine. And all the time there was Amelia ... Ernestine would never have done *that* for *me*." And on a little pang of regret for the impossible he fell asleep.

Amelia went on living. She was not the sort that dies even of such a thing as happened to her on that night, when for the first and last time she held her love in her arms and knew him for the murderer he was. It was only the other day that she died, a very old woman. Ernestine who, beloved and surrounded by children and grandchildren, survived her, spoke her epitaph:

"Poor Amelia," she said, "nobody ever looked the same side of the road where she was. There was an indiscretion when she was young. Oh, nothing disgraceful, of course. She was a lady. But people talked. It was the sort of thing that stamps a girl, you know."

The Sumach
Ulric Daubeny

"How red that Sumach is!"

Irene Barton murmured something commonplace, for to her the tree brought painful recollections. Her visitor, unconscious of this fact, proceeded to elaborate.

"Do you know, Irene, that tree gives me the creeps! I can't explain, except that it is not a nice tree, not a *good* tree. For instance, why should its leaves be red in August, when they are not supposed to turn until October?"

"What queer ideas you have, May! The tree is right enough, although its significance to me is sad. Poor Spot, you know; we buried him beneath it two days ago. Come and see his grave."

The two women left the terrace, where this conversation had been taking place, and leisurely strolled across the lawn, at the end of which, in almost startling isolation, grew the Sumach. At least, Mrs. Watcombe, who evinced so great an interest in the tree, questioned whether it actually was a Sumach, for the foliage was unusual, and the branches gnarled and twisted beyond recognition. Just now, the leaves were stained with splashes of dull crimson, but rather than droop, they had a bloated appearance, as if the luxuriance of the growth were not altogether healthy.

For several moments they stood regarding the pathetic little grave, and the silence was only broken when Mrs. Watcombe darted beneath the tree, and came back with something in her hand.

"Irene, look at this dead thrush. Poor little thing! Such splendid plumage, yet it hardly weighs a sugar plum!"

Mrs. Barton regarded it with wrinkled brows. "I cannot understand what happens to the birds, May—unless someone lays poison.

262

We continually find them dead about the garden, and usually beneath, or very near this tree."

It is doubtful whether Mrs. Watcombe listened. Her attention seemed to wander that morning, and she was studying the twisted branches of the Sumach with a thoughtful scrutiny.

"Curious that the leaves should turn at this time of year," she murmured. "It brings to mind poor Geraldine's illness. This tree had an extraordinary fascination for her, you know. It was quite scarlet then, yet that was only June, and it had barely finished shooting."

"My dear May! You have red leaves on the brain this morning!" Irene retorted, uncertain whether to be irritated or amused. "I can't think why you are so concerned about the color. It is only the result of two days' excessive heat, for scarcely a leaf was touched, when I buried poor old Spot."

The conversation seemed absurdly trivial, yet, Mrs. Watcombe gone, Irene could not keep her mind from dwelling on her cousin's fatal illness. The news had reached them with the shock of the absolutely unexpected. Poor Geraldine, who had always been so strong, to have fallen victim to acute anemia! It was almost unbelievable, that heart failure should have put an end to her sweet young life, after a few days' ailing. Of course, the sad event had wrought a wonderful change for Irene and her husband, giving them, in place of a cramped suburban villa, this beautiful country home, Cleeve Grange. Everything for her was filled with the delight of novelty, for she had ruled as mistress over the charmed abode for only one short week. Hilary, her husband, was yet a stranger to the more intimate of its attractions, being detained in London by the winding-up of business affairs.

Several days elapsed, for the most part given solely to the keen pleasure of arranging and rearranging the new home. As time went by, the crimson splashes on the Sumach faded, the leaves becoming green again, though drooping as if from want of moisture. Irene noticed this when she paid her daily visits to the pathetic little dog grave, trying to induce flowers to take root upon it, but do what she might, they invariably faded. Nothing, not even grass, would grow beneath the Sumach. Only death seemed to thrive there, she mused in a fleeting moment of depression, as she searched around for more dead birds. But none had fallen since the thrush, picked up by Mrs. Watcombe.

One evening, the heat inside the house becoming insupportable, Irene wandered into the garden, her steps mechanically leading her to the little grave beneath the Sumach. In the uncertain moonlight, the twisted trunk and branches of the old tree were suggestive of a rustic seat, and feeling tired, she lifted herself into the natural bower, and lolled back, joyously inhaling the cool night air. Presently she dropped asleep, and in a curiously vivid manner, dreamt of Hilary; that he had completed his business in London, and was coming home. They met at evening, near the garden gate, and Hilary spread wide his arms, and eagerly folded them about her. Swiftly the dream began to change, assuming the characteristic of a nightmare. The sky grew strangely dark, the arms fiercely masterful, while the face which bent to kiss her neck was not that of her young husband: it was leering, wicked, gnarled like the trunk of some weather-beaten tree. Chilled with horror, Irene fought long and desperately against the vision, to be at last awakened by her own frightened whimpering. Yet returning consciousness did not immediately dissipate the nightmare. In imagination she was still held rigid by brutal arms, and it was only after a blind, half-waking struggle that she freed herself, and went speeding across the lawn, towards the lighted doorway.

Next morning Mrs. Watcombe called, and subjected her to a puzzled scrutiny.

"How pale you look, Irene. Do you feel ill?"

"Ill! No, only a little languid. I find this hot weather very trying."

Mrs. Watcombe studied her with care, for the pallor of Irene's face was very marked. In contrast, a vivid spot of red showed on the slender neck, an inch or so below the ear. Intuitively a hand went up, as Irene turned to her friend in explanation.

"It feels so sore. I think I must have grazed the skin, last night, while sitting in the Sumach."

"Sitting in the Sumach!" echoed Mrs. Watcombe in surprise. "How curious you should do that. Poor Geraldine used to do the same, just before she was taken ill, and yet at the last she was seized with a perfect horror of the tree. Goodness, but it is quite red again, this morning!"

Irene swung round in the direction of the tree, filled with a vague repugnance. Sure enough, the leaves no longer drooped, nor were they green. They had become flecked once more with crimson, and the growth had quite regained its former vigor.

"Eugh!" she breathed, hurriedly turning towards the house. "It reminds me of a horrid nightmare. I have rather a head this morning; let's go in, and talk of something else!"

As the day advance, the heat grew more oppressive, and night brought with it a curious stillness, the stillness which so often presages a heavy thunderstorm. No bird had offered up its evening hymn, no breeze came sufficient to stir a single leaf—everything was pervaded by a silence of expectancy.

The interval between dinner and bedtime is always a dreary one for those accustomed to companionship, and left all alone, Irene's restlessness momentarily increased. First the ceiling, then the very atmosphere seemed to weigh heavy upon her head. Although windows and doors were all flung wide, the airlessness of the house grew less and less endurable, until from sheer desperation she made her escape into the garden, where a sudden illumination of the horizon gave warning of the approaching storm. Feeling somewhat at a loss, she roamed aimlessly awhile, pausing sometimes to catch the echoes of distant thunder, until at last she found herself standing over Spot's desolate little grave. The sight struck her with a sense of utter loneliness, and the tears sprang to her eyes, in poignant longing for the companionship of her faithful pet.

Moved by she knew not what, Irene swung herself into the comfortable branches of the old Sumach, and soothed by the reposeful attitude, her head soon began to nod in slumber. Afterwards it was a doubtful memory whether she actually did sleep, or whether the whole experience was not a kind of waking nightmare. Something of the previous evening's dream returned to her, but this time with added horror; for it commenced with no pleasurable vision of her husband. Instead, relentless, stick-like arms immediately closed in upon her, their vice-like grip so tight that she could scarcely breathe. Down darted the awful head, rugged and lined by every sin, darting at the fair, white neck as a wild beast on its prey. The foul lips began to eat into he skin ... She struggled desperately, madly, for to her swooning senses the very branches of the tree became endowed with active life, coiling unmercifully around her, tenaciously clinging to her limbs, and tearing at her dress. Pain at last spurred her to an heroic effort, the pain of something—perhaps a twig—digging deep into her unprotected neck. With a choking cry she freed herself, and nerved by a sudden burst of thunder, ran tottering towards the shelter of the house.

Having gained the cozy lounge-hall, Irene sank into an arm-chair, gasping hysterically for breath. Gusts of refreshing wind came through the open windows, but although the atmosphere rapidly grew less stagnant, an hour passed before she could make sufficient effort to crawl upstairs to bed. In her room, a further shock awaited her. The bloodless, drawn face reflected in the mirror was scarcely recognizable. The eyes lacked luster, the lips were white, the skin hung flabby on the shrunken flesh, giving it a look of premature old age. A tiny trickle of dry blood, the solitary smudge of color, stained the chalky pallor of her neck. Taking up a hand-glass, she examined this with momentary concern. It was the old wound reopened, an angry-looking sore, almost like the bite of some small, or very sharp—toothed animal. It smarted painfully...

Mrs. Watcombe, bursting into the breakfast room next morning, with suggestions of an expedition to the neighboring town, was shocked at Irene's looks, and insisted on going at once to fetch the doctor. Mrs. Watcombe fussed continually throughout the interview, and insisted on an examination of the scar upon Irene's neck. Patient and doctor had regarded this as a negligible detail, but finally the latter subjected it to a slightly puzzled scrutiny, advising that it should be kept bandaged. He suggested that Irene was suffering from anemia, and would do well to keep as quiet as possible, building up her strength with food, open windows and a general selection of pills and tonics. But despite these comforting arrangements, no one was entirely satisfied. The doctor lacked something in assurance, Irene was certain that she could not really be anemic, while Mrs. Watcombe was obsessed by inward misgivings, perfectly indefinable, yet none the less disturbing. She left the house as a woman bent under a load of care. Passing up the lane, her glance lighted on the old Sumach, more crimson now, more flourishing in its growth than she had seen it since the time of Geraldine's fatal illness.

"I loathe that horrid old tree!" she murmured, then added, struck by a nameless premonition, "Her husband ought to know. I shall wire to him at once."

Irene, womanlike, put to use her enforced idleness, by instituting a rearrangement of the box-room, the only part of her new home which yet remained unexplored. Among the odds and ends of the rubbish to be thrown away, there was a little notebook, apparently unused. In idle curiosity, Irene picked it up, and was surprised to learn, from an inscription, that her cousin Geraldine had intended to use it as a diary. A date appeared—only a few days prior to the poor girl's death—but no entries had been made, though the first two pages of the book had certainly been removed. As Irene put it down, there fluttered to the ground a torn scrap of writing. She stooped, and continued stooping, breathlessly staring at the words that had been written by her cousin's hand—*Sumach fascinates m—*

In some unaccountable manner this applied to her. It was obvious what tree was meant, the old Sumach at the end of the lawn; and it fascinated her, Irene, though not until that moment had she openly recognized the fact. Searching hurriedly through the notebook, she discovered, near the end, a heap of torn paper, evidently the first two pages of a diary. She turned the pieces in eager haste. Most of them bore no more than one short word, or portions of a longer one, but a few bigger fragments proved more enlightening, and filled with nervous apprehension, she carried the book to her escritoire, and spent the remainder of the afternoon in trying to piece together the torn-up pages.

Meanwhile, Mrs. Watcombe was worrying and fretting over Irene's unexpected illness. Her pallor, her listlessness, even the curious mark upon her neck, gave cause for positive alarm, so exactly did they correspond with symptoms exhibited by her cousin Geraldine, during the few days prior to her death. She wished that the village doctor, who had attended the earlier case, would return soon from his holiday, as his *locum tenens* seemed sadly wanting in that authoritative decision which is so consoling to patients, relatives, and friends. Feeling, as an old friend, responsible for the welfare of Irene, she wired to Hilary, telling him of the sudden illness, and advising him to return without delay.

The urgency of the telegram alarmed him, so much so that he left London by the next train, arriving at Cleeve Grange shortly after dark.

"Where is your mistress?" was his first enquiry, as the maid met him in the hall.

"Upstairs, Sir. She complained of feeling tired, and said she would go to bed."

He hurried to her room, only to find it empty. He called, he rang for the servants; in a moment the whole house was astir, yet nowhere was Irene to be found. Deeming it possible that she might have gone to see Mrs. Watcombe, Hilary was about to follow, when that lady herself was ushered in.

"I saw the lights of your cab—" she commenced, cutting short the sentence, as she met his questioning glance.

"Where is Irene?"

"Irene? My dear Hilary, is she not here?"

"No. We can't find her anywhere. I thought she might have been with you."

For the space of half a second, Mrs. Watcombe's face presented a picture of astonishment; then the expression changed to one of dismayed concern.

"She is in that tree! I'm certain of it! Hilary, we must fetch her in at once!"

Completely at a loss to understand, he followed the excited woman into the garden, stumbling blindly in her wake across the lawn. The darkness was intense, and a terrific wind beat them back as if with living hands. Irene's white dress at length became discernible, dimly thrown up against the pitchy background, and obscured in places by the twists and coils of the old Sumach. Between them they grasped the sleeping body, but the branches swung wildly in the gale, and to Hilary's confused imagination it was if they had literally to tear it from the tree's embrace. At last they regained the shelter of the house, and laid their inanimate burden upon the sofa. She was quite unconscious, pale as death, and her face painfully contorted, as if with fear. The old wound on the neck, now bereft of bandages, had been reopened, and was wet with blood.

Hilary rushed off to fetch the doctor, while Mrs. Watcombe and the servants carried Irene to her room. Several hours passed before she recovered consciousness, and during that time Hilary was gently but firmly excluded from the sickroom. Bewildered and disconsolate, he wandered restlessly about the house, until his attention was arrested by the unusual array of torn-up bits of papers on Irene's desk. He saw that she had been sorting out the pieces, and sticking them together as the sentences became complete. The work was barely half finished, yet what there was to read, struck him as exceedingly strange:

The seat in the old Sumach fascinates me. I find myself going back to it unconsciously, nay, even against my will. Oh, but the nightmare visions it always brings me! In them

I seem to plumb the very depths of terror. Their memory preys upon my mind, and every day my strength grows less.

Dr. H. speaks of anemia...

That was as far as Irene had proceeded. Hardly knowing why he did so, Hilary resolved to complete the task, but the chill of early morning was in the air before it was finished. Cramped and stiff, he was pushing back his chair when a footstep sounded in the doorway, and Mrs. Watcombe entered.

"Irene is better," she volunteered immediately. "She is sleeping naturally, and Doctor Thomson says there is no longer any immediate danger. The poor child is terribly weak and bloodless."

"May—tell me—what is the meaning of all this? Why has Irene suddenly become so ill? I can't understand it!"

Mrs. Watcombe's face was preternaturally grave.

"Even the doctor admits that he is puzzles," she answered very quietly. "The symptoms all point to a sudden and excessive loss of blood, though in cases of acute anemia—"

"God! but—not like Geraldine? I can't believe it!"

"Neither can I. Oh, Hilary, you may think me mad, but I can't help feeling that there is some unknown, some awful influence at work. Irene was perfectly well three days ago, and it was the same with Geraldine before she was taken ill. The cases are so exactly similar.

"Irene was trying to tell me something about a diary, but the poor girl was too exhausted to make herself properly understood."

"Diary? Geraldine's diary, do you think? She must mean that. I have just finished piecing it together, but frankly, I can't make head or tail of it!"

Mrs. Watcombe rapidly scanned the writing, then studied it again with greater care. Finally she read the second part aloud.

"Listen, Hilary! This seems to me important."

"Dr. H. speaks of anemia. Pray heaven, he may be correct, for my thoughts sometimes move in a direction which foreshadows nothing short of lunacy—or so people would tell me, if I could bring myself to confide these things. I must fight alone, clinging to the knowledge that it is usual for anemic persons to be obsessed by unhealthy fancies. If only I had not read those horribly suggestive words in Barrett...

"Barrett? What can she mean, May?"

"Wait a moment. Barrett? Barrett's *Traditions of the Country*, perhaps. I have noticed a copy in the library. Let us go there; it may give the clue!"

The book was quickly found, and a marker indicated the passage to which Geraldine apparently referred.

At Cleeve, I was reminded of another of those traditions, so rapidly disappearing before the spread of education. It concerned an old belief in vampires, spirits of the evil dead, who by night, could assume a human form, and scour the countryside in search of victims. Suspected vampires, if caught, were buried with the mouth stuffed full of garlic, and a stake plunged through the heart, whereby they were rendered harmless, or, at least, confined to that one particular locality.

Some thirty years ago, an old man pointed out a tree which was said to have grown from such a stake. So far as I can recollect, it was an unusual variety of Sumach, and had been enclosed during a recent extension to the garden of the old Grange...

"Come outside," said Mrs. Watcombe, breaking a long and solemn silence. "I want you to see that tree."

The sky was suffused with the blush of early dawn, and the shrubs, the flowers, even the dew upon the grass caught and reflected something of the pink effulgence. The Sumach alone stood out, dark and menacing. During the night its leaves had become a hideous, mottled purple; its growth was oily, bloated, unnaturally vigorous, like that of some rank and poisonous week.

Mrs. Watcombe, looking from afar, spoke in frightened, husky tones.

"See, Hilary! It was exactly like that when—when Geraldine died!"

When evening fell, the end of the lawn was strangely bare. In place of the old tree, there lay an enormous heap of smoldering embers—enormous, because the Sumach had been too sodden and sticky sap, to burn without the assistance of large quantities of other timber.

Many weeks elapsed before Irene was sufficiently recovered to walk as far as Spot's little grave. She was surprised to find it almost hidden in a bed of garlic.

Hilary explained that it was the only plant they could induce to grow there.

The Green Death

H. C. McNeile

I.

"And why, Major Seymour, do they call you Old Point of Detail?"

The tall, spare man, with a face tanned by years in the tropics, turned at the question, and glanced at the girl beside him. At the time when most boys are still at school, force of circumstances had sent him far afield into strange corners of the earth—a wanderer, and picker-up of odd jobs. He had done police work in India; he had been on a rubber plantation in Sumatra. The Amazon knew him and so did the Yukon, while his knowledge of the customs of tribes in Darkest Africa—the very names of which were unknown to most people—was greater than the average Londoner has of his native city. In fact, before the war it would have been difficult to sit for an evening in one of those clubs which spring into being in all corners where Englishmen guard their far-flung inheritance without Bob Seymour's name cropping up.

Then had come the war, and in the van of the great army from the mountains and the swamps which trekked home as the first shot rang out, he came. As his reward he got a D.S.O. and one leg permanently shortened by two inches. He also met a girl—the girl who had just asked him the question.

He'd met her just a year after the Armistice; when he was wondering whether there was any place for a cripple in the lands that he knew. And from that day everything had changed. Even to himself he wouldn't admit it; the thought of asking such a glorious bit of loveliness to tie herself to a useless has-been like himself was out of the question. But he let the days slip by, content to meet her occasionally at dinner—to see her, in the distance, at a theatre. And now, for the first time, he found himself staying under the same roof. When he'd arrived the preceding day and had seen her in the hall, just for a moment his heart had stopped beating, and then had given a great bound forward. She, of course, knew nothing of his feelings; of that he felt sure. And she must never know; of that he was determined. The whole thing was out of the question.

Of course—naturally. And the only comment which a mere narrator of facts can offer on the state of affairs is to record the remark made by Ruth Brabazon to a very dear friend of hers after Bob Seymour had limped upstairs to his room.

"That's the man, Delia," she said, with a little smile. "And if he doesn't say something soon, I shall have to."

"He looks a perfect darling," remarked the other.

"He is," sighed Ruth. "But he won't give me the chance of telling him so. He thinks he's a cripple."

With which brief insight into things as they really were, we can now return to things as Bob Seymour thought they were. Beside him, on a sofa in the hall, sat the girl who had kept him in England through long months, and she had just asked him a question.

"The Old, I trust, is a term of endearment," he answered, with a smile, "and not a brutal reflection on my tale of years. The Point of Detail refers to a favourite saving of mine with which my reprobate subalterns—of whom your brother was quite the worst—used to mock me."

"Bill is the limit," murmured the girl. What was the saying?"

"I used to preach the importance of Points of Detail to 'em," he grinned. "One is nothing; two are a coincidence; three are a moral certainty. And they're very easy to see if you have eyes to see them with."

"I suppose they are, Old Point of Detail," she replied, softly.

Was it his imagination or did she lay a faint stress on the Old?

"It was certainly a term of endearment," she continued, deliberately, "if what Bill says is to be believed."

"Oh! Bill's an ass," said Seymour, sheepishly.

"Thank you," she remarked, and he noticed her eyes were twinkling. "I've always been told I'm exactly like Bill. I know we always used to like the same things when we were children." She rose and crossed the hall. "Time to dress for dinner, I think."

In the dim light he could not see her face clearly: he only knew his heart was thumping wildly. Did she mean—? And then from half-way up the stairs she spoke again.

"Two are certainly a coincidence," she agreed, thoughtfully. "But the third would have to be pretty conclusive before you could take it as a certainty."

II.

"Well, Major Seymour, hitting 'em in the beak?" The Celebrated Actor mixed himself a cocktail with that delicate grace for which he was famed on both sides of the Atlantic.

"So—so, Mr. Trayne," returned the other. "All the easy ones came my way."

The house-party were in the hall waiting for dinner to be announced, but the one member of it who mattered to Bob Seymour had not yet appeared.

"Rot, my dear fellow," said his host, who had come up in time to hear his last remark. "Your shooting was magnificent—absolutely magnificent. You had four birds in the air once from your guns."

"Personally," murmured the Celebrated Actor, "it fails to appeal to me. Apart from my intense fright at letting off lethal weapons, I have never yet succeeded in hitting anything except a keeper or—more frequently—a guest. I abhor violence—except at rehearsals." He broke off as a heavy, bull-necked man came slowly down the stairs. "And who is the latest addition to our number, Sir Robert?"

"A man who did me a good turn a few weeks ago," said the owner of the house, shortly. "Name of Denton. Arrived half an hour ago."

He moved away to introduce the new-comer, and the Actor turned to Bob Seymour.

"One wonders," he remarked, "whether it would be indiscreet to offer Mr. Denton a part in my new play. Nothing much to say. He merely drinks and eats. In effect, a publican of unprepossessing aspect. One wonders—so suitable." He placed his empty glass on the table and drifted charmingly away towards his hostess, leaving Bob Seymour smiling gently. Undoubtedly a most suitable part for Mr. Denton.

And then, quite suddenly, the smile died away. Bill Brabazon, who was standing near the fireplace, had turned round and come face to face with the new-comer; For a moment or two they stared at one another—a deadly loathing on their faces; then with ostentatious rudeness Denton turned his back and walked away.

"My God! Bob," muttered Bill, coming; up to Seymour. "How on earth did that swine-emperor get here?"

His jaw was grim and set, his eyes gleaming with rage; and the hand that poured out the cocktail shook a little.

"What's the matter, Bill?" said Seymour, quietly. "For Heaven's sake, don't make a scene, old man!"

"Matter!" choked Bill Brabazon. "Matter! Why—"

But any further revelations were checked by the announcement of dinner, and the party went in informally. To his delight, Bob Seymour found himself next to Ruth, and the little scene he had just witnessed passed from his mind. It was not until they were half-way through the meal that, it was recalled to him by Ruth herself.

"Who is that dreadful-looking man talking to Delia Morrison?" she whispered.

"Denton is his name," replied Seymour, and every vestige of colour left her face.

"Denton," she muttered. "Good heavens! it can't be the same." She glanced round the table till she found her brother, who was answering the animated remarks of his partner with morose mono-syllables. "Has Bill—"

"Bill has," returned Seymour, grimly. "And he's whispered to me on the subjects. What's the trouble?"

"They had the most fearful row—over a girl," she explained, a little breathlessly. "Two or three months ago. I know they had a fight, and Bill got a black eye. But he broke that other brute's jaw."

"Holy smoke!" muttered Seymour. "Their meeting strikes the casual observer as being, to put it mildly, embarrassing. Do you known how the row started?"

"Only vaguely," she answered. "That man Denton got some girl into trouble, and then left her in the lurch—refused to help her at all. A poor girl—the daughter of someone who had been in Bill's platoon. And he came to Bill."

"I see," said Seymour, grimly. "I see. Bill would."

"Of course he would!" she cried. "Why, of course. Just the same as you would."

"I suppose that isn't pretty conclusive?" He said, with a grin. "As a third point, I mean."

But Ruth Brabazon had turned to the Celebrated Actor on her other side. He had already said, "My dear young lady" five times without avail, and he was Very Celebrated.

Neglected for the moment by both his neighbours, Bob proceeded to study the gentleman whose sudden arrival seemed so inopportune. He was a coarse-looking specimen, and already his face was flushed with the amount of wine he had drunk. Every now and then his eyes sought Bill Brabazon vindictively, and Seymour frowned as he saw it. Denton belonged to a type he had met before, and it struck him there was every promise of trouble before the evening was out. When men of Denton's calibre get into the condition of "drink-taken," such trifles as the presence of other guests in the house do not deter them from being offensive. And Bill Brabazon, though far too well-bred to seek a quarrel in such surroundings, was also far too hot-tempered to take any deliberate insult lying down.

Suddenly a coarse, overloud laugh from Denton sounded above the general conversation, and Ruth Brabazon looked round quickly.

"Ugh! what a horrible man!" she whispered to Bob. "How I hate him!"

"I don't believe a word of it," he was saying, harshly. "Fraud by knaves for fools. For those manifestations that have been seen there is some material cause. Generally transparent trickery." He laughed again, sneeringly.

For a second or two there was an uncomfortable silence. It was not so much what the man had said, as the vulgar, ill-bred manner in which he had said it, and Sir Robert hastily intervened to relieve the tension.

"Ghosts?" he remarked. "As impossible a subject to argue about as religion or politics. Incidentally, you know," he continued, addressing the table at large, "there's a room in this house round which a novelist might weave quite a good ghost story."

"Tell us, Sir Robert." A general chorus assailed him, and he smiled.

"I'm not a novelist," he said, "though for what it's worth I'll tell you about it. The room is one in the new wing which I used to use as a smoking-room. It was the part built on to the house by my predecessor—a gentleman, from all accounts, of peculiar temperament. He had spent all his life travelling to obscure places of the world; and I don't know if it was liver or what, but his chief claim to notoriety when he did finally settle down appears to have been an intense hatred of his fellow-men. There are some very strange stories of the things which used to go on in this house, where he lived the life of an absolute recluse, with one old man to look after him. He died about forty years ago."

Sir Robert paused and sipped his champagne.

"However, to continue. In this smoking-room in the new wing there is an inscription written in the most amazing jumble of letters by the window. It is written on the wall, and every form of hiero-glyphic is used. You get a letter of Arabic, then one of Chinese, then an ordinary English one, and perhaps a German. Well, to cut a long story short, I took the trouble one day to copy it out, and replaced the foreign letters—there are one or two Greek letters as well—by their corresponding English ones. I had to get somebody else to help me over the Chinese and Arabic, but the result was, at any rate, sense. It proved to be a little jingling rhyme, and it ran as follows:—

When 'tis hot, shun this spot.
When 'tis rain, come again.
When 'tis day, all serene.
When 'tis night, death is green."

Sir Robert glanced round the table with a smile.

"There was no doubt who had written this bit of doggerel, as the wing was actually built by my predecessor—and I certainly didn't. That's a pretty good foundation to build a ghost story on, isn't it?"

"But have you ever seen anything?" inquired one of the guests.

"Not a thing," laughed his host. "But"—he paused mysteriously—"I've smelt something. And that's the reason why I don't use the room any more.

"It was a very hot night—hotter even than this evening. There was thunder about—incidentally, I shouldn't be surprised if we had a storm before to-morrow—and I was sitting in the room after dinner, reading the paper. All of a sudden I became aware of a strange and most unpleasant smell: a sort of fetid, musty, rank smell, like you get sometimes when you open up an old vault. And at the same moment I noticed that the paper I held in my hand had gone a most peculiar green colour and I could no longer see the print clearly. It seemed to have got darker suddenly, and the smell be-came so bad that it made me feel quite faint.

"I walked over to the door and left the room, meaning to get a lamp. Then something detained me, and I didn't go back for half an hour or so. When I did the smell was still there, though so faint that one could hardly notice it. Also the paper was quite white again." He laughed genially. "And that's the family ghost; a poor thing, but our own. I'll have to get someone to take it in hand and bring it up-to-date."

"But surely you don't think there is any connection between this smell and the inscription?" cried Denton.

"I advance no theory at all." Sir Robert smiled genially. "All I can tell you is that there is an inscription, and that the colour green is mentioned in it. It seemed to me most certainly that my paper went green, though it is even more certain that I did not die. Also there is at times in the room this rather unpleasant smell. I told you it was a poor thing in the ghost line."

The conversation became general, and Ruth Brabazon turned to Bob, who was thoughtfully staring at his plate.

"Why so preoccupied, Major Seymour?"

"A most interesting yarn," he remarked, coming out of his reverie. "Have a salted almond, before I finish the lot."

III.

To have two hot-tempered men who loathe one another with a bitter loathing in a house-party is not conducive to its happiness. And when one of them is an outsider of the first water, slightly under the influence of alcohol, the situation becomes even more precarious. For some time after dinner was over Bill Brabazon avoided Denton as unostentatiously as he could, though it was plain to Bob Seymour and Ruth that he was finding it increasingly difficult to control his temper. By ten o'clock it was obvious, even to those guests who knew nothing about the men's previous relations, that there was trouble brewing; and Sir Robert, who had been told the facts of the case by Bob, was at his wits' end.

"If only I'd known," he said, irritably. "If only someone had told me. I know Denton is a sweep, but he did me a very good turn in the City the other day, and, without thinking, I asked him to come and shoot some time. And when he suggested coming now, I couldn't in all decency get out of it. I hope to Heaven there won't be a row."

"If there's going to be, Sir Robert, you can't prevent it," said Seymour. "I'm sure Bill will do all he can to avoid one."

"I know he will," answered his host. "But there are limits, and that man Denton is one of 'em. I wish I'd never met the blighter."

"Come and have a game of billiards, anyway," said the other. "It's no use worrying about it. If it comes, it comes."

When they had been playing about twenty minutes, Ruth Brabazon and Delia Morrison joined them, the billiard-room being, as they affirmed, the coolest room in the house.

"We'll have rain soon," said Sir Robert, bringing off a fine losing hazard off the red. "That'll clear the air."

And shortly afterwards his prophecy proved true. Heavy drops began to patter down on the glass skylight, and the girls heaved a sigh of relief.

"Thank goodness," gasped Ruth. "I couldn't have stood—" She broke off; abruptly and stared at the door, which had just opened to admit her brother. "Bill," she cried, "what's the matter?"

Bob Seymour looked up quickly at her words; then he rested his cue against the table. Something very obviously was the matter. Bill Brabazon, his tie undone, with a crumpled shirt, and a cut under his eye of the cheek-bone, came into the room and closed the door.

"I must apologize, Sir Robert," he said, quietly, "for what has happened. It's a rotten thing to have to admit in another man's house, but the fault was not entirely mine. I've had the most damnable row with that fellow Denton—incidentally he was half drunk—and I've laid him out. An unpardonable thing to do to one of your guests, but—well—I'm not particularly slow tempered, and I couldn't help it. He went on and on and on—asking for trouble: and finally he got it."

"Damnation!" Sir Robert replaced his cue in the rack. "When did it happen, Bill?"

"About half an hour ago. I've been outside since. Meaning to avoid him I went to the smoking-room in the new wing, and I found him there examining that inscription by the window. I couldn't get away—without running away. I suppose I ought to have." An uncomfortable silence settled on the room; which was broken at length by Sir Robert.

"Where is the fellow now, Bill?"

"I haven't seen him—not since I socked him one on the jaw. I'm deucedly sorry about it," he continued, miserably, "and I feel the most awful sweep, but—"

He stopped suddenly as the door was flung open and the Celebrated Actor rushed in. The magnificent repose which usually stamped

his features was gone: it was an agitated and frightened man who
stood by the billiard table, pouring out his somewhat incoherent
story. And as his meaning became clear Bill Brabazon grew white
and leaned against the mantelpiece for support.

Dead—Denton dead! That was the salient fact that stood out
from the Actor's disjointed sentences.

"To examine the inscription," he was saying. "I went in to examine it—and there—by the window..."

"He can't be dead," said Bill, harshly. "He's laid out, that's all."

"Quick! Which is the room?" Bob Seymour's steady voice served
to pull everyone together. "There's no good standing here talking—"

In silence they crossed the hall, and went along the passage to
the new wing.

"Here we are," said Sir Robert, nervously. "This is the door."

The room was in darkness and in the air there hung a rank,
fetid smell. The window was open, and outside the rain was lash-
ing down with tropical violence. Bob Seymour fumbled in his
pocket for a match; then he turned up to the lamp and lit it. Just
for a moment he stared at it in surprise, then Ruth, from the doorway, gave a little stifled scream.

"Look," she whispered. "By the window—"

A man was lying across the windowsill, with his legs inside the
room and his head and shoulders outside.

"Good heavens," muttered Sir Robert, touching the body with
a shaking hand. "I suppose—I suppose—he is dead?"

But Seymour apparently failed to hear the remark.

"Do you notice this extraordinary smell?" he said, at length.

"Damn the smell," said his host, irritably. "Give me a hand with
this poor fellow."

Seymour pulled himself together and stepped forward as the
other bent down to take hold of the sagging legs.

"Leave him alone, Sir Robert," he said, quickly. "You must leave
the body till the police come. We'll just see that he's dead, and then—"

He picked up an electric torch from the table and leant out of the
window. And after a while he straightened up again with a little shudder.

It was not a pretty sight. In the light of the torch the face seemed
almost black, and the two arms, limp and twisted, sprawled in the
sodden earth of the flower-bed. The man was quite dead, and they
both stepped back, into the middle of the smoking-room with obvious relief.

"Well," said Brabazon, "Is he—?"

"Yes—he's dead," said Seymour, gravely.

"But it's impossible," cried the boy, wildly. "Why, that blow I gave him couldn't have—have killed the man."

"Nevertheless he's dead," said Seymour, staring at the motionless body, thoughtfully. Then his eyes narrowed, and he bent once more over the dead man. Ruth, sobbing hysterically, was trying to comfort her brother, while the rest of the house-party had collected near the door, talking in low, agitated whispers.

"Bob—Bob," cried Bill Brabazon, suddenly. "I've just remembered. I couldn't have done it when I laid him out. I told you I was walking up and down the lawn. Well, the light from this room was streaming out, and I remember seeing his shadow in the middle of the window. He must have been standing up. The mark of the window-sash was clear on the lawn."

Seymour glanced at him thoughtfully.

"But the light was out, Bill. How do you account for that?"

"It wasn't," said the other, positively. "Not then. It must have gone out later."

"We'll have to send for the police, Sir Robert," said Seymour, laying a reassuring hand on the boy's arm. "Tell them everything when they come."

"I've got nothing to hide," said the youngster, hoarsely. "I swear to Heaven I didn't do that."

"We'd better go," cried Sir Robert. "Leave everything as it is. I'll ring the police up."

With quick, nervous steps he left the room, followed by his guests, until only Seymour was left standing by the window with its dreadful occupant.

For a full minute he stood there, while the rain still lashed down outside, sniffing as he had done when he first entered. And, at length, with a slight frown on his face, as if some elusive memory escaped him, he followed the others from the room, first turning out the light and then locking the door.

IV.

It was half an hour before the police came, in the shape of Inspector Grayson and a constable. During that time the rain had stopped for a period of about twenty minutes; only to come on again just before a ring announced their arrival.

The house-party were moving aimlessly about in little scattered groups, obsessed with the dreadful tragedy. In the billiard-room Ruth sat with her brother in a sort of stunned silence; only Bob Seymour seemed unaffected by the general strain. Perhaps it was because in a life such as his death by violence was no new spectacle; perhaps it was that there was something he could not understand.

Who had blown the light out? That was the crux. Blown—not turned. The Celebrated Actor was very positive that the light had not been on when he first entered the room. It might have been the wind, but there was no wind. A point of detail—one. And then the smell—that strange, fetid smell. It touched a chord of memory, but try as he would he could not place it.

His mind started on another line. If the boy, in his rage, had struck the dead man a fatal blow, how had the body got into such a position? It would have been lying on the floor.

"Weak heart," he argued. "Hot night—gasping for breath—rushed to window—collapsed. That's what they'd say."

He frowned thoughtfully; on the face of it quite plausible. Not only plausible—quite possible.

"Major Seymour!" Ruth's voice beside him made him look up. "What can we do? Poor old Bill's nearly off his head."

"There's nothing to do, Miss Brabazon—but tell the truth," said Seymour, gravely. "What I mean is," he explained, hurriedly, "you've got to impress on Bill the vital necessity of being absolutely frank with the police."

"I know he didn't do it, Bob," she cried, desperately. "I know it."

Bob! She'd called him Bob. And such is human nature that for a moment the dead man was forgotten.

"So do I, Ruth," he whispered, impulsively. "So do I."

"And you'll prove it?" she cried.

"I'll prove it," he promised her. Which was no rasher than many promises made under similar conditions.

"Thank goodness you've come, Inspector." Sir Robert had met the police at the door. "A dreadful tragedy."

"So I gather, Sir Robert," answered the other. "One of your guests been murdered?"

"I didn't say so on the 'phone," said Sir Robert. "I said—killed."

The inspector grunted. "Where's the body?"

"In the smoking-room." He led the way towards the door.

"I've got the key in my pocket," said Seymour; and the inspector looked at him quickly.

"May I ask your name, sir?" he remarked.

"Seymour—Major Seymour," returned the other. "I turned out the light and locked the door while Sir Robert was telephoning for you, to ensure that nothing would be moved."

The inspector grunted again, as Seymour opened the door and struck a light.

"Over in that window, Inspector—" began Sir Robert, only to stop and gape foolishly across the room.

"I don't quite understand, gentlemen," said Inspector Grayson, testily.

"No more do I," muttered Bob Seymour, with a puzzled frown.

The window-sill was empty; the body was gone.

"I left him lying, as we found him, half in and half out of the window," said Seymour. "His legs were inside, his head and shoulders from the waist upwards were outside."

It was the constable who interrupted him. While the others were standing by the door he had crossed to the window and leaned out.

"Here's the body, sir," he cried. "Outside in the flower-bed."

The inspector went quickly to the window and peered out; then he turned and confronted Sir Robert and Seymour.

"He's dead right enough *now*," he said, gravely. "It seems a pity that you gentlemen didn't take a little more trouble to find out if he was dead in the first place. You might have saved his life."

"Hang it, man!" exploded Seymour, angrily, "do you suppose I don't know a dead man when I see one?"

"I don't know whether you do or don't," answered the other, shortly. "But I've never yet heard of a dead man getting up and moving to an adjacent flower-bed. And you say yourself that you left him lying over the window-sill."

For a moment an angry flush mounted on the soldier's face; then, with an effort, he controlled himself. On the face of it, the inspector was perfectly justified in his remark: dead men do not move. The trouble was that Bob Seymour had felt the dead man's heart and his pulse; had turned the light of his torch from close range into his eyes. And he *knew* that he had made no mistake; he *knew* that the man was dead when he turned out the light and left the room. He *knew* it; but—dead men do not move. What had happened in the room during the time they were waiting for the police? The key had been in his pocket: who had moved the body? And why? Not Bill Brabazon: that he knew.

With a puzzled frown he crossed slowly towards the two policemen, who were hauling the limp form through the open window. And once again he paused and sniffed.

"That smell again, Sir Robert," he remarked.

"What smell?" demanded the inspector as they laid the dead man on the floor.

"Don't you notice it? A strange, fetid, rank smell."

The inspector sniffed perfunctorily. "I smell the ordinary smell of rain on dead leaves," he remarked. "What about it?"

"Nothing, except that there are no dead leaves in June," returned Seymour, shortly.

"Well, sir," snorted the inspector, "whether there are dead leaves or not, we've got a dead man on the floor. And I take it he wasn't killed by a smell, anyway."

In the full light of the room Denton was an even more unpleasant sight than when he had lain sprawling over the window-sill. The water dripped from his sodden clothing and ran in little pools on the floor; the dark, puffy face was smeared with a layer of wet earth. But it was not at these details that Bob Seymour was staring: it was an angry-looking red weal round the neck just above the collar that riveted his attention. The inspector, taking no further notice of the two spectators, was proceeding methodically with his examination. First he turned out all the pockets, laying the contents neatly on the table; then, with the help of the constable, he turned the body over on its face. A little fainter, but still perfectly discernible, the red weal could be traced continuously round the neck; and after a while the inspector straightened up and turned to Sir Robert.

"It looks as if he had been strangled, sir," he remarked, professionally. "I should imagine from the size of the mark that a fairly thin rope was used. Have you any idea whether anyone had a grudge against him? The motive was obviously not robbery."

"Strangled!" cried Sir Robert, joining the other three. "But I don't understand." He turned perplexedly to Bob Seymour, who was standing near the window absorbed in thought. Then, a little haltingly, he continued: "Unfortunately there was a very severe row between him and another of my guests earlier in the evening."

"Where did the row take place?"

"Er—in this room."

"Was anyone else present?"

"No. No one heard them quarrelling. But Mr. Brabazon, the guest in question, made no secret about it—afterwards. He told us in the billiard-room that—that they had come to blows in here."

"I would like to see Mr. Brabazon, Sir Robert," said the inspector. "Perhaps you would be good enough to send for him."

"I will go and get him myself," returned the other, leaving the room.

"A very remarkable affair," murmured Seymour, as the door closed behind his host. "Don't you agree with me, Inspector?"

"In what way?" asked the officer, guardedly.

But the soldier was lighting a cigarette, and made no immediate answer. "May I ask," he remarked at length, "if you've ever tried to strangle a man with a rope? Because," he continued, when the other merely snorted indignantly, "I have. During the war—in German East Africa. And it took me a long while. You see, if you put a slipknot round a man's neck and pull, he comes towards you. You've got to get very close to him and kneel on him, or wedge him in some way, so that he can't move, before you can do much good in the strangling line."

"Quite an amateur detective, Major Seymour," said the other, condescendingly. "If you will forgive my saying so, however, it might have been better had you concentrated on seeing whether the poor fellow was dead."

He turned as the door opened, and Bill Brabazon came in, followed by Sir Robert.

"This is Mr. Brabazon, Inspector," said the latter.

The officer eyed the youngster keenly for a moment before he spoke. Then he pointed to a chair, so placed that the light of the lamp would fall on the face of anyone sitting in it.

"Will you tell me everything you know, Mr. Brabazon? And I should advise you not to attempt to conceal anything."

"I've got nothing to conceal," answered the boy, doggedly. "I found Denton in here about half-past ten, and we started quarrelling. I'd been trying to avoid him the whole evening, but there was no getting away from him this time. After a while we began to fight, and he hit me in the face. Then I saw red, and really went for him. And I laid him out. That's all I know about it."

"And what did you do after you laid him out?"

"I went out into the garden to cool down. Then when the rain came on. I went to the billiard-room and told Sir Robert. And the first thing I knew about this," with a shudder he looked at the dead body, "was when Mr. Trayne came into the billiard-room and told us."

"Mr. Trayne! Who is he, Sir Robert?"

"Another guest stopping in the house. Do you wish to see him?"

"Please." The inspector paced thoughtfully up and down the room.

"The light was on, wasn't it, Bill, when you left the room?" said Seymour.

"It was. Why, I saw his shadow on the lawn, as I told you."

"Did you?" said the inspector, watching him narrowly. "Would you be surprised to hear, Mr. Brabazon, that this unfortunate man was strangled?"

"Strangled!" Bill Brabazon started up from his chair. "Strangled! Good God! Who by?"

"That is precisely what we want to find out," said the inspector.

"But, good heavens! man," cried the boy, excitedly, "don't you see that that exonerates me. I didn't strangle him: I only hit him on the jaw. And that shadow I saw," he swung round on Seymour, "must have been the murderer."

"You wish to see me, Inspector?" Trayne's voice from the doorway interrupted him, and he sat back in his chair again. And Seymour, watching the joyful look on Bill's face, knew that he spoke the truth. His amazement at hearing the cause of death had been too spontaneous not to be genuine. In his own mind Bill Brabazon regarded himself as cleared: the trouble was that other people might not. The majority of murderers have died, still protesting their innocence.

"I understand that it was you, Mr. Trayne, who first discovered the body," said the inspector.

"It was. I came in and found the room in darkness. I wished to study an inscription by the window to which Sir Robert had alluded at dinner. I struck a match, and then—I saw the body lying half in half out over the sill. It gave me a dreadful shock—quite dreadful. And I at once went to the billiard-room for assistance."

"So whoever did it turned out the light," said the inspector, musingly. "What time was it, Mr. Trayne, when you made the discovery?"

"About half-past eleven, I should think."

"An hour after the quarrel. And in that hour someone entered this room either by the window or the door, and committed the deed. He, further, left either by the window or the door. How did you leave, Mr. Brabazon?"

"By the door," said the youngster. "The flower-bed outside the window is too wide to jump."

"Then if the murderer entered by the window, he will have left footmarks. If he entered by the door and left by it the presumption is that he is a member of the house. No one who was not would risk leaving by the door after committing such an act."

"Most ably reasoned," murmured Seymour, mildly.

But the inspector was far too engrossed with his theory to notice the slight sarcasm in the other's tone. With a powerful electric torch he was searching the ground outside the window for any trace of footprints. The mark in the ground where the body had lain was clearly defined; save for that, however, the flower-bed revealed nothing. It was at least fifteen feet wide; to cross it, leaving no trace, appeared a physical impossibility. And after a while the inspector turned back into the room and looked gravely at Sir Robert Deering.

"I should like to have every member of the house-party and all your servants in here, Sir Robert, one by one," he remarked.

"Then you think it was done by someone in the house, Inspector?" Sir Robert was looking worried.

"I prefer not to say anything definite at present," answered the official, guardedly. "Perhaps we can start with the house-party."

With a shrug of his shoulder, Sir Robert left the room, and the inspector turned to the constable.

"Lend a hand here, Murphy; we'll put the body behind the screen before any of the ladies come in."

"Great Scot! man," cried Seymour. "What do you want the ladies for? You don't suggest that a woman could have strangled him?"

"You will please allow me to know my own business best," said the other, coldly. "Shut and bolt the windows, Murphy."

The rain had stopped as the policeman crossed the room to carry out his orders. And it was as he stood by the open window, with his hands upraised to the sash, that he suddenly stepped back with a startled exclamation.

"Something 'it me in the face, sir," he muttered. Then he spat disgustedly. "Gaw! what a filthy taste!"

But the inspector was not interested—he was covering the dead man's face with a pocket handkerchief, and after a moment's hesitation, the constable again reached up for the sash, and pulled it down. Only the soldier had noticed the little incident, and he was staring like a man bereft of his senses at a point just above the policeman's head.

"Don't move," he ordered, harshly. "Stand still, constable."

With a startled look the policeman obeyed, and Seymour stepped over to him. And then he did a peculiar thing. He lit a match and turned to the inspector.

"Just look at this match, Inspector," he murmured. "Burning brightly, isn't it?" He moved it a little, and suddenly the flame turned to a smoky orange colour. For a moment or two it spluttered; then it went out altogether.

"You can move now, constable," he said. "I didn't want any draught for a moment." He looked at Inspector Grayson with a smile. "Interesting little experiment that—wasn't it?"

Grayson snorted. "If you're quite finished your conjuring tricks, I'll get on with the business," he remarked. "Come along over here, Murphy."

"What is it, Bob?" Bill Brabazon cried, excitedly.

"The third point, Bill," answered the other. "Great Scot! what a fool I've been. Though it's the most extraordinary case I've ever come across."

"Think you can reconstruct the crime?" sneered the inspector.

"I don't think—I know," returned the other quietly. "But not to-night. There's the rain again."

"And might I ask what clues you possess?"

"Only one more than you, and that you can get from Sir Robert. I blush to admit it, but until a moment ago I attached no importance to it. It struck me as being merely the foolish jest of a stupid man. Now it does not strike me quite in that light. Ask him," he continued, and his voice was grim, "for the translation of that inscription under the window. And when you've got that, concentrate for a moment on the other end of the dead man—his trousers just above his ankles."

"They're covered with dirt," said the inspector, impressed, in spite of himself, by the other's tone.

"Yes—but what sort of dirt? Dry, dusty, cobwebby dirt—not the caked mud on his knees. Immense amount of importance in dirt, Inspector."

But Mr. Grayson was recovering his dignity. "Any other advice?" he sneered.

"Yes. Hire a man and practise strangling him. Then buy a really good encyclopedia and study it. You'll find a wealth of interesting information in it." He strolled towards the door. "If you want me I shall be in the billiard-room. And, by the way, with regard to what I said about strangling, don't forget that the victim cannot come towards you if his feet are off the ground."

"Perhaps you'll have the murderer for me in the billiard-room," remarked the inspector, sarcastically.

"I'm afraid not," answered the other. "The real murderer, unfortunately, is already dead. I'll look for his accomplice in the morning."

With a slight smile he closed the door and strolled into the hall. The house-party were being marshalled by Sir Robert preparatory to their inquisition; the servants stood huddled together in sheepish groups under the stern eye of the butler.

"Have you found out anything, Major Seymour?" With entreaty in her eyes, Ruth Brabazon came up to him.

"Yes, Miss Brabazon, I have," answered the man, reassuringly. "You can set your mind absolutely at rest."

"You know who did it?" she cried, breathlessly.

"I do," he answered. "But unfortunately I can't prove it to-night. And you mustn't be alarmed at the attitude taken up by the inspector. He's not in a very good temper, and I'm afraid I'm the cause."

"But what does he think?"

"I should hesitate to say what great thoughts were passing through his brain," said Seymour. "But I have a shrewd suspicion that he has already made up his mind that Bill did it."

"And who did do it, Bob?" She laid her hand beseechingly on his arm as she spoke.

"I think it's better to say nothing at the moment," he answered, gently. "There are one or two points I've got to make absolutely certain of first. Until then—won't you trust me, Ruth?"

"Trust you! Why, my dear—" She turned away as she spoke, and Bob Seymour barely heard the last two words. But he did just hear them. And once again the dead man was forgotten.

V.

"May I borrow your car, Sir Robert? I want to go to London and bring back a friend of mine—Sir Gilbert Strangways." Bob Seymour approached his host after breakfast the following morning. "I'll have to be back by three, in time for the inquest, and it's very important."

"Strangways—the explorer! Certainly, Seymour; though I'm not keen on adding to the house-party at present."

"It's essential, I'm afraid. They can only bring in one verdict this afternoon—Murder. That ass Grayson was nosing round this morning, and he, at any rate, is convinced of it."

"What—that Bill did it?" muttered the other.

"He's outside there now, making notes."

"You don't think the boy did it, do you, Seymour?"

"I *know* he didn't, Sir Robert. But to prove it is a different matter. May I order the car?"

"Yes, yes, of course. Anything you like. Why on earth did I ever ask the poor fellow down here?" Sir Robert walked agitatedly up and down the hall. "And anyway, who did do it?" He threw out his hands in despair. "He can't have done it himself."

"All in good time, Sir Robert," said the other, gravely. "The lucky thing for you is that you have practically never used that room."

"What do you mean?" muttered his host, going a little white.

"If you had, the chances are that this house-party would never have taken place," answered Seymour. "At least, not with you as the host."

"My God!" cried the other. "You don't mean to say that there's anything in that inscription!"

"It's the key to everything," returned the other, shortly. "To put it mildly, your predecessor had a peculiar sense of humour."

Ten minutes later he was getting into the car, when Inspector Grayson appeared round the corner.

"You won't forget the inquest is at three, Major Seymour?" he said, a trifle sharply.

"I sha'n't miss it," answered the soldier.

"Found the murderer yet?" asked the detective.

"Yes—this morning," returned the other. Haven't you?"

And the officer was still staring thoughtfully down the drive long after the car had disappeared round a bend. This confounded soldier seemed so very positive, and Grayson, who was no fool, had been compelled to admit to himself that there were several strange features about the case. The inscription on the wall he had dismissed as childish; from inquiries made in the neighbourhood, Sir Robert Deering's predecessor had obviously been a most peculiar specimen. Not quite all there, if reports were to be believed. To return to the case, however, a complete *alibi* had been proved by every single member of the household, save one kitchen-maid, Mr. Trayne, and— Bill Brabazon. The kitchen-maid and Mr. Trayne could be dismissed— the former for obvious reasons, the latter owing to the impossibility of having done the deed in the time between leaving the drawing-room and arriving in the billiard-room with the news. And that left —Bill Brabazon. Every single line of thought led ultimately to— Bill Brabazon. Motive, opportunity, capability from a physical point of view—all pointed to him. A further exhaustive search that morning of the flower-bed outside the window had revealed no trace of any footprint; it was impossible that the murderer should have entered by the window. Therefore—he shrugged his shoulders. The house-party again—and Bill Brabazon. Blind with fury, as he admitted himself, he had first knocked the dead man down and then strangled him, turning out the light lest anyone should see. Then, taking off the rope, he had left him, almost, but not quite, dead on the floor. In a last despairing gasp for air, Denton had staggered to the window and collapsed—still not quite dead. Finally, he had made one more convulsive effort, floundered on to the flower-bed, and had there died.

Such was the scene as Inspector Grayson reconstructed it, and yet he was far from satisfied. Why strangle? An un-English method of killing a man. Still—facts were facts—the man *had* been strangled. Un-English or not, that was the manner in which he had met his death; and since suicide could be ruled out, only murder remained. If the soldier could prove it was not young Brabazon— well and good. Until he did, Mr. Grayson preferred to bank on facts which were capable of proof.

The result of the coroner's inquest was a foregone conclusion. Death after strangulation, with a rider to the effect that, had prompt assistance been given on the first discovery of the body, life might have been saved.

Bob Seymour, seated beside another lean, sun-tanned man, heard the verdict with an impassive face. He had given his evidence, confining it to the barest statement of fact; he had advanced no theory;

he had not attempted to dispute Inspector Grayson's deductions. Once he had caught Ruth's eyes fixed on him beseechingly, and he had given her a reassuring smile. And she—because she trusted him—knew that all was well; knew that the net which seemed to be closing so grimly round her brother would not be fastened. But why—why didn't he tell them now how it was done? That's what she couldn't understand.

And then, when it was all over, Bob and his friend had disappeared in the car again.

"There's no doubt about it, Bob," said Strangways. "What a diabolical old blackguard the man must have been."

"I agree," answered Seymour, grimly. "One wishes one could get at him now. As it is, the most we can do is to convince our mutton-headed friend Grayson. I owe the gentleman one for that rider to the verdict."

The car stopped first at a chemist's, and the two men entered the shop. It was an unusual request they made—cylinders of oxygen are generally required only for sick rooms. But after a certain amount of argument, the chemist produced one, and they placed it in the back of the car. Their next errand was even stranger, and consisted of the purchase of a rabbit. Finally, a visit to an ironmonger produced a rose such as is used on the end of a hosepipe for watering.

Then, their purchases complete, they returned to the house, stopping at the police-station on the way. Grayson came out to see them, a tolerant smile on his face. Yes, he would be pleased to come up that evening after dinner.

"Do you want to introduce me to the murderer, Major?" he asked, maliciously.

"Something of the sort, Inspector," said Seymour. "Studied that encyclopedia yet?"

"I've been too busy on other matters—a little more important," answered the other, shortly.

"Good," cried Seymour, genially. "By the way, when you want to blow out a lamp what is the first thing you do?"

"Turn down the wick," said Grayson.

"Wise man. I wonder why the murderer didn't."

And for the second time that day, Inspector Grayson was left staring thoughtfully at a retreating motor-car.

It was not till after dinner that Bob Seymour reverted to the matter which was obsessing everyone's mind. Most of the house-party had left; only Mr. Trayne and Ruth and her brother remained. And even the Celebrated Actor had been comparatively silent throughout the meal, while Bill had remained sunk in profound gloom. Everything at the inquest had pointed to him as the culprit; every ring at the bell and he had imagined someone arriving with a warrant for his arrest. And Bob had said nothing to clear him—not a word, in spite of his apparent confidence last night. Only Ruth still seemed certain that he would do something; but what could he do, exploded the boy miserably, when she tried to cheer him up. The evidence on the face of it was damning.

"About time our friend arrived, Gilbert." Bob Seymour glanced at his watch, and at that moment there came a ring at the bell.

"Who's that?" said Bill, nervously.

"The egregious Grayson, old boy," said Bob. "The experiment is about to begin."

"You mean—" cried Ruth, breathlessly.

"I mean that Sir Gilbert has kindly consented to take the place of Denton last night," said Bob, cheerfully. "He'll have one or two little props to help him, and I shall be stage-manager."

"But why have you put it off so long?" cried Bob, as the inspector came into the room.

"'When 'tis day. All serene,'" quoted Bob. "Good evening, Mr. Grayson. Now that we are all here, we might as well begin."

"Just as well," agreed the inspector, shortly. "What do we begin with?"

"First of all a visit to the smoking-room," answered Seymour. "Then, except for Sir Gilbert Strangways, we shall all go outside into the garden."

In silence they followed him to the scene of the tragedy.

"I trust you will exonerate me from any charge of being theatrical," he began, closing the door. "But in this particular case the cause of Mr. Denton's death is so extraordinary that only an actual reconstruction of what happened would convince such a pronounced sceptic as the inspector. Facts are facts, aren't they, Mr. Grayson?"

The inspector grunted non-committally. "What's that on the floor?" he demanded.

"A cylinder of oxygen, and a rabbit in a cage," explained Seymour, pleasantly. "Now first to rearrange the room. The lamp was on this table—very possibly placed there by the dead man to get a better view of the inscription under the window. Otherwise, nothing needs moving; so that we may proceed to what happened.

"First, Inspector, Mr. Brabazon entered the room, and, as he has already described, he and Mr. Denton came to blows, with the result that he laid Denton out. Then Mr. Brabazon left the room, as I propose we shall do shortly. And, after a while, Mr. Denton came to his senses again, and went to the window for air, just as Sir Gilbert has done at the present moment."

"You can't prove it," snapped Grayson.

"True," murmured Seymour. "Just logical surmise—so far; from now onwards—irrefutable proof. The murderer is admirably trained, I assure you. Are you ready, Gilbert?"

"Quite," said Strangways, bending down and picking up the rabbit-cage, which he placed on the table by the lamp.

"Perhaps, Inspector, you would like to examine the rabbit?" remarked Seymour. "No! Well, if not, I would just ask you to notice Sir Gilbert's other preparations. A clip on his nose; the tube from the oxygen cylinder in his mouth."

"I don't understand all this, Major Seymour," cried Grayson, testily. "What's the rabbit for, and all this other tommyrot?"

"I thought I'd explained to you that Sir Gilbert is taking the place of the murdered man last night. The tommyrot is to prevent him sharing the same fate."

"Good God!" The inspector turned a little pale.

"Shall we adjourn to the garden?" continued Seymour, imperturbably. He led the way from the room. "I think we'll stand facing the window, so that we can see everything. Of course, I can't guarantee that the performance will be *exactly* the same; but it will be near enough, I think. Nor can I guarantee exactly when it will start." As he spoke they reached a point facing the window. The lamp was burning brightly in the room, outlining Sir Gilbert's figure as he stood facing them, and with a little shudder Ruth clutched her brother's arm.

"Even so did Denton stand last night." Seymour's even voice came out of the darkness. "You see his shadow on the grass, and the shadow of the sash; just as Mr. Brabazon saw the shadow last night, Inspector."

Silence settled on the group; even the phlegmatic inspector seemed impressed. And then suddenly, when the tension was becoming almost unbearable, Sir Gilbert's voice came from the window.

"It's coming, Bob."

They saw him adjust his nose-clip and turn on the oxygen; then he stood up as before, motionless, in the window.

"Watch carefully, Inspector," said Seymour. "Do you see those dark, thin, sinuous feelers coming down outside the window? Like strands of rope. They're curling in underneath the sash towards Sir Gilbert's head. The lamp—look at the lamp—watch the colour of the flame. Orange—where before it was yellow. Look—it's smoking; thick black smoke; and the room is turning green. Do you see? Now the lamp again. It's going out—even as it went out last night. And, by this time last night, Inspector, Denton, I think, was dead; even as the rabbit on the table is dead now. Now watch Sir Gilbert's shirt front."

"Great heavens!" shouted Sir Robert. "It's going up."

"Precisely," said Bob. "At the present moment he is being lifted off his legs—as Denton was last night; and if at this period Denton was not already dead, he could not have lasted long. He would have been hanged."

"Oh, Bill, it's awful!" cried Ruth, hysterically.

"Then came the rain," continued Seymour. "I have here the hosepipe fitted with a rose." He dragged it nearer the window, and let it play on the side of the house as far up as the water would reach. Almost at once the body of Sir Gilbert ceased rising; it paused as if hesitating; then, with a little thud, fell downwards half in half out of the window, head and arms sprawling in the flower-bed.

"And thus we found Mr. Denton last night, when it was still raining," said Seymour. "All right, Gilbert?"

"All right, old boy!" came from the other.

"But if he's all right," said the inspector, wonderingly, "why wasn't the other?"

"Because Sir Gilbert, being in full possession of his senses when the hanging process started, used his hands to prevent strangulation. To continue—the rain ceased. We were out of the room waiting for your arrival, Mr. Grayson, and while we were out—Look! look!"

Before their eyes the top part of Sir Gilbert's body was being raised till once again he stood straight up. Then steadily he was drawn upwards till his knees came about the level of the sill, when, with a sudden lurch, the whole body swung out and then back again, while the calves of his legs drummed against the outside of the house. "Do you remember the marks on the trousers, Inspector? And then the rain came again." Seymour turned on the hose. Once more the body paused, hesitated, and then crashed downwards into the flower-bed.

"All right, Gilbert?"

"All right," answered the other. "Merely uncomfortably wet." He rose and came towards them.

"And now, Inspector," murmured Seymour, mildly, "you know exactly how Mr. Denton was killed."

"But, good Lord! gentlemen," said Grayson, feebly, "what was it that killed him?"

"A species of liana," said Sir Gilbert. "In my experience absolutely unique in strength and size—though I have heard stories from the Upper Amazon of similar cases. It's known amongst the natives as the Green Death."

"But is it an animal?" cried Grayson.

"You've asked me a question, Inspector," said Sir Gilbert, "that I find it very difficult to answer. To look at—it's a plant—a climbing plant, with long, powerful tendrils. But in habits—it's carnivorous, like the insect-eating variety in England. It's found in the tropical undergrowth, and is incidentally worshipped by some of the tribes. They give it human sacrifices, so the story goes. And now I can quite believe it."

"But, hang it, sir," exploded the inspector, "we aren't on the Upper Amazon. Do you mean to say that one of these things is here?"

"Of course. Didn't you see it? It's spread from the wall to the branches of that old oak."

"If you remember, Inspector, I pointed it out to you this morning," murmured Seymour, mildly. "But you were so engrossed with the flower-bed."

"But why did the lamp go out?" asked Ruth, breathlessly.

"For the same reason that the rabbit died," said Bob. "For the same reason that the match went out last night, and gave me the third clue. From each of the tendrils a green cloud is ejected, the principal ingredient of which is carbon dioxide—which is a gas that suffocates. The plant holds the victim, and they suffocate him. Hence the oxygen and the nose-clip; otherwise Sir Gilbert would have been killed to-night. By the way, would you like to see the rabbit, Inspector?"

"I'll take your word for it, sir," he grunted, shortly. "Only, why the devil you didn't tell me this last night I can't understand."

"For the very simple reason that you wouldn't have believed me," returned Bob. "I'd have shown you—only the rain had come on again. And you must admit I advised you to get an encyclopedia."

VI.

"Bob, I don't understand how you did it," cried Ruth. It was after breakfast the following morning, and the sound of axes came through the open window from the men who were already at work cutting down the old oak tree.

The other laughed. "Points of detail," he said, quietly. "At first, before the police arrived, I thought it possible that Bill had been responsible for his death. I thought he'd hit him so hard that the man's heart had given out, and that in a final spasm he'd staggered to the window and died. It struck me as just conceivable that Denton had himself blown out the lamp, thinking it made it hotter. But why not turn it out? And would he have had time if he was at his last gasp? Then the police came, and the body had moved. I *knew* the man was dead when he was lying over the sill, though I hadn't seen the mark round his neck. I therefore knew that some agency had moved the body. That agency must have been the murderer—anyone else would have mentioned the fact. Therefore it couldn't have been Bill, because he was in the billiard-room the whole time, and I'd locked the door of the smoking-room. Then I saw the mark round his neck—strangled. But you can't strangle a powerful man without a desperate struggle. And why should the strangler return after the deed was committed? Also there were no footmarks on the flower-bed. Then I noticed the grey dust on his trousers just below the knee, and underneath the window outside, kept dry by the sill, which stuck out, was ivy—dusty and cobwebby as ivy always is. How had his legs touched it? If they had—and there was nowhere else the dirt could have come from—he must have been lifted off the ground. Strangulation, certainly, of a type—hung. The dirt had not been there when we first found the body lying over the sill. And if he'd been hung—who did it? And why hang a dead man? What had happened between the time Bill left the room and the police found the body? A heavy shower of rain, during which we found the body; then clear again, while we were out of the room; then another shower, when the police found the body. And then I thought of the rhyme:—

When 'tis hot, shun this spot;
When 'tis rain, come again.

Could it be possible that there was some diabolical agent at work, who stopped, or was frustrated, by rain? It was then I saw the green cloud itself over the constable's head—the cloud which extinguished my match.

"Incredible as it seemed, I saw at once that it was the only solution which fitted everything—the marks on the back of his trousers below the knee—everything. He'd been hung, and the thing that had hanged him had blown out the lamp—or extinguished it is a more accurate way of expressing it—even as it extinguished my match. The smell—I'd been searching my memory for that smell the whole evening, and it came to me when I saw that green gas—it's some rank discharge from the plant, mixed with the carbon dioxide. And I last saw it, and smelt it, on the Upper Amazon ten years ago. My native bearers dragged me away in their terror. There was a small animal, I remember, hanging from a red tendril, quite dead. The tendril was round its neck, exuding little puffs of green vapour. So I got Gilbert to make sure. That's all."

"But what a wicked old man he must have been who planted it!" cried the girl, indignantly.

"A distorted sense of humour, as I told our host," said Bob, briefly, starting to fill his pipe.

"Bill and I can never thank you enough, Major Seymour," said the girl, slowly, after a long silence. "If it hadn't been for you—" She gave a little shudder, and stared out of the window.

"Some advantages in wandering," he answered, lightly. "One does pick up odd facts. Suppose I'll have to push off again soon."

"Why?" she demanded.

"Oh, I dunno. Can't sit in England doing nothing."

"Going alone?" she asked, softly.

"Do you think anybody would be mug enough to accompany me?" he inquired, with an attempt at a grin. Dear heavens! If only he wasn't a cripple—

"I don't know, I'm sure," she murmured. "You'd want your three points of detail to make it a certainty, wouldn't you? We only reached the coincidence stage two nights ago."

"What do you mean, Ruth?" he whispered, staring at her.

"That for a clever man—you're an utter fool. With a woman one is a certainty. However, if you'll close your eyes, I'll pander to your feeble intellect. Tight, please."

And it was as the tree fell with a rending crash outside that Ruth Brabazon found that, at any rate as far as his arms were concerned, Bob Seymour was no cripple. And Bob—well, a kiss is pretty conclusive. At least, some kisses are.

Si Urag of the Tail

Oscar Cook

Dennis sat on the verandah of his bungalow and gazed meditatively around him. He could not look at the view, because there was none to speak of since the house was built on an island in the middle of the Luago River. On all sides of the island grew the tall rank elephant-grass and nipa-palm. Here and there a stunted, beetle-ridden coconut tree just topped the dense vegetation, a relic of some clearing and plantation commenced by a native, then left to desolation and the ever-encroaching jungle.

Dennis was bored. He was two years overdue for leave; also the day was unusually hot. The hour was about four, but though the sun was beginning to slant there was no abatement in the fierceness of its rays. After lunch he had followed the immemorial custom and undressed for a short siesta, but sleep was denied him. The mechanical action of undressing had quickened his brain. The room seemed stifling; the bed felt warm. He bathed, dressed and betook himself to the verandah. Here he smoked and thought.

And his thoughts were none too pleasant, for there was much that was troubling him. Throughout the morning he had been listening to the endless intricacies of a native land case—a dispute over boundaries and ownership. He had reserved his judgment till the morrow, for the evidence had been involved and contradictory. He had meant to go over the salient points during the afternoon, and instead, here he was seated on his verandah smoking and thinking of an entirely different matter. Try as he would, his mind would not keep on the subject of the land, but roamed ever and ever over the mystery that was fast setting its seal of terror and fear on the district.

From a village in the *ulu* (source) of the river, strange rumours had come floating downstream. At first they were as light and airy as thistledown—just a passing whisper—a fairy story over which to smile; then they passed, but came again, more substantial and insistent, stronger and sterner and not to be denied. Their very number compelled a hearing; their very sameness breathed a truth. Inhabitants from the village had gone forth and never returned; never a trace of them had been found. First a young girl, then her father. She had been absent six days, and he had gone to look for her. But he looked in vain and in his turn disappeared. Then a young boy, and next an aged woman. Then, after a longer period a tame ape, and finally the headman's favourite wife.

Fear settled on the village; its inhabitants scarce dared leave their houses, save in batches to collect water and food. But fear travels fast, and the rumours reached Klagan and came to Dennis's ears. In the end the mystery caught him in its toils, weaved itself into his every waking moment and excited his interest beyond control.

An idle native story: the tale of a neighbouring village with an axe of its own to grind. He was a fool to worry over it. Such mare's nests were of almost daily occurrence, thus Dennis argued; and then from two other villages came similar tales. Two little girls had gone to bathe in the height of the noonday sun. At moonrise they had not returned. Nor in the days that passed were they ever seen again. Two lovers met one moonlight night and waded to a boulder in midstream of the river. Here they sat oblivious of the world around them. They were seen by a couple of natives passing downstream in their boat and then—never again.

Down the river crept the cold, insidious Fear like a plague, taking toll of every village in its path. In their houses huddled the natives, while crops were unsown and pigs uprooted the plantations; while crocodiles devoured untended buffaloes, and squirrels and monkeys rifled the fruit trees. From source to mouth the Fear crept down and in the end forced Dennis's hand, compelling him to action.

Thus as he sat on his verandah and cursed the heat of the sun and the humidity of the tropics, unbidden and unsought the mystery filled his thoughts; and he began to wonder as to if and when his native sergeant and three police would return. For he had sent them to the *ulu* to probe and solve the meaning of the rumours. They had been gone three weeks, and throughout this time no word had been heard of or come from them.

In the office a clock struck five. Its notes came booming across to Dennis. Then silence—not complete and utter stillness; such is never possible in the tropics, but the silence of that hour when the toilers—man and animal—by day realize that night is approaching; when the toilers by night have not yet awakened.

Lower and lower sank the sun. In the sky a moon was faintly visible. Dennis rose, about to call for tea, then checked the desire. From afar upstream came the chug, chug, chug of a motor-boat. Its beat just reached his ears. He looked at his wrist-watch. In ten minutes he would go down to the floating wharf. That would give him plenty of time to watch the boat round the last bend of the river. In the meanwhile ...

But he went at once to the wharf after all, for mystery gripped him, causing him feverishly to pace up and down the tiny floating square. Chug, chug, chug, louder and louder came the noise; then fainter and fainter, and then was lost altogether as the dense jungle cut off the sound as the boat traversed another bend of the river. Chug, chug, chug, faintly, then louder and stronger. A long-drawn note from the horn of a buffalo smote the air, and the boat swung round the final bend. Only a quarter of a mile separated it now from Dennis.

As the boat drew nearer he saw that she was empty save for the *serang* (helmsman) and boatmen. Then the Fear gripped him too, and he quickly returned to the house. With shaking hand he poured out a whisky-and-soda, flung himself into a chair and shouted for his "boy".

"*Tuan!*" The word, though quietly spoken, made him flinch, for the "boy" had approached him silently, as all well-trained servants do. Quickly, too, he had obeyed the summons, but in that brief space of time Dennis's mind had escaped his body and immediate wants to roam the vast untrodden fields of speculation and fear.

With an effort he pulled himself together.

"The motor-boat is returning. Tell the *serang* to come to me as soon as he has tied her up. See that no one is within earshot."

"*Tuan.*" And the boy departed.

Scarcely had the boy left than the *serang* stood in front of Dennis. His story was brief, though harrowing, but it threw no light upon the mystery. For two days, till they reached the rapids, they had used the motor-boat. Then they transhipped into a native dug-out, leaving the motor in charge of a village headman. For three days they had paddled and poled upstream till they came to the mouth of the Buis River. Here the sergeant and police left them, telling them to wait for their return, and struck inland along a native track. For sixteen days they waited, though their food had given out and they had taken turns to search the jungle for edible roots. Then on the sixteenth day it happened—the horrible coming of Nuin.

The boatmen had gone to look for roots. The *serang* was dozing in a dug-out. Suddenly it shook and rocked. Something clutched the *serang's* arm. It was Nuin's hand. Startled into wakefulness, the *serang* sat up; then he screamed and covered his eyes with his hands. When he dared look again Nuin was lying on the river bank. His clothes were in rags. Round his chest and back ran a livid weal four inches wide. His left leg hung broken and twisted. His right arm was entirely missing. His face was caked in congealed blood.

As the *serang* looked, Nuin opened his lips to speak, but his voice was only a whisper. Tremblingly, haltingly, the *serang* went to him and put his ear to his mouth. "Sergeant—others—dead—three days—west—man—with—big—big—others." The whisper faded away; Nuin gave a shudder and was dead.

They buried him near the river and then left, paddling night and day till they reached the rapids. A night they spent in the village, for they were racked with sleeplessness, and they left the next morning, reaching Klagan the same day.

Such was the *serang's* report.

The Fear spread farther down the river till it reached the sea and spread along the coast.

In the barracks that night were two women who would never see their men again; was born a baby, who would never know his father; wept a maiden for the lover whose lips she would never kiss again.

As the earliest streaks of dawn came stealing across the sky, the chugging of a motor-boat broke the stillness of the night. Dennis himself was at the wheel, for the *serang* was suffering with fever. With him were nine police and a corporal. They carried stores for twenty days.

The journey was a replica of the *serang's,* save that at the village by the rapids no friendly headman or villagers took charge of the motor-boat. The village had fled before the Fear. On the fifth day Buis was reached as the setting sun shot the sky with blood-red streamers.

On the banks of the river the earth was uprooted; among the loosened earth were human bones and the marks of pigs' feet. Among the bones was a broken tusk, sure sign of some fierce conflict that had raged over Nuin's remains.

Dennis shuddered as he saw the scene; his Murut police, pagans from the interior of North Borneo, fingered their charms of monkeys' teeth and dried snake-skins that hung around their necks or were attached to the rotan belts around their waists, that carried their heavy *parangs* (swords).

Occasionally throughout the night the droning noise of myriad insects was broken by the shrill bark of deer or kijang. Sometimes the sentry, gazing into the vast blackness of the jungle, saw the beady eyes of a pig, lit up for a moment by the flames of the campfire. Sometimes a snake, attracted by the glare, glided through the undergrowth, then passed on. Once or twice a nightjar cried and an owl hooted—eerie sounds in the pitch-black night. Otherwise a heavy brooding stillness, like an autumn mist, crept over the jungle and enveloped the camp. Hardly a policeman slept; but dozed and waked and dozed again, only to wake once more and feel the Fear grow ever stronger. Dennis, on his camp-bed under a *kajang* awning, tossed and tossed the long night through.

Dawn broke to a clap of thunder. Rain heralded in the new day.

"Three days—west." This was all Dennis knew; all he had to guide him. For this and the next two days the party followed a track that led steadily in a westerly direction.

On the evening of the third day it came out into a glade. Here Dennis pitched his camp. The tiny space of open sky and glittering stars breathed a cooler air and purer fragrance than the camps roofed in by the canopy of mighty trees. Thus the tired and haunted police slept, and Dennis ceased his tossing. Only the sentry was awake—or should have been. Perhaps he too dozed or fell fast asleep, for a few unconscious moments. If so he paid a heavy penalty.

Dennis awoke the next morning at a quarter to six to see only the smouldering remains of the campfire.

"Sentry!" he called. But no answer was vouchsafed. "Sentry!" he cried again, but no one came. Aroused by his voice, the sleeping camp stirred to wide and startled awakeness.

The corporal came across to Dennis, saluted, then stood at attention, waiting.

"The fire's nearly out; where's the sentry?" Dennis queried.

The corporal looked around him, gazed at the smouldering fire, counted his men, then looked at Dennis with fear-stricken eyes.

"*Tuan!*" he gasped; "he is not—there are only eight men!"

"Is not? What d'you mean? Where's he gone?" As Dennis snapped his question cold fear gripped his heart. He knew; some inner sense told him that the man had disappeared in the same mysterious fashion as those early victims. Here, in the midst of his camp, the terrible, unseen thing had power!

"Where's he gone?" Dennis repeated his question fiercely to quench his rising fear. "What d'you mean?"

For answer the corporal only stood and trembled. His open, twitching mouth produced no sound.

With an oath Dennis flung himself from his bed. "Search the glade, you fool," he cried, "and find his tracks! He can't be far away. No, stay," he added as the corporal was departing. "Who is it?"

"Bensaian, *Tuan,*" gasped the terrified man.

Dennis's eyes narrowed and a frown spread over his face. "Bensaian!" he repeated. "He was Number Three. His watch was from twelve till two."

"Tuan!"

"Then he's never been relieved. From two o'clock at least, he's been missing!"

"*Tuan!* I must have slept. I saw Auraner relieve Si Tuah, but I was tired and—"

"Search for his tracks," Dennis cried, breaking in on his protestations, "but see no man enters the jungle."

In that tiny glade the search was no prolonged affair, but no traces of the missing man were found—save one. A brass button, torn from his tunic, lay at the foot of a mighty billian tree. But where and how he had gone remained a mystery. Only the regular footprints as he had walked to and fro on his beat were just discernible, and these crossed and recrossed each other in hopeless confusion.

Over the tops of the trees the sun came stealing, bathing the glade in its warming light, but Dennis heeded it not.

"Three days—west." The words kept hammering in his brain as he sat on the edge of his bed and smoked cigarette after cigarette. Up and down the glade a sentry walked. Round the fire the police were crouched cooking their rice; over another Dennis's boy prepared his *tuan's* breakfast.

At length, when ready, he brought it over to him, poured out his coffee and departed to join the whispering police. But though the coffee grew cold and flies settled on the food, Dennis sat on, unmoved, deep in his distraction.

This was the fourth day! For three days they had journeyed west, following Nuin's almost last conscious words. The glade was hemmed in by the impenetrable jungle; no path led out of it save that along which they had come. It formed a *cul-de-sac* indeed! And Bensaian was missing!

As Dennis sat and pondered, this one great fact became predominant. Bensaian was missing. Then what did it mean? Only that here the thing had happened, lived or breathed or moved about. Here, then, would be found the answer to the riddle! In this little glade of sunlight must they watch and wait. Into the trackless jungle he dared not enter, even if his men could hack a path. To return the way they had come would make his errand worse than fruitless. Watching and waiting only remained.

So they waited. Day turned to evening and evening into night; the dawn of another day displaced the night; the sun again rode over the tops of the jungle. But nothing happened. Only the policemen grew more frightened; only Dennis's nerves grew more frayed. Then once again the night descended, but no one in the camp dared really sleep.

Up and down walked the sentry, resting every now and then, as he turned against the billian tree. A gentle breeze stirred the branches of the encircling trees, bearing on the air a faint aromatic smell, that soothed the nervous senses of the resting camp, as a narcotic dispels pain. One by one the police ceased whispering and gently dozed, calmed by the sweet fragrance. Dennis ceased his endless smoking; stretched himself at ease upon his bed. The sense of mystery seemed forgotten by all; a sense of peace seemed brooding over them.

Midnight came and the wakeful sentry was relieved. His relief, but half awake, railed at his fate—the half-unconscious dozing was so pleasant, and this marching up and down the glade, while others rested, so utterly to his distaste.

As for the fortieth time he turned about at the base of the great billian tree, he lowered his rifle, rested for a few seconds with his hands upon its barrel, then leaned against the dark ridged stem; just for a moment he would rest, his rifle in his hands—just for a moment only, then once again take up his beat.

The wind in the trees was gradually increasing; the fragrance on the air became more pronounced. The camp was almost wrapt in slumber. On his bed Dennis sleepily wondered whence came the pleasing, soothing odour, that seemed to breathe so wondrous a peace. Against the billian tree the sentry still was leaning; his rifle slipped from the faint grasp of his hands, but he heeded not the rattle as it struck the ground.

Peace in the glade from whence came so much mystery! Peace while the dread, though unknown, agent drew near apace!

Down from the top of the billian tree it slowly descended, branch by branch; slowly, carefully, silently, till it rested on the lowest branch still thirty feet above the sentry.

The bark of a deer broke the stillness of the night. From afar came an answering note. Somehow the sound awakened the sentry. He looked around him, saw the fire was burning bright, picked up his fallen rifle and commenced to walk about.

Down the far side of the tree a bark rope descended till its weighted end just rested on the ground. Down the rope a man, naked save for a bark-made loin-cloth, descended till he too reached the earth. Then, pressed flatly to the great tree's trunk, he waited.

Across the glade the sentry turned about. With listless, heavy steps he was returning. Nearer and nearer he approached. At the foot of the billian tree he halted, turned and leaned against its trunk. The tension of his limbs relaxed. The rifle slipped from his grasp, but hung suspended by the strap that had become entangled over his arm. A light unconsciousness, hardly to be designated sleep, stole over him. From the camp there was no sign of wakefulness.

Slowly a figure crept noiselessly round the tree and stood gazing at the policeman. Naked indeed he was save for the *chavat* (loin-cloth) of bark; his thick black hair hung over his neck and reached beyond his shoulders, framing a face out of which gleamed two fanatical shining eyes. His body to the waist was covered with tattoo. From each of his breasts the designs started, spreading to waist-line and round to the back. The nipple of each breast gleamed a fiery burnished gold, while from their fringe spread outward, like a full-blown flower, five oval petals of wondrous purple hue. From the golden centre of each flower ten long pistils spread, curving downward and round his body. At their source they too were of a purple hue, but as they reached the petals their colour turned to gleaming gold which slowly changed to glistening silver as their ridged ends were reached. These ridged ends were circular, and their silver rims framed brilliant scarlet mouths, shaped like the sucking orifice with which the huge and slimy horse-leech gluts its loathsome thirst for blood.

The man's arms were unusually long; his finger-nails had never been clipped; the splay of his toes, especially between the big and the next one, uncommonly wide.

One hand still clutched the bark rope; the other hung loosely at his side. Though he was tall, standing five feet ten inches, and heavily built, he moved as lightly as a cat.

Lightly he let go the rope and extended his two long arms toward his unconscious prey. The cry of a nightjar sounded close at hand. The somnolent sentry stirred as the sound just reached his brain. With a spring the man was upon him. One hand upon his mouth; one arm around his chest pinioning his arms to his side. With a swiftness incredible he reached the far side of the tree, let go his grasp upon the sentry's mouth, and using the rope as a rail, commenced to climb step over step with an amazing agility.

"*Tolong!*" (Help!) The cry, laden with overwhelming Fear, rent the stillness of the night. "*Tol—*"

All further sound ended in a gurgle as the relentless pressure round the sentry's chest squeezed out all breath from his body. The camp at that sudden cry of human agony and fear awoke to life. Instinctively the police seized their rifles; the corporal blew fiercely on his whistle; Dennis hurriedly pulled on his mosquito boots and picked up his revolver from under his pillow.

"Corporal!"

"Tuan!"

"*Siapa itu?*" (Who's that?)

The cries rent the air simultaneously. Then came silence for the fraction of a second, as everyone stared hopelessly at one another as they realized the glade was empty of the sentry.

"Si Tuah! Tuah!" Dennis's voice rose in a long cry, breaking the sudden silence that followed the camp's awakening. "Tu-ah," he called again.

Somewhere from among the trees came a sound—a kind of muffled sob—a choking, gurgling cry of fear. To the edge of the jungle close to the billian tree Dennis and the corporal darted.

"Look, *Tuan*, a rope!" the latter gasped.

"My God!" Dennis whispered. "What does it mean?"

"It's made of bark and—" began the corporal, but the rest of his words were drowned by a loud report.

"*Jaga! Tuan, Jaga!*" (Look out!) he cried, as a jumbled shape came hurtling down from the branches of the tree and the frayed ends of the rope came writhing about them. The snapping of a twig overhead, and a smoking rifle fell at their feet.

As the shape reached the ground with a sickening bump, two figures fell apart and then lay still.

"Seize that man and bind him!" Dennis cried, pointing to the naked form, as he bent over the prostrate figure of Si Tuah. "Gently, men, gently," he added, as four police picked him up and carried him over to their *kajang* shelter.

His left arm hung loosely by his side, two ribs were also broken, but his heart still faintly beat. Dennis poured a little brandy down his throat. Slowly Si Tuah came to. He tried to rise to sitting posture, but fell back with a groan of pain.

"He came upon me from behind the tree—I must have dozed," he muttered. "He picked me up—the pressure of his grasp was awful—and then commenced to climb the tree, holding the rope as a rail and walking up step by step. I struggled—just as we neared the branches his grip slackened—I could not cry—I had no breath— I only groaned, I struggled once again—my foot kicked the butt of my rifle—my toe found the trigger and I pressed and pressed—there came a report—we fell—and—"

Si Tuah had fainted again. Dennis's eyes met those of the corporal. "The shot must have severed the rope," he whispered.

"*Tuan,* his *nasib* (fate) was good," the corporal answered, and they crossed to where the human vulture lay, one leg twisted under him, his *chawat* all awry. As the policemen rolled him over on his face to knot the ropes—they showed but little pity for his unconscious state—the *chawat* came undone and slipped from his waist.

"Look, *Tuan,* look!" the corporal gasped, and pointed with shaking finger. "Look, he has a tail—it's not a man—it has a tail!" And feverishly he fingered the charms that hung around his neck.

Dennis looked, following the pointing finger, then bending down, looked long and closely. It was as the corporal said. The man possessed a tail—a long, hard protuberance that projected from his spine for about four inches.

"Bring him to the camp," he ordered. "Place two sentries; one over him, one on the camp. He is only stunned; there are no bones broken. In the morning when Tuah's better we'll learn some more."

Dennis walked across to his bed. The Fear was gone, but the mystery was still unexplained. The camp-fire burnt brightly, giving out a smell of pungent wood smoke. The soothing aromatic scent of an hour ago was no more. From the police came intermittent whisperings; from the man with the tail naught but heavy breathing. On his bed Dennis tossed and wondered.

As the early dawn first faintly flooded the sky, shriek upon shriek rent the air. Si Tuah had become delirious. The man with the tail awoke and listened. From a group of police squatting over a fire their voices reached him. His eyes blinked in perplexity. Quietly as he lay, he dug with his nails a small round hole in the earth about five inches deep. Then gingerly he moved, and in spite of his bonds sat up. From his bed Dennis watched him. Into the hole he fitted his tail, then looked at his bonds and the group of police: He opened his mouth, but no sound came forth. His tied hands he stretched out to them. His face expressed a yearning. It was as if their voices brought a comfort or recalled a past. Then tear after tear rolled down his cheeks.

Calling the corporal, Dennis crossed to the weeping man. At Dennis's approach he looked up, then with a cry buried his face in his bound hands and rocked his body to and fro. He was afraid— afraid of a white man, the like of which he had never seen before.

"Peace, fool," the corporal said roughly, speaking unconsciously in Murut; "stop your wailing, the *tuan* is no ghost but a man, albeit all-powerful."

Slowly the tailed being ceased his weeping and looked up. "A man!" he muttered. "A man and the colour of the gods!" He spoke a bastard Murut and Malay that caused Dennis to start and the corporal to frown in perplexity, for his meaning was clear, though many of the words, akin to either language, were yet unlike either. But they understood him.

"And your name?" Dennis asked in Malay, but the being only shook his head in fear, extending his hands in supplication.

"Loosen his bonds," Dennis commanded. "Ask him his name and tribe and village."

The corporal obeyed, and then translated.

The man's name was Si Urag. He came of a Murut race that years ago had captured some Malay traders. All had been killed except the women. These had been made to marry the head-men. Then came a plague and nearly all died. The remnants, according to custom, moved their village. For days and days they walked in the trackless jungle. Then from the trees they were attacked by a race of dwarfs who lived in houses in the branches. All save him were killed. He lay stunned; when he recovered consciousness he saw that the dwarfs had tails and that they were disembowelling the dead and dying and hanging their entrails round their necks. Fear seized him. He tried to rise and run away. He staggered to his feet, tottered a yard or two and then collapsed. Terrified, face downward, he waited for his foes. With a rush of feet they came. He waited for the blow. It never fell. Suddenly he felt a gentle pull upon his tail—the tail over which all his life he had been ridiculed; then came a muttering of voices. From the face of the moon a cloud passed by. He was in a glade and lying near a pool. Over the air a heavy scent was hanging. Suddenly the waters stirred. Out of their depths a flaming gold and purple flower arose. Ten tentacles spread out with gaping, wide-open, blood-red mouths. Shriek upon shriek of utter agony rent the air. Into the flaming golden centre each tentacle, curving inward, dropped a dwarf. Into the depths of the pool the flower sank down. All was still. Si Urag was alone.

That night he slept in a house among the branches of a tree. The surviving dwarfs had fled.

In the morning he collected the corpses of his friends and placed them near the lake. That night from his tree-house he watched. The moon was one day off the full. When at its highest point in the sky, the waters of the pool became disturbed. Again the golden-purple flower arose from its depths and the soothing scent spread over the jungle. Again the red-mouthed tentacles spread over the shore and sucked up the corpses, curved themselves in toward the golden centre, dropped in its bell-shaped mouth the stiffened bodies. Once again the human-feeding flower sank beneath the waters. Once again all was still. Gradually the narcotic smell grew less; slowly the moon sank in the west. All was dark and silent.

On the next and two following nights the flower appeared. Each night the hungry tentacles sought for food—human or animal. Then with the waning of the moon the flower rose up no more. Still in his tree-house Si Urag watched and lived. Where else was he to go? His tribe was killed; the dwarfs had fled, and of them he was afraid. On account of his tail he was shy to intermingle with other humans, even if he knew where to find them. Here was his house, safe from wild beasts that roamed at night; in the pool were many fish, in the jungle many roots and fruit. Here was the wondrous flower that fed on men, that spread its wondrous scent, to whom he felt he owed his life. Here, then, he would live and consecrate his life in a kind of priesthood to the flaming gold-and-purple orchid.

The corporal ceased and his eyes met those of Dennis. There was no need to answer the unspoken question in them. The mystery of those disappearances was explained.

"And that?" Dennis pointed to the tattooing on the prisoner's body.

Si Urag understood the gesture, if not the words.

"Is the picture of the flower I serve," he answered, looking at the corporal. "Two nights ago I fed it with a man clothed like that"— and he pointed to the police. "A night ago I caught a pig and deer; last night I caught a man"—he pointed to where Si Tuah lay in his delirium— "but a magic spoke from out a tube that flashed fire and the rope was severed and ..." He shrugged his shoulders with a world of meaning, then, "I am hungry; give me some rice," he begged.

For a while he ate his fill. Then when the sun rose high over the little glade Dennis questioned him further, and from his answers formed a great resolve.

The glade of the golden-purple flower was but a few miles away. A little cutting of the jungle, and a hidden path—Si Urag's path— would be found. That night the moon would be but two days past its zenith, the wondrous flower would rise for the last time for a month—or rise never to rise again, hoped Dennis.

Si Urag was complacent. Was it fear or cunning? Who could tell? His face was like a mask as he agreed to lead the little party to the pool where dwelt the sacred flower. The hour was after midnight. In the camp three police watched the delirious Si Tuah. Along a narrow track that led from the jungle to a pool, silently stole eight men. In the west a clipped moon was slowly sinking. Out of the jungle crept the men, into a glade silvered by the light of the moon.

"To the right ten paces ex—" Dennis's whispered orders faded away, giving place to a breathless gasp of surprise. There in the middle of the pool was the great golden-purple flower, its centre flaming gold, its petals deepest purple, its ten pistils curling and waving about—curling and waving toward the little group of men as they emerged from the track; the blood-red, silver-rimmed mouths opening and shutting in hungry expectation. Over the glade lay the heavy aromatic scent.

Speechless, spellbound, the little party looked at the wondrous, beautiful sight. The deadening spell of that narcotic scent was spreading through their veins. Lower and lower slowly sank the moon.

Si Urag fell upon his knees, covered his face with his hands and commenced to mumble a prayer. His action jerked the rope with which he was attached to Dennis and the corporal. With a start the former awoke as from a trance. All the waving pistils were pointing and stretching toward the huddled group. The moon was nearly touching the farther edge of the sky. Soon—soon ...

"To the right ten paces extend!" Like pistol shots Dennis's words broke in upon the night. Unconsciously, automatically, the police obeyed. Si Urag remained in prayer. "Load!" The one word cut the stillness like a knife. The waving pistils changed their curves—followed the extending men, stretched and strained their blood-red mouths.

"At point-blank—fire!" Six tongues of flame; one loud and slightly jagged report. Four pistils writhed and twisted in an agony of death. In the flaming golden centre, a jagged hole. The heavy aromatic scent came stealing stronger and stronger from the maimed and riddled centre. The moon just touched the far horizon. Slowly the wondrous flower began to sink, the waters became disturbed, the pistils seemed to shrink.

Si Urag rose from his knees and prayers; uncovered his ears, over which he had placed his hand at the sound of the report. From Dennis to the corporal he looked in mute and utter supplication. From head to foot he trembled.

Slowly the moon and flower were sinking. One pistil, bigger, stronger, fuller-mouthed than the rest, seemed reluctant to retreat, but pointed and waved at the silent three.

Into his *chawat* Si Urag dived his hand. Quick as lightning he withdrew it. A slash to the right, another to the left, and he was free. A mighty spring, a piercing cry and he hurled himself, as a devotee, into the great ravenous, blood-red mouth. Slowly the pistil curved inward. Over the golden bell-shaped centre it poised. Then it bent its head; its silver rim distended and then closed. Si Urag was no more.

The moon sank down out of sight; the wondrous flower with its maddened, fanatical victim slipped beneath the waters of the pool. The stillness of the jungle remained; the scent of dew-laden earth arose. Darkness—and a memory—surrounded the group of seven.

The tropic sleepiness of 3 p.m. hung over Klagan. Suddenly the chugging of a motor-boat was heard coming from afar upstream. Down to the tiny floating wharf the populace descended, headed by the *serang*. Round the last bend swung the motor-boat, drew alongside the wharf and came to rest. Out of it silently stepped Dennis and the weary police. One of them carried two rifles, which told the wondering people of a death. Two of them supported Si Tuah, which told them a struggle had taken place. Over his features spread a smile as his hands met those of his wife. "'Twas a near thing, Miang," he murmured, "and it happened at the dead of night. A man with a tail and a golden-purple orchid which he worshipped."

From the people rose a gasp of wonder and cries of disbelief. Then Dennis raised his hand.

"Si Tuah speaks the truth," he said, "but Si Urag of the Tail no longer lives, and the flower no more can blossom. The Fear is dead."

Then unsteadily he walked to his house.

Green Thoughts: A Story
John Collier

The orchid had been sent among the effects of his friend, who had come by a lonely and mysterious death on the expedition. Or he had bought it among a miscellaneous lot, "unclassified," at the close of the auction. I forget which, but one or the other it certainly was; moreover, even in its dry, brown, dormant root state, this orchid had a certain sinister quality. It looked, with its bunched and ragged projections, like a rigid yet a gripping hand, hideously gnarled, or a grotesquely whiskered, threatening face. Would you not have known what sort of an orchid it was?

Mr. Mannering did not know. He read nothing but catalogues and books on fertilizers. He unpacked the new acquisition with a solicitude absurd enough in any case towards any orchid, or primrose either, in the twentieth century, but idiotic, foolhardy, doom-eager, when extended to an orchid thus come by, in appearance thus. And in his traditional obtuseness he at once planted it in what he called the "Observation Ward," a hothouse built against the south wall of his dumpy, red dwelling. Here he set always the most interesting additions to his collection, and especially weak and sickly plants, for there was a glass door in his study wall through which he could see into this hothouse, so that the weak and sickly plants could encounter no crisis without his immediate knowledge.

This plant, however, proved hardy enough. At the ends of thick and stringy stalks it opened out bunches of darkly shining leaves, and soon it spread in every direction, usurping so much space that first one, then another, then all its neighbors had to be removed to a hothouse at the end of the garden. It was, Cousin Jane said, a regular hop-vine. At the ends of the stalks, just before the leaves began, were set groups of tendrils, which hung idly, serving no apparent purpose. Mr. Mannering thought that very probably these were vestigial organs, a heritage from some period when the plant had been a climber. But when were the vestigial tendrils of an ex-climber half or quarter so thick and strong?

After a long time sets of tiny buds appeared here and there among the extravagant foliage. Soon they opened into small flowers, miserable little things: they looked like flies' heads. One naturally expects a large, garish, sinister bloom, like a sea anemone, or a Chinese lantern, or a hippopotamus yawning, on any important orchid; and should it be an unclassified one as well, I think one has every right to insist on a sickly and overpowering scent into the bargain.

Mr. Mannering did not mind at all. Indeed, apart from his joy and happiness in being the discoverer and godfather of a new sort of orchid, he felt only a mild and scientific interest in the fact that the paltry blossoms were so very much like flies' heads. Could it be to attract other flies for food or as fertilizers? But then, why like their heads?

It was a few days later that Cousin Jane's cat disappeared. This was a great blow to Cousin Jane, but Mr. Mannering was not, in his heart of hearts, greatly sorry. He was not fond of the cat, for he could not open the smallest chink in a glass roof for ventilation but that creature would squeeze through somehow to enjoy the warmth, and in this way it had broken many a tender shoot. But before poor Cousin Jane had lamented two days something happened which so engrossed Mr. Mannering that he had no mind left at all with which to sympathize with her affliction or to make at breakfast kind and hypocritical inquiries after the lost cat. A strange new bud appeared on the orchid. It was clearly evident that there would be two quite different sorts of bloom on this one plant, as sometimes happens in such fantastic corners of the vegetable world, and that the new flower would be very different in size and structure from the earlier ones. It grew bigger and bigger, till it was as big as one's fist.

And just then, it could never have been more inopportune, an affair of the most unpleasant, the most distressing nature summoned Mr. Mannering to town. It was his wretched nephew, in trouble again, and this time so deeply and so very disgracefully that it took all Mr. Mannering's generosity, and all his influence too, to extricate the worthless young man. Indeed, as soon as he saw the state of affairs, he told the prodigal that this was the very last time he might expect assistance, that his vices and his ingratitude had long cancelled all affection between them, and that for this last helping hand he was indebted only to his mother's memory, and to no faith on the part of his uncle either in his repentance or his reformation. He wrote, moreover, to Cousin Jane, to relieve his feelings, telling her of the whole business, and adding that the only thing left to do was to cut the young man off entirely.

When he got back to Torquay Cousin Jane had disappeared. The situation was extremely annoying. Their only servant was a cook who was very old and very stupid and very deaf. She suffered besides from an obsession, due to the fact that for many years Mr. Mannering had had no conversation with her in which he had not included an impressive reminder that she must always, no matter what might happen, keep the big kitchen stove up to a certain pitch of activity. For this stove, besides supplying the house with hot water, heated the pipes in the "Observation Ward," to which the daily gardener who had charge of the other hothouses had no access. By this time she had come to regard her duties as stoker as her chief *raison d'être*, and it was difficult to penetrate her deafness with any question which her stupidity and her obsession did not somehow transmute into an inquiry after the stove, and this, of course, was especially the case when Mr. Mannering spoke to her. All he could disentangle was what she had volunteered on first seeing him, that his cousin had not been seen for three days, that she had left without saying a word. Mr. Mannering was perplexed and annoyed but, being a man of method, he thought it best to postpone further inquiries until he had refreshed himself a little after his long and tiring journey. A full supply of energy was necessary to extract any information from the old cook; besides, there was probably a note somewhere. It was only natural that before he went to his room, Mr. Mannering should peep into the hothouse, just to make sure that the wonderful orchid had come to no harm during the inconsiderate absence of Cousin Jane. As soon as he opened the door his eyes fell upon the bud; it had now changed in shape very considerably, and had increased in size to the bigness of a human head. It is no exaggeration to state that Mr. Mannering remained rooted to the spot, with his eyes fixed upon this wonderful bud, for fully five minutes.

But, you will ask, why did he not see her clothes on the floor? Well, as a matter of fact (it is a delicate point), there were no clothes on the floor. Cousin Jane, though of course she was entirely estimable in every respect, though she was well over forty, too, was given to the practice of the very latest ideas on the dual culture of the soul and body—Swedish, German, neo-Greek and all that. And the orchid-house was the warmest place available. I must proceed with the order of events.

Mr. Mannering at length withdrew his eyes from this stupendous bud and decided that he must devote his attention to the gray exigencies of everyday life. But although his body dutifully ascended the stairs, heart, mind, and soul all remained in adoration of the plant. Although he was philosophical to the point of insensibility over the miserable smallness of the earlier flowers, yet he was now as much gratified by the magnitude of the great new bud as you or I might be, hence it was not unnatural that Mr. Mannering while in his bath should be full of the most exalted visions of the blossoming of his heart's darling, his vegetable godchild. It would be the largest known, by far: complex as a dream, or dazzlingly simple. It would open like a dancer, or like the sun rising. Why, it might be opening at this very moment! At this thought Mr. Mannering could restrain himself no longer; he rose from the steamy water, and, wrapping his bath-towel robe about him, hurried down to the hot-house, scarcely staying to dry himself, though he was subject to colds.

The bud had not yet opened: it still reared its unbroken head among the glossy, fleshy foliage, and he now saw, what he had had no eyes for previously, how very exuberant that foliage had grown. Suddenly he realized with astonishment that this huge bud was not that which had appeared before he went away. That one had been lower down on the plant. Where was it now, then? Why, this new thrust and spread of foliage concealed it from him. He walked across, and discovered it. It had opened into a bloom. And as he looked at this bloom his astonishment grew to stupefaction, one might say to petrification, for it is a fact that Mr. Mannering remained rooted to the spot, with his eyes fixed on the flower, for fully fifteen minutes. The flower was an exact replica of the head of Cousin Jane's lost cat. The similitude was so exact, so lifelike, that Mr. Mannering's first movement, after the fifteen minutes, was to seize his bath-towel robe and draw it about him, for he was a modest man, and the cat, though bought for a Tom, had proved to be quite the reverse. I relate this to show how much character, spirit, *presence*—call it what you will—there was upon this floral cat's face. But although he made to seize his bath-towel robe, it was too late: he could not move; the new lusty foliage had closed in unperceived, the too lightly dismissed tendrils were everywhere upon him; he gave a few weak cries and sank to the ground, and there, as the Mr. Mannering of ordinary life, he passes out of this story.

Mr. Mannering sank into a coma, into an insensibility so deep that a black eternity passed before the first faint elements of his consciousness reassembled themselves in his brain.

For of his brain was the center of a new bud being made. Indeed, it was two or three days before this, at first almost shapeless and quite primitive lump of organic matter, had become sufficiently mature to be called Mr. Mannering at all. These days, which passed quickly enough, in a certain mild, not unpleasant excitement, in the outer world, seemed to the dimly working mind within the bud to resume the whole history of the development of our species, in a great many epochal parts.

A process analogous to the mutations of the embryo was being enacted here. At last the entity which was thus being rushed down an absurdly foreshortened vista of the ages arrived, slowing up, into the foreground. It became recognizable. The Seven Ages of Mr. Mannering were presented, as it were, in a series of close-ups, as in an educational film; his consciousness settled and cleared; the bud was mature, ready to open. At this point, I believe, Mr. Mannering's state of mind was exactly that of a patient who, struggling up from vague dreams, wakening from under an anesthetic, asks plaintively, "Where am I?" Then the bud opened, and he knew.

There was the hothouse, but seen from an unfamiliar angle; there, through the glass door, was his study, and there below him was the cat's head and there—there beside him was Cousin Jane. He could not say a word, but then, neither could she. Perhaps it was as well. At the very least, he would have been forced to own that she had been in the right in an argument of long standing; she had always maintained that in the end no good would come of his preoccupation with "those unnatural flowers."

Yet it must be admitted that Mr. Mannering was not at first greatly upset by this extraordinary upheaval in his daily life. This, I think, was because he was interested, not only in private and personal matters, but in the wider and more general, one might say the biological, aspects of his metamorphosis; for the rest, simply because he *was* now a vegetable, he responded with a vegetable reaction. The impossibility of locomotion, for example, did not trouble him in the least, or even the absence of body and limbs, any more than the cessation of that stream of rashers and tea, biscuits and glasses of milk, luncheon cutlets, and so forth that had flowed in at his mouth for over fifty years, but which had now been reversed to a gentle, continuous, scarcely noticeable feeding from below. All the powerful influence of the physical upon the mental, therefore, inclined him towards tranquility. But the physical is not all. Although no longer a man, he was still Mr. Mannering. And from this anomaly, as soon as his scientific interest had subsided, issued a host of woes, mainly subjective in origin.

He was fretted, for instance, by the thought that he would now have no opportunity to name his orchid or to write a paper upon it and, still worse, there grew up in his mind the abominable conviction that, as soon as his plight was discovered, it was he who would be named and classified, and that he himself would be the subject of a paper, possibly even of comment and criticism in the lay press. Like all orchid collectors, he was excessively shy and sensitive, and in his present situation these qualities were very naturally exaggerated, so that the bare idea of such attentions brought him to the verge of wilting. Worse yet was the fear of being transplanted, thrust into some unfamiliar, draughty, probably public place. Being dug up! Ugh! A violent shudder pulsated through all the heavy foliage that sprang from Mr. Mannering's division of the plant. He awoke to consciousness of ghostly and remote sensations in the stem below, and in certain tufts of leaves that sprouted from it; they were somehow reminiscent of spine and heart and limbs. He felt quite a dryad.

In spite of all, however, the sunshine was very pleasant. The rich odor of hot, spicy earth filled the hothouse. From a special fixture on the hot-water pipes a little warm steam oozed into the air. Mr. Mannering began to abandon himself to a feeling of *laissez-aller*. Just then, up in the corner of the glass roof, at the ventilator, he heard a persistent buzzing. Soon the note changed from one of irritation to a more complacent sound; a bee had managed to find his way after some difficulty through one of the tiny chinks in the metal work. The visitor came drifting down and down through the still, green air, as if into some subaqueous world, and he came to rest on one of those petals which were Mr. Mannering's eyebrows. Thence he commenced to explore one feature after another and at last he settled heavily on the lower lip, which drooped under his weight and allowed him to crawl right into Mr. Mannering's mouth. This was quite a considerable shock, of course, but on the whole the sensation was neither as alarming nor as unpleasant as might have been expected; indeed, strange as it may sound, the appropriate word seemed to be something like ... refreshing.

But Mr. Mannering soon ceased his drowsy toyings with the *mot juste* when he saw the departed bee, after one or two lazy circlings, settle directly upon the maiden lip of Cousin Jane. Ominous as lightning, a simple botanical principle flashed across the mind of her wretched relative. Cousin Jane was aware of it also, although, being the product of an earlier age, she might have remained still blessedly ignorant had not her cousin, vain, garrulous, proselytizing fool, attempted for years past to interest her in the rudiments of botany. How the miserable man upbraided himself now! He saw two bunches of leaves just below the flower tremble and flutter and rear themselves painfully upward into the very likeness of two shocked and protesting hands. He saw the soft and orderly petals of his cousin's face ruffle and incarnadine with rage and embarrassment, then turn sickly as a gardenia with horror and dismay. But what was he to do? All the rectitude implanted by his careful training, all the chivalry proper to an orchid-collector, boiled and surged beneath a paralytically calm exterior. He positively travailed in the effort to activate the muscles of his face, to assume an expression of grief, manly contrition, helplessness in the face of fate, willingness to make all honorable amends, all suffused with the light of a vague but solacing optimism; but it was all in vain. When he had strained till his nerves seemed likely to tear under the tension, the only movement he could achieve was a trivial flutter of the left eyelid—worse than nothing.

This incident completely aroused Mr. Mannering from his vegetative lethargy. He rebelled against the limitations of the form into which he had thus been cast while subjectively he remained all too human. Was he not still at heart a man, with a man's hopes, ideals, aspirations—and capacity for suffering?

When dusk came and the opulent and sinister shapes of the great plant dimmed to a suggestiveness more powerfully impressive than had been its bright noonday luxuriance, and the atmosphere of a tropical forest filled the orchid-house like an exile's dream or the nostalgia of the saxophone; when the cat's whiskers drooped, and even Cousin Jane's eyes slowly closed, the unhappy man remained wide awake, staring into the gathering darkness. Suddenly the light in the study was switched on. Two men entered the room. One of them was his lawyer, the other was his nephew.

"This is his study, as you know, of course," said the wicked nephew. "There's nothing here. I looked round when I came over on Wednesday."

"Ah! well," said the lawyer. "It's a very queer business, an absolute mystery." He had evidently said so more than once before; they must have been discussing matters in another room. "Well, we must hope for the best. In the meantime, in all the circumstances, it's perhaps as well that you, as next-of-kin, should take charge of things here. We must hope for the best."

Saying this, the lawyer turned, about to go, and Mr. Mannering saw a malicious smile overspread the young man's face. The uneasiness which had overcome him at first sight of his nephew was intensified to fear and trembling at the sight of this smile.

When he had shown the lawyer out the nephew returned to the study and looked around him with lively and sinister satisfaction. Then he cut a caper on the hearthrug. Mr. Mannering thought he had never seen anything so diabolical as this solitary expression of the glee of a venomous nature at the prospect of unchecked sway, here whence he had been outcast. How vulgar petty triumph appeared, beheld thus; how disgusting petty spite, how appalling revengefulness and hardness of heart! He remembered suddenly that his nephew had been notable, in his repulsive childhood, for his cruelty to flies, tearing their wings off, and for his barbarity towards cats. A sort of dew might have been noticed upon the good man's forehead. It seemed to him that his nephew had only to glance that way and all would be discovered, although he might have remembered that it was impossible to see from the lighted room into the darkness in the hothouse.

On the mantelpiece stood a large unframed photograph of Mr. Mannering, His nephew soon caught sight of this and strode across to confront it with a triumphant and insolent sneer. "What? You old Pharisee," said he, "taken her off for a trip to Brighton, have you? My God! How I hope you'll never come back! How I hope you've fallen over the cliffs, or got swept off by the tide or something! Anyway ... make hay while the sun shines. Ugh! you old skinflint, you!" And he reached forward his hand, on which the thumb held the middle finger bent and in check, and that finger, then released, rapped viciously upon the nose in the photograph. Then the usurping rascal left the room, leaving all the lights on, presumably preferring the dining room with its cellarette to the scholarly austerities of the study.

All night long the glare of electric light from the study fell full upon Mr. Mannering and his Cousin Jane, like the glare of a cheap and artificial sun. You, who have seen at midnight, in the park, a few insomniac asters standing stiff and startled under an arc light, all their weak color bleached out of them by the drenching chemical radiance, neither asleep nor awake, but held fast in a tense, a neurasthenic trance, you can form an idea of how the night passed with this unhappy pair.

And towards morning an incident occurred, trivial in itself, no doubt, but sufficient then and there to add the last drop to poor Cousin Jane's discomfiture and to her relative's embarrassment and remorse. Along the edge of the great earth-box in which the orchid was planted ran a small black mouse. It had wicked red eyes, a naked, evil snout, and huge, repellent ears, queer as a bat's. This creature ran straight over the lower leaves of Cousin Jane's part of the plant. It was simply appalling: the stringy main stem writhed like a hair on a coal-fire, the leaves contracted in an agonized spasm, like seared mimosa; the terrified lady nearly uprooted herself in her convulsive horror. I think she would actually have done so, had not the mouse hurried on past her.

But it had not gone more than a foot or so when it looked up and saw, bending over it, and seeming positively to bristle with life, that flower which had once been called Tib. There was a breathless pause. The mouse was obviously paralyzed with terror, the cat could only look and long. Suddenly the more human watchers saw a sly frond of foliage curve softly outward and close in behind the hypnotized creature. Cousin Jane, who had been thinking exultantly, "Well, now it'll go away and never, never, never come back," suddenly became aware of hideous possibilities. Summoning all her energy, she achieved a spasmodic flutter, enough to break the trance that held the mouse, so that, like a clockwork toy, it swung round and fled. But already the fell arm of the orchid had cut off its retreat, the mouse leaped straight at it; like a flash five tendrils at the end caught the fugitive and held it fast, and soon its body dwindled and was gone. Now the heart of Cousin Jane was troubled with horrid fears, and slowly and painfully she turned her weary face first to one side, then to the other, in a fever of anxiety as to where the new bud would appear. A sort of sucker, green and sappy, which twisted lightly about her main stem, and reared a blunt head, much like a tip of asparagus, close to her own, suddenly began to swell in the most suspicious manner. She squinted at it, fascinated and appalled. Could it be her imagination? It was not. ...

Next evening the door opened again, and again the nephew entered the study. This time he was alone, and it was evident that he had come straight from table. He carried in his hand a decanter of whiskey capped by an inverted glass. Under his arm was a siphon. His face was distinctly flushed, and such a smile as is often seen at saloon bars played about his lips. He put down his burdens and, turning to Mr. Mannering's cigar cabinet, produced a bunch of keys which he proceeded to try upon the lock, muttering vindictively at each abortive attempt, until it opened, when he helped himself from the best of its contents. Annoying as it was to witness this insolent appropriation of his property, and mortifying to see the contempt with which the cigar was smoked, the good gentleman found deeper cause for uneasiness in the thought that, with the possession of the keys, his abominable nephew had access to every private corner that was his.

At present, however, the usurper seemed indisposed to carry on investigations; he splashed a great deal of whiskey into the tumbler and relaxed into an attitude of extravagant comfort. But after a while the young man began to tire of his own company; he had not yet had time to gather any of his pothouse companions into his uncle's home, and repeated recourse to the whiskey bottle only increased his longing for something to relieve the monotony. His eye fell upon the door of the orchid-house. Sooner or later it was bound to have come to pass. Does this thought greatly console the condemned man when the fatal knock sounds upon the door of his cell? No. Nor were the hearts of the trembling pair in the hothouse at all succored by the reflection.

As the nephew fumbled with the handle of the glass door, Cousin Jane slowly raised two fronds of leaves that grew on each side, high up on her stem, and sank her troubled head behind them.

Mr. Mannering observed, in a sudden rapture of hope, that by this device she was fairly well concealed from any casual glance. Hastily he strove to follow her example. Unfortunately, he had not yet gained sufficient control of his—his limbs?—and all his tortured efforts could not raise them beyond an agonized horizontal. The door had opened, the nephew was feeling for the electric light switch just inside. It was a moment for one of the superlative achievements of panic. Mr. Mannering was well equipped for the occasion. Suddenly, at the cost of indescribable effort, he succeeded in raising the right frond, not straight upwards, it is true, but in a series of painful jerks along a curve outward and backward, and ascending by slow degrees till it attained the position of an arm held over the possessor's head from behind. Then, as the light flashed on, a spray of leaves at the very end of this frond spread out into a fan, rather like a very fleshy horse-chestnut leaf in structure, and covered the anxious face below. What a relief! And now the nephew advanced into the orchid-house, and now the hidden pair simultaneously remembered the fatal presence of the cat. Simultaneously also, their very sap stood still in their veins. The nephew was walking along by the plant. The cat, a sagacious beast, "knew" with the infallible intuition of its kind that this was an idler, a parasite, a sensualist, gross and brutal, disrespectful to age, insolent to weakness, barbarous to cats. Therefore it remained very still, trusting to its low and somewhat retired position on the plant, and to protective mimicry and such things, and to the half-drunken condition of the nephew, to avoid his notice. But all in vain.

"What?" said the nephew, "What, a cat?" And he raised his hand to offer a blow at the harmless creature.

Something in the dignified and unflinching demeanor of his victim must have penetrated into even his besotted mind, for the blow never fell, and the bully, a coward at heart, as bullies invariably are, shifted his gaze from side to side to escape the steady, contemptuous stare of the courageous cat. Alas! his eye fell on something glimmering whitely behind the dark foliage. He brushed aside the intervening leaves that he might see what it was. It was Cousin Jane.

"Oh! Ah!" said the young man, in great confusion. "*You're* back. But what are you hiding there for?"

His sheepish stare became fixed, his mouth opened in bewilderment; then the true condition of things dawned upon his mind.

Most of us would have at once instituted some attempt at communication or at assistance of some kind, or at least have knelt down to thank our Creator that we had, by his grace, been spared such a fate, or perhaps have made haste from the orchid-house to insure against accidents. But alcohol had so inflamed the young man's hardened nature that he felt neither fear nor awe nor gratitude. As he grasped the situation a devilish smile overspread his face.

"Ha! Ha! Ha!" said he, "but where's the old man?"

He peered about the plant, looking eagerly for his uncle. In a moment he had located him and, raising the inadequate visor of leaves, discovered beneath it the face of our hero, troubled with a hundred bitter emotions.

"Hullo, Narcissus!" said the nephew.

A long silence ensued. The nephew was so pleased that he could not say a word. He rubbed his hands together, and licked his lips, and stared and stared as a child might at a new toy.

"You're properly up a tree now," he said. "Yes, the tables are turned now all right, aren't they? Ha! Ha! Do you remember the last time we met?"

A flicker of emotion passed over the face of the suffering blossom, betraying consciousness.

"Yes, you can hear what I say," added the tormentor, "feel, too, I expect. What about that?"

As he spoke, he stretched out his hand and, seizing a delicate frill of fine, silvery filaments that grew as whiskers grow round the lower half of the flower, he administered a sharp tug. Without pausing to note, even in the interests of science, the subtler shades of his uncle's reaction, content with the general effect of that devastating wince, the wretch chuckled with satisfaction and, taking a long pull from the reeking butt of the stolen cigar, puffed the vile fumes straight into his victim's center. The brute!

"How do you like that, John the Baptist?" he asked with a leer. "Good for the blight, you know. Just what you want!"

Something rustled upon his coat sleeve. Looking down, he saw a long stalk, well adorned with the fatal tendrils, groping its way over the arid and unsatisfactory surface. In a moment it had reached his wrist, he felt it fasten, but knocked it off as one would a leech, before it had time to establish its hold.

"Ugh!" said he, "so that's how it happens, is it? I think I'll keep outside till I get the hang of things a bit. *I* don't want to be made an Aunt Sally of. Though I shouldn't think they could get you with your clothes on." Struck by a sudden thought, he looked from his uncle to Cousin Jane, and from Cousin Jane back to his uncle again. He scanned the floor, and saw a single crumpled bath-towel robe lying in the shadow.

"Why?" he said, "*well!* ... Haw! Haw! Haw!" And with an odious backward leer, he made his way out of the orchid-house.

Mr. Mannering felt that his suffering was capable of no increase. Yet he dreaded the morrow. His fevered imagination patterned the long night with waking nightmares, utterly fantastic visions of humiliation and torture. Torture! It was absurd, of course, for him to fear cold-blooded atrocities on the part of his nephew, but how he dreaded some outrageous whim that might tickle the youth's sense of humor and lead him to *any* wanton freak, especially if he were drunk at the time. He thought of slugs and snails, espaliers and topiary. If only the monster would rest, content with insults and mockery, with wasting his substance, ravaging his cherished possessions before his eyes, with occasional pulling at the whiskers, even! Then it might be possible to turn gradually from all that still remained in him of man, to subdue the passions, no longer to admire or desire, to go native, as it were, relapsing into the Nirvana of a vegetable dream. But in the morning he found this was not so easy.

In came the nephew and, pausing only to utter the most perfunctory of jeers at his relatives in the glass house, he sat at the desk and unlocked the top drawer. He was evidently in search of money, his eagerness betrayed that; no doubt he had run through all he had filched from his uncle's pockets, and had not yet worked out a scheme for getting direct control of his bank account. However, the drawer held enough to cause the scoundrel to rub his hands with satisfaction and, summoning the housekeeper, to bellow into her ear a reckless order upon the wine and spirit merchant.

"Get along with you," he shouted, when he had at last made her understand. "I shall have to get someone a bit more on the spot to wait on me; I can tell you that."

"Yes," he added to himself as the poor old woman hobbled away, deeply hurt by his bullying manner, "yes, a nice little parlor-maid ... a nice little parlor-maid."

He hunted in the *Buff Book* for the number of the local registry office. That afternoon he interviewed a succession of maidservants in his uncle's study. Those that happened to be plain, or too obviously respectable, he treated curtly and coldly; they soon made way for others. It was only when a girl was attractive (according to the young man's depraved tastes, that is) and also bore herself in a fast or brazen manner, that the interview was at all prolonged. In these cases the nephew would conclude in a fashion that left no doubt at all in the minds of any of his auditors as to his real intentions. Once, for example, leaning forward, he took the girl by the chin, saying with an odious smirk, "There's no one else but me, and so you'd be treated just like one of the family; d'you see, my dear?" To another he would say, slipping his arm round her waist, "Do you think we shall get on well together?"

After this conduct had sent two or three in confusion from the room, there entered a young person of the most regrettable description, one whose character, betrayed as it was in her meretricious finery, her crude cosmetics, and her tinted hair, showed yet more clearly in florid gesture and too facile smile. The nephew lost no time in coming to an arrangement with this creature. Indeed, her true nature was so obvious that the depraved young man only went through the farce of an ordinary interview as a sauce to his anticipations, enjoying the contrast between conventional dialogue and unbridled glances. She was to come next day. Mr. Mannering feared more for his unhappy cousin than for himself. "What scenes may she not have to witness," he thought, "that yellow cheek of hers to incarnadine?" If only he could have said a few words!

But that evening, when the nephew came to take his ease in the study, it was obvious that he was far more under the influence of liquor than had been the case before. His face, flushed patchily by the action of the spirits, wore a sullen sneer, an ominous light burned in that bleared eye, he muttered savagely under his breath. Clearly this fiend in human shape was what is known as "fighting drunk"; clearly some trifle had set his vile temper in a blaze.

It is interesting to note, even at this stage, a sudden change in Mr. Mannering's reactions. They now seemed entirely egotistical, and were to be elicited only by stimuli directly associated with physical matters. The nephew kicked a hole in a screen in his drunken fury, he flung a burning cigar-end down on the carpet, he scratched matches on the polished table. His uncle witnessed this with the calm of one whose sense of property and of dignity has become numbed and paralyzed; he felt neither fury nor mortification. Had he, by one of those sudden strides by which all such development takes place, approached much nearer to his goal, complete vegetation? His concern for the threatened modesty of Cousin Jane, which had moved him so strongly only a few hours earlier, must have been the last dying flicker of exhausted altruism; that most human characteristic had faded from him. The change, however, in its present stage, was not an unmixed blessing. Narrowing in from the wider and more expressly human regions of his being, his consciousness now left outside its focus not only pride and altruism, which had been responsible for much of his woe, but fortitude and detachment also, which, with quotations from the Greeks, had been his support before the whole battery of his distresses. Moreover, within its constricted circle, his ego was not reduced but concentrated, his serene, flowerlike indifference towards the ill-usage of his furniture was balanced by the absorbed, flowerlike single-mindedness of his terror at the thought of similar ill-usage directed towards himself.

Inside the study the nephew still fumed and swore. On the mantelpiece stood an envelope, addressed in Mr. Mannering's handwriting to Cousin Jane. In it was the letter he had written from town, describing his nephew's disgraceful conduct. The young man's eye fell upon this and, unscrupulous, impelled by idle curiosity, he took it up and drew out the letter. As he read, his face grew a hundred times blacker than before.

"What?" he muttered, "'a mere race-course cad ... a worthless vulgarian ... a scoundrel of the sneaking sort' ... and what's this? '... cut him off absolutely ...' What?" said he, with a horrifying oath, "Would you cut me off absolutely? Two can play at that game, you old devil!"

And he snatched up a large pair of scissors that lay on the desk, and burst into the hothouse. ...

Among fish, the dory, they say, screams when it is seized upon by man; among insects, the caterpillar of the death's-head moth is capable of a still, small shriek of terror; in the vegetable world, only the mandrake could voice its agony—till now.

The Walk to Lingham
Lord Dunsany

"There's a kind of idea that I can't tell a story," said Jorkens, "without some kind of a drink. How such ideas get about I haven't the faintest notion. A story crossed my mind only this afternoon, if you call an actual experience a story. It's a little bit out of the way, and if you'd care to hear it I'll tell it you. But I can assure you that a drink is absolutely unnecessary."

"Oh, I know," I said.

"All I ask," said Jorkens, "is that if you pass it on, you'll tell it in such a way that people will believe you. There have been people, I don't say many, but there have been people that treated those tales I told you as pure fabrication. One man even compared me to Munchausen, compared me favourably I admit, but still he made the comparison. Painful to me, and painful, I should think, to your publisher. It's the way you told those tales; they were true enough every one of them; but it was the way you told them, that somehow started those doubts. You'll be more careful in future, won't you?"

"Yes," I said, "I'll make a note of it."

And with that he started the story.

"Yes, it's distinctly out of the way. Distinctly. But I imagine you will not disbelieve it on that account. Otherwise everyone that ever told a story of any experience he'd had would have to select the dullest and most ordinary, so as to be believed; an account of a railway journey, we'll say, from Penge to Victoria station. We've not come to that, I trust."

"No, no," I said.

"Very well," said Jorkens.

A couple of other members sat down near us then, and Jorkens said: "I can remember as if it was yesterday a long road in the East of

330

England, with a border of poplars. It must have been three miles long, and poplars standing along it all the way on both sides of the road; right across flat fen-country. They had drained the fens, but patches of marsh remained, and here and all along ditches the pennons of the rushes were waving, like an army that had warred with ill success against man, scattered but not annihilated. And they hadn't contented themselves with draining the fens, for they had begun to cut down the poplars. That was what they were at when I first saw the road, with its two straight rows of poplars over the plain like green and silvery plumes, and I must say they were felling them very neatly. They were bringing them down across the road, as it was easier that way to get them on to the carts, and the amount of traffic they interfered with wasn't worth bothering over: in any case they could see it coming for three miles each way, if any ever came, and I never saw any, except the thing that I'll tell you about. Well, they were cutting one down that had to fall between two others across the road without making a mess of their branches, and there was only just room to do it with not two feet to spare. And they did it so neatly that it never touched a leaf: it came down with a huge sigh between the two other trees, and all the little leaves that were turned towards it waved and fluttered anxiously as it went past them with that great last breath. It was done so neatly that I took off my hat and cheered. Anyone might have done so. One doesn't set out to rejoice over those that are down, at least not openly. But one does not always stop to think, and it was perhaps five minutes before I began to be ashamed of that cry of triumph of mine echoing down the doomed avenue.

"It was the last tree they felled that day, and soon I was walking back alone to the village of Lingham where stood the nearest human habitations three miles away over the fenland. And the glimmers of evening began to mellow the poplars. The woodmen with their carts and their fallen trees went the other way; their loud clear voices in talk, and their calls to their horses, soon fading out of all hearing. And then I was in a silence all unbroken but for my own footfall, and but for the faintest sound that seemed sometimes to murmur behind me, that I took for the sound of the wind in the tops of the poplars, though there was no wind blowing.

"I hadn't gone a mile when I had a sense, based on no clue, yet a deeply intense feeling, growing stronger and stronger for the last ten minutes, growing up from a mere suspicion to sheer intuitive certainty, that I was being furtively followed. I looked round and saw nothing. Or rather, partly obscured by a slight curve of the road I must have seen what I afterwards saw too clearly, and yet never credited what was happening. After that the more my sense of being followed increased, the less I dared look round. And none of the kinds of men that I tried to imagine as being what was after me seemed quite to fit my fears. I hadn't gone another quarter mile; I'd barely done another four hundred yards, when: but look here, I'm damned dry. I never had another experience like it, and looking back on it even today has parched my throat till I can hardly speak. I doubt if any of you have ever known anything of the kind."

"I'm sure we haven't," I said, and signed to the waiter, for there was no doubt that there was something in Jorkens' memory that could shake him even now. When he was quite himself again the first thing he did was to thank me, like the good old fellow he is, and then he went on with his tale.

"I hadn't gone another four hundred yards, when it was clear to me with some awful certainty that whatever was after me was nothing human. The shock of that was perhaps worse than the first knowledge that I was followed. There was no longer the very faintest doubt of pursuit; I could hear the measured steps. But they were not human. And, you know, looking over the fields all empty of men, level and low and marshy, I got the feeling, one got it very easily all alone as I was, that if there was anything there that had something against man, I was the one on whom its anger must fall. And the more that the fading illumination of evening made all things dim and mysterious the more that feeling got hold of me. I think I may say that I bore up fairly well, going resolutely on with those steps getting louder behind me. Only I daren't look round. I was afraid when I knew I was followed; I freely admit it; I was more afraid when I knew it was nothing human, yet I held on with a certain determination not to give way to my fears, except that one about not looking round. It wasn't the memory of anything I've told you yet that made my throat go dry just now." Jorkens stopped and took another long drink: in fact he emptied his tumbler.

"A frightful terror was still in store for me, a blasting fear that so shook me then that I nearly dropped on the road, and that sometimes even now comes shivering back on me, and often haunts my nights. We, you know, we are all so proud of the animal kingdom, and so absolutely preoccupied with it, that any attack from outside leaves us staggered and gasping. It was so with me now, when I learned that whatever was after me was certainly nothing animal. I heard the clod clod of the steps, and a certain prolonged swish, but never a sound of breathing. It was fully time to look round, and yet I daren't. The hard heavy steps had nothing of the softness of flesh. Paws they were not, nor even hooves. And they were so near now that there must have been sounds of large breathing, had it been anything animal. And at such moments there are spiritual wisdoms that guide us, intuitions, inner feelings; call them what you will. They told me clearly that this was none of us. Nothing soft and mortal. Nor was it. Nor was it.

"Those moments of making up my mind to look round, while I walked on at the same steady pace, were the most frightful in my life. I could not turn my head. And then I stopped and turned completely round. I don't know why I did it that way. There was perhaps a certain boldness in the movement that gave me some mastery over myself which just saved me from panic, and that would have of course been the end of me. Had I run I must have been done for. I spun right round and back again, and saw what was after me.

"I told you how I had cheered when the poplar fell. I was standing right under its neighbour. And men had been cutting down poplars for weeks. I remembered the look of that tree by which I had stood and cheered; chanced to note the hang of its branches. And I recognized it now. It was right in the middle of the road. One root was lifted up, with clods of earth clinging to it, and it was stumping after me down the road to Lingham. Don't think from any calmness I have as I tell you this that I was calm then. To say that I wasn't utterly racked with terror, would be merely to tell you a lie. One thing alone my reeling mind remained master of, and that was that one must not run. Old tales came back to me of men that were followed by lions, and my mind was able to hold them, and to act as they had taught. Never run. It was the last piece of wisdom left to my poor wits.

"Of course I tried to quicken my pace unnoticed. Whether I succeeded or not I do not know: the tree was terribly close. I turned round no more, but I knew what it looked like from the sound of its awful steps, coming up crab-like and elephantine and stumping grimly down, and I knew from the sigh in the leaves that the twigs were all bending back as it hurried after me. And I never ran.

"And the others seemed to be watching me. There was not that air of aloofness that inanimate things, if they really be inanimate, should have towards us; far less was there the respect that is due to man. I was terribly alone amongst the anger of all those poplars; and, mind you, I'd never cut one of them.

"My knees weren't too weak to have run: I could have done it: it was only my good sense that held me back, the last steady sense that was left to me. I knew that if I ran I should be helpless before the huge pursuit of the tree. It stands to reason, looking at it reasonably, as one can sitting here, that anything that is after you, whatever it is, is not going to let you get right away from it, and the more you try to escape the more you must excite it. And then there were the others: I didn't know what they would do. They were merely watchful as yet, but I was so frightfully alone there, with nothing human in sight, that it was best to go calmly on as though nothing was wrong, and making the most of that arrogance, as I suppose one must call it, that marks our attitude towards all inanimate things. As evening darkened the snipe began to drum, over the empty waste that lay flat and lonely all round me. And I might have felt some companionship, in my awful predicament, from these little voices of the animal kingdom, only that somehow or other I could not feel so certain as to what side they'd be on. And it is a very uneasy sound, the drumming of snipe, when you cannot be sure that it is friendly: the whole air moans with it. Certainly nothing in the sound decreased the pursuit of the tree, as one might have hoped it would, had any allies of the animal kingdom been gathering to befriend me. Rooks moved over, utterly unconcerned, and still the pursuit continued. I began to forget, in my terror, that I was a man. I remembered only that I was animal. I had some foolish hope that, as the rooks went over and the snipe's feathers cut through the air, these awful watchful poplars and the terror that came behind me might drop back to their proper station. Yet the sound of the snipe seemed only to add to the loneliness, and the rooks seemed only to aid the gathering darkness, and nothing turned the poplar as yet from its terrible usurpation. I was left to my miserable subterfuges; walking with a limp as though tired, and yet making a longer or quicker step with one leg than the other. Sometimes longer, sometimes quicker; varying it; and seeing which deceived the best. But these poor antics are not much good; for whatever is quietly following you is likely to judge your pace by the space between it and its prey, as much as by watching your gait, and to match its own accordingly. So, though I did increase my lead now and then, there soon grew louder again the swish of the air in the branches, and that clod clod that I hear at nights even now, whenever my dreams are troubled, a sound to be instantly recognized from any other whatever.

"Three miles doesn't sound far: it's no more than from here to Kensington: but I knew a man who was followed for far less by only a lion, and he swore it was longer than any walk he had ever walked before, or any ten. And only a lion, with breath and blood like himself; death perhaps, yet a death such as comes to thousands; but here was I with a terror from outside human experience, a thing against which no man had ever had to steel himself, a thing that I never knew I should one day have to face. And still I did not run.

"A change at last seemed coming over the loneliness. It wasn't merely the lights that began to shine from Lingham, nor the smoke from chimneys, the banner of man in the air; nor any warmth from the houses that could beat out as far as this: it was a certain feeling wider than warmth could go, a certain glow that one felt from the presence of man. And it was not only I that felt it: the poplars along the road were no longer watching me with quite that excited interest with which a while ago they had seemed to expect my slaughter."

"How did they show it?" said Terbut who can never leave Jorkens alone.

"If you had studied poplars for years and years," said Jorkens, "or if you had watched them as I watched them on that walk, when vast stretches of time seem condensed in one dreadful experience, you too would have been able to tell when poplars were watching you. I have seldom seen it since, and never again so as to be quite certain, but it was unmistakable then, a certain strained tensity in every leaf, twigs like the fingers of a spectre saying Hush to a village; you could not mistake it. But now the leaves were moving again in the soft evening air, the twigs seemed to be menacing nothing, and nothing about the trees was pointing or hinting or waiting; if you can use so mild a word as 'waiting' for their dreadfully strained expectancy. And better than all that, I had a hope—I could not yet call it any more—that my frightful pursuer was slowly dropping behind. And as I neared the windows the hope grew. Their mellow light, some reflecting the evening, some shining from lamps already, seemed throwing far over the marshes the influence of man. I heard a dog bark then, and, immediately after, the healthy clip clap clop of a good cart-horse, going home to his byre. The influence of these sounds on all nature can scarcely be estimated. I knew at once that there had been no revolution. I knew the animal kingdom was still supreme. I heard now unmistakably a certain hesitance come in the frightful footsteps behind me. And still I plodded on with my regular steps, whatever my pulse was doing. And now I began to hear the sound of geese and ducks, more cart-horses and now and then a boy shouting at them, and dogs joining in, and I knew I was back again within the lines of the animal kingdom; and had it not been for that terrible clod clod clod that I still heard behind me though fainter, I could have almost brought myself to disbelieve in the tree. Yes, as easily as you can, Terbut," for Jorkens saw he was about to say something, "sitting safely here." And in the end Terbut said nothing.

"When at last I reached the village the steps were far fainter, and yet I was still pursued, and only my fears could guess how far the revengeful tree would dare to penetrate into Lingham to face the arrogant mastery, and even the incredulity, of our kind. I hurried on, still without running, till I came to an inn with a good stout door. For a moment I stood and looked at it, door, roof and front wall, to satisfy myself that it could not easily be battered in, and when I saw it was really the shelter I sought, I slipped in like a rabbit.

"The brave appearance I kept up in front of the poplar dropped from me like a falling cloak, as I sat or lay on a wooden chair by a table, part of me on the table and part on the chair; till people came up and began to speak to me. But I couldn't speak. Three or four working men, in there for their glass of beer, and the landlord of the Mug of Ale, all came round me. I couldn't speak at all.

"They were very good to me. And when I found that the words would come again I said I had had an attack. I didn't say of what, as I might have blundered on to something that whiskey was bad for, and my life depended on a drink. And they gave me one. I will indeed say that for them. They gave me a tumbler of neat whiskey. I just drank it. And they gave me another. Do you know, the two glasses had no effect on me whatever. Not the very slightest. I wanted another, but before I took that there was one thing I had to be sure of. Was there anything waiting for me outside? I daren't ask straight out.

"'A nice village,' I said, lifting up my head from the table. 'Nice tree outside.'

"'No tree out there,' said one of the men.

"'No tree?' I said. 'I'll bet you five shillings there is.'

"'No,' he said, and stuck to it. He didn't even want to bet.

"'I thought I noticed something like a:' I daren't even say the word poplar, so I said 'a tree' instead. 'Just outside the door,' I added.

"'No, no tree,' he repeated.

"'I'll bet you ten shillings,' I said.

"He took that.

"'Well, go and have a look, governor,' he said.

"You don't think I was going outside that door again. So I said, 'No, you shall decide. I mayn't trust your memory against mine, but if you go outside and look, and say whether it's there or not, that's quite good enough for me.'

"He smiled and thought me a bit dotty. Oh Lord, what would he have thought me if I'd told him the bare truth.

"Well, he came back with the news that thrilled all through me, the golden glorious news that I'd lost my ten shillings. And at that I paid my bet and had my third tumbler of whiskey, which I did not dare to risk while I didn't know how things were. And that third whiskey won. It beat my misery, it beat my fatigue and my terror, and the awful suspicion which partly haunted my reason, that this unquestioned dominion that animal life believes itself to have established was possibly overthrown. It beat everything, and I dropped into a deep sleep there at the table.

"I woke next day at noon immensely refreshed, where the good fellows had laid me upstairs on a bed. I looked out over ruddy tiles; there was a yard below, with poultry, among walls of red brick, and a goat was tied up there, and a woman went out to feed him; and from beyond came all the ancient sounds of the farm, against which time can do nothing. I revelled in all these sounds of animal mastery, and felt a safety there in the light of that bright morning that somehow told me my dreadful experience was over.

"Of course you may say it was all a dream; but one doesn't remember a dream all those years like that. No, that frightful poplar had something against man, and with cause enough I'll admit.

"What it would have done if I'd run doesn't bear thinking of."

And Jorkens didn't think of it; with a cheery wave of his hand he made the sign to the waiter, that drowns memory.

Also Available

About Time:
The Forerunners of Time Travel
and Temporal Anomalies in
Science Fiction and Fantasy

ISBN 1-930585-55-1

15 classic stories, from Rip Van
Winkle and Peter Rugg to tales
by Rudyard Kipling, H. G. Wells,
and Algernon Blackwood.

The Historical Bigfoot

ISBN 1-930585-30-6

Stories of large hairy manlike apes
(wild men, yahoos, circus gorillas)
in North America, before the term
"Bigfoot" was even coined.

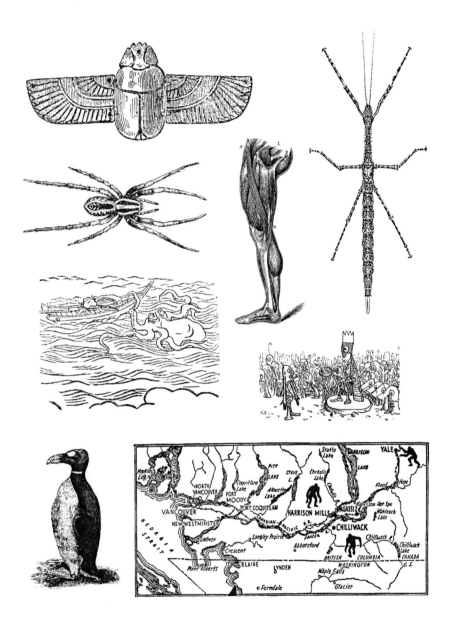

Printed in the United Kingdom by
Lightning Source UK Ltd., Milton Keynes
136539UK00001B/174/P